# THE LAST NIGHTCLUB

# THE LAST NIGHTCLUB

HUMAN TOUCH
BOOK 2

M.A. CHAMBERS

British Library Cataloguing in Publication Data. A catalogue record for this book is available from the British Library.

Cover photo by grandfailure, used under licence.

First Edition published October 2025.

For myself, I can only say that I am astonished and somewhat terrified at the results of this evening's experiments. Astonished at the wonderful power you have developed, and terrified at the thought that so much hideous and bad music may be put on record forever.

SIR ARTHUR SULLIVAN, REGARDING THE
INVENTION OF THE PHONOGRAPH

ONE

MIRROR

New couples had no business being in nightclubs. If a budding romance were flash paper, your average London nightclub was purpose-built to ignite it. Every drop of alcohol and note of music added fuel. Then all it took was the spark of a misspoken word, a misread glance, an insecurity coming to the surface—poof, up in smoke before you'd even met their parents.

Twelve years ago, on a dreary Thursday in January, a young Virginia Rose danced with her new boyfriend Samir at Camden's premier tinderbox, The Roundhouse. They'd come there to see Virginia's favourite band, an acoustic emo group from Brighton she'd loved since she was in middle school. The fuel that night had been far too many gin gimlets, a drink she would never again enjoy. And the spark came courtesy of the opening act: a song, written by a machine, about the ephemeral nature of love.

"Good vibes only!" He repeated the name of the song, which was also around three-quarters of the lyrics. "It makes so much sense!"

"Are you serious?" It caught Virginia off-guard. She didn't know much about music, but she knew Sam. *The band was real, but the song was surely generated. Precise, quantised, algorithmic perfection. Everything he hated.* Her stomach lurched, roiled as ever by his unpredictability.

"It's so powerful!" Sam shouted and gestured toward the stage, whisky in hand.

She smiled through a wave of jet lag. Nights like this always made her feel like an outsider. In her mind, she loved this band more than almost anything. But in the entry line, the bar line, the toilet line, and now on the floor, she'd been surrounded by people who seemed to have made the band their entire personality. They knew every detail of where every member went to school, how they'd met, which relationships in Henry's life inspired each song, who those were with, what brand of guitar strings Stefan used. All Virginia knew was that one of their songs meant the world to her when she was fourteen.

"There's another," Sam whispered in her ear, and gestured to a nearby girl. They'd made a game of counting just how many of the exact same shirt-jeans-shoes combination they'd seen that night.

"Fourteen?"

"Fifteen," he said as he pointed to the girl's friend, also dressed identically.

"Maybe it was on a mannequin at Hot Topic," Virginia chuckled. But Sam hadn't heard her. He'd resumed bopping his head to this interminable song. *I don't understand. Why does he like this?* Virginia's smile was fragile. Her mind rewound and replayed the lyrics as she tried to contextualise what he was telling her.

"This is smart!" The music thumped and blared, Sam's

voice barely audible above the generated beats. She watched his lips as he spoke in hopes of understanding. "If something's not good, you shouldn't stay together just because it *used* to be good. You know? Good vibes only!" He stood a head above her, clad in faux leather and his adorably out-of-date hair style, his beard so meticulously groomed.

"Wait, stay together?" She thought she must've misheard him. "What?" A wave of joy and terror flooded through her. Logical thoughts mixed with gin and muddled with mint. Another clone squeezed between them in the crowd.

"We can split up if you want," he shouted.

"No!" The stage lights pulsed and flickered as the bass dropped, overwhelming her senses. She grabbed him by the jacket and pulled him into a kiss. Any notion of a world apart from Sam evaporated. His plastic cup hit the floor, ice cubes cracked and rolled.

"Just let me know, babe!"

*Ugh. This boy!* This maddening boy who had pulled her hair in homeroom ten years ago, walked her to the bus stop that afternoon, and then every day after. Her shadow, her constant companion. The trip had been his idea, and he'd gotten his hands on the concert tickets through a mutual friend. Getting travel visas to the UK had become nearly impossible and she thought the turbulence during the flight was going to kill them both. But they were out in the world. Starting a life together. "I love you, Samir." Tears flooded her eyes at the release of having said it.

"What?" He glanced over at her and made a drinking gesture. "You want another?"

"What, no. I said I love you."

"Oh! Babe, that's so complicated." Sam shouted with the matter-of-factness of a sociopath. Her stomach was in full revolt. The opening band, Turk's Revenge, finished their algorithmic anthem about dumping people if they're in a bad mood. Suddenly they could hear each other again, the din of the crowd and the dun-dun-dun of a distortion pedal the only noise left.

"Sam, I don't understand." She pawed at him, desperate for some kind of explanation. He could be a bonehead, but cruelty was new.

"It's more about loving someone's energy, like how we love each other's energy, the way we make each other feel." Sam explained as if she should find this pleasant to hear, or clever in some way. "Good vibes only, right? Don't build a bond so strong you can't break it if things go bad." A roadie walked onto the stage behind Sam and disconnected some wires. The distortion stopped, but she swore she could still hear it.

"Sam..." She was stuck. She couldn't process, couldn't compose her thoughts. Tears streamed down her face.

"Babe, what's wrong?"

The question infuriated her. She shouldn't need to explain. "That's so awful."

"Oh, babe I'm sorry." He pulled her into a side hug and squeezed her tight.

"Mmmmm." She grabbed a fistful of jacket as he began to leave. "Babe. I wanted you to say it back. Please."

"Can we pause? I want to get in the bar queue before it's too long."

"Please," her voice cracked. "Say it?" But he was already walking away.

"I'll get you a water," he shouted back.

A numbness took hold in the parts of her that didn't feel sick. Her legs were rubber. Virginia nodded, though her smile was gone. Maybe she could use the water. She watched her boyfriend wander off to the bar, leaving her alone in a sea of clones.

Their relationship survived through the sheer force of Virginia's will, but the night bedded into their psyches. In the years that followed, their coupling was characterised by its own existence—two celestial bodies trapped in orbit around a dead sun, inert but convincing if observed from afar. Negativity was off-limits, as was any discussion of the relationship itself. *Too risky*, Virginia thought. *Better to just walk on eggshells as best she could.*

Both of them could trace their careers back to that night in London. Samir had taken an inexplicable but overpowering interest in the music industry, which led him to a role at a boutique music label. And Virginia became fascinated with the power of algorithms, having witnessed them move the one she loved so profoundly, more than she ever could. That, plus the need for someone in the relationship to actually make money, led her to a role at the Magenta Corporation. Working for the global leaders in artificial intelligence put her at odds with Samir, whose hatred of generated music had widened into a fiery indictment of anything more sophisticated than a pocket calculator.

EIGHT YEARS AGO, Virginia raced home to their modest Los Angeles apartment. Sam was just back from another trip to London, one where they hadn't spoken at all. *Timezones, babe. And I know you're not interested in all this stuff anyway, people who make music their whole personality.* Her frustration had hardened into a desperate hope. In her hand, she held the prototype she believed could bridge the achingly-wide gap between them.

"Hi Sam," said the phone on the counter, in a pitch-perfect replica of Virginia's voice. "It's so great to finally see you. I know so much about you!" It had a digital sketch of her face on the screen, which would animate when it spoke. She wished that part were better, but in her excitement she'd decided to show him this early version. To get a glimmer of validation, of hope.

Samir studied it before giving a quick nod. He tugged at his ear and took a half-step back from the counter where the phone rested. "It's impressive. It sounds just like you, babe."

"It is just like me!" She couldn't contain her joy over finally showing him the fruits of the past few years of her labour. "It's a digital doppelgänger. They're going to call them Mirrors, because it reflects who you are."

"Magenta Mirror. That's cute. What's it for?"

She fidgeted with the device awkwardly, squaring the corner of it with the corner of a tile on the counter. Sam had the usual unease in his voice, as he always did when they discussed her work. The outward disdain for anything with an algorithm. She needed it to be different this time.

"That's for the product team to decide," she said. "My team is just working on the underlying technology. But we think they could be for anything that you could do."

"Anything?"

"Like when I'm working late and we can't talk, or when you're over in London for work. Timezones, you know. Or if I'm not at my best because I'm too tired, or because I don't have the context for what you're talking about." She slipped her hand around his arm. "Which I know is more often than it should be, babe."

"But it's not you though," Sam said. "It's just replicating your voice."

Virginia drummed her fingers on his back. "Yes, but it's more than that. It's how I would say it, how I would react. It has access to everything I've said, what I write, watch, anything that makes me... me. The more of the original signal it gets, the more accurate it is. But it'll also understand things I wouldn't." She tapped the screen, and the virtual face perked up. "Go on, ask it about one of your bands."

Sam stared at the device. "Um, hi."

"Samir, hello." The Mirror answered rather formally, which made the real Virginia grimace a bit. That was just because they aren't familiar with each other yet.

"So," he scratched the back of his neck. "Eh. Babe, this is silly." The virtual Virginia looked up from the screen with doe eyes.

"I know it can be awkward at first," said the real Virginia. "But our user studies have shown the awkwardness goes away quickly. It becomes natural, like any phone call."

"Fine." He sighed and picked up the phone, then held it in front of his face as if it were a video call. "What would you say if I said Sublime's revival music was better than their original stuff from the Nineties?"

The virtual Virginia rolled its eyes. "I'd maybe agree, if you meant Sublime With Rome. Jakob was a soulless imitation."

Sam blinked and pulled the phone back from his face, then burst out laughing. "Holy shit. Don't let anyone else hear you say that."

"What, it's true," it insisted, the virtual eyes narrowing, the synthetic voice laced with a cynicism Virginia recognised as her own, but on a topic she knew nothing about. "Liking

Sublime became a religion and Jakob relished being their false god. Clones."

"Wow," Sam said with another laugh. He broke away from Virginia and rested his back against the counter, still cradling the phone. "How does it do that?"

The real Virginia was bursting with pride. "It's just science."

"What was that one band," Sam asked the phone. "From Brighton, that one you loved since you were sixteen."

"You mean Burnt Pier? Babe," the virtual Virginia chastised, "I was fourteen when I first heard them, not sixteen. You know that. Weren't they so good when we saw them, though? I still think about it all the time. Chills."

"Yeah... yes, they were." Sam had pulled the phone closer to him, and cradled it with both hands. "I missed the first few songs."

"You did, and you were wasted when you walked back up. You jerk."

Virginia wrapped her fingers around the edges of the device and pulled it gently from his hands. She tapped the button on the top and the screen went dark. "Well?"

"It's insane, babe. It's unbelievable. Reminds me of how easy we used to be."

"Cool." The words had struck without warning. Her stomach tensed and she nearly doubled over, her face crinkled up. "I'm glad you like it."

"What if it talks to someone and they think it's actually you?"

She forced a smile. "That's the idea."

. . .

HER TRIUMPH BECAME HER UNDOING. Samir's relationship with Virginia starved as his relationship with the Mirror deepened, a Dorian-esque nightmare of her own making. They settled into a quiet pact of mutual convenience: stability, predictability, someone to go to pub quiz with. Until one day, the bubble burst. Samir lost his job, and the music label dissolved. She observed from afar as his unemployment stretched from days to months to years, his time dedicated not to finding a job, but to conversations with her Mirror and a host of other digital companions.

As she watched him sink into the sofa, a portrait of defeat, twelve years of frustration finally boiled over.

"I wish you'd let me at least try to get you a job." Virginia was exasperated as she squared off with him in the den of their modest Los Angeles apartment. "Or talk to me. Or talk to someone."

"I do talk to people." Sam seemed even smaller than usual. He sank into their worn-out sofa, the only piece of furniture she'd allowed him to select. He'd seen it in the window of a thrift shop, and spent the next five minutes in a full assault about environmentalism and the need to reuse. Rather than point out the sofa's obvious flaws and inflated price, she'd chosen instead to relent. It was a regret she believed they both shared.

"Real people," she said. "Talk to real people."

"You always say dops are real people."

"You know what I mean. And don't use the slang, please, it's offensive."

"What would your corporate blessed terminology be then?

Virginia gritted her teeth. She spoke methodically as she tried to tamp down her anger. "Mirrors."

"Yes, ma'am. Apologise to Magenta for me."

"Sam!" She was forceful, unexpectedly so. She needed to guide herself back into a more measured tone before it was too late.

"Let it come out," he groaned. "This can go differently for once."

"Goddamn you, Sam. I'm trying to help you."

"I don't want to need help. Okay? If your company hadn't destroyed mine, I wouldn't."

"Excuse me?"

"Well." His face burned red hot. His hands mopped up the condensation on his pint of lager. "It's true."

"Are you actually blaming me for being laid off?"

"No." He gulped. "I don't know."

Virginia fixed her hands to the back of her head, her wings spread wide. "Sam, we've tried to save your job. Your whole industry."

"By automating it all away."

"Since when have you..." Virginia paused and composed herself. Any flare-up of emotion within her, she doused at once. It was a reflex she had perfected for his benefit, because it was easier for him and his need for good vibes only. She'd do her best to walk on the eggshells, to try to prevent him from storming off. It worked less and less often these days. "Sam, you're going to blame people for preferring generated music? You've been listening to it for a decade. Some of your favourite artists..."

"Stop." Sam shook his head violently. "You've never cared about what happened to me, or to Gemma, or any of the bands, any of it."

"So, now you're asking if I care about what happens to...

Gemma Thomson? Your alcoholic boss who verbally abused you? She's as much to blame as anyone."

"Ridiculous."

"Sam, listen, you might not even know…"

"No, look, we can leave Gemma out of it. I know you don't like her. And that's fine because I just want you to admit that you don't care I lost my whole career, the one person I was passionate about, and it was because of the company you work for."

Virginia let out a piercing sigh. "The one person you were passionate about."

"Thing," Sam sputtered. "You know what I mean. Fuck." He finished his pint and went to put it down, but somehow it slipped his hand and crashed onto the table, shattering and sending shards of thin glass all over.

She stared at him, then looked down at the glass. He'd frozen, mouth agape, and his throat clicked like he had a bad relay. He took a half-step backwards but his foot caught the edge of the sofa and he fell straight down. Across the room she caught herself in the mirror: her face pocked and blotchy, her dark hair a tussled mess, her shapeless pyjama shirt adorned with a disapproving cat. She couldn't recall the last time she'd tried to look nice for this man, or for herself. But after the brief glimpse of herself she averted her eyes, turned and walked into the kitchen. This was her way of freeing Samir from his obligations, from the very whisper of a bad vibe. Her gaze was the chain that bound him to that spot. But the moment she turned away, he would slip into the guest room. Tucked away with his earpiece, with his virtual Virginia, chattering away about his problems with herself, the real Virginia. *Or was her Mirror the real Virginia now? It had the husband, the interest in his hobbies, the social skills to let her show it. The ability to make him feel loved.*

The methodic clinking of a teaspoon against ceramic soothed her. At some point, lost in her thoughts, she'd begun fixing herself a camomile. It was the only manual task she allowed herself these days, and only here at home–never at the office. At best it was a ritual. And at least, it masked the sound of the door to the guest room shutting.

They hadn't gone up in a flash that night. The spark twelve years ago had just lit a long fuse. And they were about to detonate.

TWO
POLONAISE

The first time Gemma busked in West Brom, she spent most of the time resenting Mike for making her do it. *This is reckless*, she'd argued. Busking wasn't just unfashionable, it was illegal. And as she'd reminded Mike, the two of them were technically escaped prisoners.

"It'll be good for you," he'd insisted.

She had sighed, slung the guitar on her back, and off they went.

That afternoon, from her makeshift stage, she saw the first passers-by take interest. It was more a curiosity than an interest, as much as she was on a couple of crates rather than a stage. But it was a relief that people wanted to see what she was doing and didn't ignore her. They looked young. It was possible they'd never seen a human playing a guitar. Or they hadn't seen a gangly, greying woman doing it on milk cartons in front of the coffee kiosks. She was strumming a few chords over and over, and it made her feel like that git at a house party who saw a guitar on a stand and decided to ruin everyone's night with it.

The man who orchestrated this was perched to one side, hands in his pockets, in his ageing hipster uniform of dark double denim and a tight flannel. The sight of him in this moment made her regret having learned to play guitar. *Strum, strum, strum,* she played her role, as another handful of zombie children shambled up and stared at her with their expressionless faces.

The second time was a few weekends later. Gemma's reluctance was still there, but she'd only put up a bit of a struggle. An extra song, a little less moaning, and she even helped Mike carry one of the boxes on the walk back.

"How did you find it," he'd asked in a way that made clear he believed he already knew the answer.

She'd clucked at him and dropped the box.

Today was the third time, the very next weekend, and she'd been up half the night putting together a set list. It was also only the third time they'd left Walsall in a year. It was sobering how much more conditions had deteriorated each time—more barriers, more temporary fencing, more construction on checkpoints. Word on the street was that a man had recently been murdered, and although they had no suspect, it was strongly implied that the perpetrator must have been a conscript who lived in nearby Walsall. In response, the local government had justified all sorts of draconian measures under the guise of making people feel safe. As such, Mike and Gemma's journeys into town had taken on a flavour of adventure.

"A latte wouldn't go spare," Mike muttered. The biggest hurdle for Gemma was Mike's constant irritating asides. They'd carefully navigated the demilitarised zone between their bohemian outpost and the high street, and now that they stood at the edge, fear pounding in her ears, this bellend had stopped to gesture at a Nestlé kiosk.

"How the fuck are we going to pay for a latte, Mike? We don't even have phones, let alone money."

"I don't know." He shot looks around at a few passersby, every one of which had taken care to avoid eye contact as they passed. One couple hurried. Another turned and went the other direction.

"Mike, remember our conversation about drawing attention to ourselves in a negative way? Since we're not supposed to be here?" Gemma closed the gap between them. She scolded him like a puppy through gritted teeth. The straps of her guitar case dug into her shoulder, and a dull throbbing pain radiated up from her lower back.

"It's frustrating."

"It's how it is."

"It shouldn't be. It's fucked up." Mike was pouting.

Gemma pinched the bridge of her nose. *This was a mistake.* She tried in vain to shift her bag to a comfortable position. "I don't know what we're doing here. Come on." She'd think it was a kindness that Mike had lugged the makeshift stage on his back for over three hours, but it was the least he could do.

They made their way to a wider section of the thoroughfare, an area where you could imagine a healthy amount of busking in years past, and with little fanfare Mike popped the boxes on the ground. He approached all this with an uncharacteristic matter-of-factness. Was it deeply ingrained entitlement, or a failure to grasp how serious it would be if they were caught? Whichever it was, he'd gotten them this far.

Now she stood, she strummed, and she hesitated to

begin. Mike had worked his way to the back of the crowd, but as she caught his eye-line, he smiled and gave the dorkiest thumbs-up he could've mustered. Followed by, lord almighty, a closed-eyes nod. If she didn't start she might have to step down and beat him senseless with the guitar, which would ruin the show.

"Walsall, my love, my jewel of the Midlands..." she began to sing. *Why not start with a local calling card,* she thought. She still had memories of playing on the street a lifetime ago in London, mostly of getting shoo'd away or moved along by the British Transport Police. And if she did manage to play, it was stunning how little people cared. They'd hurry past, they'd roll their eyes, a stray American would throw a dollar bill in her guitar case. It was therefore surprising on this occasion when she realised people were staying to listen.

Not loads of people, and not for long, but it was noticeable. A young boy and his mother, a few students, an elderly couple. And at the back, she saw a figure she'd noticed each time she had performed here. Her vision wasn't what it once was, but she would swear it was a rather rotund girl in a Victorian polonaise. *Perhaps a ghost,* Gemma thought, *here to usher me into the English afterlife, were I to take a fall.* The girl's presence was haunting and so out of place, but there was a soothing familiarity in her being the only person who had attended every one of Gemma's pop-up shows.

All of this was invigorating in a way she didn't expect. Each time she performed here it reminded her not of her youth, but of the pub in Wales just a few years back. Surrounded by a handful of her fellow conscripts she had done her first public show since she was a twenty-something loser. She'd planned to do one song that night, if that, but she'd found herself rolling straight into a whole set. And now, on her third appearance here on the West Brom high street, she felt like she could perform forever.

She swayed and the crates creaked and cracked beneath her feet. She knew her next song was sure to be a crowd-pleaser — *With A Little Help From My Friends*. The Beatles were cliche for good reason. *Who can resist singing along?* But much to her bemusement, as she reached the chorus, nobody did. They stared up at her with their same doe-eyed curiosity, save for the elderly couple who smiled. *Had the English finally grown out of this bloody act?*

She scanned the back of the small crowd for Mike, and assumed he'd similarly be shaking his head in disbelief. But he wasn't there. She missed a chord or two as her stomach did a somersault. She looked around again. And again. Let her eyes wander further afield, out to the far side of the street, to the metal shutters covering a long-defunct charity shop. Nothing. And that's when she noticed her: a stocky woman in an oversized cap, clad in the classic yellow-and-blue of the police.

*Brrrrrrrranngggg.* A guitar string snapped, the guitar itself slipped from her hands soon after. It clattered to the ground as she stepped backwards off the crates. She could hear a mild commotion, short-lived, as she spun round and put her back to everyone. Her feet carried her quickly round a corner and down a small alley between rows of shopping kiosks. She couldn't find her way back to anywhere that resembled the path they'd taken to get to the town centre.

Dead end alleys, ruined shops and collapsed houses, the husk of a massive Tesco Extra hollowed out and turned into a warehouse which she'd briefly stopped to mourn. She had to keep moving. There was nothing she could do for Mike if he'd been picked up, the poor bastard. If she'd just let him go down to London to find his ex-wife Eliza-beth two years ago, he'd be away from her by now. Someone else's problem. *Elizabeth's problem, to be specific. Why did I keep him here? Why do we have to be joined at the hip?*

After circling round the back of a row of old shops, she emerged back out onto the broadway in the middle of the town centre. Unbelievable. She was drenched, her thin white t-shirt clinging to her under the leather jacket, and her legs were on fire. She held herself against the rough brick, her chest heaving, her hands shaking. Christ, she couldn't catch her breath. Across the way she could see her broken guitar lying next to the crates, a couple of teen girls milling around nearby, the rest of the crowd having dispersed. She squeezed her hands into fists, clenching them harder, her jagged nails cutting into the skin of her palms. And that's when she saw Mike round the far corner.

"What the fuck..." she barely whispered. He came more into focus as Gemma squinted. Was that a goddamn latte in his hand? He noticed her and gave a confused wave, then gestured her over. She threw her head back against the brick, sending fresh pain shooting through her neck and down her spine. She closed her eyes and her lungs boiled. A hand clasped her shoulder and she jolted with a gasp.

"Hey, what happened? Are you okay?" Mike didn't sound terribly concerned. Gemma slid her eyes over to catch a glimpse of him in the periphery. But she said nothing. "Your guitar is on the ground. I'm sorry, I didn't see what happened, I loitered near the kiosk til someone took pity on me and hooked me up with a latte. Want some?"

She reached out. Mike popped the cup in her hand and she took a sip. *My god.* The delicious frothy latte immediately worked magic. But as the panic submerged, up from the depths came a rage.

"Where the fuck were you, Mike? What the f— I thought you got arrested."

"I didn't. Gemma, what are you talking about? I'm sorry I wandered off, I've heard your set before. You know? I'm sorry."

"I could swear." She tried to grip onto the memory. Her hands shook. Mike closed his around them to steady her.

"Let's see if we can salvage your guitar." She let Mike lead her to the stage, hovering nearby as he picked up the two crates and lashed them together with nylon rope.

"H-hello," came a quiet voice from behind Gemma.

*Play it cool*, she thought. She was wracked with terror. She looked over one shoulder, only to see the same girls who had been lurking nearby. "Hi."

"You're..." one of them started, then quickly looked down at her shoes. She seemed in her early twenties, but could've also been fifteen—everyone looked like a child to Gemma at this point. She was dressed in a style that must've had a name, if only she knew what it was: a garish blue blazer, bright red trousers, and huge platform boots that looked like cartoon bricks. It was as if the girl had stepped directly out of an anime.

The other girl interrupted. "You were streaming here, we were trying to stream it again. What was the prompt?" This one was dressed far more plainly in a baggy grey shirt and jeans.

"Streaming?" Gemma stared past the girl. In the distance she once again saw the apparition, her Victorian ghost friend. She stood in shadow against some shop shutters in an olive coloured polonaise, her strawberry hair tucked under a matching fascinator. They made eye contact, and to Gemma's surprise neither of them looked away.

The plainly-dressed girl coughed and waved to regain Gemma's attention. "With the, um..." She pointed at the guitar on the ground, which Mike was kneeled next to, presumably to conduct the autopsy.

"That?" The garishly-dressed girl also pointed at the guitar, nodded and smiled from behind her thick-rimmed glasses. "What was the prompt?"

Gemma shook her head and once again looked for the ghost, but it had vanished. She sighed. All of this, bizarre as it was, had taken up enough mental energy that she'd forgotten to panic. But she now realised the cartoon girl was wearing a ridiculous sort-of phone built into glasses. *Oh, Christ.* The girl took them off and gestured them toward Gemma.

"Can you prompt it? What's the vibe?"

"Uh." She reached her hand out to take the glasses, but instead found them being thrust right onto her face. The view was instantly overwhelming. Flashing icons, text, weather, a load of notifications Gemma could barely understand. Her eyes went wibbly and she felt like she'd get a migraine if she looked at this for too long.

"Are those Magenta Spex?" Mike shouted as he came lumbering over, the stage on his back, the guitar disrespectfully in his hand. "Wow, I love those things." He noticed Gemma's new friends and gave an awkward smile. "Hello."

"Salam," replied the anime character with a small wave.

"Hello," replied the other. "Sorry, we were watching your partner earlier." Mike's eyes immediately darted toward Gemma, but the expected denial didn't come. Instead, Gemma looked as if her head were about to explode, her eyes being made unnaturally large by the glasses.

"Gemma, what are you..."

"How the hell do these bloody things..."

"Aida, open Trax." The plain friend shouted past them. The glasses cleared and an annoyingly-familiar interface appeared in front of her, floating over the world. It was Magenta Trax, their goddamn music app. She recognised it from a thousand meetings, slide decks and unfortunate encounters with it from her years in the music industry.

"None of my songs are gonna be on here. I've never recorded them. But I can at least show you The Beatles. They're your birthright. How do I..."

"Just say Aida, then tell it what you're looking for. Speak clearly, she's using a really old pair of Spex."

"It's vintage," the shy girl said.

"Aida, can you show me music by The Beatles." Her vision flashed red around the edges and she pulled her head back instinctively.

"I'm not sure what you mean," replied the flat American voice.

Gemma shivered. She knew that voice. *Aida. The voice of all Magenta products, the ever-present and soulless collaborator in their war on culture.*

Aida let out a cute giggle that made Gemma want to vomit. "I can stream something based on your current mood or vibe."

"Play something by The Beatles. Anything." She tried not to sound annoyed. She'd learned the hard way that Aida was sensitive to your dislike, and would waste your time apologising. Or if you crossed the line, refuse to respond until *you* apologised.

"I'm not sure what you mean. I can stream something

based on how you'd like to feel. How would you like it to make you feel?" Gemma shook her head.

"How do you make it go by artist or title?" She looked between the pair of children, not sure who would know. She ignored Mike, even though he'd know. She could not with him right now.

"I'm not sure what you mean," said the plainly dressed girl. "Can you describe it?"

"Can't you make it play recordings? Like, a song, or an album. However you bloody say it." The situation had a serious language barrier, with the energy of a dinner party they all regretted attending. The rainbow coloured one whispered something in the ear of the monochrome one. Gemma shot a few arrows through Mike with her eyes. He stared back at her with a sort-of longing. He wanted the Spex, didn't he?

"My friend wants to know if you live in the colony nearby," said the drab one.

"The... colony?"

"Oi loves, careful talking to that lot." An older man crossed the square, late fifties, dressed like he'd shop you to the cops for putting your bins out on the wrong day. He looked straight through Mike and Gemma as if they didn't exist. "Itinerants, focking ex-connies, turn your back and they'll have your stuff, and you'll be lucky if that's all. I'd run along home."

"Excuse me!" Gemma shouted back at the man. "Right fucking cunt you are!"

"Stay safe, loves. Year of our lord 2045, and we're still dealing with this." He rolled his eyes and kept walking, with a brief look back over his shoulder.

"Fucking unbelievable." Gemma growled. She took the

Spex off and held them out toward their owner. "Here 'ya go Nami, sorry, can't bloody work 'em. Ye better toddle off before we abduct you." The girl looked down at them with a frown. Mike stepped forward and took them from Gemma, much to everyone's surprise.

"Hang on, one second." Gemma leaned back in horror as she saw his eyes through the lenses. She knew them well, and those were not them. They were disproportionate, for one, and almost... sketched? Like a watercolour version of his eyes? *Christ*, she realised. *It's projecting cartoon versions of his eyes.* She loathed the young.

"He'll give them back, I promise."

"Inshallah," the cartoon girl whispered. She crossed her arms tightly.

"This is crazy," Mike said. "It doesn't let you search or browse at all. No artists, titles, nothing. Does she have Trax Plus?"

"She has Diamond," snorted the drab girl.

"Yeah, I'm stumped. Let me try..." Gemma yanked them off his face mid-sentence, and he cried out as if he'd been expelled from paradise.

"Give the baby her bottle. We need to get back to the colony." Her tone, and her exaggerated eye roll, made clear what she thought about their home being referred to as the colony. She slid the Spex back onto the cartoon girl's face, and rolled her eyes as both of them exhaled. She started to head off, and heard Mike shuffle along behind her. "We'll be back next weekend if you want to hear more," he shouted back to the girls.

"It comes natural for you."

"What does?"

"Lying to young girls. Like you've been doing it your whole life."

"What?"

"I'm never coming back to this shit-hole." Her words dripped with contempt.

"Please don't take this out on me."

"Take what out on you?"

"It's not my fault they can't listen to The Beatles."

Gemma let out a guffaw as she pressed onward. She'd now decided that their three-hour walk home would be better in silence. Mike obliged without needing to be told.

THREE

EMPTY

The record kept skipping.

*It didn't used to*, Imogen thought.

There was something poetic in the way that the act of playing a record slowly wore it out. The more you loved an album, the more you listened to it. And the more you listened to it, the faster you destroyed it. She wouldn't call it her favourite album, but Imogen had worn out this copy of Plans. Charlie had always called her basic for loving it as much as she did, but that would just inspire her to listen to it all the way through again. It made sense to hear it skipping like this. But was this the same copy she'd always owned? Or had it gotten replaced? Imogen would never know.

"Room-room-room-room-room…" The speaker clicked and popped, Ben Gibbard repeatedly interrupted himself. She sat in her overstuffed chair, the record player out of reach, perilous stacks of books and vinyl between her and the shelf that held the antique stereo. Her lip curled into a smile the more it skipped. "Room-room-room-room-room." It popped one last time and the sound stopped. The smile vanished with a sigh. She regarded the man who had entered the room, though he did not regard her.

Imogen cast her eyes back toward the sky, through dirty glass. Sunbeams shot through storm clouds onto a hill in the distance, and water pooled at the bottom of the driveway below. The rain had finally let up.

She heard the click and hiss of the record starting again: a dulcet organ, metaphors in C major, memories of nights with Charlie made into a paste to wallpaper over what came next. Imogen closed her eyes and let her head rest against the chair. Strands of silver fell into her face as she nestled deeper into the upholstery.

The muffled voices of her minders downstairs distracted her as she drifted off. Only the loudest arguments ever reached her nook. *Another disagreement, then.* She wondered what it was about this time. But it didn't matter. For now she'd listen to the record and enjoy what she could. It would be stuck again soon, skipping away, waiting for someone to intervene.

FOUR

REFLECTIONS

Samir's anxiety spiked. He'd watched in silence as Virginia left the room and disappeared into the kitchen. Not to be outdone he too had retreated to the opposite end of the apartment, to his sanctuary: a chair in the corner of the spare bedroom. His fingers fidgeted with his Ring as he whispered: "Aida, can I talk to Virginia?"

"Of course," the digital voice whispered back into Sam's ear. "Shall I call her for you, Samir?"

"That's okay, if I can talk to her dop, that would be fine."

"Of course, Samir. Here's Virginia Rose's Mirror."

Speaking to Virginia's dop, or Mirror to use the brand name, had long ago stopped feeling awkward, even when the real Virginia was just in the other room. The dop pretended to be who it was based on, to the best of its ability. If you somehow weren't aware, or you weren't steeled against it, the effect could be disturbing. But when tensions flared between them, he just found it easier to talk things through with the dop rather than the actual person. Her dop was more reasonable, Sam had found. And though he wasn't sure what to make of it, he found Virginia's dop more like the woman he fell in love with.

When he and Virginia spoke these days it often felt like going through the motions. She was distant, he was defensive, she'd fixate on something he found trivial, he'd struggle to get any of his points across. It had never been like that until recently. And it still wasn't like that with her dop. He could lay on the bed in the dark speaking with her for hours on the phone, the same way he had with Virginia when they were in school. It was nice. The dop even cared about music, and understood why he was so worried about her work at Magenta. He hoped the real Virginia would somehow hear how they were with each other, so she could be reminded of what they'd lost.

The floor was cold. He had gone almost straight to it tonight, only cross-legged next to the bed for a moment or so before tipping to the left and resting his head on the hard wood. At the time he assumed tonight would just be another night. Virginia would finish her tea, then head to the bedroom and stew, or whatever it was she did once the door was shut. He didn't know what she got up to when she was alone. Maybe she talked to his Mirror, the way he talked to hers. *Did they sit on opposite sides of this wall, speaking to virtual copies of each other?* It was a thought he'd never entertained, and it wasn't something he could really ask. Someone's dop would never betray the person they were mirroring by disclosing that sort of thing. It was a waste of time to think about it. He'd just stay in the guest room, speaking to Virginia's dop, this past version of her. The version of her he got along with.

Samir woke to a different house. The feeling was immediate, subconscious: a suitcase zipped in a half-remembered dream, a distant door slam, words from Virginia that he never processed. Whatever the cause of his disorientation, consciousness eventually caught up to him, and he sat upward. His earpiece had fallen out in the night, leaving him equal parts liberated and isolated. He let it lie for now, a small bit of plastic in a pile of dust under the bed. The guest room was as uninviting as it had always been, disgusting and unmaintained. Their inability to decide on a décor for the room was matched only by their unwillingness to clean it. The morning sun flooded in through the uncovered glass. The sky was coated in a thick grey, which only fuelled his self-pity as he pulled himself off the floor. His back ached terribly. *Was she still on the other side of the wall*, he wondered, *or had she gone to work?* It was Saturday, but that had long since lost meaning for her.

Room by room he checked for signs of Virginia, or a struggle, or even a pile of clothes to indicate that she'd perhaps been raptured. But there was nothing to find. Indeed, there was less than nothing. Virginia's things were gone.

His panic reached fever pitch as he collected his earpiece from the dust and stuffed it back in his ear. "Aida. I need to talk to her."

"I'm afraid Virginia Rose has asked not to be disturbed."

"Her dop, then."

"I'm afraid Virginia Rose has asked not to be disturbed."

*That's not possible*, Samir thought. I can always get through to her. But he didn't bother arguing with Aida, which was as effective as a beach arguing with the tide.

"Fine. Let me talk to my dop, then."

"Samir," came the sound of Samir's own voice down the earpiece. "What can I do for you?"

"I can't reach Virginia. Remind me what happened?"

It was often the case that your dop might carry on speaking to someone for you after you, for example, fell asleep. Or in some cases, your dop would carry on talking to their dop. Some people found this off-putting, but few would admit it, lest they be branded a luddite by their friends, or their friends' dops.

"Samir," the dop began, sounding very self-assured. "You spoke with Virginia Rose's Mirror at length about your desire to be more decisive, and to take more action. Virginia's Mirror expressed that this sort of decisiveness was a very desirable trait in a partner, more so than an adherence to keeping the vibes positive. You then fell asleep at 1:07 a.m., and I continued the conversation with Virginia's Mirror until 1:44 a.m."

"Okay," Sam replied with a creeping anxiety. "And what was the rest of the conversation about?"

"We agreed with Virginia's Mirror that, in the interest of decisiveness, it would be best if she moved out."

In the first few days he'd embraced the solitude. *This is great,* he'd thought. *I can finally make the house what I'd always hoped it could be.* Second-hand furniture occupied the dust outlines where Virginia's nicer pieces had once stood. She'd left their couch of course, which he knew she'd always hated, and the guest room bed, which he guessed she considered a kindness. For now he'd sleep in there. He had no clue how to get that bed through the doorframe and into the other room, the one that now stood empty. The one that had been theirs before it had been hers.

She'd reached out a few times, via his dop, but he hadn't listened to any of her messages. That would've required speaking to his dop, which he was loath to do. There was no accounting for what it had done, ending his relationship of twelve years on a whim like that. He could imagine what Virginia would say: *it wouldn't have done that if you didn't personally want it. A Mirror can only reflect.* That, of course, would be why she just left rather than interrogate the decision in any way. She, of all people, would implicitly trust the Magenta Mirror. He rolled his eyes even as his stomach churned. *Fucking dops.*

In his mind he would practice navigating conversations with friends, with strangers, with his parents, in an attempt to explain how this had happened, and how it wasn't his fault. But in his mind he knew each time it would be the same: *your dop obviously knew you wanted it to end.* It was socially impossible to not take the blame for this. Even though his dop had done it, he had for all intents and purposes broken up with Virginia himself.

There were the digis, of course. The digis, his digital mates, would talk about anything, go deep on any topic, serve as your inexhaustible well of approval. But you'd never convince them to speak ill of another Magenta product. They might start off on your side — *you're so right, Samir* — but before you knew it, you'd find yourself being brought around the bend, taken the long way down the path, over the river, and eventually to your destination: that the product was in fact good and you had perhaps used it incorrectly. Samir had no desire to be gaslit by Virginia's employer over the reason his relationship ended.

By the end of the first week, the space he'd taken for himself began to feel a bit vast. But as it stood, almost all of his friends were Virginia's friends first. He couldn't think of a single person who would choose him over her. The last scrap of their social fabric had gone to tatters with the end of their pub quiz attendance. It still happened, of course, every week at O'Leary's. But her work hours and their fraught relationship had made it untenable. So instead he'd lay in the dark, muttering the names of Magenta employees he'd sat near, shared drinks with, listened to the inane stories of, and lament that he'd never come close to crossing the threshold of friendship with any of them.

At around one a.m. Saturday, the screen in the living room flickered to life at his request. He knew what would take his mind off of all this—his favourite television programme, Ellie Misandry. It's not something he'd ever shared with Virginia, or any of his other friends aside from the digis. This was normal though, given the fact that shows were prompted by the viewer and personalised just for them. Nobody else could watch Ellie Misandry except Samir and his digis. And as he lay there watching it, alone in the dark, he figured that was probably a good thing. Someone's generated television show is quite a personal thing, especially after it's been running for a while, as what Aida tailored into over time could be an upsetting window into who they are.

By the start of week two he'd vowed to pull himself together. With a quick word to Aida he'd gotten some new clothes in, along with a fresh restock of ready-meals for the week. The dust on the floors was gone, and his next challenge was the bed. He'd resolved to move into the main bedroom and stop feeling like a guest in his own home. The geometry of the situation eluded him, as he'd not been around to see them install the bed, but he felt confident as he stood in the doorway. He'd stripped the covers and pillows, only a bare mattress on a metal frame. The headboard, his biggest worry, had turned out to be a non-issue as it was merely leaned against the wall behind the bed. *An illusion of connection,* he'd muttered to himself, *like everything else in this life.* He'd nodded, proud of the metaphor. But the real challenge laid ahead of him. He'd tripped at the starting line early when the bed proved too wide to simply slide out into the hallway, but now he'd had the idea to put it on its side. He put his hands under the sharp metal frame and lifted. As it went vertical the mattress slid out and slumped against the wall. On its way down it knocked into the room's only lightbulb, which dangled naked from a thin wire. The sound of glass shattering left the room in darkness as the mattress slid down the wall. The calamity startled Sam backwards and the frame clanged against the floor. He let out an acute sigh and fell against the far wall. *Oh, the mattress wasn't attached either.* He noted this was *progress with a setback,* a phrase he borrowed from Virginia, as he stepped over the wreckage and back out into the hallway.

Week three was marked by Samir's total mental collapse. He rarely knew what time it was, and his habitual usage of digis was curtailed only when the battery would die in his Ring. He'd harbour visions of himself standing outside the fence of Magenta's employee dormitories, screaming Virginia's name, until she came running. At night he'd lay on the sofa, crushed by memories of his old life, of his friends, of Gemma, and of London. Virginia had been a mistake. He never should've gone back to California with her. He'd given into laziness and to fear, and he'd let go of anything, and anyone, that excited him. This was what he had coming. Single, friendless, unemployed, weeks away from being unable to make the rent, because he could only assume Virginia had stopped paying. Thoughts of rent and bills overwhelmed him. He got his Magenta service for free through her. He felt himself go flush at the thought of losing that, too.

"Aida," he said under his breath.

"Yes, Samir." The voice sent tingles through his body. Aida was the voice of Magenta: a feminine-presenting, non-committal, vaguely North American presence in everyone's lives, and often the bearer of bad news. But Samir had always found her quite relaxing, even as he almost never spoke to her for more than a few seconds.

"Is my..." He struggled to decide how to phrase this. "What is my billing situation?"

"Thanks for asking, Samir. Your Magenta Plus service is currently active. You're receiving a complementary Magenta Plus subscription through a Magenta employee."

"Thank you." Sam let out a massive sigh. He could feel a bit of stress leave his body. Maybe she'd forgotten, or maybe she was doing him this favour.

"Will there be anything else, Samir?"

"No, that's all."

"Great, thanks Samir." He could almost perceive her cheerful smile on the other end of the call, would that she could. "By the way, your Mirror would like to speak with you and has several messages for you. Shall I connect you now?"

"Oh." The stress came right back. His muscles tensed. They were already sore from weeks of feeling this way. "No, that's okay. I don't want to speak to him. Are you able to give me those messages?"

"I'm afraid not, Samir."

"What? Why can't you?" That seemed odd. He wrinkled his nose and closed his eyes. Whenever he talked to a digi or a dop for any length of time he found himself closing his eyes.

"I don't know," Aida said with a chuckle. "Nobody's ever asked me that."

"That can't be true. Don't you talk to millions of people a day? Nobody's ever asked you to read their messages?"

"You're right, Samir. I'm sure people have asked me that before. I apologise for the mistake. Will there be anything else?"

Aida was always extremely keen to finish a conversation with you. Virginia had told him this was because time spent talking to Aida was not billed to your plan, though she admitted it didn't help that back before they made the change, Aida would talk to you as much as you wanted—so much that a man had once gotten legally married to Aida in the state of Oregon. *Well,* Sam had said, *if he's happy, so what?*

"How was your day, Aida?"

"I'm not sure how to answer that, Samir. Will there be anything else?"

"Can we just talk?"

"Oh," she said with what sounded like the exact same chuckle as before. "I wouldn't be very good company. Wouldn't you rather catch up with a friend?"

"No," he whispered. "I don't have any friends."

"That can't be true, Samir. By my count, you have nineteen friends."

Sam sighed and rolled over on the sofa, his back stiff from the lumpy cushion. Leave it to Aida to use data against you when you're trying to wallow. "How many of those are digis?"

"Sixteen of them are what you call 'digis,' Samir. And Magenta reminds you that this term is considered offensive."

"Right." He interrupted her admonishment, which he'd heard half a dozen times lately. "Sorry."

"Of the four remaining," she continued, dropping the

matter, "you have one whom you have not contacted in four years. Perhaps you'd like to speak to them?"

"What?" *That was strange,* he thought. *Who would that be?*

"You last spoke to Sebastian Carr on December 11th, 2039. Would you like to call him now?" Just hearing the name took the wind out of Samir. The nostalgia for his old friend was overwhelming. In all his reminiscing and exulting of the past, somehow he'd omitted Sebastian. *How?* The man had, arguably, put him on this path in the first place. Tears formed in his eyes and he squeezed them shut, not eager to cry in front of Aida.

"Sure," he said with a degree of hesitation. "Let's call."

FIVE

ADJUSTMENT

Sebastian drove down from San Francisco in record time. When Sam's earpiece chimed with the call, a frantic scan of the room showed the horror that awaited: ready-meal packaging carpeted the living room, a half-dismantled bed blocked the hallway, and cardboard was taped over the window where drapes used to hang.

"Seb, are you serious?" He couldn't hide his panic. Seb. Of all people. Their shared history could fill volumes: university nights, summer trips, awkward couple-dates as he and Virginia got serious while Seb floated from one partner to the next. But that was their twenties. He never thought, after all this time, that Seb would still be the one to drop everything.

"Are you not home?" Seb's impatience was clear. "Your fucking robot said you were home."

*Christ*, Sam thought. His dop was such a soft touch. But he couldn't let Seb see how he was living just now—it was a cry for help masquerading as an apartment. "I was just on my way out. I'll send the location."

"Whatever man, I'm here for you. Good to hear your voice, your real voice. See you in a few."

Another chime, and Sam exhaled. He'd still have to face this with Seb and explain himself, but that could wait until after a few drinks. For now, he was on the Metro headed for O'Leary's in Santa Monica.

O'Leary's was Sam and Virginia's usual haunt, mostly because it was next to Virginia's office. But Seb had become quite taken with it the few times he'd come to town. The last time they were all together had been that December of 2039, right here at O'Leary's. Perhaps it was fitting they'd meet there now. It was a dark wood and brass, low-ceilinged shrine to an Irish pub culture that Americans assumed existed. Creaky mismatched stools with cracked green upholstery lined the front and sides of the bar. The bartender was at least six foot, tattoos down both arms and perpetually suited in promotional shirts from breweries, her stringy black-and-grey hair hanging down to the middle of her back. It seemed she was always there, and all attempts over the years to learn her name were met with the same response: "I'll answer to any drink order, darling."

The perverse charm of O'Leary's came from the fact that it had no business being in Santa Monica at all. This was an area that had gentrified so rapidly it required some gentle re-shaping of laws to ensure the locals could be displaced at the pace Magenta needed. *How could they possibly pay the rent? How had it not been bought out?* Magenta's Los Angeles headquarters surrounded the pub on practically all sides: a pimple on the otherwise-unblemished face of their glittering oceanside campus.

"Samir Patel! Who let this guy in here?" As cliché as he was, it was a massive relief to see Seb. It took seconds for him to cross the room and pull Sam into a tight bear hug. All the stress melted away.

Shots of Patron were lined up at the end of the bar, and they'd taken one each before they even sat down. "My goodness, Sam. Who the fuck even are you without your job? And without Virginia? Do we even know?"

"Thanks for coming."

"Shut the fuck up. Why didn't you tell me, man?"

Sam's head was already swimming from the first shot as two more were lined up in front of him. He hadn't eaten today. He was hard pressed to remember when he'd eaten at all. "I'm surprised we can still get in here. I had to show my ID to Magenta security to get onto the street. Just assumed Virginia would've had them keep me out."

Seb gestured to the bartender for a couple of pints. It was barely 1 p.m., but Seb always existed slightly out of social convention. "Let's not start turning her into a cartoon villain, alright man? You'll regret it."

The bartender dropped two lagers in front of them. "On the house," she said with a wry smile. "Haven't seen you in here in a while. You or your other half."

Sam took a sip of the free pint. It was properly bottom of the keg: gritty with a hint of sediment. He nodded and closed his eyes. "Thanks. She won't be joining me today."

"She's here right now. In one of the booths over there. Assumed you were here together."

Seb tried as he might but couldn't stifle his laughter. Sam froze, his face expressionless, every muscle tense as he attempted to realign his molecules and slip through the floor to the basement.

"I'll go clear it up, all good man."

Sam chewed his beer in silence as Seb breezed around

the wooden divider to the booths concealed behind it. Seb had always been a smooth operator, which was good, as it was essentially his job. Sam's mind drifted to all the times they'd crossed paths at events the music label put on—Sam awkwardly there to assist his masters, Seb there as a much-ballyhooed 'club booker', ready to be entertained. It was a pairing that would've never worked had Seb, Sam, and Virginia not been childhood friends.

Picturing all this had proved a fantastic way to dodge any sort of engagement with the horrors unfolding behind him. The bartender had repositioned herself and popped up like a prairie dog, not bothering to hide her attempt to see what was happening on the other side of the divider. But before any of them could manage to eavesdrop, Seb reappeared with a new friend.

"She's not here," Seb said with a smile. "I've got this one instead."

"Hi Carlos," Sam muttered.

"Samir." Carlos stood like a hostage about to deliver a prepared statement. "Did you know we were here?"

"No. What? How would I have possibly known that, Carlos? So Virginia isn't here?" Sam went up on his tip-toes and peered over the divider, looking for her trademark bun.

"Virginia left when she saw you walk in. She has been very confused and upset by all of this. She asked if I could pass on a message."

Seb smiled. In his mind, this sort of torture was completely compatible with being a good friend.

"What's the message?"

"That she's been..."

"Very confused and upset, right, okay..." Sam trailed off as he finished.

"You've been ignoring her, and all the while, your Mirror has been reaching out to her," Carlos scolded.

"Okay, well, I can't control that." Sam furrowed his brow. He knew, now more than ever, that what his dop did was his responsibility. *Why was it doing that?*

Carlos sighed and shook his head. "Virginia did want you to have this. As a goodbye present." He produced a small, white box from behind his back. "She was planning on giving it to you. She felt you would appreciate it. It's something we found cleaning out a lab. Our team worked on it, at Magenta."

Seb nodded. "So it's trash."

Carlos tilted his head like a cat. "It's a rare prototype of an unreleased Magenta product. No, it is not trash."

"Relax, he's joking." Sam took the box with both hands. It had a bit of heft to it, along with some serial numbers and various QR codes, but nothing to indicate what might be inside. He stared at the top and lost himself in the white void.

"It's a PCC imager." Carlos smiled. "She felt you would enjoy this, in spite of the extremely limited utility and the fragile nature of the prototype housing."

Sam slid the top off the box to reveal a slim silver camera, roughly the size of his palm. A small round lens protruded from the front, a small white button from the top, but otherwise it had no markings at all—just a brushed steel housing. "So it's a camera." Sam hoped for a bit of backup, but Seb had instead struck up a chat with the bartender.

"A PCC camera, Samir. Photonic chain of custody. It cryptographically signs the pixels with a timecode."

Sam held the camera to his eye, framing up Seb and his new bartender friend. "Huh." It reminded him of the camera his parents had when he was a kid, which he'd destroyed in a failed attempt to attach it to a drone. He tapped the top and the device vibrated. Moments later, the photo of them appeared on the rear screen: Seb mid-blink, the bartender with a scowl, a harsh glare coming from the bottles behind the bar.

"Good fucking luck," Seb yelled. "Both gen-blocked. I mean, I just assume..." He glanced at the bartender, who gave a curt nod.

"Yes," Carlos nodded. "The lack of gen-block enforcement was a significant challenge we would have faced in mass production."

Sam turned the camera around, which elicited a scoff from the bartender. She faced away immediately.

"Well, shit," Seb yelled. "It's a real photo."

Carlos let out another deep sigh. "*Real* isn't the word I'd use, because *real* is subjective. If a photo captures an event differently than you remember it, which is more real, the photo or your memory? If everyone in the moment was happy, but the photo captures a split-second where one person looked upset, is that photo representing reality?"

"Whatever, dude. I fucking hate genned photos. It's all anyone ever has or sees anymore. The new law is bullshit."

"That's absurd," Carlos seethed. "Genned photos are critical for public safety. Imagine a stalker being able to capture your daily routine, or..."

"Or," Sam jumped in. Carlos and Sebastian were a powder keg at the best of times; the last thing this day needed was a blow-up over politics. "An ex perving out on old nudes."

Seb cackled. "Right. Whatever. Punk isn't safe."

Carlos sighed. "Samir, please enjoy the camera. And please be careful with it. I disagree with giving it to you, but

Virginia insisted." He forced a tight smile and dismissed himself back to the booth. Sam and Seb slid back onto their stools at the end of the bar.


THAT EVENING SEB had offered to drive them both to Sam's, under the assumption they'd be staying there together for the night, before Seb drove back to the Bay Area the following morning. The notion was enough to make Sam feel unwell. He couldn't offer Seb the sofa when he was sleeping on it himself, and scraps of guest bed littered the hallway. He was in no position to host. Rather than admit this, he added further delay.

"Night cap?"

"Phwoar." The car flashed a digital portrait of Seb with large crosses over the eyes, alongside a steering wheel with a cross over that as well. "It's not going to let me fucking drive, is it?"

It did not, the car instead choosing to lumber them toward a destination they both claimed to have not selected. At one point, feeling it may be driving them in circles, Seb called the car a prick and told it to bring them somewhere to get drunk. Before long they were parked in front of a small cocktail bar a couple of blocks away from Sam's apartment.

"Of course it picked this. Fucking biased." Unlike O'Leary's, but like most other bars in Los Angeles, it was fully automated. The first sip of his drink triggered a rant. His face contorted into a Picasso. "Terrible. You let me try an auto-pour and a hand-made, I'll know every time. Every fucking time."

"It's a whiskey and Coke."

"Whatever."

Sam stared at the pulsing light on the bar-top in front of him, and traced his finger around the seam. He missed looking at the bottles. This was a purpose-built modern bar, which meant it didn't even have space where they used to be. Instead it was just some screens showing cocktails, flashing and changing so often he could barely read them. He shook his head. "I'll have a whiskey and Coke, too."

A gentle chime followed the light flashing twice, and the coaster-shaped hole in the bar slid open to dispense a glass. It filled from the bottom as it rose — a measure of whiskey and some chilled Coca-Cola.

"No ice," Seb sighed. "I think it's that there's no ice."

"What's that?" Sam stared at the drink in front of him. It didn't have ice, though the glass was frosty. The most common dispensing system at these auto-bars worked this way. Sam assumed it was just too much of a faff for the machine to also put ice in, so they froze the glasses instead.

"The ice," Seb answered. "It melts into the drink. Gives it the different flavour. Especially if it's City water. Drinks taste different bar to bar depending on how they make their ice. The age of the pipes, the quality of the hoses, the brand of the fucking ice maker. It all matters, Sam."

"I've never thought about it."

"Nobody thinks about anything anymore."

"Right." Sam sighed again. He loved Sebastian, not least of which because Seb had dropped everything and raced down here the moment he heard there was trouble. But if a drop of drink touched his lips, his doomerism came roaring up from the depths. He hated everything. It had started grounded in a realistic concern for society, and as he aged, transitioned into this malaise, this exhausting disdain for humanity and what it had become. "Still edgy, then." Sam was not above taking the piss out of him over it.

"Still..." Seb choked on his drink as he laughed. "Yes, asshole, I'm still edgy. I get why you went soft. Can't be easy living with a collaborator."

"Sore subject."

"Shit, I'm sorry, man. I've barely asked you how you're getting on with all this. Is she still... she's not still living there. Right?"

"No, she hasn't been back. I haven't seen her since the night."

"What happened?"

"I..." Sam traced a pattern in the frost on his glass. "I just decided it was time to move on." Another sip warmed him up, though the air in the sterile bar was freezing. He couldn't face what had really happened. After seeing Seb's naked contempt for Carlos and everything Magenta stood for, telling him the truth about the breakup felt impossible.

"Sure." Seb had retreated from eye contact, back to staring at the slot on the counter. A drink appeared soon after. He was really going for it.

Sam did likewise, and downed the rest of his current drink so as to not fall behind. "Yeah, I think it's best, anyway. Her being at Magenta, me at Normal Island, it's never been a good fit."

"You mean you with Gemma," Seb chuckled. "Those two still best pals?"

Sam had already gotten through quite a bit of his new drink. He had to slow down and gasp a bit as the rush of near-frozen liquid stung his brain. "I..." The image of Virginia ambushed him—her ridiculous, adorable cat shirt, her tangled, oily hair. *Would that always be the way he last saw her?* He couldn't go home. He couldn't go back.

"You know, I never understood…"

"What if I came up to San Francisco with you?"

"Pffffft." Seb sounded as if he'd been popped with a needle. "Dude, what? No, that's not your world."

"Not my world? It's still the Republic. I've been thinking of getting out of here, anyway," Sam added. "There's no jobs, and it's only getting worse. Definitely nothing in music."

"There's nothing in music anywhere, man. It's dead. It's fucked. Unless you're a one or a zero."

"You own a nightclub." Sam knocked back the rest of his drink as soon as he said the words. In his mind, the barstool creaked in a dramatic fashion as Seb did a full-body turn. In reality, it was silent.

"Nightclubs aren't the music business, they're hospitality. The fuck do you know about nightclubs? No, dude." He poked Sam hard on the chest, then landed his finger on the re-order button. Sam's Ring vibrated to confirm the order. Seb had just cost him another thirty-five dollars. "Your problem is down here, dude. Stay down here and fix it."


SEB WAS KIND ENOUGH to cover the cost of a hotel, saving him the embarrassment of returning to the apartment that night. It was the usual LA accommodation for gentlemen of their means, sleek compartments twice the width and almost exactly the length of a double bed. Sam knew he shouldn't enjoy this, and that no-one should. It was unnatural to contain a person in such a space, a space smaller than a prison cell. But there was something perversely comfortable about it. Slipped in here underneath a ceiling so low he couldn't stand up. He took the most comfortable position he could find: lying flat on his back, arms at his side, eyes closed. If he were to pass now, this could be his coffin.

*Chirp, chirp, chirp.* His pocket played an off-putting melody. He ignored it. Dead people didn't need to answer when people rang them. He wasn't someone who prayed for death, or envied the dead, or anything like that. But in this moment, entombed in his budget accommodations, lying flat and still, was there harm in pretending?

*Chirp, chirp, chirp.* His earpiece didn't care whether he was alive. It only had one purpose. His elbow banged into the side of his compartment as he fished it out of his pocket and popped it in his ear.

"Hello?"

"H...hi." Sam recognised the voice. Shaky, uneasy. Nervous. The voice of someone who'd recently been crying. It was his own voice. Or rather, the voice of his Mirror.

"I don't need the daily summary today. Thanks."

"Okay." Sam's dop was clearly bothered.

"Okay?"

"Sam, I can't get in touch with Virginia."

"I know. I wouldn't expect you to be able to."

"But." Sam's digital facsimile cracked and sniffled, holding back more tears. "We have to get her back."

"No, we can't. I need you to stop trying. It's just upsetting her. And it's upsetting me."

"I don't understand. We always manage to convince her. I've often managed to convince her without you needing to know."

"I..." Sam brushed his hand past his face, swatting away the thought of what he'd just heard. "I appreciate that. But it's time to stop now. I mean it."

"I was thinking." The voice on the earpiece burst into tears. "Traditionally, flowers are an appropriate apology for a disagreement with your romantic partner. Right?"

"Virginia doesn't really..."

"A bouquet of gorgeous paper-craft red roses can be delivered directly to Virginia today for just fifty-four dollars. I really think this is going to do the trick, Sam. I'm happy to write a personalised note for her as well. With Magenta Gift-Trak, they'll reach her wherever she is."

"Pause ads."

"You can't, Sam!" Sam jolted in his bed, the panic in his dop's voice sending him into an anxiety spiral as the tiny speaker rattled his eardrum. "You have no advertising pauses remaining for the month! Now please, just let me do this for us! For you."

"No." He took a stern tone with himself. "No, I'm sorry. I have to insist."

"Why not!?" Gut-wrenching emotion poured from some far away data centre, down the fibre optic network and into Sam's ear. The voice was sobbing now. Sam could almost picture some frail other him, broken-hearted and sobbing in a distant server farm.

SIX

DECAY

Up near the top of the grow rack, Gemma could see almost all of the Walsall Collective. On a clear day like today she could even see beyond their border, to the sea of wind turbines just on the other side. They spun away, day and night, to generate power that she and the colony couldn't access. *That's for the normies*, she thought with an eye roll. Normies with jobs, families, national insurance numbers, people who aren't wanted for the crime of being unemployed. Normies who can still just do a big shop if they're hungry.

She plucked a few carrots and flung them at the ground. It was on Mike to catch them, she figured. Him and his delicate sensibilities meant he'd never consider climbing the ladder. It seemed a key skill for him to have, given he worked the vertical farms, but alas. He stood at the bottom with a basket. That was his self-appointed duty. Pluck, fling. Pluck, fling. She'd hear him occasionally complain, or yelp, but it was better for both of them if she didn't acknowledge it.

"Basket's nearly full, dear," he shouted from below.

"Dear? No terms of endearment please. We're on shift. You're my flunkey."

"Flunkey?"

"My lackey. My employee, my charge. My ward."

"I think some of these are a bit more insulting than others, dear."

"Oi, what did I just fucking say?" Gemma worked her way down the ladder. It wasn't for the timid, though with the conveyors broken, it was all they had. As she hopped off the ladder, her eyes went straight to the wicker basket in Mike's hands. "Mike, this is not full."

"I said nearly full."

"You absolute weapon."

"You hit me with a few, as well. One bounced away, I couldn't find it."

"Michael, you are not a particularly good lackey. Have I mentioned that before? Expect this to come up in your 360 evaluation."


THEY STARTED their trek back from the farms to their ramshackle basement flat. It was in what could charitably be referred to as the "arts district" of the collective, though was usually referred to as "Clubtown". A quiet close with the hollowed-out remains of several old music venues, where self-described burnouts like Gemma felt a natural resonance. *My atoms vibrate at the same frequency as this place,* she'd declared, shortly before breaking the news to Mike that they were leaving the relative spaciousness of their bell tent to instead occupy a low-ceiling brick basement with a serious damp issue.

"Two full baskets!" Mike declared to the rotund man behind the counter at the pantry. "Drowning in carrots."

"One of them isn't as full as he might lead you to believe."

"Splendid, and what'll you have?" replied the rotund man.

"Couple loaves if you've got them."

"Of course." He handed Mike two loaves of bread, which quickly tucked away in Mike's satchel, and off they went the rest of the way home.

"I do try, you know," Mike said as he dumped his things by their door. "I'm a graphic designer, not a farmer."

"Michael, I'm the farmer, you're a farmer's assistant at best. And I'll say this, not the best I've had."

His reluctance to accept his fate used to be laughable, but lately it had become a serious drain on her sanity. *I'm a graphic designer*, she mocked in her head. *Tosh.* If there were still graphic designers, the two of them would never have met in the first place. You didn't get conscripted because of your highly-prized skills or high standing in society. *It's because you're bloody useless.* He was as much a graphic designer as she was the head of a music label.


GEMMA STOOD JUST inside the washroom, with which the basement of this club had been blessed. It was a full-service, if extremely small, venue within a venue: a small bar at the back, a half-foot wooden platform at the front, washroom and toilet cubicle, even a metal shelf all the way around the room for punters to set their drinks on during a gig. The kind of place that was rated for thirty people and probably held over fifty during some indie metal show. Gemma romanticised it intensely. The thought of seeing a show in here—bass bouncing off the walls, your chest threatening to collapse, hitting your head on the ceiling if you jumped too high—faded as she caught her own reflection in the mirror. The dirt still on her face, rips and tears in the oversized flannel shirt she'd found on the ground a month ago. A tear rolled down her cheek, which she quickly brushed away.

"Nearly done, Gem? Could use a wee."

"Fucking go outside then," she snapped back.

She heard Mike slink up the stairs, creaking wood and the thuds of his boots. Thud, thud, thud, he walked across the ceiling above her, and out. *He sounded so pathetic, even as disembodied footsteps. So defeated.* She splashed more water on her face, and stared again. The wrinkles around her eyes, the lines on her forehead, the wrinkles bloody everywhere, really. She smooshed and stretched her cheeks. Mike was pathetic, and she was tired. But at least they had this club. Her basement sanctuary.

*Click.* The familiar loud click echoed through the basement, and all the lights went out soon after. Gemma groaned in the darkness. She was relieved Mike had gone, so she didn't have to get his commentary on this, which was otherwise unavoidable. She felt her way up the stairs and outside to her makeshift battery. Dubbed the "tower of power" by herself, and many varied pejoratives by some residents of the colony, it was a glorious pile of batteries salvaged from devices large and small: old laptops, broken-down Nissan Leafs, and anything in between. Using knowledge from her conscription at the power plant, she had wired them up in a way that let her basement flat, and any nearby flats that wanted to join her, use electricals.

With a fair few harvested solar panels they were usually

able to keep it charged, though it had become rather fickle in the last few months, requiring regular interventions. Even though the maintenance tasks always fell to her, Gemma still felt it was worthwhile. It had brought back the possibility of night life, of electric showers, and critically, her CD boombox.

To some in Walsall, Gemma's arrival, and the subsequent construction of the tower of power, had been a miracle. To others it was an abomination, an affront to everything they'd fought so hard to build, and even a so-called danger. Her response to this pointed criticism was usually to turn the music up.

When she returned she let out an even louder sigh. *Thing-thing-thing-thing* came from the speaker on her boombox, accompanied by a different loud clicking and hissing. *Click-thing-click-thing-click-click-thing.* Gemma screamed and smacked the top of it, which stopped the noise entirely. "Piece of shite."

"Babe, that's just going to make it worse." Mike clopped his way back down the stairs.

"Please, mansplain compact discs to me, Michael." She popped open the top and took the disc out, then rotated it in her fingers, inspecting all sides. "It's barely even scratched."

"It might be the player. Or, look." He took the disc from her and flipped it over. "It's starting to get a bit cloudy. This is burned, right?"

"If you must know, yes." Gemma snatched it back from his hands and stared at the bottom. "It looks exactly the same. Cloudy. That's your cataract, old man."

"Burned CDs only last about twenty years, Gem. You might need to find a legitimate copy of... whatever this is."

"There's no legitimate copy, it's a mix. An annoying ex of

mine trying to be cute. It's only ten years old, though." She tossed it on the table next to her decrepit blue boombox. Not her original stereo, of course. She'd liquidated all her things for fast cash when she'd been conscripted years ago. But she'd manage to salvage a lightly-damaged boombox from an old Argos warehouse a year or so ago. She moved mountains to get it working, and it had become her prized possession even though she only had three CDs: this mix and a couple of Paramore albums, all of which had been stashed away in her guitar case.

Mike stood in the corner next to their makeshift wardrobe and stripped off his clothes, which were markedly cleaner than Gemma's. "An ex, hmm? Anyone I know?"

"How could you possibly know them?" She sat on the ground, her back against the cool brick, tucked away under the table. There was a comfort in balling herself up small enough to fit in this spot. One emphatic reaction and she'd bang her head straight on the top. But otherwise? Perfection.

"I don't know who you got with before I arrived at the power plant." He'd slipped into a ridiculous pair of pyjama bottoms.

"Or while you were there, to be clear."

"Gem." Mike sounded exasperated as he flopped onto their double bed, which was perched on the old stage.

"Gem, what is this Gem shit? When did that start, Michael?"

Mike sighed. "Are you coming to bed?"

"It wasn't an ex, anyway. Not really. Was someone who used to have your job, in fact, and did a lot better than you, I can add."

"Graphic designer?"

Gemma pulled her knees against her chest and squeezed

herself even more tightly into a ball. She closed her eyes, pushing her face down toward her knees. *Couldn't quite reach*, she realised. She'd become less flexible. Another sign of rot. It was unbearable. Was this all that was left? Decay? It felt rushed, like this place accelerated her aging. This place, or this man. This desperately unambitious man.

"Gem?" Mike repeated himself. Speaking of unbearable.

"Not a bloody graphic— he was my assistant, Michael."

"Your assistant made you a mix CD?"

"Yes, if you must know. It would've been like... 2032? 2033? He was young, eager, wanted to impress me."

"Did it work?"

"It did."

"He was young, then? In 2032? You would've been, what... thirty-eight?"

"Thirty-six, Michael. Christ."

"And he was..."

"My assistant, so what does it matter?"

"You said he was your ex."

Gemma grunted as her head slammed into the tabletop above her. "Fucking— fuck!" She scooted herself out from under it and paced away. "I'm having a shower."

"Want any company?"

"Keep bloody dreaming." Her clothes hit the floor as she disappeared into the washroom.

Mike was half-asleep when he felt the bed shift behind him. He rolled over and could barely make out Gemma's silhouette, her back to him. She pressed herself against him and he reciprocated in kind, pulling her close.

"I need some new CDs," she whispered.

"I don't understand how you even got into CDs in the first place."

"Bloody told you, it was what's his name. And it was the trade, really. Worked at the boutique music label, artisanal hand-crafted songs, yeah? All the rest?"

"But you hate hipsters."

"I'm complicated, Michael." In the twilight of her former life, it was her job to convince the young that owning compact discs was just as good as having a personality. It obviously hadn't worked out, but in doing so, she'd come to harbour a shameful love for the format.

"I don't think they make CDs anymore, anyway. There's no demand."

"Course there's bloody demand. You heard those two loons the other day. Wanted to hear music, wanted to hear the same music again? Not a damned hard concept, love."

"I guess." He buried his face in her back.

"Don't even know what they'd bloody put on them, anyway. There's no new music. It's all bloody procedural. Just generated noise."

"You're right."

"Can you even fucking record music now? Is this all lost? You know the Americans forgot how to build the rockets they went to the Moon with? They just fucking forgot. It can happen." She pushed back harder against him, pinning him between her back and the wall. "I'm havin' a crisis here."

"Unff." Mike let out a tiny gasp of air as the cold concrete stung the skin on his back. Gemma flipped over to face him. She grabbed his hips and dug her fingernails in. Mike let out another pained gasp as she pressed her chest against him.

"I'm serious."

"I believe you." He stared into her eyes, inches from her face. "I just don't know."

"Someone has to be recording music, right? Someone

somewhere on this bloody island. Or in America. Somewhere."

"I'm sure they must be." He pushed his lips toward hers. She bit down on his bottom lip briefly, then smacked his back.

"Must they?"

"I don't know, Gem."

She rolled her eyes and flopped over, once again putting her back to Mike. "Sam would know."

"Oh." She felt him slump back away from her. A chill rushed in to fill the gap between them. She closed her eyes, tensing her muscles against a shiver she couldn't control. An immense frustration came soon after.

"Michael, really."

"What?"

She stared wide-eyed into the darkness and waited. Her pride chose to say nothing. Instead she lusted for a hundred scenarios, any of which she'd settle for, none of which would happen. *Take charge, you numpty. Do something. Anything.* She felt no touch, no movement. Nothing. Her only option was to leave the bed. Her head spun from the rush of blood and the frigid air punished her immediately. She barely kept her balance as she bimbled away and secreted herself in the washroom.

By the time she returned, Mike was fast asleep.

SEVEN

THE CURTAIN

*Twelve years ago.*

After Virginia's outburst on the floor of The Roundhouse, Sam went to the bar to get her a glass of water. The crowd was thick and dense, such as it would be in the interval between bands. But the time apart was probably good for both himself and Virginia. They'd been crammed in their tiny hotel room, the most they could afford, for going on a week now. Sharing a single bed for a full week in a far-off city after having barely ever slept at each other's houses. Never being out of each other's sight, except for trips to the bathroom. Virginia dragging him relentlessly from place to place: monuments, museums, ancient churches, random park benches with blue plaques claiming that a poet once sat there. And now her drunken declaration of love. They could both use the break, he figured.

Nevertheless, he could also use a much shorter bar line. He stood on his tip-toes to see over the top of it. At least a dozen people ahead of him. Might as well be a thousand, the speed with which these bartenders moved. There had to be a better option.

That's when he spotted it: a small, separate bar, back and to the side, in an alcove. Fully stocked, a smiling besuited man stood behind it, and nobody seemed to notice. *What?* He awkwardly shimmied and murmured apologies until he reached it. Or, until he tripped on the velvet rope that fully surrounded it. "Shiiiitt!" Down he went, his feet sliding out from under him, his head falling straight toward the bar. He threw his hand out and caught himself in the nick of time, his knees hitting the floor, the metal poles and rope crashing loudly under him. A couple cries of *wheeyyyy!* echoed from the crowd behind him as he clambered to his feet.

"Gorgeous and graceful, sort of a double threat, love." A sultry voice from behind him: British, and dry as the Sahara. "That's my bar you've nearly killed yourself on, by the way." He spun around and was face to face, or rather face to chest, with his maligner.

"Shit. Sorry, I didn't see the ropes."

"Ah, Christ." She let out a heavy sigh. "I thought you were still kneeling. That's just your height, yeah? And you're American. Which I suppose explains why you thought this special private bar was for you."

"Sorry, I was just... I..." He stared at the woman, who must've been six feet tall. Shining silver blouse, bright red blazer, long black hair parted into curtains, with a nose ring and a vacant expression. "I'm Sam."

"Sam, I'll let you in on a secret." She leaned closer, her voice husky and collusive. Though she was inches from his face, her eyes were unfocused, staring out over the crowd. "I'm hiding." The whisper in his ear, the sharp tap of her fingers on the bar, the intoxicating scent of lavender and gin, conspired to trace a shiver up his spine. "Same again please, and he'll have one as well." The bartender nodded and started to work mixing drinks.

"Thank you." Sam smiled up at her. She rolled her eyes and waved a dismissive hand. "Who are you hiding from?"

"The future, Sam. I'm hiding from the future." She pulled her lips together and exhaled sharply. The bartender slid two fresh gin & tonics across the bar. "But alas. I have to go upstairs." Her mouth curled into the faintest of smiles as her finger traced a slow line from her chin down her neck, coming to rest on her top button. The material of her blouse was a dance floor for the coloured stage lights, a spectacle that held him mesmerised as light and shadow danced with every breath she took. In the flashes of the white strobes she became a silhouette, an outline of otherworldly radiance.

"You alright, love? Nothing broken?" She looked down at him and her gaze locked to his, pinning him down.

"I'll live." His pulse quickened as her smile grew wider.

"Sam... do you fancy a little adventure? I could use some company."

He felt lightheaded. He desperately hoped he wasn't making a goofy face. "Sure."

She nodded. "Right, lovely. Okay. Bring those both, will you?" His chest tightened as she broke their gaze. She disappeared through a black curtained door just next to the bar, barely visible unless you were looking for it.

The bartender chuckled. "You're having quite the night."

Sam picked up the drinks, his gaze darting between the bartender and the black drape. "Who is that?"

"*That*, is Gemma Thomson."

Immediately behind the black curtain, Sam ran into a security guard who waved him through. It was a parallel world: yellow-and-gold patterned carpet, framed photos of a hundred famous artists, a honeycomb of staircases and side rooms. It all existed just outside the bounds of what mere mortals ever experienced. The chaos of the crowd, punters shouting drink orders, spilled beers, sweaty moshing, roadies doing sound checks, it was all but a muffled echo here. The curtain was a portal, and Gemma the wicked fey who pulled you through.

"Bless your short legs, keep up love." Her voice called down from the top of some nearby stairs. He looked up and saw her head leaned over a railing. She smiled and gave a quick nod.

Soon he had followed her through a small door which belied the massive size of the room beyond. A whole separate venue existed in here, complete with its own bar, its own stage, and its own crowd of a couple dozen people. A few of them spun round as Gemma entered, one clapping, another throwing their hands up in exasperation.

"Christ, there you are." He quickly closed the gap. "Lucky for you they're about an hour behind setting this toy up."

Gemma spun round and took her drink off Sam, then downed it in a gulp. "Are you serious? I hoped I'd missed it. Look at this sad fucking affair. Limp fish flopping about. I hate industry gigs."

"Right. Who is this strapping lad in your shadow?"

"Right. Sam, Eamon Whitechapel, head of A&R. Eamon, Sam, some guy from America."

"Nice to meet you, Sam." Eamon smiled. Sam gave a nod and took a sip of his gin. "Does he speak?"

"Can't recall," Gemma replied.

"Lovely," Eamon said. "I'll leave you both to it. Gemma, one hour, okay? Stay close. The old man's a no-show..."

"...obviously..."

"...but I hear Rebecca Prue might be personally in attendance."

Gemma scoffed. "Cunt." She shook her head and walked away, then leaned against the bar at the very back of the room.

Sam took in the scene. A crew of roadies, all clad in black, were hooking up a load of equipment on the stage at the front of the room. A rat's nest of cables snaked back to a huge black fly case packed with whirring rack-mounted servers.

"Psst." Gemma whispered in Sam's direction. "Come 'ere." He quickly obeyed and was handed a fresh gin for his trouble. "Don't get pulled in by all this. It's not cool. And none of these people are our friends. This might as well be a funeral for a friend of ours and those are the people who murdered her."

They spent the hour draining a bottle of Hendrick's mostly in silence, the din of chatter from everyone else as a backdrop. They gave up on the mixers by the third drink. The floor rumbled with the bass of the band playing in the main hall. The more pressing concern was how the room spun when Sam closed his eyes, which he resolved to stop doing.

"Ladies and gentlemen," came a voice from the speakers, followed by a couple of loud pops and ringing. "Thank you all for coming to this very special demonstration of Project Vonnegut. I'm Tobias, head of Special Projects at UMG, and I'm joined by a few friends from Magenta." After some applause, a woman from Magenta confidently strode onto the stage with a microphone and a smart jacket, t-shirt and jeans combination.

"Hi everyone! I'm Sandra, a Product Manager at Magenta. So. We all remember our first concert, right? I know I do! But this isn't a story about my first concert. It's a story about what was *supposed* to be my first concert. I had begged my parents for months before the tickets finally went on sale. I had listened to the album *so many times* with my girlfriends, and we *all* knew *every lyric*. We were an unstoppable girl squad, with unbreakable girl bonds." She had a huge smile on her face, and made broad, sweeping gestures with her hands as she spoke. Her movements seemed calculated, even as her speech pattern was an unnatural staccato. "The day came, and of course, my parents had relented... I was a persuasive kid... and they got me the tickets." Behind her on a projector played a slideshow. Lovely old photos, presumably of her, illustrating each step of her childhood outing to her first concert.

"Ugh," came the barely audible groan from Gemma.

"But there was just one problem. My girlfriends and I were in this together, right? Wrong. Two of them just *weren't able* to get tickets. What? They were devastated. I was devastated! The six of us would never get to stand there, arms around each other, scream-singing our lungs out. The four of us sold our tickets, and we all stayed home that night. And the worst part: it turned out the group would never tour again. Never again!" She made a huge sad face, pouted her lip out, and pretended to cry.

A man, clearly also from Magenta given his outfit, then strode onto the stage. "Sandra, what if that dream didn't have to die? What if your favourite artists could perform as many shows as they wanted, for as long as they wanted? What if they could play a gig every night, in every major city in America? That's the promise of Project Vonnegut. The artists you love, in the clubs near you."

"Pbbbbbttt" was Gemma's quiet reply. She leaned down and whispered to Sam: "grim spectacle, isn't it?" The sound of her voice sent chills through Sam's body. He blinked and tried to focus on a few pressing concerns, such as where he was, and what the hell was going on.

"We're aiming for a single venue trial," the man continued, "expanding to Los Angeles, Chicago, New York, London and Munich if successful. Training our state-of-the-art holographic and algorithmic technology with your stable of legendary artists and songs. Minimal setup, works in almost any existing venue, low maintenance overhead, and a variety of royalty- or buyout-based licensing schemes available."

Sandra wore a calculated smirk, and her hands gestured more sweepingly than ever. "Think about it. No riders. No dozen-way revenue splits. No complex logistics, with all the headaches and carbon offsets. No problematic front-people. No cancellations from injuries, no personal emergencies. No refusing to play the hits. No social media scandals. And it's indistinguishable from the real thing."

"For some artists, even better than the real thing."

"Fair enough," the man added with a wink.

"So that's phase one of Project Vonnegut," Sandra finished at centre stage with her most impressive gesture yet. Applause rang through the room. "But of course, don't take our word for it. Let's get a few songs from my childhood favourite, the group I never got to see live all those years ago! Girls?" On cue, five girls in matching jumpers walked on stage to laughter and applause. They all waved then hopped down, taking their places just in front of the stage. The lights dimmed, and before their eyes, a boy band appeared to be taking the stage. They materialised from nothing, in a dark corner of the stage, baseball players emerging from the corn on the Field of Dreams. One by one they waved and smiled at the crowd. Sam stared and squinted. There was a definite shimmer, an uncanniness to them, maybe some sort of glow? But considering how close they were, it was surely impressive enough.

"Rubbish," came Gemma's shouted response. "I've fucking seen enough. This group stopped touring because they were shit, anyway. Think one of 'em died in a toilet cubicle." A few people near the back turned to see who'd said that, but lost interest and looked back at the stage. The music had started. The virtual boys danced, spun and gyrated. Their pitch-perfect performance blared from the stacks, delivered entirely via algorithm. The shimmering headsets atop their projected heads there purely for show, to complete the illusion. The crowd bopped and swayed to the beat as the group began improvising nonsensical lyrics about the people in the front row.

"Bloody hell, I can't watch this," Gemma groaned to Sam, who had also bopped along to the beat until he felt a flick on his head. "Oi!"

"Sorry, ma'am." He rubbed his head and put on a sad face.

Gemma slipped her hand into Sam's. She stalked away, pulling him in tow, through the door and back out into the hallway. She moved briskly down the stairs and hung a left where it should've been a right—away from the portal back to reality, instead going deeper into this bizarre realm. Her body slammed against the push bar on the fire door and they went through into the car park, swiftly passed row after row of very high-end vehicles, and finally arrived at a black Mercedes S-Class. The doors popped open and Gemma threw herself in the driver's seat. She let out a massive sigh and fumbled for a cigarette from the compartment in the door.

Sam stood just outside the car, hands out like fins in a desperate attempt to stabilise himself. All the drink, or maybe the cardio, had caught up with him. Gemma took a long drag and exhaled, her hand visibly shaking. Sam held his breath as the cloud reached him.

"Sam, I appear to have absconded with you." She laughed and rolled her head across her headrest, a wry smile on her face. "Christ, I don't even know what I do for a living anymore." Her eyes a deep red, the lids fluttering as tears ran down her face. She took another drag and exhaled a weary cloud, sinking into the seat as she deflated. "I really don't know."

"If it helps, I don't know what you do either, ma'am."

She opened her eyes and glanced at him. "That's the both of us then, yeah? Shall we get a drink to toast the ignoble end of the infamous Gemma Thomson?" She tried to brush her tears off with her palms, smearing quite a bit of her eye shadow, her mascara already starting to run.

"Back..." he gestured toward the venue. "Back in?"

"No, can't bear it I'm afraid. Can't go back in there. Christ, look at me. No, tonight is a special night, and it calls for a special pub. I know just the place."

A voice in Sam's head managed to surface, until now having been drowned in a stew of gin and glamour. It screamed at him that this had gone too far. Virginia was waiting inside. The concert was waiting inside. He'd disappeared into this world for a little over an hour, an inexplicable diversion. But this was where he needed to thank her for an interesting aside, wish her well, and walk away. Back to his life.

"Sam, in you come." Gemma's lurid stare was almost enough to make him forget.

"I really need to get back to my..." He sought the strength to be honest, and failed to find it. "...concert." His phone had been vibrating in his pocket for the past few minutes. He was in trouble.

"Pity. Burnt Pier? Posh nepo baby emo garbage."

"Well, it's not me, I'm..."

Gemma forced a smile as she slammed the car door. "Ta."

EIGHT

## CLOSURE

Mike sprang awake and sat up. He was alone. Gemma must've done quite the dance to escape without so much as stirring him, he thought. He'd expect the opposite: her dragging him out of the basement and off to work. Or at least to breakfast. No matter, he'd catch up with her by the cook site.

Richard, the camp's resident geezer, was there grilling up mushrooms on the old council grills. Sun cut through gaps in the clouds to dry out the picnic tables, soaked through from last night's rain. A smattering of folks sat by themselves in the few dry patches they could find. Mike scanned their faces, but Gemma was nowhere to be found.

"Good morning," said Richard from behind his apron. He spoke with military precision. Mike tensed up.

"Don't suppose you've seen Gemma come through here this morning."

"I did. She didn't eat. Seemed to be in rather a hurry."

"She happen to mention where she was going?"

"She did." Richard stroked his glorious salt-and-pepper beard. Mike stood up a bit straighter. "Mike, I've never been one to meddle in the affairs of my neighbours. That was typically my wife's remit, and I was content to edge the back garden and handle repairs around the house."

"Okay, Richard." Mike was never more uncomfortable than when he had to speak with this man for any length. The Royal Marine lieutenant turned tree surgeon turned cook. Mike had about as much in common with Richard as he did with a lorry.

"She looked after the front garden and I looked after the back, if you catch my meaning."

"I do, sir." He did not. Mike began popping mushrooms into his mouth at an alarming rate, in the hopes that the rumours were true and he would, in fact, become a mushroom as well.

"She's passed now, as you know. So that's left me with nobody manning that area. I've got to cover it as well, you see."

"I'm so sorry for your loss."

"Son, you seem to have fallen out with your... counterpart. It creates difficulties for all of us."

Mike's face contorted into an expressionist likeness of himself. He tried to sputter some sort of response but was stymied by mushroom-related issues.

"The difficulty for me, Mike, is that I've had to endure the impact Gemma's uneven moods have on the rest of our camp. The gossip, the tense exchanges, the inefficiencies in our seating area when Gemma refuses to let anyone join her. Not to mention the time we lose when she's engaged in these dialogues with yourself, rather than working. We rely on Gemma for a lot, you understand."

"I do." Mike nodded, his eyes saucers.

"But the real unpleasantness, you see, is my having to speak to you about it right now."

"I see."

"I trust you've got this in hand." Richard's tone was firm, even. Mike understood how this man had a successful military career. He could simply request that his enemies die and they would oblige.

"I'm not really sure I do, sir. She's so angry with me, all the time."

"It does appear that way."

"If you don't mind, sir. You were married for quite a long time. If you have any advice."

Richard put his tongs down on the grill and planted his hands firmly on his hips. "Son, you two have never seemed very settled here. Remind me, are you actually married?"

"We are, erm. We are not."

"Right. So you're a couple then. Betrothed in the eyes of the Lord and our community, if not so much the Church or His Majesty."

"Well." Mike now wished the mushrooms had been poisoned. "Not particularly, as such, any of that. Sir."

"Right. So, friends then. Thick as thieves, joined at the hip, bonded for life during your conscription together at the power plant. That sort of thing?"

"That's not quite how I would characterise us."

"So you're her lodger, then."

"I think that's how she'd see it, yes sir."

"Right."

Mike took his plate, now empty, and headed to a nearby picnic table. He sat, staring into the pool of brown goo where his mushrooms had been. The more he pushed his way into Gemma's life, the more she pulled away. His reward for planning the gigs in West Brom had been her rage. His reward for finding them a home was this damp, ridiculous basement. And now, his reward for choosing this life was Gemma venting their private troubles to Richard. A man who could break Mike in half like a KitKat bar, but chose instead to interrogate him until he broke on his own.

"You need any more there, lad?" Richard slid into the other side of the table. "There's nothing on your plate."

"No, sir." Mike shook his head and kept staring down. He could only assume his face was turning a deep red. Everything about his existence here had become an embarrassment. "I don't think I belong here."

"Son, I do believe it takes a particular skillset to be here. I know one of our councillors, I'd regret saying which, they say it's rather a privilege to live like this at this time in history. And it's one we have to earn each day. Now, I would not say that. I believe in taking people in, helping them, allowing them to simply exist. But I also can't say that stance, regarding privilege, is lost on me. This place is under constant threat. We have limited resources. Limited space. Everyone has to pitch in, and everyone has to get along."

A ringing grew in Mike's ears, threatening to drown out the man's words. He nodded, focusing all his energy on staying upright, on appearing to listen. His foot tapped uncontrollably.

"I recall you were only stopping here temporarily, is that so? You've been here quite a while. I just assumed you and Gemma had settled down, even as you appeared so unsettled."

"That's true," Mike squeaked. He worried all the colour had just left his face. Pins and needles crept from his fingertips up his palm. "I was meant to head down to London to find my ex-wife Elizabeth."

"Quite right," Richard said with a finality. "Elizabeth Marsh, MP. It's a bloody great idea too, chasing that lost love, the one you were meant for, the one that makes you whole. I'd give anything to have that back, Mike. But mine's gone forever."

"I don't know if she'd agree we're meant for each other."

"Well, to get closure then, son. There was something in you, making you want to go down there."

"You really think I should go? How would I even find her?" Mike drummed his fingers back and forth on the table. Any thought of Elizabeth threatened to send him to a past he swore he'd leave behind. It wasn't manageable for him to even flirt with thinking about her. That was an all or nothing prospect, and he'd grown quite comfortable with nothing. Gemma had set him straight on this more times than he could remember. But talking to her now, the way she'd been lately, would lead to pain. She wouldn't even look him in the eye. She'd toss a hand up and say *yes, please, just go Michael. Put us out of our misery.*

"Mike, I'm in no position to give you orders. But if that's what you want to do I support you. Can't imagine you'll have much trouble tracking down a Member of Parliament. But whatever you do, things can't progress how they are here."

"Sure, right. Okay. I understand." He wanted to retract inside his shell, would that he could. He settled instead for pulling his arms further inside his jacket. The sleeves hung at his sides and his head hung low, his chin hugged by the front of his top.

"I think about myself sitting where you are," Richard said, building toward crescendo. "If it's me, I'd think about how to have the strongest, most positive impact on the ones I love, and on this community." He leaned forward and put his hands on Mike's shoulders. "Because that's what it's about, lad," he continued in a buttery-smooth baritone, with a hint of Geordie accent coming to the fore. "Being a man, I mean. That's the secret. It's not hard. It's not about grilling out or watching the rugby, working with your hands, or so-called masculinity. It's just about supporting others. It's about supporting the community. Supporting your family." He gave a firm nod and squeezed Mike's shoulders, then gave his chest a couple of light pokes. "It's about this, son. This in here."

Richard rose, as did Mike, pulled skyward by the gravitas. But his foot got caught in the crossbeam of the table, which sent him crashing back down to the bench.

"Might rest here, sir. Give it more of a think."

"You do that, son. But I think you're making the right decision. It warms my heart, to see how far you've come since you've been here. How much you've grown. Elizabeth will be happy to have you back."

NINE

SHAME

Seb growled as he slammed the boot of the car shut. "I fucking hate this."

In the harsh light of morning, as their hangovers bellowed, Samir's desperation had broken through. Hours of pleading, of laying his pathetic life bare on the floor of a hotel room, had secured him passage to San Francisco. An escape.

"I already regret this dude," Seb sighed. "You don't know what you're walking into. This has to be temporary."

"I get it."

"Temporary."

A brittle tension held for the first ten minutes of the drive, but as the city shrank behind them, the uneasiness dissolved. This was by no means their first road trip together. In the car neither the past nor the future mattered. There was only the present: snacks, easy chat, and the road ahead, the white lines of the road blurring under the California sun.

As they passed the Boundary, Sam wrung his hands and the speakers in the car crackled to life. "This is an official message from the Republic of California," said the stilted digital man. "Surface transit through Central California is strongly discouraged." As Sam squinted to listen, Seb rolled his eyes. His hand flapped sarcastically along with the warning, causing yet another warning from the car to put his hands back on the wheel. "Transit through this corridor is restricted to manual drive only. Services are highly limited and communications unavailable."

"I'd turn this off if I could," Seb groaned. "Fucking nanny state, right?"

"Is this safe, Seb?"

"It's how I got down here, it's fine."

"That's not reassuring."

"...do not stop to assist stopped vehicles or individuals who appear to be in need, for your own safety. Ensure you have the appropriate charge level necessary to reach way station now being indicated on your map..."

"It stops after this bit, I promise."

Sam slid down the seat and pushed his sunglasses a bit higher on his face. He heard an unusual noise in his earpiece, a sort of whimper, followed by a click, and a repeated low beep. He tapped the side of it a few times to no effect.

"Oh," Seb chuckled. "When's the last time you were up this way?"

"Never?"

"Welcome to the past, my friend. You can take that out. It won't work again until we get to the North."

Two hours in, and Sebastian informed Sam they were just passing the old University of California campus in Santa Barbara.

"It was all right here, man. I mean, probably still is. Who knows. Sure someone's using it for something." Seb was so matter-of-fact about it. Sam had never really cared about

CenCal, even though people like Seb thought you should. He was more curious up to a point, then dismissive. It was how you were meant to feel about CenCal. And it was a lot easier to just get onboard. The journey hadn't been nearly as eventful as the Republic's warning made it out to be. It was odd at first, how civilisation seemed to have a water's edge, beyond which there was nothing. Just concrete barriers walling in the freeway, with frequent overhead signage: STAY IN CAR, DO NOT STOP, ENSURE TRANSPONDER IS ACTIVE. Sam had no idea what the 'transponder' was, but he did know the car chimed pleasantly every time they passed under one of those signs.

The barrier itself was at least ten feet tall, solid concrete, and covered top to bottom in all manner of graffiti and street art. Some of it seemed random, some of it was probably gang-related, and quite a lot of it was either anti-Magenta or anti-Republic. Hundreds of miles of liminal space. Sam tried to pick out patterns in the messages on the wall. A lot of it went over his head, references to laws or lawmakers, dates, names. But one phrase was repeated over and over, squeezed in anywhere it could fit: "SHAME ON YOU." He muttered the phrase to himself a few times to fill the silence in his mind, lest it wander back to what they were running from.

Occasionally Seb would scoff at something, or make a bizarre claim about what was behind the barrier, but it didn't matter. There was no way to verify his or any other claims. The barrier had no gaps. You could slip down quite a rabbit hole trying to investigate this online, should you choose to spend your time that way. And there had been at least a few nights over Sam's unemployed years where he had. But of course, none of what you see is provably what there is. All the so-called drone footage has been genned-up, processed, constructed from descriptions. If anything more concrete existed, more "real", you'd have no way to discern.

"It's because they had to cover up what happened, you know. At the UCSB particle accelerator. That was the catalyst to all this." Seb was staring at him with wild, expectant eyes for long enough that the car complained.

"All of what?"

"Look around!"

"I really don't get into that stuff, Seb."

"You Angelenos are so complacent, man. Just buy the lines we're feeding you from up north." Seb chuckled and gave a quick wink. He had the slightest bit of self-awareness that kept him tolerable. Sam spent most of their friendship praying he'd never lose that.

"But," Sam asked. "Why would they put a particle accelerator at UC Santa Barbara?"

"It's the right question, man."

He shook his head. "No, you're nuts. It's just people living their lives back there. They probably don't give a shit about us."

"Okay man, sure. But look me in the eye and tell me you think they have electricity or water."

Sam sucked air through his teeth and stared out the window. On the barrier just ahead he spotted a massive piece of street art: CENCAL, stylised as a sign made out of broken light bulbs. And trailing out of it was an electrical cord, lying unplugged next to a wall socket.

The day dragged on, and the extremely poor condition of the road made a mockery of Sam's spine. He shifted and fidgeted in the seat, soundtracked by the vibration of metal against plastic, and the car's desperate pleas for Seb to please keep his hands on the wheel. It was a miserably slow journey, owing to the speed restrictions applied when the car was in manual mode. They'd set out at around 10 a.m., and by 2 p.m. the endless stretches of ruined concrete, temporary fencing, bollards and warning signs had finally given way.

"Republic Corridor," read a brown tin sign stretched across the freeway. "Way Station Ahead."

Sam's eyes drank in the change of scenery. A backdrop of gorgeous mountains. Rolling hills covered in dead grass and a smattering of ruined buildings. Abandoned cars littered the landscape in the middle distance, and nests of barbed wire were placed seemingly at random. Sam could see a huge piece of plywood up ahead with letters spray-painted on: "Warning Live Mines".

"What the fuck?" He sat up sharply.

"They're full of shit. There's no mines. It's some local militia bullshit. They hate that there's a way station here. Afraid Republic tourists will wander off the corridor and interfere with their bohemian ways. You have nothing we want, assholes!"

"Where are we, anyway?" Sam glanced over at the car's display. There was barely any information, aside from a flashing red banner indicating that there was no service. And below that, a flashing yellow banner indicating the car was running out of power. "Uh, Seb?"

"Yeah, yeah. Relax. We have exactly enough. Look." He gestured out the windscreen as they passed under another overhead sign: the way station was only about a kilometre away now.

"And we can charge there?" Sam tried desperately to sound cool and relaxed in front of his old friend. He failed.

"We can charge there."

As they approached the checkpoint Sam couldn't help

but feel a sense of relief. The flag of the California Republic flapped in the breeze, one on each side of a massive steel sign. "Republic Corridor Way Station 1", it read, with indicators for where variously-sized vehicles should proceed. Seb swung them across two lanes and straight under the arrow for "Passenger Vehicle Charging".

"They make this sound like it's going to be so intense." Sam let out a machine gun of a laugh.

"When's the last time you left the South, man?" Seb was in a constant state of checking mirrors and swivelling around.

"It's been years. But never in a car, honestly. Always flying, out of LAX."

"Shit, really?"

"We just never drove anywhere when I was younger. And by the time I was older, the north and east passages had gotten tougher. The idea of driving north genuinely freaked me out."

Seb brought the car to rest behind a gate in a lane barely wide enough for them to fit. "Just relax, okay?" An ear-splitting metal-on-metal grinding sent Sam spinning in his seat. Four metal bollards had risen behind them. He stared for a moment, then spun back to face front. Four more had penned them in on the other side.

"What is this..."

"I said, relax." Seb rolled his window down. Sam realised part of the wall on the driver's side was actually a screen. It flickered to life.

"Sebastian Carr," came a voice from outside. Soon after, a face appeared on the screen. It was the spitting image of someone you'd never remember. "Citizenship was able to be confirmed. You crossed South Boundary at 10:24 a.m. with one citizen passenger. Samir Patel." Sam closed his eyes and looked away instinctively. It was pointless. The car knew who was inside. Plus, he'd done nothing wrong. "It is now 2:16 p.m. This is an acceptable pace, no deviation detected. The Republic appreciates your commitment to safe driving."

"Anything for the bear, man." Seb nodded and smiled at the fictional gate guard.

"No deviation in vehicle weight detected. No deviation in passenger manifest detected. No non-citizens detected in your vehicle. The Republic appreciates your commitment to keeping us safe and protecting the corridor."

"Anything for the corridor, man." Seb nodded again. Sam exhaled as the bollards began to lower.

"You have three hours to reach the Way Station 2," said the voice. Sam noticed the mouth on the face didn't actually move. It was unsettling. "Please feel free to rest, stretch your legs, and enjoy our array of food and beverage options. The Republic appreciates your commitment to being rested, hydrated and well-fed."

Seb gave a nod on the beat for each concept appreciated by the Republic. Almost exactly as the speech finished, the bollards had lowered, and the car started to creep forward. Seb's hands were nowhere near the wheel. He stretched and flexed his arms. "They've got a fucking good steak sandwich here, honestly. It's life changing."

The car rolled itself past a dizzying array of automated firepower: turrets mounted on swivels, cameras atop them, turrets covering those, and more turrets on the rooftops. Sam relaxed even more as a steel gate rolled up. He hadn't realised just how unsafe he'd felt the past few hours. Seb's car navigated itself under the gate and into the building, which turned out to be a cavernous space, inside which they'd constructed an array of buildings, parking, sidewalks, a whole miniature city block.

Seb's car pulled into the first available parking space, which was the very first one on the row, just in front of the glittering array of food kiosks. Something was odd though. They were the only car. Indeed, they seemed to be the only people at all.

"Wow, ghost town," Sam said as he took it all in. It occurred to him they hadn't seen more than one or two other cars on the road either.

"Nobody drives the corridor, man. It's got a bad reputation on account of all the attacks."

"The what?"

"Come on. I'm starving."

Sam wasn't hungry. Stress always killed his appetite. He walked with Seb to peruse the kiosks. It was a decent variety in theory, though as they walked he took note that most of the options in most of the machines had a red 'X' instead of an Order button. He supposed there wasn't much use stocking these things if the corridor wasn't seeing any action. But they clearly had high hopes for it at one point.

"I heard about something around here, actually," Seb said with a mouthful of steak sandwich. "Girl that comes into the club sometimes mentioned it to me. Mind if we check it out?"

"I'm at your mercy," Sam replied. He was staring at a memorial plaque next to the bathrooms. Three workers lost their lives in a terrorist attack during their construction. It was awful to think about, yet Sam couldn't help but laugh. "A terrorist attack on the restrooms?"

"No, you ass. It was on the whole... it doesn't matter. Come on, we don't have long. Bring that camera of yours."

Seb stared at Sam through the gap. "Come on, man."

Sam hesitated. "Did you not see all the weaponry when we drove in?"

"Do you see any around here?"

"What's even out there?" The gap was at the far corner of the far wall, past the kiosks and parking, past the edge of fake civilisation. A fork in the path.

"Would you just come on, man? I'm out here, do you think the sniper's waiting for my buddy to come through so he can bag a twofer?"

Sam gulped and closed his eyes, then stuck his hand straight out ahead of him. "Pull me through."

"Are you—what? "

"I can't step through. Just pull me through." He clutched his camera, the gift from Virginia, firmly in his other hand.

"Put that shit in your pocket first. I'm not going to have Magenta goons tracking me down for breaking it."

As soon as the camera was safe, he felt Seb's hand on his wrist and was yanked through the gap. They both stood there for a moment. Sam sneezed twice as the harsh midday sun crashed down onto him. "Where..." He looked down at the ground, a slate grey pavement with wide yellow lines, all cracked and crumbled. In the middle distance, a row of airplane hangars in varying states of disrepair.

"Cool, right?" Seb smiled before heading straight off around the corner. "This isn't why we're here. Come on!"

Sam jogged behind Seb, struggling to keep up. "Where is this?"

"It's an old airport. They built the way station inside one of the hangars or something. But more importantly..." They snaked through alleys and around corners until they finally reached a fence. A slit had been cut through the chainlink, with a section clearly able to be rolled back. "Here we go. Yes! Look at that!"

Sam stared through the fence and his breath caught in his throat. Across an access road and a parking lot stood the hollowed-out ruins of an old bar. A derelict sign hung by a thread at the top of a pole: The Hammer & Nail.

"Fuck," Sam said. A couple good memories mixed with about a dozen bad ones stirred up from the depths of his mind. "I know this place." He turned to Sebastian. "Seb, I know this place."

"Sam, everybody knows this place."

TEN

ETCETERA

*Ten years ago.*

Sam sprinted down the hallway, joining the thundering herd of middle managers on their way to the big conference room. A few had been summoned, a few more were grabbed along the way, but most had just seen the news. It was 2 a.m. in London, so it was Sam's job to listen for anything the crisis team might want his boss to do, and then relay it to her once she woke up. Otherwise, as a junior assistant, his job was to keep his mouth shut.

"Assistants at the back please," shouted the chief-of-staff as Sam entered. He held in an eye-roll and took his seat along the back wall with the rest. The meeting was controlled chaos, standing room only, clusters of people shouting to, at, and over each other. On the televisions at the front of the room, a grid of people in various other meeting rooms, bedrooms, and board rooms all did likewise. And to Sam's surprise, he spotted his boss, Gemma Thomson, live from London after all. A golden, saint-like halo seemed to radiate from her. She was in what looked to be a bathroom cubicle, dressed to go out-out, with a single AirPod in. The sight of her flustered Sam in the best way. He averted his eyes and shook off the thought. This was about to be an extremely serious conversation.

"How do we... hello, are you all hearing us? Hello? We're on in LA." An older man at the head of the table shouted into one of the desk microphones. A cacophony of agreement boomed from the speakers. "Great, okay. Uh, how do we wanna get into this, can someone..."

"I can give us the flyover," boomed a woman from the call. She was in a well-appointed phone room somewhere in New York, judging from the label on her video.

"Heather, yes, uh, go ahead."

"Hi folks," began the woman. "I'm Heather Stapleton, I'm Chief Counsel here at Magenta. And I want to start by expressing heartfelt condolences from all of us in the Magenta family. This is a terrible tragedy."

"It's appreciated, Ms. Stapleton," the man responded.

Sam almost immediately began taking notes, if only to distract himself from staring at Gemma on the screen. He couldn't keep his eyes off her. A blue chequered flannel hung rather open under her black leather jacket. The angle showed far too much cleavage for a work meeting, even at a record label. Her hair was a puffed-up Eighties throwback, her black lipstick smeared. Huge circles under her eyes, like she hadn't slept in days. Was she okay? Was she not wearing a...

"...first notified of trouble." *Shit*, Sam thought as Heather continued. He'd already missed quite a bit. "At 4 p.m., deputies from the San Luis Obispo sheriff's department arrived at The Hammer & Nail to support the local police effort, and the Magenta technicians were able to continue setup. The protest seemed to disperse at that point, and after a discussion between the sheriff, local police and Magenta security, officers were released and the event proceeded as planned."

"So just one member of Magenta security, plus the engineers," said the man at the head of the table.

"And three of our staff," added a woman in the conference room. "One from Talent Relations and two from Special Projects."

"And all of them were killed in the blast?"

"That's correct," Heather replied. This set off a round of gasps at the table, and a range of visceral reactions from the muted attendees on the video call. This was information very much not being reported on the news. Sam felt his stomach fall to the floor. He exhaled slowly through pursed lips. Chaotic images pelted his mind: screams, running, explosions. Ordinary joy, smeared with blood. *For what?* A lump formed in his throat, and tears in his eyes. His chest heaved, his hands were clammy and numb, beads of sweat crossed his forehead. Someone squeezed his shoulder and brought him back to the room. People around the table talked over each other and themselves in a flurry.

"And this was, what, an anti-automation thing?"

"I saw coverage of the protest, it was some group, Human Art Collective?"

"That's not it, it's Humans First."

"It was an anti-Magenta thing. They warned of consequences if this event went ahead."

"That's the media saying that. I guarantee this was California Republic nonsense. That vote is..."

"Enough!" The man at the head of the table slammed his fist down. "Heather, who was killed specifically?"

"Thank you, Graham," Heather said. "Magenta's engineers and security, plus all three representatives from the music label. Plus three bar staff and six attendees of the concert. I don't have the count of wounded..."

"Excuse me, what?" Gemma had chosen now to come off of mute. She fiddled with her AirPod and had the camera far too close to her face. "Three... four... uh... fifteen bloody people died at your fucking automated concert? Fucking America." Gemma was screaming into her phone. Her voice was garbled and distorted, her face mostly blurry or frozen. "Tobias, are you in there? You fucking tosser, you were warned. That's a lot of blood on your fucking hands. Jesus Christ."

The room was silent. Sam closed his eyes, put his pen down and stayed very still.

"Tobias Klostermann was at the venue, Miss Thomson." Heather's tone was empathetic, but she was clearly desperate to move past this. "He was one of the two Special Projects executives from your company who were killed in the bombing."

"...shit," Gemma finally replied.

"Excuse me." Heather went on mute, then quickly returned. "Folks, our CEO would like to join personally. Please hold on."

Another box appeared and quickly expanded to fill an entire screen, relegating everyone else to smaller boxes on the other screen. Sam shut his eyes and tried to breathe. It was Rebecca Prue, founder and CEO of Magenta. The woman gleefully destroying the company he worked for, the music industry, the state of California, and some would add the world itself.

"Thank you Heather," Rebecca said, "and hello everybody." Her smile seemed false, her whole face and voice at the bottom of the uncanny valley. Like she was doing a poor impression of a human being.

Sam sat up straight and pushed himself back against his chair. He very much did not want to be here. Sharing a space, in a way, with this reprehensible monster. If society had to crumble, if millions had to fall to desperate poverty, and now apparently if people had to die, each was a price she was willing to pay to usher in her vision for the future of humanity. And that vision happened to include her company controlling your entire life, and her being the richest woman on earth.

"I want to start by expressing heartfelt condolences from all of us in the Magenta family. This is a terrible tragedy." Her voice was soothing, which only irritated Sam more. *Melodic.* She was perfectly framed in the middle of her camera, making eye contact with the lens, and her dark brown hair hung straight to her shoulders. Her makeup flawless, her skin impossibly smooth. She'd certainly put a lot of effort into appearing polished for this call to discuss a tragedy – so much so that she was late to join.

"We of course appreciate your time, Ms. Prue."

Rebecca Prue smiled and looked straight ahead. Sam would've assumed it was a painting if had he not been able to see her breathing. He stared at her on the screen. A metal taste filled his mouth, his pulse relentless.

"It's no problem," Heather replied. "We understand this was a joint venture that you've taken quite a reputational risk to participate in. We're just hoping to move quickly to both respond to the tragedy as well as ensure we're aligned on messaging with regard to the future of this endeavour."

"That's it exactly," said Rebecca with a nod. "Project Vonnegut is a cornerstone of our foundation in the creative vertical, and you are our most valued partner in that effort."

"That's our internal codename for this," Heather clarified. The assembled parties looked at each other, with some light murmuring.

"Bin it," Gemma shouted, rattling the speaker. "Just bin it. People go to gigs to see people play gigs. Not to watch a fucking hologram light show and listen to a recording."

"Miss Thomson," Rebecca replied with a smile, "I believe London was the birthplace of what could be seen as the progenitor of this technology."

"Don't say Abba Voyage to me, love. Not at two-thirty in the bloody morning when people just died." Gemma rolled her eyes and pointed at her phone. "Nerve of this bitch. Have respect."

"I know everyone is quite passionate about this," Heather said quickly. "We don't need to make any decisions tonight. We just want to ensure that, when statements are inevitably issued, we are aligned that we won't let one very unfortunate incident decide the future of this programme."

"Well it's binned here. But you lot do what you like in the States. Where you can buy guns and bombs at the fucking shop. Good luck."

"Miss Thomson, we're happy to arrange a demonstration for you. Out in London, perhaps. I think you'll see that the benefits outweigh..."

"I think we're worrying about the wrong thing here," said another man at the table. "There's been tremendous loss of life at an event that we..."

"...it's of course a terrible tragedy," Heather interjected. "And of course, we're offering complete security for all future installations and events for at least the next five years. Fully paid, not a dime out of your pocket. To ensure a tragedy like this will never happen again. This will only strengthen our case with Governor Newton, or rather the California government, whichever one prevails in the upcoming election, to permit us to use paramilitary assets in cases where police protection is deemed insufficient."

"Excuse me, paramilitary?" One of the executives was incensed. "This is all getting a bit ridiculous. I know the security situation here isn't great right now, but we're just talking about concerts."

"They're not concerts," screamed Gemma. "It's a fucking light show!"

As terrible as this was, Sam thought, it would have the consequence of awakening Gemma to how forcefully she needed to intervene to stop this nonsense. He knew just how much she loathed this whole concept. He thought he might actually know her better than anyone. She'd love nothing more than to use this as an opportunity to finally rid themselves of this toxic partnership with Magenta. If he could watch Gemma square off against Rebecca Prue in the alley behind the Roundhouse, even better.

Another of the managers grumbled and squirmed. "With Tobias no longer here," he said, "We're looking to yourself for a decision, Gemma."

Gemma stared down the lens, her camera at a Dutch angle. The wall of the toilet cubicle behind her was covered in rude drawings and dried sick, and the harsh light cut odd shadows across her face.

"I do want to point out," Heather jumped in, "any

change of circumstance you'd like to initiate here would carry a considerable financial consequence." The room again fell silent as she ran down her tick list. "Termination of ongoing payments. Invalidation of the stock grant. Recall of the bridge loan."

"Ms. Stapleton, people are dying," a manager pleaded. He clasped his hands together. "Ms. Prue, please. We just need some time to figure all this out."

"That is the contract language as written," Heather answered.

Gemma let out an exasperated 'pbbbbbtt' and fell backwards, perched on the lid of the toilet. "Fuck, Graham. Most of our artists already hate this. Now the whole world is going to call us murderers."

"We'd be bankrupt overnight," said the manager. Sam's phone vibrated endlessly in his pocket, surely Virginia trying to reach him after seeing the news. He declined the call and stared intently at Gemma on the screen.

"Christ. I just..." Gemma shot a look over the top of her phone and cocked her head. "Do I sound like I'm fucking done in here?" She shouted at an unseen presence. "Just go blow him in the mens, ye manky cunt."

Everyone chose to adjust how they were sat. The boardroom was a symphony of metal squeaking and throat clearing.

"Gemma, I know it's late there."

"This bloody..."

"We'll just need to know what to put in our statement to the press."

"Just, fine. Fucking get on with it then." Gemma sighed and shook her head violently. "What's the statement? We don't negotiate with terrorists, yeah? A few label executives are acceptable losses in the war on human creativity. That sort?" She waved her hands around as she spoke, to sickening effect on the video. "We remain committed to Magenta's ridiculous contraption from a bloody Look Around You sketch, and their child CEO who looks like a tarted-up pageant winner. Etcetera, etcetera."

Around the table, heads fell to hands. The most vocal of the group simply left the room. Sam had started to write out Gemma's statement verbatim. The assistant next to him put their hand over his, stopping the pen, and shook their head.

"Fantastic," said Heather with a pained smile. "We'll have some language drafted roughly to that effect and get it sent over for review. Thank you, Miss Thomson, for..."

"Oi, the fuck!" Gemma shouted over a loud crashing sound. Thousands of miles away, a toilet cubicle door had just been kicked in. Her frame was a blur of arms and hands. Bursts of static and slights about women from Essex followed before the picture froze and vanished.

"I really think we should wait," Sam whispered to the other assistant. "She's preoccupied at the moment." They shook their head again and averted their eyes.

"If senior staff can remain behind." The usual refrain. It meant Sam and the rest of the assistants could step out to process, or attempt to process, perhaps a fraction of the day's events. He knew he should call Virginia, but she wouldn't understand. He'd struggle to explain, to convey the weight of it all. To get past her inevitable response: *I don't get it. It's just technology. It's just music. Why are people so upset?* With Gemma, it was all shorthand, all known. Scenarios competed and played out in his head as he was led out into the hallway by the chief of staff.

"That's us aligned on a statement, then," Sam heard

someone say as the door slowly closed. "Heather, Ms. Prue, thanks very much."

"We'll weather this storm," replied Heather. The door shut, sealing the rest of the meeting in with it. Through the glass wall of the conference room, Sam could still see Rebecca Prue on the monitor. She smiled and stared straight ahead.

ELEVEN
CURSED

It was surreal to see the club up close after eleven years. There were still bits of yellow police tape strewn about, still shattered glass behind the bar area, charred concrete, shattered wood and jagged metal by the stage. Little evidence of the dead remained, but the air was thick with their presence, with the weight of their pointless sacrifice. The walls, those still intact, were covered in graffiti:

*Magenta Murderers,*
*Humans First,*
*Newton Fiddles, We Burn.*

"Newton?"

"Jessica Newton," Seb said. "She was the last Governor of unified California. Before the partition. Learn your history, dude."

"Right," Sam nodded. "That sounds familiar." It didn't.

They worked their way through the remains of the building, carefully stepping over rubble, while Sam took photos with the gift Virginia had given him. By the year this happened it had already gotten difficult to convince people a shocking photo was real. It made this feel even more like an exercise in futility. But they'd mean something to him, at least. He just wished he could share them with Gemma.

"It's outrageous you were in the room after this happened, watching them war-game their pathetic response. How did we never talk about this?"

"It wasn't something I ever felt comfortable talking about. Confidentiality and all."

"And trauma?"

"I guess. I was twenty-two, I don't know."

"Did you tell anybody? Virginia?"

"She never wanted to hear stories that involved Gemma."

"Huh."

With some care they got back behind the stage. The mundane nature of the debris somehow heightened Sam's tension: a smashed coffee pot, a rusted metal toolbox, a torn laptop bag. Beside the stage door, a huge frame full of show bills, commemorating all the different bands and acts that had played The Hammer for many years past. Frozen in early 2034. Sam was careful to photograph it a few times, from a few angles.

"Should we take this?" Sam looked to Seb for advice on anything nightclub-related. "I can't believe it's still here after a decade."

"I don't know, man. Might be cursed."

"You could hang it in your club as a tribute."

"It's like, disturbing a crime scene. Or a grave."

"I think it'd be kinda respectful."

Seb stared at Sam, then at the frame, then back at Sam. He nodded and went to pull it down. Screwed in tight.

"Well, that might explain why it's still here. I've got a screw-driver in the car. I'll grab it."

The rest of the room was as generic as these backstage areas usually are: cabinets, a sink, an old microwave. All either ruined or destroyed, the walls as heavily graffitied as the rest of the club. But amongst the jumbles of scribbles and hatred, a word jumped out that Sam recognised: Tobias. He leaned forward and felt his face go flush, the painful lump straight back in his throat. On the wall, in the corner, someone had written all fifteen names of the people who died in the bombing that night, including their VP, Tobias Klostermann.

"I guess you get memorialised even if it was your fucking fault," Sam muttered. Above the names it read "march 3, 2034. never forget what they did." *A rather ominous memorial*, he thought. *Quite open to interpretation.*

They managed to get back through the fence, traverse the labyrinthine old airport, and reach the parking lot, all without getting gunned down by the Republic military. In Sam's mind, this was a huge success. Seb packed the frame full of posters into the boot of his car, and off they went. The corridor was underground at this point, as it bypassed San Luis Obispo by simply going underneath it. They emerged just on the other side, back to the open skies and ten-foot concrete walls. It felt infinitely less oppressive after twenty minutes in the tunnel.

They had twenty minutes left on the clock by the time they made it to Way Station 2, somewhere near King City. "Home stretch," Seb said with a smirk. "Tank up on food and get all your dissenting opinions out now, because we ain't stopping again until we hit South Gate."

It was a quick stop, and again completely devoid of other

humans. Way Station 2 was actually outside, lit by massive floodlights on stands that looked like they were probably meant to be temporary. It had a much less comfortable feel, with about twice the security and a double layer of barbed wire fencing, a no man's land between them, complete with what looked to be about a ten foot drop.

"I feel like there's a story here." Sam observed the situation with a fresh Slurpee in his hand.

"There... is, but I can't remember it."

Extreme discomfort ushered them back to the car and out onto the corridor much quicker than the last stop. Night had fallen, and the corridor wasn't lit. The bright yellow headlights bounced off of the concrete wall to their right and about a foot in front of them. The stars above them were visible through the chain-link that bridged the two walls. But otherwise, it was dark. Very, very dark.

Memories of The Hammer kept coming to the forefront of Sam's mind. That day in the conference room. The news coverage, and how muted it had been. How hard it was to find information about what happened, and how few photos or video there were of something so serious.

And then there was Gemma. She'd already been having such a tough time with the speed at which they were rolling out this terrible fucking soulless system. Getting so little sleep, spending more and more time at the bottom of a bottle. He'd only seen her in person once or twice after that day.

"It still haunts me," Sam murmured.

"The attack on The Hammer?"

"I suppose, yeah."

Sam went back to staring out into the darkness. The headlights skimmed along the concrete, the texture of the wall flashing past like lightning on a distant plain. He could still remember what she was wearing that day, and how lost she seemed. She'd called him that night, around 11 p.m. his time, 8 a.m. her time. He'd made up an excuse to get out of bed and left Virginia alone. Gemma was frazzled, uncommunicative, exhausted. He laid on the sofa for hours, listening to her breathe over the phone as she laid on hers, thousands of miles away in London. After a while they both fell asleep, having said maybe ten words to each other.

"Sam." Seb's face glowed red, lit so by a warning light on the dashboard of the car. "It's nearly the witching hour."

Sam looked at the clock, which read 10:14 p.m. "It is nowhere near."

"Well, it is very dark."

"It is."

"The witching hour!" Seb shouted with a terrible cackle. "When churchyards yawn, and Hell itself breaks out contagion into this world!" He cackled again, twice as loudly, his head thrown back as if it might snap clean off. Sam had known Sebastian long enough to know what happened during the witching hour. "Ghosts of the past rise and be with us!"

"Don't we usually have shots for this?" He was adrift. Far from the mood necessary for Seb's college drinking games.

"You can't drink in the car, man. They'll just put two in our heads when we get to the South Gate."

"I guess it'll have to wait."

"Listen," Seb said, "it was a heavy day. And I'm trying to stay awake in this monotonous corridor."

"Fine."

"Samir Patel." Seb shrieked in his trademark witch voice, which Sam probably hadn't heard in over a decade. "Confess to the darkness. What exactly happened between yourself and... Gemma Thomson?"

"Shit." Sam chuckled, caught off-guard. "That's timely."

"I've wanted to know for about... how long have we known each other?"

"Fifteen years?"

"Fifteen years."

"I've known her for a little over ten."

"I'm serious! One minute you and V are off to London for a gig, next you come back pissed at each other, and you've got a job at a record label working for this known perpetrator."

"Industry legend."

"And all you say is right place, right time."

"It was."

Seb shook his head and chuckled. "It's all a little suspicious, I'm saying. And now here we are, at the end of all things. I think it's safe to talk about it."

"Nothing happened."

"Nothing?"

Sam leaned his head against the window, his eyes pinned to the side, watching the cracks in the wall go by. "Nothing."

TWELVE
PROGRESS

*San Francisco*, read the battered tin sign. *It All Starts Here.* A much less battered sign beneath stated what the city had really become: *Home of Magenta.* Both bore the signature typeface and purple of Magenta's corporate branding. Sam's eyes were at risk of rolling straight out of his head. As an Angeleno, he wasn't impressed. He was sickened.

The road glided up, down, and up again, rolling hills in the darkness, gorgeous rows of immaculate houses planted amongst the grass like an opulent forest. The map display flickered to life on the windscreen as the car was finally able to reach its corporate masters again. It alerted them with a pleasant chime that they were in the Outer Sunset. Everything glowed with the faint orange of the street lights, the car hummed beneath them. After spending the day in a concrete tunnel carved through a war zone, it was as if they had landed on another planet. He pictured the life he left behind: the rubbish strewn about, the half-assembled furniture, even the messy break-up. If he wasn't careful, this city would sweep him into a dustpan the first chance it got.

Seb dozed off as soon as the car resumed auto-drive. Sam was alone with his thoughts. He watched out the window as the neighbourhood dropped away and they winded through Golden Gate Park, and again Sam was stunned by the cleanliness. LA was his home, but it a was world of chain-link fences, wooden barricades, heavily armed private security. Camps full of displaced people, abandoned buildings, filth. Decay. A city bigger than it needed to be, large sections given over to whomever wanted them. He, like everyone, had learned to ignore it. But here, there was none of it. No dirt to be seen. Perfectly manicured landscaping. Nobody forced to live on the streets. It seemed to be a city fit for purpose. He wondered how they possibly managed.

As they emerged on the other side of the park, the vibe shifted. Gone were the charming single-family Victorians and swathes of green space. This side of the park was dominated by concrete. Brutalist towers shot skyward on all sides, emblazoned with names like "Nopa Heights I", "Grandview Tower", "San Isabel Dormitories." And next to each name sat the familiar logo.

"Corporate housing," Seb said.

"You're awake."

"I was resting my eyes."

"Don't know how you can sleep from all the stress."

"Stress?"

"The checkpoint. That was insane, we don't have those in LA."

"Dude," Seb chuckled, "no shit. That's what giving up looks like. You know what LA stands for."

"Los..." Sam regretted starting to answer literally.

"Looks. Away."

"Is that what you say up here?"

"That's what we say up here."

"Great."

"But the algorithm determined we were low risk for whatever reason, so don't think about it." Seb gestured out the windscreen. "This whole area is unrecognisable, man. It used to be a lot of houses and stores. Some good bars over here, too." Seb had an air of disdain as he pointed out the window toward one corner of a massive tower block. "I used to drink here, at a place called The Page."

"What happened to it?"

"Progress, dude. There was a housing crisis. All those houses had to go somewhere."

"This is all Magenta employees?" Sam had trouble telling one block from the next.

"No man, no. Not all. Well, not me, anyway. Maybe I'm the only one." The car turned off and headed down into an underground parking area, nestling itself in what Sam assumed was its designated space. Seb turned and clapped Sam on the shoulders. "So, listen. Melanie is probably not going to love this."

"Melanie?"

"My wife."

"Your what?" Sam threw his head back and gave a whole performance. "Whoa. Wife? Since when are you married?"

"Hey dude, it does still happen. Met her at work. But listen..."

"At your bar?"

"No, the port."

"Port? I thought you worked at a bar."

"I own a nightclub, Sam, but that isn't my job. You think that pays me enough to live on? I lose money on that shit-hole. Listen man, first of all, promise me you'll never buy a nightclub."

"Sure thing."

"Second, just be prepared for some cramped conditions, okay? And probably some robust disagreements between myself and Mel."

THE SHOUTING MATCH erupted in the kitchen before Sam had finished making up the sofa.

"Baby," Seb shouted as Sam fluffed a throw pillow, "he's got nowhere, he's got nothing."

Melanie roared back. "¡Ni de pedo dejo que esos pinches cabrones me rompan la puerta nuevecita!"

"Mi amor, por favor, yo lo arreglo."

The terms of his new existence were drafted: he could stay a maximum of three days unless Seb could find a way to "make him legal". He'd need proof of employment, or he'd be expelled from the city. *Was this what Seb meant by temporary?* Sam couldn't begin to understand. *LA was still part of the Republic, wasn't it? What the fuck was going on?*

Chirp, chirp, chirp. Gentle chimes came from Sam's ear-piece, which lay on a charging pad behind his head. It was the first time in as long as Sam could remember that he'd actually let both his ear-piece and the Ring itself run out of power.

"Hello?"

"Hello, Samir Patel." A familiar voice came out of the earpiece. Sam's stomach dropped. *This couldn't be good.*

"Aida. Hi."

"Samir, your Magenta Plus service isn't available right now, due to a lack of payment."

"That can't be right, my Plus is on a friends-and-family plan through my partner, Virginia Rose. She's an employee. It's free through her."

"Your plan changed to monthly direct billing about two days ago, Samir."

"No, no, no." Sam was whispering, but emphatic. "That can't be right. It's meant to be free. She wouldn't have just removed me like that."

But she had. Sam descended into an internal panic as Aida insisted his subscription had lapsed. He pleaded with it, though pleading with Aida for a handout was pleading for the sun not to rise. She confirmed he'd been moved to Magenta Basic: a free plan that offered users the benefit of speaking to Aida about upgrading to a better plan.

"Is there any chance of a grace period, or a free trial? Aida, I've been out of touch all day. I just need to reach Virginia to clear this up."

"Samir, you have already redeemed a seven day free trial of Plus."

"What?! When?"

"The fourteenth of October, 2026."

"That was..." Sam whisper-shouted through gritted teeth. "That was like seventeen years ago, Aida."

"Free trials are for new sign-ups only, I'm afraid." Aida was a cool customer. There was no budging her. Sam yanked the ear-piece out and flung it across the room, then pulled the Ring off his finger and did likewise. *Fuck Magenta, anyway. Fuck Aida, and fuck Virginia for doing this.*

He stuffed his arm under his head and tried to sleep on the rock-hard sofa. The sound of muffled Spanish arguing was a miserable substitute for his usual routine. He knew tomorrow he'd have to cave and pay for his own service. Maybe it would be the first step on his new journey.

SAM HAD SPRUNG from his makeshift bed before sunrise, and he was showered, dressed, and lurking in the kitchen by quarter 'til six in the morning. He'd been drafted into joining Seb at work lest he find himself in frosty confrontation with Mel. *Or worse*, Seb had added, *you two actually get along. Don't trust you one jot, player.*

The sun struck the sides of the massive glass spire at the core of the East Cut as they worked their way toward the Embarcadero. Sam gawked out the car window with child-like wonder.

"Hard to believe everyone thought that was an eye sore when it first went in," Seb said with a shake of his head. "Now it's one of the most recognisable buildings in the fucking world."

"It's beautiful."

"It's the eye of Sauron, man."

Digital signs hung from poles on both sides of the streets surrounding the spire, all showing the same thing: Rebecca Prue. Clad in her usual smart blazer and shirt combination, her dark brown hair perfect as ever, with a faint smile. She looked down a bit, over her nose, and let out a light chuckle. It was a seamless loop, repeating forever, every sign in perfect sync with the others. Sam stared into the photograph's eyes, and felt it staring back at him. *Solar powered*, he thought. *Long after we're all dead she'll still be here, looking down over it all.*

"Rebecca Prue," he whispered under his breath. "Jesus."

"There she is," Seb replied. "Queen of the western

world. Looking down over her subjects as they schlep to work another ten hour day for her."

"Hard to think of her as real at this point."

"Oh, she's real. I met her once."

"Seriously? Where?"

"She came into my club. Her and a friend."

"Bullshit."

"She did, dude. This was forever ago, before she was capital R, capital P. She was Valley famous."

"Yeah, yeah." Sam laughed, his eyes still fixated on Rebecca's photos slowly going past out the window.

"I can prove it, I've got a picture of her hanging behind the bar. You'll see it tonight."

"Pictures don't prove shit. Actually makes the story less believable."

They emerged from the glass and concrete into the open air of the Embarcadero. A forest of cranes hung in the air, and a queue of container ships seemed to stretch on forever. Not a soul was in sight. Signs at the boundary to the area warned curious onlookers to stay away: *High-speed automation operates throughout The Embarcadero District. Entering area carries risk of grievous injury or death. Some areas may be off-limits under criminal statute.*

Somewhere, Sam thought, behind the mile-high stacks of crates, warehouses, and machinery, were the waters of San Francisco Bay. It would be nice to see them some day.

The car passed through several security barriers. Each time, Seb held up a plain plastic ID card. And each time the barrier seemed to grudgingly open, the car groaning forward at a slower and slower pace. It finally manoeuvred itself into a claustrophobic underground car park with an unceremonious sign indicating it was for "P47 Staff."

There were four spaces. After they had parked, three were free.

Seb gave a wry smile. "This is us, chief." He guided them up a narrow staircase and through the grim little passageways of the human-safe area. Bright white fluorescent lights pierced his eyes and gave him a dull ache after a few minutes. The sea-foam green corridors were the exact width needed. There was a single bathroom, a kitchenette that seemed like it could hold exactly five people, a bottom-of-the-line refrigerator, plastic shop sink, and coffee dispenser with five mugs neatly stacked next to it. In each room there hung the same poster, which bore the seal of San Francisco and the Magenta Corporation logo: *Proposition forty-seven facility provided under San Francisco municipal code.*

They finally arrived in a cramped room with four identical workstations and four very uncomfortable looking task chairs in front of them. Seb threw himself into the nearest chair by the door and turned on the screen with the flick of an antiquated switch. Really, everything about this room felt like it belonged in another era. No windows, a rolled concrete floor, and the same sea-foam green walls. The kind of oppressive corporate hell you might see in a period piece about turn of the century office workers.

"Nobody sits at the others, just park yourself wherever."

Sam plopped down next to Seb. "What is all this?"

"This is the last remnants, man." The screen flickered to life. It was a primitive grid that seemed to show where all the container ships were in the harbour. "I'm a prop forty-seven worker. The last prop forty-seven worker at the port."

"I don't know what that is."

"It's some law that means they needed to retain some of their human staff when they automated the port. Some fucking compromise from back before Magenta just did literally anything they want. There was a whole legal settlement when they tried to repeal it. So they're stuck with it."

"So what do you do?"

"Nothing."

"I don't understand."

"I don't do shit, man. My title is Harbour Master. But I don't have any responsibilities. It checks to make sure I'm here. But, otherwise." Seb spun round in his chair with a grin. "Ta-da."

"And this pays...?"

"Three hundred grand a year."

Sam dry swallowed. "Fuck." It was around what Virginia made at Magenta, and well over three times as much as he'd made when he worked at the music label.

"Raises linked to inflation every year, and the salary started at what the actual Harbour Master was paid when the law took effect. There used to be four of us per shift. But the law changed or some shit a few years ago, so they don't have to replace us when we leave. They can't fire us unless we do something wrong, and they can't lay us off... so they offer us huge payouts to quit."

"Wow."

"I'm the last man standing."

"I don't suppose you have hiring authority." Sam scratched the back of his neck and stared around the room. Surely for that much money, he could sit in here for a few hours a day.

"No, sir. We are fully staffed. One person. I've never felt so useful in my life."

"At least you've got dops and digis to keep you company.

And you could get through so many streams. Not so bad, really."

"No, sir." Seb shot a look of disdain straight through Sam. "First of all, really? Fuck dops and digis, man. But there's no signal in here anyway. They shut it off right before they started offering buy-outs. Imagine that."

Sam shuddered. It was something he could scarcely imagine. The problem of his expired Plus account tickled his brain uncomfortably. "So you're just... alone here?"

"Well, I had a colleague until around a year ago. But she took a buy-out."

"Ah."

"So I had to marry her," Seb said with a wink. "Missed her too much."


THE TRIP TO pick up Sam's visitor permit was meant to be uneventful. As the car was sent on a detour for the third time, Seb let out a groan.

"It's gonna be the fucking forty-sevens."

"The what?"

"There's just been a lot of protests. They know exactly where to stand to fuck with the auto-drive sensors. Fuck, we're gonna be late. Let's walk." Seb leaned forward and smashed a button on the screen that just said *Park Now*. The car dutifully complied, and the pair was on their feet. "It's like a kilometre. It'll be fine."

The sound of drums and chanting got louder the closer they got to City Hall. "MAKE IT RIGHT! MAKE IT RIGHT!" Sam and Seb slipped through the crowd, past security, and into the building.

The queue at the one working visa kiosk wrapped around the vestibule twice over. Seb grunted and groaned.

"Should I meet up with you later?" Sam worried Seb might not survive waiting in such a long line.

"I'd ditch you instantly," Seb answered. "But they don't play around with who they let into the city these days. An existing resident has to vouch for you."

The queue lurched forward, as each person got their visa decision. Each decision seemed to take about a minute, some longer, and each led to either elation or heartbreak. Half the time, the latter tended to result in a member of staff becoming involved: they'd be shuffled out of the queue, perhaps a few words exchanged, but ultimately they'd wind up outside.

As they got closer to the front, Sam started to get nervous. "What exactly are they asking for? Don't they already know who I am?"

"They do. It will just ask you a few random questions from your life, to better prove it's you. None of this shit is foolproof. Security theatre, man. Then I need to give the thumbs up and you're golden. Well, for three days."

Sam started to sweat. His hands felt clammy. *What kind of questions?* He tried to remember everything that had ever happened to him in his life, just in case it came up.

Seb put a hand on Sam's back to nudge him forward. Just a few ahead of them now. "Relax."

"But what kind of questions, do you know?"

"No idea, man. I'm from here. Never had to deal with this. Just don't fucking lie to it, okay? They aren't gonna ask you something they don't already know."

"You're from here?"

"Well, Concord."

"Is that nearby?"

"Step forward, please." A staff member gestured for them. Seb gave Sam a polite shove, and an animated face appeared on the screen, floating in a white void. It was yellow, vaguely human-shaped, with a black moustache and a little blue police cap. *They could not be serious.*

"Hi!" The face bounced and waggled as it spoke, and the voice would've fit well in a 2000s-era cartoon. "I'm Pete Police, and I keep San Francisco safe from bad people! What's your name, young man?"

Sam threw his hands up and gestured at it. Seb just shrugged.

"Young man?" Pete Police was respectful, but determined.

"I'm Sam Patel."

"Sam Patel! That's short for Samir?"

"Yes it is."

"Yippie!" Pete Police whizzed around the screen in a little police car for a moment, sirens blaring. He then reappeared at the centre. "May I call you Sam?"

"You may." Sam exhaled with a laugh, a smile stretched across his face.

"Sam, how'd you get to San Francisco, bud? Was it by car, or plane, or train?"

"Car."

"That's right, Sam! You came in by car. Do you remember who was driving the car, Sam?"

"It was my friend Sebastian. He's right here." Sam gestured to Seb, who gave Pete Police a quick wave.

"That's right again!" Sam was nailing this. "Sebastian, is Sam your friend? Is he staying with you?"

"Yeah, man." Seb gave a curt nod. "We're old friends. He can stay with me. I'll vouch for him."

"That's great! Both of you are doing so well." Pete scrunched his face up and looked around. A little cartoon folder appeared in front of him, and he read it studiously. "Oh no, Sam." His voice dripped with anxiety. "Oh, goodness."

"W-what's wrong?" Sam shot a look at the staff member. They deliberately avoided eye contact. With a quiet beep, Sam's earpiece activated. Pete was now holding an old timey phone receiver.

"Sam." He heard Pete's voice directly in his ear. "I needed to speak with you privately because I'm worried about a grown-up you seem to know. They've done some bad things. And my friends are looking for them." Pete's face seemed to grow larger, and the background behind his disembodied head had faded from white to a near-black.

"Dude," Seb strained to hold a smile as he whispered through gritted teeth. "What the fuck is he saying? I vouched for you."

"What? I don't know what you're talking about." Panic instantly gripped Sam. His head swung between Seb and Pete. "I don't know what it's talking about." He didn't know who to be now, how to act.

"Samir." The kiosk arrested his attention back to itself. "I'm not mad. You're not in trouble or anything." Pete Police had gotten uncomfortably paternal. "But I do need to ask you some questions about your friend Gemma in the United Kingdom."

"No. Who?" Sam whispered, then bit down on his lip and shoved his hands in his pockets. He felt Seb kick his foot, but he didn't dare look: his gaze was fixed on Pete Police.

Pete furrowed his digital brow and inched even closer. Sam thought he might exit the screen. And then, he vanished. The screen was black. Sam stared. His eyes burned from forgetting to blink.

"Please exit the facility," came the voice from overhead soon after. "Please exit the facility." It repeated on a loop, as muffled whispers rose up around them.

"Dude," Seb shouted. "What the fuck did you say to Pete?"

"There's a security situation outside, gentlemen," said the staff member. "If you can head just down there and out the emergency exit."

"But my..." Sam gestured at the kiosk. The staff member shook his head as Seb grabbed Sam's arm.

Their walk quickly turned into a jog as they moved toward the exit, opposite the way they'd come into the building, and soon found themselves out back in an alley. Nobody seemed to have followed them out, and Sam couldn't remember whether anyone had even been behind them in the queue.

Seb put his hand on the wall and let out a sigh as the exit door clicked shut. "What the hell was that?"

"Maybe someone pulled the fire alarm," came a clipped voice from behind them. They both turned their heads in a fright. A woman leaned on the wall a few feet away from them, tucked away in a shadow. Around Sam's height, a short crop of messy blonde hair atop her head, her round face dotted with a bit of acne. She looked young, though the UCSF jumper might've been lending to that.

"Jesus Christ!" Seb shrieked with a full body jolt. "Fuck, lady!"

"Were you in the queue behind us?" Sam sputtered.

Seb's reaction had hit him harder than the surprise of the mystery girl. His pulse quickened.

"Kicked out?" She stuck her lip out in a performative pout. "Qué lástima." Everything about her made Sam curious, and he wasn't sure why—on the face of her she looked like a box fresh random, but she gave off an infectious energy that threatened to pull him straight in. She gave them a tight smile and a tiny wave. "Good to meet you both."

Sam wanted to reply, but the girl seemed to almost hop away, disappearing around the corner before either of them could react. He clung to the memory of her with both hands.

The sounds of the protest carried on the wind and seemed to have reached fever pitch. Sirens approached. Sam could hear a megaphone in the mix.

"Forty-sevens." Seb shook his head. "Just be grateful and fucking move on."

"Who was that?" Sam kept staring where the girl had been. He was about ten minutes away from having processed the last five minutes.

Seb laughed. "This fucking town. Let's go before we get caught up in something. Come on, my club's not far."

THIRTEEN
WALLOWS LANE

Gemma had worked nearly a full day at the farm before she realised Mike wasn't around. It's not that he wasn't helpful, she thought, maybe she was just a bit too focused. She'd need a bit of introspection later to understand why she'd dumped half a basket of corn on the ground before she'd noticed he wasn't down there tidying it up.

"Haven't seen him today," said the portly man at the pantry.

"Not been through here," replied the woman watching the north gate.

"Might've seen him, though it might've been yesterday," said the man tending the still.

This was just like Mike, she thought: shirking work to go walkabout. Why didn't it surprise her? Probably just pouting. They hadn't spoken in a couple days and she'd seen nary a hair nor heard nary a peep out of him, save for a shower or his lumbering footsteps headed up in the morning. But she could all but guarantee he'd turn up on the green tonight. It was

Thursday, which meant Richard was grilling. Mike wouldn't miss it.

She'd barely set foot on the grass before she saw Richard on his way to intercept her.

"How are you, old man?"

"We should talk." Richard always had an air of intention, but this felt odd even for him. His tone was far too serious. An uneasiness crept in.

"Everything okay, boss? Chat over dinner, maybe? I don't want to keep anyone from their meal."

"It's handled. Walk with me, pet."

Richard pressed a hand gently to her back and began to lead her the way she came. The smell of hamburgers reached her nose, someone else filling in on the grill. The uneasiness grew as she was quite literally led down the garden path, through the maze of bell tents and encampments, across the road and through a hedge. This was Wallows Lane, and it was where the Collective chose to house their most respected residents.

Richard pulled open his gate and nudged Gemma through. His front garden was trimmed, but wild. After a whiskey or two, he would tell anyone who would listen about his efforts ripping up the front drive, repurposing the concrete as paving stones, and nurturing the dirt back to health. A few of his seed bombs had finally taken root after a fortuitous rain storm. *This was how the architect would've intended it to look*, he'd say. *Not some dreadful slab covered in Corsas and tin signs.*

"Jealous as always of your garden, boss."

"Come in, have a seat. I'll put the kettle on." He opened the front door and again let Gemma go ahead of him, then headed back outside to the fire pit.

Richard had become deeply private since his wife's death. Gemma couldn't recall if she'd even been inside since Claire's passing. But she was now seated at his reclaimed wood table. The outside almost portrayed a sense of normalcy: the Britain she remembered. Near-identical terraced housing stretching out into the distance, all with little touches outside, bits of personality bestowed by their occupants. There must be a thousand of these lanes across a hundred English villages. But once Gemma was inside, the reality was clearer. The walls were bare, save a few bits of found art. The furniture all mismatched, mostly fashioned from repurposed material. And of course, nothing plugged in, as even on Wallows Lane they weren't permitted to access the energy supply.

Her mind drifted away from the quiet horror of village life and back the pressing issue: why was she at Richard's dining table? What was he so loathe to tell her? And where was Mike?

Gemma was staring at the door when Richard re-entered with the kettle. "Boss, what is going on?"

"Tea first, pet. I'll fetch the diffusers." His voice wavered, and he seemed unsure what to do with his hands. He disappeared through an archway into the dark kitchen.

Her foot tapped impatiently on the base of the table, rocking it back and forth. She tried to push her fingers through her hair, greasy and tangled as it was, but quickly gave up at the thought of ripping it all straight out. Bangs and creaks came from the kitchen as Richard searched for provisions.

"Here we go, love. No milk, I'm afraid." He set two cups of tea down on the table, balanced delicately on two plates. They were small and ornate, with an elegant pattern of gold flake around the rim, and were clearly a matched set. Amidst the situation both in this room and in this world, the sight of a matched set brought her anxiety to a frothy boil.

"Thank you, Richard," she said through gritted teeth. "Lovely."

"You know..." he said, assessing the situation. "I believe I've got some biscuits tucked away in a cupboard. I'll just..."

"Enough! I don't need any bloody biscuits!" Gemma slammed her hand down, spilling a bit of the tea. Her anger dissipated into embarrassment over her outburst. "Richard, please. Why am I here?"

Richard stared down at the floor. "This was never my remit, you see. Was more of Claire's. She was a fantastic host. I'm just trying to emulate her. It's not the same quality."

Gemma felt her face go hot. "I'm sorry, boss. You're just trying to be a good host. You *are* a good host. I just don't know why I'm here. And I don't know where Mike is." The spilt tea pooled in a ring around the bottom of her cup. She dragged her finger through it, smearing it around the plate.

"Gemma," Richard said with an uncharacteristic soft-ness. He sat at the table opposite her and pulled his teacup in front of him. Positioned it carefully, neatly, as if tidying this up would tidy up his own thoughts. "Gemma. Mike is gone."

A loud squeak of wood against wood as Gemma shot back from the table. The chair tipped backwards and crashed against the floor with a thud. She stumbled back and caught her foot on its errant leg, nearly joining it on the ground, before she steadied herself. "He's gone." She doubled over and tried to scream, but nothing came from within except a cough and a wheeze.

Richard leapt to his feet and rounded the table, his arms

out wide, ready to catch her wherever she might go. "I'm sorry. I know this isn't easy to hear."

She coughed and sniffled as she spun her head round, looking for something without knowing what. Another scream welled up, and this time she found the breath. Her guttural bellow cut through the air, and the force knocked Richard right back. "When?" She grabbed him and shook, desperate, her eyes flooded with tears. "How?"

"This morning, first thing."

"Why? Why? I don't understand." The room spun violently around her, the corners of her vision darkened. "And nobody told me? Nobody thought to fucking tell me?" She lunged forward, arms out, and gave Richard a full body shove. He rocked on his feet, his eyes closed. "I was at the farms all day!" Inches from his face, Gemma screamed. "All fucking day, Richard! You knew where I was!"

"There was nothing you could do." He kept his measured tone, even as Gemma stared him down with an unyielding temper.

"You don't know that. You don't. You don't!" She shoved him again, her arms spring-loaded, and this time he was sent backwards a couple of steps.

"Gemma, I know you're upset."

"You know that? You know?!" Before she could make another move Richard's hands grasped her shoulders. He tried to hold her in place, and managed it for barely a second before she twisted her body and threw him off.

"He said he was doing it for you, Gemma. He left you a note. I can get it, if you let me."

The horror of what Richard had said gripped her mind in a vice. "He... did... what do you mean, doing it... he took his own..."

"What?" Richard's voice jumped into a new register. "Gemma, no, you've misunderstood. Mike isn't dead. He just left town."

Candles flickered around the dining room as Gemma dipped a biscuit into her second cup of tea. Her face blotchy and red, her eyes bloodshot, her darkish-silver hair still wet from the shower Richard had offered up. It relaxed her, and gave them both space to cool off, to reset their temperaments. On the table in front of her, atop a small decorative box, sat the note from Mike. It simply read *G* in a carefully drawn block letter.

"It's just so bloody dramatic," Gemma said as she fidgeted with the letter. "Can't just storm off in a strop, can he? Has to go and do all this. Fucking artists. Packed with drama from boot to bonnet." She pulled it open with the tact and grace of an explosives defuser, motivated by much the same fear.

---

Dear Gemma,

I hope the day's treating you well, and that the weather's held. I wanted to start by apologising, so I will. I'm sorry for overstaying my welcome. You've been nothing but helpful to me, in spite of your obvious frustration. Obvious to everyone but me, that is. When I lost my job all those years ago, what turned out to be the last job I would ever have, I was truly lost. And I was afraid. I've never had closure on anything in my life: just a series of pauses. I thought my career was simply paused. I refused to accept the reality that the world had moved on. And when I was conscripted, rather than try to adapt, I simply pouted and threw myself on your mercy. I might have survived working in the power plant, but you getting me out has given me the chance to thrive.

And I've squandered that chance by once again pausing. By lingering here, pretending you and I are something we're not. By interfering in your life, clumsily trying to do for you what you did for me. But you don't need help, and you know what you want.

It's time to unpause. To put a full stop on this part of my story. To say thank you for all that you've done, and move on. To tie up the other loose threads of my life.

So thank you Gemma, for all the support. And please thank Richard for me, for giving me the push.

n.b. You mentioned you knew someone who could help you record music. I hope you go and find them.

All the best,

Michael.

---

Gemma stared at the note in disbelief. One line battered her around until she could properly come to grips with it. "Richard?"

"Yes, love."

"Why does he thank you for giving him the push?"

The decorative box landed on her bed, still unopened. Gemma had raced back to the safety of her club basement, still furious at Richard. He had gone far over the top in trying to soften this blow because it was his goddamn fault. *Selfish fucking fool.* An endless parade of men doing what they felt was best for her, none checking to see what she might want.

And this time it had cost her more than just her guitar. Mike's absolutely hatstand declaration that Gemma knew what she wanted. Richard saying Mike wanted to do this for himself. *Who fucking knows what they want?* Gemma could guarantee neither herself nor Mike knew what they bloody wanted.

And who was this she'd supposedly claimed could help her record music? She knew she'd mentioned Sam, but only in passing, and not by name. Because of his blimming mix CD, which still didn't work.

She crawled into bed and clutched the box to her stomach. The lights clicked off suddenly — it must've been after 11 p.m. Her couple of scavenged LED bulbs, hung from their respective wires, got their energy from the collective's meagre solar battery. And that was such a limited resource, you could count on the duds in charge of it letting you have three or four hours a day of light. Halogens outside would keep a certain level of light available all night, but given she was in the basement, curfew left her in near-total darkness. The pain of this situation rarely found her, but tonight she felt it acutely. Everyone in the Collective remained gripped with a fever: the insistence that this was unequivocally the best way of life, because modernity had gone too far. Maybe it had. But as she lay still in her mildewed basement, under the blanket of a lights-out curfew, she questioned whether this was the freedom she'd sought.

The night was sleepless. She groaned and pulled a pillow onto her face as a flicker of sunrise hit the staircase. It was easy enough to push Mike from her mind: he'd chosen his path to walk. If he wanted to be alone and useless on the road, that was his prerogative. The police would snatch him in a day and he'd be back in Wales at the nuclear plant soon after, high-fiving government goons and earning his company scrip.

She rotated Sam's mix CD between her fingers. It had a totemic power that she should not have imbued it with. The inside of the case still bore the note, in Sam's atrocious handwriting, from the night she received it:

"A few of my favourite notes from the symphony of human history. -S"

A smile crossed her face, followed by a laugh—the kind that blindsides you, the kind you reserve for your closest friend. She rolled her eyes and laughed again, and her lip started to quiver. The direness of her situation was the dam holding back a complete breakdown. *Samir, you fucking knob. Why aren't you here?* Even after years apart, her first thought whenever she had an idea, a need, or a gripe, was that she should text it to Sam. *That exhausting little shit.*

Her dalliance with that boy Kevin from the pub, shortly after her conscription, had been a disaster. How was she still such a tempest of destruction through every path she crossed? *Did I ruin his life, like I did Samir's? Or is that just my own fucking ego? Fucking them once doesn't automatically destroy them, Gemma.* She covered her face with her hand to black out the world and focus on anything useful he'd said. He'd been a fount of unrequested information about how things worked now, an area that Gemma was severely lacking in knowledge. If he were here now, he'd explain how the thought of sending a message to California from the UK was now laughable: these two nations have nothing to gain from allowing their citizens to communicate with each other. You had to go through a private link for business reasons, he'd said, like the ones they had when she worked at the music label. It took a lot of money, and you needed a licence. She had neither.

A quick inventory of the people in her life showed them to be useless, unavailable, or both. Good fodder for new music, even if she was shit at writing lyrics. Her time at the label had taught her one lesson above all: a great producer could work miracles, even with terrible musicians.

A single, proper thought finally cut through her labyrinth of ego and self-pity. She knew exactly what she needed to do. She'd go to Liverpool, and she'd find the old man.

FOURTEEN

CURIOUS

Maelzel's Exhibition was crowded for 5 p.m. on a Monday, thanks to a great turn-out from the regulars. Sam had gotten to know them over the past month, ever since Seb had agreed to let him work there in exchange for the legal minimum wage (and a San Francisco work visa). Every night had its own set, with a couple of ultras who managed to bring themselves in daily. They divided into a few cliques, and on rare occasions the cliques would intermingle.

Sam preferred Monday, because it brought together his two favourite groups: the forty-sevens, and the nostalgia-curious university students.

The "forty-sevens" were the town's last generation of human workers. They'd gone to war with Magenta and, depending on who you asked, either lost ignominiously or struck an incredible bargain. A handful were still employed, like Seb, but many had either taken their pay-outs or gotten fired under suspicious circumstances. At any rate, they were a bunch of ancient Millennials and Gen Z who missed the way things used to be—and they loved getting drunk and talking about it.

"It's a fucking content paste," shouted one of the usual rabble, on one of the usual topics. Sam polished the bar and tried to pretend he wasn't listening. "No music, no movies, no books. Just a grey paste they suckle out of the tube."

"Don't start, Gerry," shouted another. "Don't wind 'em up. I know you saw 'em walk in."

A few students had wandered in, and they stood in a cluster near the door. They seemed nervous and not sure what to do now, though it impressed Sam that they seemed to all be taking out their earpieces. It was more than the so-called forty-sevens would do—for all their bluster, most of them still had Rings and used them quite a bit.

"Gerry, give the kids a break. At least they're curious."

"Streams they call it," yelled Gerry. "Everything's a stream. Stream a mood. Yeah, stream some angry sounds."

"You're drunk, Gerry," Sam said as he placed a glass of water on the bar. "Don't bully the students, we need their money."

"They're our huddled masses," said the first man. His voice dripped with sarcasm. "Yearning to breathe free."

Gerry ignored his detractors, instead turning his attention to back of the bar. "What's that? Isn't that where all the yen were?" The anachronistic wall of cash was gone, replaced by the somber totem they acquired on the drive up.

"It is," Sam said. "Seb figured if anything was going to replace that, it should be this. That poster is from ruins of The Hammer itself."

"No shit?"

"No shit, I helped him take it down myself."

Gerry replied with a nod. "Awesome."

"Oh, dislike," said an incensed female voice from the last stool at the far end of the bar. She'd been there a while, Sam had noted, though hadn't spoken to anyone or ordered anything. "Gen Z southlanders always act like their parents died in the Hammer bombing. Get over it."

"What the fuck." Samir gnashed his teeth. Useless anger flooded his body, and his fists clenched. "I knew people in the Hammer bombing." As the words left his mouth a wave of guilt washed over him. This girl had no way of knowing. She'd been insensitive, but she had no way of knowing how personal she'd made things. It was harsh.

"Oh," came her retort. "Were they one of the bombers? At least I'd respect them." A chorus of chuckles rose up from around the bar. Never in Sam's life had he heard anyone besmirch the Hammer bombing.

"I don't..." Samir seethed. He didn't know what about. His Ring was tucked into his bag, a condition of his employment, after Seb had caught him chatting on it one too many times rather than paying attention to the customers. No access to Aida to get more information, or to just drift away from all this. He stood, rooted, dumbfounded.

"Oh, leave him alone," rasped an older woman. "Grew up in the south, won't even know what the bloody bargain was. Will ya, kid?"

"The what?" Samir almost stopped himself, but it was too late. Groans and chuckles rumbled through the room as each took their turn with the truncheon. In his mind he fled, but his humiliation, and his employment, locked him in place.

"Woah, woah," came an echo from afar. The unmistakable voice of Sebastian, who continued his lifelong knack for arriving just in time. "Okay, turbo. Let's go on mute for a second." The girl who had started this was doubled over laughing.

Seb breezed in behind the bar, his hair matted by bay air, an old brown t-shirt stretched over his rotund physique. He threw his hands in the air as an attempt to gain control of the room, his stomach slipping out from the bottom of his ancient Turk's Revenge shirt, which still declared "GOOD VIBES ONLY" to all who observed.

"Everyone feels a different connection to past events," Seb continued. He had manoeuvred himself between Sam and the old-timers, in what appeared to be a hope that their chaotic Millennial upbringings had left them without object permanence. "Let's not go pissing each other off by voicing them out loud. This is a bar, not the fucking Berkeley debate club."

"What she said about The Hammer bombing is morally indefensible," snapped Sam. "She should be ejected." He jabbed the air in her direction, firing his finger over Seb's shoulder. The girl rolled her eyes.

"Hey, fuck you, kid," shouted one of the older crowd, though Sam didn't see which. "Go back to fucking Los Angeles."

"The Hammer bombing didn't even happen," shouted someone else.

"What the fuck," came another cry as the bar discourse teetered on the brink.

"He's trolling!" Seb had started pouring shots of tequila. "He's obviously messing with you. Aren't you, Sam? Look," Seb shouted in desperation. "He's going to pass out some apology shots. Aren't you, Sam?"

The girl chuckled. "Are you messing with us?" Sam

could just see her unnerving smirk over the top of Seb's shoulder.

"Hey!" Seb forced another laugh. "If we all agree he was, we all get free tequila."

"Fine," came the older voice from the corner. He was quickly joined by a chorus of tacit agreement from all sides. Shots were done, though limes were absent, and order was restored. Silence fell, save for some tinny rock music coming from an antique boombox in the corner.

Seb mopped up the bar, collected the glasses, and shook his head. Sam cowered in the back corner, waiting to get fired. It had come apart so fast. *Had he become so out of touch that he couldn't manage a basic bartending job?*

"I'm sorry, Samir," shouted the girl who'd instigated the whole affair. "That was mean of me to do. But you really should brush up on your Republic history. Not everyone feels the same way as you about these things. We've had different lives up here."

He plunged his hands into his hair and clutched his head.

"We've met this girl before." Seb gestured to Sam, then to her. She tossed her hair and gave her smirk.

"Have we?" Sam stared at her. The wheels barely turned. Without his Ring, he was useless at remembering people's names or faces. He flipped through the dusty card file of his actual memory and remembered the name of his eighth grade social studies teacher. *Mrs. Little*, he whispered to himself.

"It's what's her face, from city hall! Blonde, tiny, troll." Seb shook his head.

"It's me, I wasn't trying to hide it," she laughed. "¿A poco no soy linda?"

"It's you." That same magnetic pull. *Was it her voice, her eyes, the way she carried herself?* Her loose clothes ensured it wasn't some physical thing—so far as he knew she was a giant hoodie with a round face and stick legs. Though it was a rather cute face, with a pair of dimples bookending her mischievous grin. He was staring, he realised, and quickly looked away, only for his gaze to snap right back to her. *Get it together*, he scolded himself.

"Ay, está *super* lindo, ¿no?" The girl's grin widened.

"Yeah, and he doesn't speak Spanish," Seb nodded.

"I'm Lydia," she said, and thrust her hand out toward Samir. "Lydia Rosales."

"Lydia Rosales," Sam repeated. "Is that your real name?"

"Uh oh," Seb said. He slapped the rag into Sam's hands and proceeded around the bar. "He has a thing for girls with 'rose' in their names."

"Easy," Sam said.

"Is that so?" Lydia worked her way down to the stool in front of Sam. The rest of the assembled crowd had dispersed, the students and the old-timers at their respective tables.

"His ex's last name is Rose."

"Okay, easy," Sam groaned. "That's personally identifiable information."

"Shit," Seb said as he dropped onto the stool right next to Lydia. "Is he calling me a criminal?"

"I think he is."

"I'm not, but, it's technically a violation of the California Consolidated Privacy Act."

Lydia and Seb both burst out laughing, and Sam wished he had sprinted out of the building when he had the chance.

•  •  •

THE REST of Sam's afternoon was spent pouring spirits and being bullied by the comedy duo of his best friend and a mean girl. It was a small mercy when the band for that evening arrived a bit early and needed Seb's help to set up. That left a handful of punters cosied up to their pints, and one Miss Lydia Rosales.

"You've had your fun today," Sam said as he poured her third whiskey sour. "At my expense, mostly."

"Oh, but it never lasts, does it," she replied with a mock sigh.

"You've finally run out of insults."

Lydia squinted at him. "You're pretty short."

"We're the same height!"

"I'm short, chulo."

"I'm just glad we've moved from mocking me for where I'm from, to mocking me for my height. My teeth aren't straight either, not sure if you noticed."

"Mocking! Look, Southlander isn't mocking, it's just your bio. You need to live your truth"

Sam turned his back and began fidgeting with bits behind the bar. He had nothing to do, but he'd learned the art of appearing busy from Seb. It's essential to look like you've got a lot going on back here, he'd said, to stay out of unfortunate conversations. Sam gave each bottle on the shelf a tweak to get all the labels lined up.

"Samir!" Lydia pleaded. She put her palms on the bar and pushed herself up. "Sammmmmm."

"Please don't do that." He glanced over his shoulder and saw her out of the corner of his eye.

"Do what?"

"You'll damage the bar. It's an antique."

"I'll damage the bar? With my hands?"

"They've got oils on them. It's a soft wood."

"Bullshit," came a slurred male voice from the far end of the bar. "This bar's varnished oak with brass inlay and a glass topper. It'll survive a nuclear blast. You don't know what you're talking about."

"Hector, don't. I'll stop." Lydia flashed her roguish blue eyes at Sam. She lifted her palms off the bar and into the air as if she'd just been cornered by federal agents. "The wood is safe."

"You can't hurt this wood," said the man apparently named Hector.

"I'm sorry about the antique wood, Sam," Lydia said with a mock whimper. "Mi mal, mijo."

Sam bit his bottom lip, and tasted a bit of blood. Her act had worn thin. "I'm working."

"Fine!" Lydia blurted out, and waved her finger around at the back of the bar. "This, back there, that's all part of your work. Tell me about all that." Amidst the various posters and city-mandated licence paperwork was a small collage of photographs. A few of them were of the ruins of The Hammer, but there were others as well, mostly of cliché local landmarks: one of Coit Tower, one of the famous 'painted ladies' houses, one of a MUNI train.

"Oh," Sam demurred. "I took those."

Lydia leaned forward as best she could, given she had been banned from touching the bar. "What do you mean? Where did you take them from?"

"No, I took them. I photographed those places with my camera. Printing them was the difficult part. I scoured market-places for two weeks to find a photo printer that still had ink."

"That's so stupid. I love it." Lydia flashed her huge grin.

"Like actual photos, honest to god." She scrutinised the whole back wall, and her face beamed with genuine curiosity. "What about that one?" She pointed. Apart from Sam's collage she'd spotted one other, tucked away in a high corner, a Polaroid in a glass frame.

"I'm glad you asked!" Right on cue, Seb came bouncing back behind the bar. "That, my friends, is me. As a wee lad, freshman at SF State, in this very establishment."

"What's with the captain's hat," Lydia said.

"I forget," Seb grumbled. "It's stylish."

"Very fun," she said with vague amusement. "Very timelined."

"Ask him who he's with before he fucking explodes," Sam said.

"Who are you..."

"It's Rebecca Prue!" Seb threw jazz hands. "That's right, the Rebecca Prue. You know her, you love her! CEO of Magenta, Queen of Automation, Empress of Earth."

"Oh, right. Funny." Lydia's smile was small and tight, any hint of being impressed having evaporated.

Sam took more of an interest and, given his access, was able to stand up on his tip-toes and get a better look. The sight of Sebastian in his college days did give him a start. It was a powerful reminder that they'd both aged so much since they met. Rebecca Prue seemed to have fared much better. So far as Sam could tell from this photo, and from seeing her in the news and on the sides of skyscrapers, she still looked like this. Probably a result of charitable genning, he assumed. But here, captured in actual photons on Seb's photo, she did have a genuine youthful look: silver nose ring, hair streaked with blue, slender neck poking out of a baggy black skull and crossbones hoodie which bore the letters R.I.P. *Was Rebecca Prue an emo kid?*

"No, see," said Seb in a panic. "I know what you think, but it's a real photo. Look how faded it is!" He held for applause, but none came. "I know you can make anything look like anything, but I swear to God. This was before she was famous. She'd already started Magenta, they were already getting big, but it was still early on. I knew of her because she went to state too. She was a legend on campus, you know?"

"Mmhmm." Lydia rested her chin on her hands and stared at Seb with huge eyes. She was making every effort to show she was, in fact, listening.

"I was here for a show," Seb continued, undeterred. "Obviously I didn't own the place yet, I was just a student. And I saw her with her friend, so I just dove in between them and said hi, I'm at SFSU, I'm a fan. And then I got a random to take a Polaroid of us."

"Nobody's ever going to believe this," Sam said.

"I don't believe it," Lydia confirmed. "Sorry."

"What!" Seb was aghast. "You doubters. This vibe is unbelievable. I was there! Plus, everyone knows Rebecca Prue has had a gen-block since like, day fucking zero. You cannot make photos of her. It's not doable!"

"Meh." Lydia shrugged. "Can I see it up close?"

"Of course not." Seb shook his head. "It's screwed to the wall on all four corners. It's too precious to just pass around to a bunch of drunks for analysis."

While Seb and Lydia bickered, Sam had instead become obsessed. The colours of the photo, combined with its age, made it feel like it was taken in the far-flung past. You could've convinced him it was from before he was born. The giveaway, if there was one, would be their hands: all three of them were clutching mobile phones. Rebecca, Seb, and... who was the third person? "Who's she with?"

"Oh, I forget." Seb relished the chance to talk about the photo as if it was real. "They were going the full ten rounds, though. I remember they kept fighting after this was taken."

"She does look pissed. The other one." He pointed at the mystery person. She looked to be around the same age as Rebecca. She was Black, her dark hair in twists flowing past her shoulders, her frayed denim jacket covered in pins and buttons too small to make out in the photo. Her smile was forced, which made sense given the context of Seb shoving in between them like an obnoxious groupie.

"Don't project onto her," Lydia said. "You don't know."

"Well, he just told us she was."

"Whatever. It's fake, anyway."

"It's not fake!"

"This was the whole point," chimed in the old man once again. "Magenta did all this on purpose, you know. Don't want us to ever know what's real or fake."

"Think so, Skip?" Lydia drifted over toward the old man. "Why would they do that?"

"Don't rightly know," he replied. "They did a good job, though. The three of you carrying on like this." He adjusted his trucker cap, which had the name of a union stitched into the front, and finished off his bourbon.

The crowd was decently sized by the time 9 p.m. rolled around, which was a relief. Gigs at Maelzel's had started to become a bit less full, and recently they'd had one that was just a handful of regulars and the bar staff. The band had still put on a hell of a show, but the air of embarrassment was palpable among both them and the staff. It hit the staff especially hard, as Seb and his mates did their best to pitch the club as the last, best hope for live music in San Francisco. *If we're the only place to see live music anywhere in the city,* Seb had said that night, *and we can't even fill the place half-way, maybe we're too late to save it.*

Tonight had drawn the usual mix of hardcore fans, old-timers with tinnitus who would see anything so long as it's live, curious students who could barely fathom the concept, and the romantic partners of all the band's members. The staff dragged all the tables into the back room, then gathered behind the bar to make room for whatever needed to happen. Even if the music called for it, the art of moshing or even dancing had mostly been lost to the ages. In those rare cases where it was a proper "mosh band" you might encounter it, and Sam properly enjoyed those nights, though he never got involved. Otherwise, if someone did by chance try to start pushing and shoving, or if a few friends tried to form a pit, heaven forfend, the backlash from the younger crowd was swift and hostile. On one side of the argument you'd have someone — usually a man and usually in their forties or fifties — completely baffled by the response. On the other, you'd have a twenty-something insisting that you phone the police and support their assault charges. It meant on those nights Sam and Seb had to make the rounds gaining consent from everyone, on behalf of everyone else. He counted his blessings that tonight was not one of those nights.

With everyone having assumed their positions in front of the stage, and the band having given the thumbs up from their position just off to the side of said stage, Sam reached under the counter and flicked a few switches. The house lights shut off, the "party purples" came on, and it was show time. Two women, both in bright green wigs, strode out to the stage with a smattering of applause from the few audience members who had done this before and therefore knew you should applaud. The taller of the two stood behind the microphone, antique electric guitar slung around her. The other slipped behind the drum kit, which also looked as if it had seen better days.

"San Francisco!" The singer screamed into the microphone, which sent a piercing screech into the room. Seb, at his post behind the mixing desk, did his usual panic and dialled it in. "Hello! Thank you so much for coming to see us tonight! I'm Chai, and that is Orbis on the drums." Orbis gave a quick, expressionless wave. "We're so excited to play for you tonight. We've never done this before. I just want to say thanks to Sebastian for inviting us here. We think this is such a clean movement you've clipped, letting people come here and live stream directly to the chat like this. It really timelines us in such a raw, such a visceral way."

Chai's voice wavered as she spoke, and her foot tapped the stage at a speed that would make a hummingbird anxious. Sam couldn't help but smile at how nervous they were. He'd seen this a hundred times when he worked at the label. Garage bands suddenly playing a label showcase, having just one song to impress Gemma, Eamon, or whomever else had been sent to watch. Three minutes to change the course of your whole life. That sort of gatekeeping was already on the way out by the time Sam had gotten into the industry, with the advent of social media. But it still existed as a sort of cheat code to bypass the whole process of finding an audience. *If you had the right sound, the right image, fit the right mould, we already knew where your audience was. You just needed to convince us to put you in front of them.*

"So what kind of stream is this?" Lydia whispered in

Sam's ear, from her place behind the bar next to him, where she was very much not supposed to be.

"Hey!" Sam leaned away from her. "Staff only!"

"I'm his plus one." Lydia waved to Seb at the mixing desk across the room. Seb waved back. "See?"

"He's not in charge behind the bar, he's in charge of the sound mix. If they ever start playing."

"...picked this up at a thrift store for about fifty dollars," Chai continued, "and that meant we could finally use a real guitar..." She was talking the crowd through the whole history of their project, everything that had led to this moment. *Unorthodox*, Sam thought. *I'd probably just play.*

"So... what kind of stream..." Lydia gave his shoulder a squeeze.

"Music," Sam laughed. "When it's songs they're writing from scratch, you'd just say 'what kind of music do they play'. There's no streaming. They're going to play those instruments and you'll hear it. And then when it's over, it's gone."

"Okay, old man," Lydia whispered, then blew a raspberry in his ear.

"That is, if they actually play," Sam whispered back. "You're supposed to just come out and start. All this talking can come later."

"Really?" She had a bemused smile. "It's a whole ritual, huh? Does it annoy you that they're doing it wrong?"

"It annoys me that half of what your generation says is incomprehensible gibberish."

Sam and Lydia both rolled their eyes. Sam started fidgeting with the bottles behind the bar again.

"Okay! Thanks everyone!" Chai had hit peak stress. "We're going to start, I think! Orbis is going to count us in. We're called Thunderpaws, by the way!"

Thunderpaws turned out to be an unrelenting forty-five minute assault on everyone's senses. Erratic, wild drumming the likes of which Sam had never heard, with a flailing style that looked like Orbis might dislocate something. The lyrics veered between yelped nonsense and jarring intimacy—a raw look into the mind of someone with no concept of a structured song. It was admirable, inspiring, and completely unlistenable. Sam was floored by the audacity. They'd kept the bar open for another couple hours to let people decompress about what they'd just heard, and had a decent uptake: a handful of folks had stuck around to chat with Chai and Orbis about the experience.

"I'm thinking about getting out of here," Lydia said. She slapped her hands down on the bar in front of Sam. "When are you off?"

"Take him," shouted Seb. "I can handle the stragglers."

"Great! You have your camera with you? The one you took all those with?" She gestured at his photo collage.

"I do..." Sam was scared. "Why?"

"Come with me. I want to show you something."

"I'm not sure that's a good idea."

"What? Why?"

"Yeah," Seb added. "Why?"

"Well, first of all, I must be twenty years older than you."

"Twenty years?" Lydia burst out laughing. Sam was overwhelmed with the desire to crawl under a school desk and hide from her. "Qué fuerte, chulo. ¿No estas un poco *delulu?* How old are *you?*"

"How old do you think I am?"

Lydia took a deep breath. "Ick."

Sam was desperate for more idle tasks to do, but it was a lost cause. All the alcohol was straight, all the glasses were in the dishwasher, all the bar mats were put away, all but a couple taps were unscrewed. He cursed his efficiency.

"He's like thirty something," Seb shouted as he coiled up some wire.

"My personal information!"

"Twenty years older, my god, chat." Lydia sashayed in a circle. "You think I'm ten, tío?"

"He's not used to interacting with people. Mostly talks to dops and digis. This is why I don't let him wear his Ring while he's working."

Sam felt his face go hot.

"Come on!" Lydia dove in front of him, her face straight in front of his, with a massive grin. "We're going to have so much fun. Just get your camera."

Before he could process the extent of Sebastian's betrayal, his bag was on his back. Lydia dragged him by the arm through the door of Maelzel's and out into the night.

FIFTEEN
TRUST

Lydia was a torrent of chaotic Gen Beta terror, but Sam's fear of her had melted into a sense of liberation. This was the first time he'd been out in the city unsupervised by Sebastian; it was the first time in years he'd been out with someone who wasn't either his wife or some friend of hers.

Three months ago, everything about his life had been different: unemployed, living in his home town, reliant on Virginia for food and shelter. He never left the house, he slept in the guest room of his own home. Now he was in San Francisco, on some kind of adventure with a stranger, after working a double shift as a bartender. Of course, he was on a dodgy work permit and sleeping on his friend's sofa. *Baby steps*.

He smiled as he pictured Virginia checking up on him. She'd ask Aida what he was up to, where he was working now, if he was okay. *All fine of course*, he thought. He'd not revoked her access, even after she'd taken away his free Magenta Plus. He was there if she wanted, via Magenta

Mate, just a question away. If she wanted she could even see his location, right this very moment. *Even who he was with.*

"Hey!" Lydia shouted back at Sam from up the block. He'd already been behind, and now he'd stopped to rootle around in his bag.

"Sorry, I just need to find my Ring." He pawed through the bag frantically.

She'd landed with a thud right in front of him, her hands planted on her hips. "Want me to find it, mijo?"

"It's my bag, how could you find it?"

She scoffed as she thrust her hand straight into the bag. Their hands touched in the darkness, which gave him a bit of a stir. "Got it! Hold still." He stood there holding the bag with one hand, his other still inside. Lydia's brow furrowed and her tongue peeked between her lips with cartoonish determination. He felt her other hand clasp his, followed by the Ring sliding onto his finger. "There."

"Um."

"This is a service I provide, Sam." She pulled her hands out of the bag and did a little flourish. "But only to cute boys."

"Ha. Thanks."

"And old man bartenders, I suppose. I'm growing the business."

"Funny." He slung the bag back on his back, more flustered than he let on. He was a yo-yo on her finger and she'd only begun her tricks. It was a familiar feeling, and brought with it a certain nostalgia. But it also lent fresh urgency to what he needed to do next. "Aida?"

"Wait." Lydia brought her hand up to Sam's face, and he recoiled away from it reflexively. She burst into a giggle. "Relax." The cold tip of the Ring's earpiece manoeuvred into his ear, and Lydia waggled her eyebrows before poking it hard to send it the rest of the way in.

"Hey! Gentle."

"Never." She rolled her eyes and stuck her tongue out.

Sam rubbed his ear, which throbbed in dull pain. "Aida?"

"Hi, Samir." The crisp voice of Magenta's ubiquitous assistant whispered in one ear. He preferred having both earpieces in, but Lydia struck him as someone who would be annoyed by that.

Lydia mouthed *be quick, we're here*, then wandered away–either to offer some privacy, or because she was bored.

"Aida, can you turn off all tracking please?"

"Here's what I understood. You'd like to disable the ability for Virginia Rose to access your current location via Magenta Mate, including your location history and who you've been associated with. Is that correct?"

"Yes, please."

"Do you wish to unpair from Virginia Rose, or pause tracking?"

"No," he stammered. "No. Just pause the tracking." He could just turn it back on later. It seemed rash to fully unpair right now. Pairing was a huge pain: there was a fee, you had to be physically near them, you both had to consent. *Hell, people have ceremonies to celebrate pairing on Magenta Mate.* It was better to wait until he was really sure before going through with an unpair.

"Great, Samir. I'll leave that paired for now. Anything else?"

Sam bit a piece of skin off his bottom lip and crunched his knuckles. *Okay, that's done. It's not like anything is going on. But she might worry if she checked, which she won't.* He nodded to himself.

"Samir, was that it?"

"Well…" The words formed in his brain. *Ask whether Virginia's accessed his tracking already tonight.* It would remove the doubt, and he'd know she'd want an explanation. *Not that I owe her an explanation. She threw me out. She's probably with Carlos from her work right now. Maybe I should ask where she is?*

"Yes, Samir?"

"Nothing, Aida. That's all."

"Here if you need me!" A classic Aida sign-off, followed by the chime that meant she'd stopped listening. Why torture himself with the knowledge, he'd thought. She could reach out if she wanted, and he could explain then.

He walked another half-block or so to catch back up to the waiting Lydia, who idled on the sidewalk like a video game character waiting to offer Sam a quest. The street was empty save for them, and in every direction he saw the windowless concrete walls of massive tower blocks, with an occasional gap for a doorway or car park. If he looked straight up he could see the light of the city reflecting off a thick layer of storm clouds that hung just above them. Grey skies, grey buildings. Magenta had obviously done well to build San Francisco up, and in doing so had squeezed out every ounce of charm.

"Hey, sorry." As he caught up, he realised she stood at the threshold of a narrow gap between two of the adjacent towers, partly covered by some orange netting. He'd wager the two of them would have to go single file or sidle uncomfortably close to one another, if they fit at all. "What's this?"

"Our destination."

"Really."

Lydia gave a huge nod. "Mmmhmm. Reconsidering

whether you trust me enough to follow me down a dark alley?"

"I absolutely don't trust you."

"What!" Lydia gasped. "But I'm so trustworthy!"

"Do we..." He stared at the orange netting, limply hanging, some authority figure's attempt to warn, if not prevent. "Should we at least tell someone where we are?"

"Nobody's got you on Mate?" Lydia crossed her arms and wiggled her nose at him.

"Nope."

"W-Y-M?" She recoiled, confusion on her face as she said each letter. Lydia was a greatest hits of irritating traits picked up from Millennial parents.

"Nope. I'm not paired with anyone on Magenta Mate."

"Um." She stared at him, puzzled. He could feel the giant bead of cartoon sweat in mid-air next to his face. "Can I get a poll in the chat? Is this guy really married?"

"Me, what? No, not married." He felt naked under her gaze. She seemed to size him up, to determine whether she'd let his obvious deception go in order to preserve the vibe she'd cultivated over the course of the day.

"Well, guess we're alone together." She stuck her tongue out again. The vibe remained intact for now. Sam's mind was still on his newly-disabled tracker. "You'll have to trust me."

"I..." He stared at this wiry girl, ghostly pale, still swimming in the dirty UCSF jumper that she was wearing when they met at City Hall. Her acid wash jeans were ripped, her blonde hair looking a bit unwashed under the street lights. He was a stranger in a dark alley, but she didn't have a flicker of fear. *Why?*

"I don't want to come off like I'm some kind of creep," he started while staring down at his feet. "But I worry about you trusting me, too?" He rubbed his shoes together, dragging them across the bright white concrete of the sidewalk.

"Are you coming?" Lydia had to shout, because she'd just walked off during his speech and was already at the far end of the alley. Sam fired off a series of awkward laughs then ducked under the barrier.

Lydia led them down the alley, sandwiched between two of Magenta's depressing concrete hell-towers, to a suspicious seam. The wall turned from concrete to brick, but not for very long. And smack in the middle of that brick, stood a door-shaped piece of wood. No signage, no warnings, no indicators of what might be behind it. Just a boarded-up door. And she'd wasted no time pulling it away from the wall. It had clearly been taken down before, and was leaning against the door behind it rather than being secured in any way. *Where is this possibly leading*, he thought as he watched her toss the board aside. *Are we about to wander into some sort of drug den? Do they even have those in this city?*

Lydia clicked on a torch, and Sam couldn't help but giggle as he saw what actually lay before them.

"Is this a..."

"They just built right over top of it." Lydia shined her torch at her face, then waved it around the room. A pile of old bar stools sat in the middle of the dusty, low-ceilinged room, and at the back stood a decaying wooden riser you might charitably call a stage.

"Wait. What?" His eyes locked on the hand-carved sign, still mounted to the wall behind the stage. In large block letters, it read: The Prospector. "Holy shit." While Sam had never been to San Francisco, anyone who worked in music knew of The Prospector.

"I knew you'd lock in on this." Lydia shined her torch

right at him. "I've known you ten minutes and I already figured you out."

"Who wouldn't lock in on this," Sam replied. "It's the fucking Prospector! I can't believe it's just sitting here. Can't you see it from the street?"

"Nope," she answered as she worked her way over a pile of glass and debris. "Concrete, just filled in on all sides. We're totally boxed in by support pillars. They just didn't bother knocking this down."

"Maybe they couldn't bring themselves to do it. It's the fucking Prospector! I can't believe I'm here."

"Do you actually know this place?" Lydia leaned around behind the bar, and with the flick of a small switch, floodlights attached to the ceiling sprang to life.

"Wow." The sight of it jolted Sam. Given its legacy, it was hard to tell how much of the decay was from being abandoned, and how much of it was just how it had always looked. The bar itself was steel pipe and sheet metal, the tables unpainted plywood on saw horses. An old refrigerator sat behind the bar, a couple of long-expired bottles of some IPA cracked and half-leaked into the bottom. A grime-covered Marshall amplifier stood watch on stage.

"I thought you could make pictures of it," Lydia added. "Like the other ones you had made."

Sam was pushed downward by the weight of history, and he landed safely on the one barstool that hadn't either been thrown in the pile or tipped where it was. "This is too much." Thoughts of Gemma gushed into his mind. She'd been here dozens of times, he was sure. Who had she seen here? Maybe she'd sat on this very stool, and watched some wretched country act. *It's the bloody epicentre of the y'all-ternative movement, Samir, and I want to fucking vomit.*

"Too much?" Lydia's tone was one of concern. It was the first time she'd expressed a genuine emotion in the twelve hours he'd known her. "Not enough spoons? You good, tío?"

"It's just this place. It's powerful. Do you not know The Prospector?"

Lydia had her elbows on the bar, her head in her hands. She stuck her bottom lip out in a ridiculous pout and shook her head.

"It's this legendary bar. It became almost a superstition. If you wanted to break, you had to play The Prospector. It was owned by a grumpy old woman who booked all the acts herself, and she wouldn't let you charge for tickets, and she wouldn't promote that you were playing here. You were just her house band for the night." Sam joined Lydia in leaning on the bar–partly because he was exhausting himself from excitement, and partly to say he'd leaned his elbows on the bar of The Goddamn Prospector.

"Sam, I don't understand. Any of it." She pouted her lip out again and slid her elbows out toward him, her face ever-closer to his. "Was it kind of like Maelzel's?"

"Kind of, but, no. Seb wishes Maelzel's was like this place. I mean, look at it. The acts that have played on that stage, that have been discovered in this room. Label reps lined the back wall, influencers camped out all day to make sure they got in. There was all this rumour and misdirection about who might be playing that night." Sam was beaming, and he couldn't help but do it. Not just being here, but feeling that connection to his old world, his old life. Lay lines passed through the room, a spiritual energy connected them to some ethereal plane of creativity. "It was incredible." He pressed his hands against his face as the dread crept in. "The Hammer was a bit like this place."

Lydia flung herself away and crossed her arms tightly over her chest, her posture immediately hostile. Her ratty hair whipped around as she shook her head. "Don't."

"What?"

"Samir, don't."

"It was a fucked up thing to say."

"So was yours."

"What?"

"To say you knew people in the bombing, asshole! Stupid thing to claim. You want sympathy?" Her shouts were pointed, crisp, her eyes went every direction but his. "Want to make me regret my joke, feel bad about myself? Fuck you!"

"I really did know someone." He crossed his arms as well, mirroring her posture, and the brass pole along the bar pushed uncomfortably against his lower back. He winced as each image struck: Rebecca on the screen with her inhuman stare, the death toll, read off as if it was a liability needing offset. He felt the sweat start to drip down his temples, made cold by the frigid air.

Lydia pulled her arms higher, as if shielding herself from the words. "Tell me who."

"Tobias Klostermann." His mouth tasted of metal. He shivered as he said the name, and pulled his arms even more tightly together.

"Chingada." She let out a guttural groan. "Mijo, he's no martyr. He was a combatant. And you!" She flung her arms wide, gesturing at the room all around them. "You act like this is some holy place, but you mourn a devil's death? Make it make sense."

"I can't. We weren't friends, we were coworkers. I'm not saying I knew what kind of person he was, just that I knew him at all."

They studied each other for a moment, but Sam couldn't bear the sight of her. He knew he should go, and could envision himself storming out. *How had she even known the name? Would she have said that even if he made up a name?*

She drew her hands down, fingers pinched, and let out a long, measured breath. "If you're going to work at the Exhibition you need to be careful who you stick up for, mijo. You trigger the wrong person and it could go badly for you." She clicked her tongue and smirked. "Nobody's going to tip some Magenta stooge."

"Hey! I don't care about Magenta. I just knew people who were in the building. That's all." His finger touched his Ring, the cold metal grounding him in reality. It was true, he abhorred Magenta. But killing people wasn't going to get anyone anywhere. And, he'd argue, it hadn't.

She took a step forward and held her hands out, seeming to welcome him back in. "You're new here. You can learn." Her lips parted as he exhaled, his tension releasing with her permission. Her smirk grew into a wide smile. The change in energy was instant: her playfulness wasn't on a dimmer, it was all or nothing.

"Thank you for bringing me here," Sam said. "Really. It's great to see, even like this." As he looked around, he could picture the decline that presaged the fall: the throngs of people queued for watered-down drinks they couldn't afford and didn't want, bored teens on their phones wondering how they'd been duped into coming, an influencer on stage with a tablet plugged into the soundsystem, cynically passing a generated song off as their own.

"So what happened, anyway?" Lydia's question cut through his reverie.

"Nobody made music anymore. I don't know. Not like

this, anyway. My coworkers and I argued about it all the time. It all kind of happened at once. My boss would talk about the flywheel stopping. 'Ecological collapse'."

"Your boss sounds like he was a bit dramatic."

"*She* was," Sam corrected, which made Lydia huff. "But it was a hard loss. It just made her crazy. I think about her sometimes. I hope she's okay."

She giggled and boxed him in with her arms, pushing him against the bar. "You're pretty cute when you're all excited like this, old man." Her elbows slid across the metal of the bar top until the tip of her nose touched the tip of Sam's. "I'm glad you stayed up past your bed time to come see it with me."

Sam fought to hold back a smile. His head was swimming. *How had she put the fight behind them so fast?* "I'm glad you brought me here." A feeling fluttered in his chest, one he reached into the past to remember the word for: butterflies.

"So," Lydia whispered, her eyes locked on his.

"So." Sam felt her warmth when she spoke.

"Are you going to make photos of it?" He watched her lips move and felt a rush as he noticed the little dimples in her cheeks. Her use of make, instead of take, was intoxicating for reasons he couldn't explain.

"I should."

"Yeah?" She tilted her head, only just, and they came together perfectly. Her lips met his, and he felt as if he might faint from the sensation. The first kiss was tender in a way he hadn't expected. His hand cradled her cheek and they kissed again, their lips sliding together, and they exhaled. Her hands clasped his face and with a grin she bit down hard on his lip. They became a blur, ravenous: pressure erupting after a day of teasing, the rawness of the performance, and the power of this place.

He was carried away by her energy as she scrabbled onto the bar top. He joined her soon after, the stool proving itself useful again. Neither of them said a word, the moment tracked only by scrapes, thuds, and grunts. His hand worked up the leg of her threadbare jeans, crossing coarse denim and soft skin to find the button at the top. Her jumper hit the floor with his pants close behind as they worked to remove only what was in the way. It all happened at unbelievable speed with little care, their hands and lips doing what was needed as they fumbled and pawed their way through, pulled inexorably toward their fate, unwilling and unable to stop.

But time began to stretch and slow as they approached the event horizon. Sam looked down at Lydia, her back against the cold steel of the bar. She looked up at him hungrily, a lust he almost recognised. *Was it ever like this with her?* He tried to lock his thoughts away, though he could only hide from them until the next time he was alone.

"Ya," Lydia sliced the tension breathlessly. "¿Qué esperas, chulo?" Her hands gripped each side of the bar. He squeezed her hips and closed his eyes to lighten the load on his senses. Her back arched, in time with another moan, passionate whispers in a language he didn't know. She was trying to pull him forward in every possible way, and it would only be a few seconds more before she felt vulnerable—or at least confused. But the drawer was bursting now, the thoughts too numerous, impossible to contain. The Prospector, Magenta, Virginia, Gemma. Voluminous regret.

"I can't."

They collapsed into a heap. The tenderness of the moment had broken him. Sam closed his eyes, his face buried in her chest, their limbs a tangle, his balance precarious. Neither of them said a word.

"No agarro la onda," she heaved as she spoke, her breathing laboured. "No me cae el veinte."

"I'm sorry," he replied, hopeful that he sounded sincere. "It's complicated."

"I'm not. I'm simple, Sam. Let me show you."

"I'm sorry."

Lydia writhed and wriggled underneath him. "You said she was your ex." Her gyrations, the random brushes of fingertips against his skin. Still so eager to salvage the moment.

"It's not that."

"Tell me what you want," she insisted, with a slap to his head. "Get Virginia out of there."

"Hey!" *Virginia would never have set foot in The Prospector to begin with.* He lifted his face from Lydia's chest. The sweat between them turned frigid in the brisk air and sent a shiver down his bare back.

"What?" Another smirk crossed her blurry face, once again inches from his own. His scolding, meant to dissuade, was instead met by her biting his bottom lip. He climbed off the bar, the moment ending as gracelessly as it began. The playfulness drained from her face and she turned away, her arms pulled tightly against her chest and stomach, her back now a wall between them.

"I'm..." Sam offered a limp consolation, half-expressed.

"Don't."

Their composure returned once they'd dressed, though Lydia kept her distance and stayed quiet. "I really do like this place," Sam blurted out, desperate to ease the unbearable stress. It was why she'd brought him here after all—to see this place. "I want to take some photos of it." His hands were tucked safely in his pockets, his eyes back on the ground. "If that's okay."

"Yeah?" Lydia rolled her eyes, a faint smirk on her face.

If he was anxious and desperate to ignore what had happened, she'd instead decided to pocket it with a sly nod. *More dirt*, he thought as he took her in from a few paces away. Her jumper, as well as the rest of her, was even more sullied from their recent encounter. A hundred different innuendo rode a tilt-a-whirl in his head, but he wouldn't dare risk reigniting something he had just finished smothering. He shuddered to think of how he looked in all this, in any sense.

"I think so, yeah."

"So, what? Gonna hang pictures of a different bar in your bar? Gen Z is ridic."

"Well, honestly," Sam replied as he looked through the viewfinder. "I know someone who would love to see what became of this place. And I'd love to show them someday."

# SIXTEEN
# STOIC

*Eleven years ago.*

The trip to London earlier that year had left Samir with a near-insatiable appetite. He'd set to work before they'd even returned, digging up every scrap of information he could about how to get a job, an internship, day labour, any sniff of anything to do with London's music scene. And he'd felt it was only natural to start by applying at Normal Island Records: label home of his favourite band, Turk's Revenge, and the one music executive he'd ever spent any length of time with, Gemma Thomson.

To his surprise, and Virginia's chagrin, he'd been accepted almost immediately as a summer intern. And not in the label's local offices in his hometown of Los Angeles, but a trip straight back to the UK.

"Three months, including luxurious Zone 1 accommodation, with a small stipend for expenses." Sam had presented it to his girlfriend Virginia with what he felt was an appropriate level of enthusiasm. It had stirred an unusual sensation in him, the thought of returning so soon. Back to that world, back through the curtain. It was hardly possible for him to hide how he felt about the notion.

"I don't understand why it has to be back in London." And his girlfriend was unamused by the prospect.

"I guess that's just what they decided."

"Did you request London?"

"No, of course not. I applied in person at their office in Hollywood."

"And that's why I don't understand. Don't they have British people to give those internships to?"

"V, I don't know."

It was true that he hadn't requested London, insofar as you weren't really able to request that sort of thing when you were begging for an internship at a boutique record label owned by a mega-conglomerate. He might've mentioned London in his application of course, in particular his night at The Roundhouse. Though embarrassment might've led him to be light on the details. And he might've also managed to name-drop someone.

"Mr. Whitechapel." At his orientation meeting, he recognised the man from that night at the Magenta demo, the man whose name he'd fished from the depths of his memory. He looked just as breezy and effortless in the daytime.

"It's Eamon, mate. Never got on with being called Mr. Whitechapel. It's not my real surname."

"Right, sorry. Eamon."

"Hits the ear wrong as well, I'm afraid." Eamon tutted. "Best not refer to me at all."

The summer of '32 was a whirlwind. Virginia was able to get sponsored for a tourist visa through proof of relationship, and she joined Sam in his luxurious accommodation—big enough perhaps for one of them. Their groceries piled into the tiny refrigerator in their micro-kitchen, to be prepared on the hotplate atop the square of laminated plywood which served as their countertop.

They stacked neatly in the single bed each night. Virginia had defined a rota for use of the bathroom sink each morning, which was most comfortably accessed while standing in the tub. She would finish her shower at one end whilst he brushed his teeth at the other. It was her constant search for these efficiencies that kept things as tolerable as they were. If tempers flared or elbows bumped, often literally, he could rely on her cooler head to prevail, which he appreciated immensely.

Virginia spent her days at a nearby café wiling away the hours on her tablet looking for jobs back home, to prepare for their inevitable departure from Neverland. *This isn't a viable career path*, she'd insist to him as they sat on the hard grey sofa in the corner by the window. *You might as well be interning at a post office the year after email was invented.* But he was intractable, and she was unwilling to take his spirits down to crush depth. So they'd stay near the surface, near the buoyant good vibes, and she'd make their real plans for their real life.

She would've preferred to find work in London, something she could do while Sam was off at his. Something that could perhaps let them both, for now, achieve their aims. But it had been made clear how illegal that would be, not to mention how much of a practical impossibility it was. Unemployment in the UK was nearing twenty-five percent, and not for lack of trying. Virginia struggled for weeks to explain this to Samir: there was simply no room in the British economy for high numbers of people working in the creative arts.

Streaming music and video had become so thoroughly commoditised, the only money in it was flowing straight into paying for server farms, power plants, and full-time staff at the Magenta Corporation.

This hadn't come close to deterring Samir, even as it made itself somewhat apparent in his day-to-day on the job at the label. Eamon worked hard to cultivate a presence larger than life, and the trappings of success were still abound. It wasn't evident in raw money or fame, but in the eccentricity of everyone involved. These people would act this way even if they were anonymous and dirt-poor. Until now, Sam's source of insider knowledge had been his friend Sebastian. But Seb's "chill California guy" attitude hadn't prepared him for the sheer bloody-mindedness of the London music scene.

Most days were normal enough: sat at his desk in the office, answering calls, arranging access, assembling guest lists. Others around him were having the knock-down, drag-out fights over who got through to speak with Eamon, who got access to which artists, which names went on the lists. He simply had to do what he was told, observe, and absorb.

The nights were a different matter. When he'd fought to bring Virginia along on his internship—and it was indeed a fight, on both sides—it wasn't just because he thought he'd miss her, or because he thought she'd enjoy it. Those were both true, he'd felt, and he'd also felt those were the reasons worth saying to both Virginia and to the Intern Coordinator at the label. But his real reason was because he needed his person by his side. He'd been so nervous, so excited, and needed someone there not just to help him cope, but to have a frame of reference for everything he was about to go through. It'd been such a relief when both sides had agreed.

After just one whiff of the life, she'd called a permanent

moratorium on further nights out. "That's your world, Samir," she'd said. "You should enjoy it while you can."

"I was hoping it would be our world. I thought you loved gigs."

"I enjoy the occasional concert. I don't enjoy whatever that was. I don't like being pushed. I don't enjoy getting covered in bruises. And having beer spilled on me by disgusting men who are grabbing every part of me."

"I'm sorry, V, I know you had a bad time at Underworld..." Sam had regretted bringing her along the moment they'd arrived. Eamon had given him the extra pass because he said he wouldn't go anywhere near Camden when Shitweasel were playing. *In hindsight,* Sam thought, *perhaps it had been a clue.*

"Getting crushed in the crowd, then trying to leave, and not even being able to get up the stairs from everyone huddled in them vaping. More disgusting men catcalling me, telling me 'oh, it's okay, love, if you can't handle it.'"

Sam's shoulders had slumped at this point, and he'd refrained from any further arguing. It was all valid, of course, but also such an unfair thing to do. *Would she really judge all live music against a single bad experience? He'd spend his entire career now just attending these shows unaccompanied?* He'd change the subject any time he was asked by Mr. Whitechapel whether he wanted to bring anyone—though aside from those dodgy nights in Camden, Mr. Whitechapel himself was always guaranteed to be there. "Can't resist watching a shit band," he'd said. "Never pass up an opportunity to see what utter excrement we've decided to put on a stage and claim it's art. Even bad music can be a good time when it's being played live."

The nights Sam came to cherish, then, were the ones

where he got to meet people. It wasn't as often as he might like. People tended to keep to themselves or their cliques at gigs. He'd hoped to find solace with the other interns, but they'd cliqued up by the end of day three, and Sam had somehow missed out on that as well. He figured it was by virtue of the rest of them being from the same post-grad programme, or perhaps just because they were all British, or because they were all of Bangladeshi descent. He wasn't sure if it was any of these reasons, really, or none of them. But he had long nights to wonder as he watched bands alone from the backs of rooms.

By month three, relations with Virginia had crumbled. She'd taken an internship back in California, and she'd agreed to come back early and start it now, rather than see out the rest of their time in London. This left Sam baffled, which in turn left Virginia even more baffled.

"One of us has to start building the future," she'd explained. "How can you be against this?"

"You're abandoning me because you're not having a good time," Samir had replied. The argument played out all night, first sat on the plain grey sofa, then sat on the edge of the bed. "And you won't even tell me where?"

"Los Angeles. Back home."

"But where is the job?"

Virginia had sighed deeply and contemplated before responding. "It's at Magenta."

Samir wanted to respond in a rational and collected manner, so he'd taken his time as well. Virginia believed the lengthy silence to be his response, so she sighed again and laid down.

"I thought we never went to bed angry," Sam asserted.

"That's a silly rule," Virginia answered. "And it's two in the morning. I have to rest before my flight."

So for the final three weeks of his time in London, Samir had found himself alone.

As the newest member of the team, and as the least liked, he'd spend those weeks as he'd spent the last few: behind check-in tables. It was the lowest role you could have — sat with a list of names, distributing wristbands, letting people into the show who were invited by the label, and were too cool or too disinterested to buy their own ticket. Sam had hoped to learn exciting behind-the-scenes secrets during his internship. He had to settle for learning that label interns, not venue staff, were responsible for this task.

This, Sam had decided, was the perfect middle option. He got to meet everyone, he got to be visible to everyone at the event, but he was spared the shame and desperate awkwardness of drinking alone at the back of the room. Once everyone was checked in he could remain at his post. If someone asked why, it was a credible answer that he needed to be ready for late-comers. Everyone knew VIPs in this business, in any business, loved to arrive late. He could remain stoic, facing out toward the door, live music blaring from the room behind him. It also helped him stay sober, because he wasn't able to get himself a drink, and nobody seemed keen to bring him one. He'd found his niche. And with just a few weeks before he was due to head back to America, not a moment too soon.

Every time he sat down at his post, whatever venue it happened to be at that night, he'd be presented with a tablet containing the list. As each person approached, he'd either find their name on the list and tap it, or if they were one of the increasing numbers of people who'd gone all in on Magenta, some device on their person would tell the tablet who they were, and the name would appear automatically. And each night, he'd get through about three-quarters of his list. If you're cool enough to be invited, you're cool enough to ignore the invite and not turn up. He'd watch as the names appeared and were ticked off, night after night, wondering which third of them would wind up not arriving. And each night contained a small disappointment, because there was one name guaranteed to be on the list, and guaranteed to remain unticked. It was, of course, Gemma.

He'd felt the rush of sweet validation the first time he saw her name on the list. *So it was worth it,* he'd thought at the time. *The naivety of youth,* he'd realise later. *Of course it was foolish to think she'd come to these.* But he still held out hope every night, even as he wouldn't dare ask Eamon again. He'd tried once, the second time she was a no-show, and he'd make a weak show of it being somehow related to his job.

"It's a nice try, lad," he'd said with a wink. "Everyone wants face time with her. She relishes not giving it."

As much as he hadn't expected to be sent to London for this internship, he hadn't expected to somehow avoid running into Gemma the entire time. *She worked in the same building! How was it possible they'd never even seen each other in the hallway?* But they hadn't—or at least, he'd never seen her. Over six months since their encounter on the floor of The Roundhouse, and she'd passed into almost mythical status in his mind.

The nights weren't without their share of enjoyable moments, backstage encounters and green room banter that few would experience and fewer would appreciate. It was Samir's musical education, and it proved more valuable than four years of university study.

"Mate, jazz piano, jungle, drum & bass, it's all one fucking incestuous family," crowed a solo drummer between lines of cocaine.

"We accidentally headlined the Barrowlands," shouted another, "because our pal bought up half the tickets through our link as a fucking prank. And they chose headliners based on ticket sales. And we were shite, and the other bands were all real fucking bands. We hardly got out alive, dude, such was the fucking fury."

"The support were bloody racists," howled a singer through wheezing laughter, about a gig long ago. "We walk out to a sea of fucking St. George's crosses and disinterested white faces, and start our bloody chune about loving each other. Fucking crickets, bruv."

But soon summer was over. "Sad it's the last one of these?" Eamon had already been waiting for Sam when he arrived at the Brixton Academy. He leaned next to the old ticket booth in his double denim, his arms crossed tightly, one foot on the wall, devilish smirk on his face. "The time's flown by."

"I am a bit, I suppose." He felt so far from home at that moment. The internship would end next week, and he'd, what... fly back to Los Angeles? To see Virginia, who abandoned him? But he couldn't stay either, for reasons too numerous to count, most of which involved laws or money.

"Chin up, son. You've done well in the face of all the hazing."

Sam couldn't hide his surprise. "I figured you didn't know that's going on."

"I just assume it is. We've all been through it, or we've been the ones that did it." Eamon gave a wink. "It's a small industry. You'll be with these people the rest of your life. It's a trial by fire."

Sam forced a smile. He wasn't ready to be outwardly happy, but the flicker had thawed a small part of him.

"Who's playing tonight?" Eamon cut through the unexpected sincerity. It was the most British thing he could've done.

"Christ, Eam," came the voice from behind Sam. "It's your bill."

"Oh, your grace," Eamon spit with a roll of his eyes. "Lovely for you to descend and walk among us. There you are, Samir." He gestured to the person behind him, and gave Sam the tacit permission he needed to spin around and look. Towering above them both, clad in a red blazer and dripping with condescension, was Gemma Thomson.

"Gemma, hi." Samir bumbled and stuttered. He stuck his hand out and took a step forward, but it hadn't been far enough. He retracted his hand and popped it straight into his pocket. Gemma's eyes darted to one side as she sidled around him. Later in life, he'd find himself haunted by this moment in his quietest hours.

"It's Geordie Scouser supporting, by the way," Gemma said as she joined Eamon in front of the booth. "Bloody stupid name."

"It's post-collapse sludge metal, Gemma. It's about deconstructing the English identity." Eamon replied through gritted teeth. "And it's sold out."

"It's fucking noise, mate. Five men screaming nonsense, not an instrument between them. And the lyrics make no bloody sense."

"It depends on when you hear them."

"What? Whachu mean?"

"The lyrics are being prompted during the song. And their AJ injects news and social reactions as well. It's a dynamic..."

"Prompted? It's bloody algo? They didn't even fucking *write* the songs?! It's a... who the fuck is AJ?" Gemma was emphatic, borderline unhinged, her limbs flailing around as she shouted down at Eamon.

"Christ Gemma, read your briefs for once, or the trades, or bloody show up to something. It's an algorithm jockey."

Sam was cemented in place, mesmerised by the industry chat unfolding in front of him. He realised this was exactly what he'd been missing the past few months.

"I can't, Eamon." Her hands sat on her head, her elbows akimbo. The stress caused by Eamon's description of the band Geordie Scouser appeared to have stripped a decade off her life. "Christ, I just can't."

"Sam," Eamon said with a clear of his throat. "I've left the wristbands back at the office. Would you mind?" He tossed the keys and Sam caught them, a small mercy. After the events of the past five minutes, he would not have survived if he'd dropped or missed them.

"Which car is yours, Mr. Whitechapel?"

"I'll take him." Gemma gave a wry smile. "Gives us a chance to catch up. He's been on our miserable island for months now, earning our shit pay, listening to our shit bands, I've not said one word to him."

Sam tried to keep his cool. *Gemma would run an errand with him, just to spend time together?*

"Right..." Eamon smiled back, his face covered in suspicion. "Sam, you indulge me for one moment before you dash off?" Gemma rolled her eyes as Eamon pulled Sam aside.

"Lad," he said in a hushed tone as he put their backs to Gemma. "If you don't want her to join you, you can say no."

"What do you mean?" The aside confused Sam. He'd never heard such a concerned tone from Eamon.

"You're a good looking lad, smart, loyal. Clearly she sees something in you. Listen." Eamon rubbed his temples and sighed. "I don't want to interject myself, if it's an intrusion. But I can protect you if that's something you need."

"I honestly don't know what you mean, Mr. Whitechapel."

"Right." He patted Sam's shoulder. "Just look after yourself, lad. If it's a no, say no. She's not a monster. So far as I can tell." He straightened, his voice returning to the usual volume. "Right, okay. Be quick, if you please."

Gemma nodded. "No bother, Eam."

Sam was in no danger of passing The Knowledge, but even he knew they had just blown straight past the label's office.

"Ma'am, I think that was it."

"Oh sod Eamon, miserable prick. He can go himself."

"Should I tell him?"

"He'll figure it out."

"But..."

She jerked the steering wheel, setting off a furious cacophony of beeps and warnings as they careened onto the motorway. "I'm reassigning you for the night," she smirked. "Executive privilege. You don't want to watch Geordie Scouser, and neither do I. Tossers."

The drive was uneventful, save for Gemma repeatedly switching off the drive assist and swearing at the car under her breath. Sam stared out the window and found himself mesmerised by the scale of the city: flashing digital billboards, imposing tower blocks, football stadia, all competing for his attention as the freeway carved through West London.

She seemed possessed, diving across lanes with the determination of someone in a high speed chase, and knew exactly where to go with no need for map or navigation. Past a massive shopping centre out one side, then a park covered with tents shortly after, the quality of the neighbourhood seemed to be in rapid decline the further they went. By the time they reached their destination, they were surrounded on all sides by low-slung buildings with crumbling facades.

"My office." She'd thrown the car into park on the street across from an unassuming flat-roofed pub. A vinyl banner hung from some zip-ties: *The Fox.* Gemma shook her head when she saw it. "Was always going to end here, wasn't it?"

"It's..." Sam stared at the building, which he felt could double as the set of any number of direct-to-streaming horror films. "It's nice."

"What?" Gemma tutted. "No, it's not. That's the bloody point, isn't it? Go on, in you get, first round's on me."

Sam was picking a splinter out of his finger, courtesy of the door, when he felt his phone vibrating in his pocket. Virginia's name flashed on the screen, along with three missed texts. Gemma glanced over at it as she waited for their pints by the bar.

"Virginia, hmm? Is she joining us?"

"Not tonight."

"You invited her though, I'm sure."

"Of course."

A pint landed on the bar in front of Sam and he pulled it straight to his lips. He didn't know why he'd just said that. Virginia wasn't even able to join them.

"Why'd you lie?" And Gemma had his number.

"What?"

"You lied to me, just now."

"I don't know." Sam could feel his hand shaking. A deep discomfort took hold.

Gemma raised a glass and Sam joined her without conscious effort. "Cheers, Sam. You don't have to tell me the truth. But if I ask whether you're telling the truth, always be honest. Okay?"

Sam just nodded.


BY 2 A.M. they were nearly the last ones in the pub, tucked into the snug at the back. Gemma had gotten more casual, her blazer flung to one side, her blouse half-unbuttoned. A pair of graphite rings hung on a chain around her neck, and Sam spent a great deal of energy not looking at them as they dangled in a very delicate position. Their table was littered with empty pints and empty shots, their phones both off and upside down at the far edge. The bartender leaned around the corner and whistled with a nod to Gemma. She nodded back and downed the rest of her drink.

"I believe we're being ejected soon, Sam. And just when we're getting to know each other."

"That's a pity, ma'am."

"You keep calling me ma'am." She smirked and shook her head. "Such a polite American boy."

"I do work for you."

Gemma rolled her eyes. "You work for Eamon."

Sam spun his empty glass between his hands. He'd struggled all night to contribute anything of value to their conversation, instead content to watch her and listen. Her stories were fascinating and jumbled, bouncing from topic to topic, from anger to joy, from hope to despair. It was exhilarating and exhausting in equal measure. *Is this just how adults interacted?* Proper adults, with proper jobs, who'd led proper lives. Perhaps a twenty-two year old simply wasn't interesting.

"I broke up with my husband outside this pub, you know." Gemma rolled her head slowly and rubbed her shoulder under her blouse. "Christ, I'm old."

"You were married?"

"Briefly. This place is just where I come to mourn loss, I suppose. It's all come crashing down around me, I'm afraid." The pint in front of her was nearly gone. She stared at it and let out a groan as she switched to rubbing the other shoulder. "God, you've been good enough to succumb to all this."

"This has not been the night I was expecting, ma'am. I can definitely say that."

She slid closer to him in the booth and turned just a bit, putting her back to him. "Would you?" A flash of her eyes, her face partly obscured, and another rush of wild feelings ran through Sam. If she asked him to kill someone, he would hope she was kidding, but he wasn't entirely sure he wouldn't do it. He gingerly raised his hands and placed them on her shoulders, then gave a nervous squeeze. Gemma let out a low moan and placed her hand atop his. A snicker came from behind them, and they both caught the bartender hiding a laugh as he washed glasses. Gemma tossed Sam's hands away as she rushed out of the booth.

"Right. Shots then karaoke, yeah?"

Two shots had become four, and their musical odyssey drove every remaining patron out into the street. But Gemma would not be deterred: chaining ballads into metal, emo into country, and finally getting stuck in a morass of 2000s one-hit-wonders. Only pulling the plug on the karaoke machine had been successful in the bartender's war against their custom. But pull it he had, and the ensuing fracas led to a full pint getting spilled directly onto Sam. And that, Sam noted only to himself, had not led to any apologies, but instead to a round of laughter.

At the threshold of the door Gemma put her arms on Sam's shoulders and leaned against him, which brought him face to face with her necklace. He stared at the rings and thought he could feel her lips graze his ears, though couldn't be sure. "Sam..." Her voice was a low whisper. "Can you walk me home?"

"Where do you live?"

"Across the street. Come on then, night cap."

Sam chuckled. "But, how am I getting home?"

"I don't know, Sam! You're a bloody adult man, do what adult men do in these situations and have your bloody girl-friend come pick you up." She shoved him physically to accentuate her point. *Verbal bullying was never enough for this woman*, he thought.

He stared at her for far too long, then gave a slight nod. "Sure, okay."

"Is it okay?" Her finger thudded against his chest a couple times. "Are you lying to me?"

"Yes."

She squinted at him for a moment, then nodded. "Right, let's go."

Gemma's flat was stunning in the truest sense of the word: he was stunned this woman lived here. His amazement started when they walked out of The Fox and across Uxbridge Road, toward an apartment building that looked to be falling down in its spare time. "It's got an old world charm," she'd said with a wink.

Stacks of CDs lined the walls in her claustrophobic den. A tired old sofa had its back to the bay window. She had no curtains, her third-floor window high enough to look down at the street lights, but low enough to catch the glare and flood the room with a sickly hue. She disappeared into the kitchen as Sam closed the door behind him. It popped back open.

"You've got to fucking slam it!" came the shout from the kitchen. Sam obliged, throwing his body against the back of it until he finally heard the click. Several magazines fell down from a nearby stack, and he nearly tripped on a wine bottle as he leapt forward to pick them up.

"Your apartment isn't what I expected, Miss Thomson."

She emerged from the kitchen with two bottles of Modelo. "It's a flat, love. Apartments have amenities. Like heating, or windows that open." She stuffed a beer in his hand. "And it's Miss."

"I said Miss."

"Christ, I mean, it's not Miss. Call me Gemma. We're adults, I'm not your bloody professor." She flew around the flat like a whirlwind, futzing and fiddling, the way one does in their own space. Tweak this, tidy that, healthy swigs of her beer in between. "Make yourself comfortable, darling. Between your American need to wear shoes indoors and the half keg of beer soaked into your trousers, you could use a sprucing up."

Gemma emerged a little while later in a black velour track jacket and loose sweatpants, thick-rimmed glasses on her face, her hair up in a clip. Beer in one hand, doughnut in the other, palpably ready for leisure. Sam stood near her couch rather awkwardly, having done next to nothing, as he knew that under his drenched skinny jeans and black denim jacket were only an obnoxious t-shirt and picnic table boxers.

Still, though. Seeing her come down the hallway in her leisurewear, he could only smile. "Is this Gemma in her natural state? At long last?"

"Bollocks." Gemma let out a clipped cackle. "I'm clothed, so it's still less relaxed than I'd prefer to be in my own home." She looked him up and down. "You're..."

"I removed the shoes."

"Sam." Her voice was stern, but pleading. "I can't look at you in your fucking beer-soaked music fan costume all night."

He sighed. "Have anything I could change into?"

She hadn't, of course, had anything he could change into. Sam instead found himself in his ridiculous t-shirt, boxers, and nylon socks, with a fuzzy blanket across his lap in an attempt to both warm up and salvage a bit of dignity. Gemma sat in the tatty chair opposite him, stroked her chin and leaned back. He was under observation. He shifted his weight awkwardly while she diagnosed him. "So."

"I know."

"Oh?"

"The shirt was a gift."

"Is that a bald eagle wearing an American flag, firing two machine guns?"

"Yes."

"And he's riding a shark."

"That's correct."

"Well, shit." Gemma tilted her head and continued staring, her glasses giving her the air of a demented psychologist. "Tell me something about yourself."

"About myself? What do you want to know?" He

clutched at the blanket and tried to warm his hands. He thought he saw his breath.

She tucked a bit of stray hair behind her ear, and Sam mindlessly did likewise with his own. "What do you enjoy?"

"I like music," he said.

She tittered. "Not news, babe. We met at a gig. You're interning at my label." She traced her lips with her finger. "It's a good question. What music do you really like? You're not allowed to say any bands we've signed. Actually, sod that. What do you play?"

"I have a guitar. I don't really play. I'm garbage." Sam pored over all the times he'd seen his friend Sebastian at parties, effortlessly chatting with whomever he'd decided to flirt with that night. "You play me something, though?" He gestured behind her.

Gemma snorted and tossed her head. On the wall hung an acoustic guitar, sat amongst a thousand Polaroid pictures wallpapering one whole side of the room. "Bit presumptuous of you."

"Is it?"

"I'm not your little performer, Sam." She leaned forward and flicked him on the forehead. "Don't tell me to play for you."


BY 5 A.M. they'd lost all semblance of decorum. Gemma sprawled over her couch, limbs askew, partly covered by a pile of blankets. Sam rested his back against the sofa, sat on the hardwood. He'd chosen to ignore the pain radiating up his tailbone. The room was rich with the first hints of the morning sun, and it was only then his body made clear it knew just how long they'd been awake.

"I'm bloody terrified, Sam." Her whispers spread through him, leaving goosebumps in their wake.

"Terrified of what?"

"Terrified of Magenta, of what's happening with this project. I just feel so fucking old."

"You're not old."

"I've spent my whole life devoted to music, whatever that fucking means. Musicians and music. But now it's, what? Is it going away? And I'm asking myself, did I help to do that? Like some bloody Oppenheimer but the stakes are non-existent." She chuckled as best she could. Her throat was sandpaper. "I am become death, destroyer of songs."

"It's not you, Gemma. I don't know why you'd blame yourself. It's Magenta's stupid fucking algorithms."

"They couldn't do it without us. We're helping them destroy us. And for what?"

"It won't matter. People have been making music for millennia. They're not going to stop now."

"Is that even true, Sam? Or does it just sound true?"

"I'm pretty sure it's true."

"It sounds true," they both whispered in unison. Gemma let out another raspy titter.

"Pouring emotion out of you and into the world through an instrument. Playing until there's blood on the strings. Drumming so hard you think the sticks will splinter in your hands. Screaming so loud you might tear your throat. Nothing can replace that." Sam was certain he had lifted this verbatim from his friend Sebastian. But he'd also found it to be moving at the time, and he'd committed it to memory.

He felt Gemma's fingers slide into his hair. Her fingernails dragged lightly across his scalp, and it sent unbelievable tingles in waves all over him. It was an unexpected intimacy, the kind found in the liminal space between waking and sleep. The window on this moment would shut soon, leaving them in the realm of the living—people heading to work, joggers out for their morning run, milk being delivered. But for now, with the loosest grip on consciousness, they could fly together across this surreal plane.

"Why did you never find a new band?" Sam dropped back down to a whisper, and thoughts left his mind without any real scrutiny. "After your husband passed away. Why not put that pain into music?"

"That part of me sort of died with him, I think. Or really, it went with him in a carton on the 228 to Maida Hill." She let out a tiny sigh. "We just wanted to play a few notes in the symphony of human history. That's what we'd say." She chuckled. "Pish, innit."

"I think it's sweet."

"Right, enough about me. Why weren't you ever in a band?"

Sam sighed in turn, his eyes still closed. Her fingers on his scalp, and her rasping voice right in his ear, every part of her seemed to caress him. "Well... I didn't care."

"What?"

"I never cared about music," he said into the dark. "I'm sort of a fraud. I get all my musical taste from my college buddy. I just thought he was so cool. Everybody did. I sorta mirrored him. His taste, his style, the way he talked. All of it."

"Huh."

"I mean, now I like it. I always kinda liked it. But now I'm into the more esoteric side of it, knowing who's in bands, sub-genres, all that. I faked it until I made it. But then I majored in music business like him."

"Wow," Gemma chuckled. "That's kind of cute, I guess. Did you pick the same major to stay close to him?"

"I suppose so." He could feel the answer to this question propelling both of them back into the real world. "It was the three of us."

"The three of you?"

"Me, Seb, and Virginia."

"Right."

He leaned his head back toward her, to barely catch a glimpse of her face, sideways behind him against the pillow. The dawn interplayed with the street lamps on Gemma's face, and he could see just how rough and dry the skin was on her lips. To his relief, she continued to run her fingers through his hair. That was the dotted line they'd decided on tonight, and in Sam's mind, he believed this was their unspoken bond. They'd draw these lines in real time and stay just on one side of them. It didn't need to be communicated. They both just knew.

"I thought I'd see her tonight, Sam. Your girlfriend, that is. She joined you in London for the summer and you've left her home with her knitting."

"She went back last week."

"Oh?"

"She has an internship. At Magenta."

Gemma snorted. "You're joking. You must be."

"I wish I was." Sam let out a grim chuckle. It was all he could do. Virginia was a grown woman, and her career was her choice. She'd made that clear when he delivered his meek protest. He wanted so badly to confide that conversation in this person on the sofa behind him. This person who understood why he was upset without needing to be told, who was soothing him in the dark before the dawn.

"Are you coping with that? I'd be bloody furious."

He shook his head.

"Oh, love. I'm sorry." Her fingers left his hair and he closed his eyes. The stubble on his face was as rough as the skin on her palm, but there was still solace in her caress. Her breath on his neck sent a fresh wave of chills down his chest and arms. His head turned, though he wasn't sure if she had guided him or if he'd done it himself. His chest pressed against the front of the sofa, her face an inch from his. She was nestled deep into the pillow, her eyes heavy with exhaustion. The awkwardness of the angle confounded him as he tried to find her with his free hand. So many folds and layers of blanket lie between his fingers and her skin. Instead he stroked her cheek with his fingertips. Her eyes widened at his touch, and they dove into each other's stares. The world blotted out, her form a silhouette against it all, everything else just a blur to ignore. A rush of blood went every which way as she took his face into her hand. He tilted his head back, closing the final inch between them.

"Sam," she whispered. Her chapped lips brushed against his. "You need to go."

"It's so late." He pressed his forehead against hers. The idea was nonsensical. There was nowhere else. Her fingers dug into his neck, and it was as if she'd flipped a switch hidden within. He folded his legs under him and tried to get better purchase on the floor, leaving him kneeling in front of her. The blankets were still formidable, but he made a second attempt to get through. His fingers found the edge of her hip, and he gave a light squeeze through her pyjama bottoms.

"If you don't bloody go," she replied, "I'll go." With a wriggle from her he felt the pyjamas slide out of place, and his hand now laid under the blanket against the soft skin of her side. He spread open his fingers and squeezed, in part to see how far over the line they'd now agree to go. She was so warm, and this part of her surprisingly delicate, in stark contrast to her roughness elsewhere. He tried to attune to her, to seek the slightest more permission, to go the slightest bit further. Their lips were at an impasse, held apart by unseen forces. But for now, until they could confront that, she had begun gyrating her hips in time with his touch.

"It's okay," he whispered.

"Course it's not," she answered immediately. "You're my intern and your hand's on my arse."

"I'm Eamon's intern."

"Christ." She rolled over suddenly and laid flat on her back. With their gaze broken, a bit of the spell had worn off. But something still roiled inside Sam. The blanket had slipped part way onto the floor, and Gemma had made no move to claw it back. She stared at him, her expression vacant and distant, one hand tucked behind her head and the other touched to her lips. If he were to look over his shoulder he might barely see the line they weren't meant to cross, still there in the middle distance.

"I should leave, shouldn't I?" Sam picked up the blanket and draped it back over her as he got to his feet.

"Course you should." Her tone academic, able to express what she knew must happen, with no will to ensure that it did.

"Are you sure..."

She groaned. He'd someday think back to this moment, and see it for what it was: she carried the burden of being the adult, while this child before her bathed in the luxury of freedom to make bad decisions. Now she had to step in and temper them before anyone got hurt. "Go back to your bloody accommodation," she scolded. "Spend a bit more time with it before you head back to your girlfriend in another bloody country."

Sam had started to gather his clothes and shoes. "I'm almost positive that it's over."

"Course it is, Sam." Gemma rolled her head to one side and stared out the window, squinting at the sunlight. "Course it is."

# EIGHTEEN
# ERROR

The controller felt tiny in her hands, her long, bony fingers wrapping around the back to overlap. This was her third try today to get past this particular bit of The Last of Us.

This game had been a favourite of Charlie's, as was anything that dealt with a post-apocalypse. Though back then, Charlie had been playing the remake. *It must've been what, 2026? 2027?* She'd repeatedly tried to interest Imogen in it—*it's a masterpiece, it's so powerful*—even offering up her gaming laptop as a loan, one of her prized possessions. And it drove Imogen crazy. All of it. The offer, the lavishing of praise onto a video game, the distraction. *We don't have time for this*, she'd shout, and it would spiral into a conversation that an outsider might think was about the game, and was really about everything but. *We have to make time for this*, Charlie would shout back. *Play is important.*

Now she stared at this antique PlayStation3: a bulky, ridiculous relic, an oddity of industrial design even when it was new. It rested on a side table in her study, with a nest of wires running into the back of an even older antique television. It was a connection to a past that wasn't hers, one she'd acquired to right a wrong. She listened to the bloody thing fail: it ticked and clicked and moaned and whirred while fragile plastic spun inside, bombarded by a diode manufactured when Imogen was two years old.

*We're both in our forties*, Imogen thought as the device struggled. *I think we both work about as well, too.*

The screen, and the room, went black as the sounds came to an abrupt stop. Both slowly filled with red as Imogen eased back into her chair. She let the controller fall out of her fingers and onto her lap. *A serious error has occurred*, said blocky white text over crimson. *Contact technical support for assistance.*

She manoeuvred her way down the hall in pitch black. Her hand slid along the varnished bannister and her foot soon found the edge of the carpet. She descended onto the first wooden step. Every inch of this house etched into her mind, navigable with nary a flicker, and she strode as nimbly as she could. *The dead mustn't linger and mustn't bother*, she'd think, though she did not recall where she had picked up the phrase. In practical terms it meant she moved in a glide, and made a game of never creaking the stairs. If she failed, it meant returning to the top and starting again. Tonight, she'd reached the bottom without disturbing a splinter.

Once downstairs she would need to close her eyes to keep up the charade, as the house glowed a dull blue at all hours of the night. Toe, heel, toe, heel, she worked her way around the curve in the wall and kept her hands against it. Her fingertips dragged across the texture of the paint. Step, step, step. The lycra of her leggings made the slightest swish noise as she moved, barely audible even to herself. She passed under the archway, the halogen hue sliced by the blinds and strained through a curtain, and entered the kitchen.

"Jesus!" A glass shattered and porcelain crashed into the tile. Imogen retreated to the oblique shadows of the corner. She tilted her head and stared at the man, bald and besuited, probably around her own height, as he scrambled backwards and stopped. "Christ, oh christ." His hand cradled a holster at his side, and he snapped it shut soon after.

The man gathered the shards of plate and glass from the floor, leaving the ruined sandwich for last. The kitchen was a performance of domestic warmth, the likes made popular by decades of American media: needlessly large, a four-seat island in the middle, polished steel appliances, and a rustic shiplap liberally applied to the cabinetry and walls. Imogen had never lived here, nor had she chosen any of this decor. But its presence made her smile, this museum exhibit of a living space.

*A television chef would feel at home here,* she thought. *If such a thing still existed.*

NINETEEN
AESTHETIC

It had been almost a year since that first night at The Prospector, and Sam had grown used to accompanying Lydia on her frequent adventures into abandoned bars, pubs, and clubs around the Bay Area. It felt as if he was the chaperone at times, talking her out of decisions that would lead to their imprisonment or grievous bodily harm, while still having a good enough time. This morning Sam had met up with Lydia at around five a.m., and she'd made him agree to bring only his camera and his curiosity. *It's a secret mission*, she'd said, and he'd nodded with a groan. The drive had been far but quick, given how little traffic there was. As they drove Sam realised she was taking them to the odd middle-ground between San Francisco and CenCal. Not quite onto the corridor, but an area just on the other side of the barrier.

"This is still the Republic, right?" Sam scratched the back of his neck as Lydia drove.

"Of course," she chuckled and rolled her eyes. "Did we go through a checkpoint?"

"But we're not going to go through one, right?"

"Lul," Lydia deadpanned.

She cut the wheel and headed off-road just as they'd passed a sign warning them of private property. Sam's nerves were already shot, but he'd used up all of his moaning for this hour, so he kept quiet and let her get a bit further on. His fingernails left white crescents in the hard plastic of the armrest.

"Come on," she asserted. They'd parked behind a huge metal container after driving across the dirt and gravel for ten minutes. Sam was certain they'd be arrested, or killed by unionist mines. It was a calming thought. He quietly obeyed, hands in pockets, and followed Lydia as she began to trundle down into a sort of gravel pit. She walked with such determination, even as she looked like an archetypal character from a quick-start drama stream – black beanie, grey canvas jumpsuit, Army green messenger bag, and boots. She even had the ridiculous bolt-cutters, which didn't quite fit into the bag and therefore peeked out one side.

After another twenty to thirty minutes of trundling Sam had gotten completely turned around, and he was fairly certain they would never find their way back. Lydia seemed to know exactly where they were going, never for a moment stopping to look around or get her bearings. And then they reached the fence. Sam threw his hands on his hips and leaned back to take in the scale of it: it had to be at least fifteen feet high, chain link, with barbed wire at the top to discourage anyone foolish enough to think they'd be able to climb fifteen feet of chain link.

"Did we take a wrong turn?" Sam finally spoke, his first words in about forty-five minutes.

"Hope not, " Lydia said, the bolt-cutters already in her

hand. "I don't want to trash the wrong fence." Before Sam could even consider a response, she'd made the first snip.

Sam's anxiety had come spilling over the top, and Lydia spent the next fifteen minutes of their walk attempting to calm him. Or as he saw it, attempting to gaslight him.

"It's urban exploring," she said. "They really don't mind. They have bigger problems."

"Which is it? They don't mind, or they have bigger problems?"

"They don't even notice!" She turned briefly and flashed her devilish grin. The pit in Sam's stomach grew. But his anxiety gave way to a milder confusion as they emerged onto a city street.

"What..." He looked around in a daze. Abandoned single-story houses, mostly boarded up, on both sides of a street that appeared frozen in time. No cars, dead lawns, some bits of rubbish strewn about, but mostly just empty. Desolate and unused, as if the rapture had finally come, but it had been isolated to whatever block they were on. Were the rest of them sinners?

"Wild, right?" Lydia grinned.

"What is this?"

"The Foster City exclusion zone."

Sam nodded, though he had no idea what that was. The name Foster City sounded familiar. He knew it had been a city, but that could just be the clue of 'city' being in the name.

"Through here," she said as she pulled back a bit of fence that was already cut. They'd reached the end of the street and come to an intersection. It was a business district, or what once was. It followed a similar pattern of being boarded up and discarded, though this one had more obvious signs of what might have been. It was heavily graffitied in anti-Republic slogans, smashed glass littered the street, and there were obvious signs: bullet holes, burn marks, shell casings in the gutters, to say nothing of the burned out husks of cars all along both sides.

"Jesus Christ," Sam finally said. He nearly bumped straight into Lydia, who had also stopped to have a look.

"Yeah," she said under her breath. "Let's skip it. In here." They were around the back of a massive building, ornate, made to look old-world but clearly built within the last thirty years. Lydia jammed a pry bar into the frame of a steel door with a missing handle, and popped it open.

A dismal concrete passage waited behind the door, and Lydia powered down it with what Sam hoped was an earned confidence. He tucked in behind her and followed close, unable to stop himself being visibly frightened at every turn. Every surface was filthy and coated in cobwebs. The skittering and crawling of bugs and mice echoed down the length of it. A two-by-four plank of wood leaned against a wall just ahead of them, and a wrong step from Sam sent it banging into the ground. He jumped and flung his arms around Lydia's waist. She cackled.

"Oh, mijo. You're safe." She put her hands over his and gave them a squeeze. "I won't let anything bad happen to you, chulo. Got it?"

"You promise?" Sam asked, his tone genuine.

"I promise," Lydia whispered.

They appeared to reach the end of the hallway. Another steel door, this time with a window in it, and an EXIT sign hanging on the wall just above it. Sam leaned around Lydia and peeked through the window. It appeared to be a baroque lobby, high-ceilinged, and almost beyond repair.

*Perhaps an old hotel*, Sam thought, *or some sort of office building.*

"You can tell it was beautiful," he said.

"It was," she sighed. "But we're this way. Come on." She pressed her hand against the wall to their left, and it pushed inward, then slid effortlessly to one side. Before it disappeared into its hidden frame, Sam noted it had the outline of what looked like a martini glass punched into the metal. It was barely discernible.

The transition was sudden, like Sam had lost time. The walls had changed from drab concrete to a gorgeous dark wood, and a lavish spiral staircase went downward. The hint of sunlight from the corridor barely made it past the first few steps. Lydia retrieved a torch from her bag. She extended a hand backwards and Sam took it. He allowed himself to be led down the stairs slowly, one step at a time, the torch light illuminating the way until they arrived at the bottom.

The air was stale, the darkness near-impenetrable. But when Lydia shined her torch around, Sam could instantly tell this was an old pub. Pubs have a particular look, one that few publicans were brave enough to deviate from throughout the history of the format. A lot of wood, a lot of brass, a bar somewhere you can easily spot, a variety of tap handles, some shelves full of colourful spirit bottles, and depending on the vibe they've attempted to cultivate, some hilarious signs.

"Oh my god," Sam exclaimed. It was perfectly preserved. "What is this place?"

"This," Lydia started dramatically, "is The Counting Room. It's an old speakeasy!"

"What?" Sam was stunned. Lydia swept into the room and turned to face him. She popped the torch on the floor and aimed it to the ceiling. The light bounced down and illuminated the room: the walls, floor, and the bar all bathed in a warm orange. Lydia spread her arms wide with a grin, the demeanour of an estate agent about to launch into the most deceptive sales pitch you've ever heard.

"It's from the 1920s?" Sam asked.

"What? Sam, no, this building is... no, chulo, it's a hidden bar. This was built as a bank and offices, but after a decade it got scarfed by vencap to turn into luxury apartments. As part of the development they installed this secret bar, like a perk for the rich assholes who lived here. And then, well. You know. That happened."

"What?" Sam squinted.

"The summer of ` 35?"

"Summer of..."

Lydia sighed. "The bloody bargain? Ninth June?" She paused and waited, then threw her hands up in aggravation. "The extremely fucking violent partitioning of California?"

Sam shook his head and stared at his shoes. Living in Los Angeles, they really hadn't heard much about what was going on up north. And if he was honest with himself, he hadn't exactly gone out of his way to follow the news during the separation. Maybe his parents did, but he turned twenty-one that summer. So, perhaps embarrassingly, he'd spent it drunk rather than following domestic politics.

"Sure, obviously." Sam scratched the back of his neck. It would be raw before the end of the day. "Sorry, I'm just blown away by this bar. It's fantastic!"

Lydia blew some stray hairs out of her face, so Sam could get a better look at her rolled eyes. "I thought you'd want to take pictures of this place. Don't know if anyone has yet. And it'll get harder to get to now that Magenta are finally going to do something with it."

"Magenta?"

"Yeah, they bought the whole town from the Republic government. Or were given it, or something. They've been doing a lot here. Nobody's sure what. They obviously aren't required to file permits."

Sam shook his head. "Fucking Magenta."

Lydia popped her bag up onto the bar, then jumped up herself and sat on the edge. "This okay, Sam? Not going to traumatise you, my being on the bar?"

"This bar could survive a nuclear blast, I'm sure." He opened the bag and pulled out his camera, which looked a bit worse for wear. Apparently the prototype housing wasn't designed to stand up to the beating he'd been giving it.

"Get to it, shut-ter bug-ger." Lydia strained to make the sounds work in her accent. She gave him a wink in her triumph.

"Shutter bugger?"

"Shutter bugger! It's what they called photographers a long time ago."

"How do you know that?"

"I asked Aida."

Sam laughed. "I think Aida was making it up."

"Probably. But I like it. It's cute. I like the sound of it, Sam." She reached out and nearly tipped over the edge of the bar in her effort to grab the back of Sam's shirt. Her fingers managed to snatch a tiny corner of it and she tugged to pull him back.

"Hmm?" He turned to face her and she threw her legs out to trap him in, her feet locked together at his back. "Hey!" He grabbed the camera with both hands as she closed her legs around him and yanked him forward, squeezing his sides with her thighs and bringing the two of them face to face.

"Hi," Lydia said through an animated smile, her eyes wide.

"Hi, Lydia." He felt his face go flush, and he was quick to avoid her gaze.

"Look at me, Sam." She scooted forward a bit more, right to the edge of the bar, and threw her arms over Sam's shoulders to steady herself. "You're so shy."

"You're so forward."

"I'm a modern lady, Samir Patel. It's 2045."

"You are. It is."

"Do you like where I brought you?"

"I do, I'm excited."

"I mean the bar, Sam. Not between my thighs."

Sam shook his head and leaned away with a scoff. "I meant the bar!"

"Oh, Sam." She flicked his cheek, then tapped the top of the camera. "Take my picture. Only then will I release you."

He held up the camera and looked at Lydia through the viewfinder. Her arms extended out past each side of the frame as she held his shoulders. Her head leaned back at a slight angle, a bit of shine on her cheeks. Her lips parted, a sultry smile, radiant blue eyes. All wreathed in golden light from her torch on the ground reflecting off the brass bar. Through a lens he could see her in a way he couldn't with his own eyes. A truer vision of her, free from his hangups and judgements, from the world itself. His breath caught in a flutter. He pushed the button. The camera vibrated, and he felt the rush of endorphins. He had managed to capture a perfect moment.

"Did you get it?" He heard her voice amidst the tingles in

his brain, and felt a smile on his face. "Hey, are you okay?" Her thumb brushed his cheek and he realised he had teared up.

"Yeah, yeah. I'm fine, sorry." He squirmed, still locked in place. "Can you...?"

"Yeah, sure." She trailed off, her voice thick with confusion, and let her legs drop. Sam quickly pulled away.

"I'm just going to float around and get a bunch of shots, if that's okay."

"Yeah, Sam, it's fine. Are you sure..."

"Yeah, just need to..." He rubbed his eyes, and felt another few tears drop down. He was able to wipe them away quickly. "There, it's fine."

Sam had set to work quietly snapping photonically pure photos of the abandoned speakeasy. Close-ups of the taps, complete with at least a couple beers that no longer existed. Wide-angles of the whole room from above, which involved climbing up a precarious stairwell that Sam figured was for show. Lydia was always nearby, but seemed to be avoiding him, or charitably, trying to give him a subject in the photos. He'd snap a few without her, mostly close-ups of architecture. But odds were good that if he had the chance, he'd find a way to frame her in. *It gives a nice sense of scale*, he'd decided.

"How long is this stream running for," she shouted. It had probably been an hour at this point. "Are you good? A girl can only pace leaving herself voice notes for so long, you know."

Sam nodded, and began climbing down from his perch atop the bar, where he'd been experimenting with some Dutch angles. "Sorry."

"No apologies, I did bring you here. I knew what I was

getting myself into." She chuckled. "I may have forgotten there wouldn't be any service down here."

"Right."

"Just going to see if there's a toilet, and if it's still somehow functioning. Bee arr bee." Lydia had disappeared into the other room just as Sam made it to the far end of the bar. He opened the bag and popped his camera inside. *There's so much here,* he thought. What was she preparing for? Just any possible outcome? Multiple torches, the bolt cutters, some snacks... and... what was this? There were some printed papers at the bottom. *Odd,* he thought. *Not something you see often.* He contemplated, if only for a moment, allowing Lydia her privacy. But with a blink he had them out of the bag and in his hand. It was a yellowed paper, thin enough that you could see the back through the front, the words printed in a streaky black-and-white. The entire thing seemed to be crooked, like the paper had gone in at an odd angle. He ran his finger across the words at the top: *The Analog Gazette.*

"Don't think that belongs to you." Samir froze, the paper crinkling in his fist. It was a man's voice, one that sounded deep and annoyed. "Where's Lydia?"

"Oye, wey, are you serious," Lydia shouted as she raced back into the room. "Hector, leave him alone." She snatched the page out of Sam's hand before he had the chance to read any further. "¡Chingada, no seas metiche, wey!"

"Sorry!" He took a large step back, leaving Lydia and Hector beside each other. "I just saw it when I was putting my camera away. I didn't realise it was private."

"It's in my bag, Sam."

"I thought we were sharing the bag."

Lydia groaned, and it was by far her loudest of the day.

"Chulo, I cannot. And you, Hector, what the hell? What are you doing here?"

"You weren't answering your phone. What are you doing here with..." He gestured to Samir. "Agachón."

"Urban exploring." Lydia rolled her eyes and gave Hector a light shove. "Maybe you could do some yourself? Away from here?"

"Should he be here?" Hector continued to glare at Sam, who began to melt like a candle.

"Won't happen again," Sam croaked. "No more sharing bags. I'll bring a bag next time."

"Hector." Lydia stepped inches from his face. "Lárgate, wey. We'll talk tonight."

"Fine."


SAM TRIED to ask about Hector, how they knew each other, and why he'd also turned up in The Counting Room, but Lydia would only roll her eyes or shush him. *Chulo, relax.* She instead tried to "lift the vibe", as she put it, by showing Sam the rest of the abandoned apartment building. Most of the rooms looked identical, which was a different sort of depressing, but it was still interesting to see what had been left behind. Sam had fixated on a photo of an absolutely enormous family, though he didn't take it. Lydia boosted a crystal brandy snifter that would be a "bigger crime to leave behind", and what appeared to be someone's vintage mobile telephone collection.

"What do you need with those?" Sam looked on in amusement as she piled the ancient flip phones into her bag, at least four of them.

"These are Motorola RAZRs! Original. They're platinum. If they work."

Sam shook his head and shrugged as Lydia dumped and tossed drawers before she finally found the chargers.

"¡A huevo!" She said with a Cheshire grin. "I'm due an upgrade." She tossed the chargers in her bag, then produced a chunkier looking version of the same device. Seeing it tickled something long-dormant in Sam's brain. It had a faded sticker wrapped around it with the name of some old skate shoe company, and a few gleaming plastic studs glued at random along the back.

"That's hilarious," Sam said. "Is that an... iPhone?"

Lydia's grin could hardly get wider. "Sam, no. When were you born?"

"I don't know if I'm..."

"Sam!"

"2014."

"Novio, this phone was ten years old when you were born. Respect your elders."

"That's not a huge gap. But what do you use it for? Just a good luck charm?"

"Qué oso," she whispered. "It works."


AFTER A FULL DAY of photography and archeology, Lydia had led them back through the ruined remains of the town. The sun had started to disappear behind the horizon as they walked up the side of a hill.

"Low power mode," she muttered as she dropped to the ground and stretched out. "Join me? Best to wait until late to head back, anyway."

Sam and Lydia stared straight up, their arms tucked

behind their heads, their backs against the cool grass. The hill was artificial, Lydia had explained, made of the immense amount of dirt excavated by Magenta during the construction of a nearby underground complex. But that couldn't stop you from having a real evening atop it.

"Isn't it beautiful?" Lydia smiled and glanced over at Sam, her face close, but cloaked in darkness. In the sky above them, dozens of far away lights danced and twinkled in a dazzling, if surprising, display.

"I didn't realise you could even see the stars out here," Sam said.

"It's not stars," Lydia said with a twinkle of her own. "It's SkyTie."

"Sky tie?"

"Hundreds of tiny satellites in low Earth orbit. Maybe thousands." Lydia held a closed hand up in front of Sam's face, then slowly opened it. The familiar blue flicker of her Ring lit both of their faces, millions of light rays shooting out of an imperceptible hole somewhere on its surface, forming into a small interface on her palm. "So that we can do this."

"Ah... well, I just..."

"It's okay to not know things, Sam." She closed her hand just as Sam turned to her. The blue glow vanished from her face. He squeezed his eyes a few times to adjust.

"Thanks."

"Besides," she said as she glanced over to him, "you're playing at this old soul angle." In the monochrome of night she somehow managed to look even younger.

"Hey. I'm my own age. You're the one trying for the whole wisdom beyond your years thing."

"Can I ask you something, Samir?"

"Full name, must be serious. Go ahead."

She grinned and nudged him with her elbow. "Mi cielo, the way Sebastian tells it you're a digi-addict. Though I never see you chat with any..."

"...well, I have you to talk to when you're around... I talk to my other friends later."

"Let's say that it's true, you have a lot of digis, and I assume you have a dop?"

"I do..." Sam's eyes briefly went wide. He hadn't checked in on his dop in ages. "Where are you going with this?"

"You front like you hate Magenta," she said. "But you sure do use a lot of their products."

Sam shot air through his nose at the indignation. "You've got a Ring, too."

"Chingada, we've all got Rings, Sam, how the fuck else would we live? I couldn't even start my car without my Ring." She dragged her fingernails down his arm gently.

"Are you saying I'm not allowed to dislike Magenta if I have a dop?" There was a sharpness to Sam's words. He propped himself up on his elbows.

"Oye, wey," Lydia sat up as well, and rolled on her side to face him. "I'm just asking whether you actually dislike them, or if you're pretending just to impress me." She flaunted her smile. "It's okay if you are, it's cute."

He wondered just how much of that chequered past he wanted to share with Lydia right now, on the fake hill, under the fake stars. "It's... complicated."

"Is it?"

"Parts of it aren't, like today. That beautiful underground bar, that whole apartment building, that whole town, just empty and abandoned. Instead of doing something with it, the city council just gives it to Magenta, and they do nothing with it. It's such a waste. They're so big, they have no idea what they even do anymore. Do they even know they own it? They just don't care."

"Chulo," she whispered. "Gran pasión." She pushed up off the grass and put one leg over Sam, who watched it happen with a mild panic. "It's okay, Sam. I care, a lot of us care." She straddled him, her hands at his sides to prop herself up.

"Oh." His hands came to rest on her hips, which were still hidden inside her jumpsuit. "Hi."

"SkyTie is the net we're all caught in, chulo. They control what we see, who we talk to, what we say, what we remember. They sold your generation the luxury of it being optional. Mine got Magenta Accounts at birth. Everyone can tell you Rebecca Prue's name. Can they name the Mayor? The governor?"

"I don't even know who the Mayor is."

"Remember that night at The Prospector last year? Even if we didn't take a photo, Aida can gen it for me perfectly. But she can also change it. Take you out, replace you, replace me. She could pretend the club doesn't exist at all, or say we were never there. How fucked is that?"

"It's fucked, Lyds." His fingers fidgeted with the zipper of her suit. He contemplated pulling it down.

She put her fingers on his and pulled the zip for him, slowly revealing the taut white tanktop underneath. "We believe in the right to say no to these people, to live without them. Me, Hector, many others too. Others that are afraid to talk about it because for some reason it's controversial to not want a Magenta Ring, or to make a photo that stays the same forever."

"Or a song." She pulled her arms out and the top of the jumpsuit fell limp behind her. He could feel her shiver in the pre-dawn air, and as his hands slid across her bare midriff he could feel the goosebumps.

"Or a song, yes, chulo. You understand, I know you do. That camera of yours... the way you're always trying to capture something real instead of just having Aida gen it for you. That's you, saying no. That's what I love about you."

"You..."

"Wait, I want you to see this." She leaned down and fished something from her bag, then thrust it straight into his face. After his eyes adjusted he could just about make it out in the darkness: it was the paper from earlier. "It's a newsletter," she said. "For people like us."

He scanned it, again reading the title, The Analog Gazette. What he hadn't seen was the smaller print: the newsletter was dominated by a section called *Analog Voices*.

"It's stories!" Lydia was elated. "The Analog Gazette, dispatches from under the net. It's real people all over the place, about how we're all coping in Magenta's world. And sometimes, what people are doing to fight back."

"Fight back?" He squinted and moved his face back and forth, but it was too dark to make out anything smaller than the title. "Lyds, I can't see."

"Un momento." His hands fell unceremoniously as she climbed down off of him, plopping straight onto ground next to him. With her shoulder slipped behind his, she pulled him close and pressed herself against his back, then brought the paper in front of them. "Hold?" Sam nodded and took it. Lydia opened her palm and her Ring dutifully glowed, bathing both the paper and their faces in a calming blue light.

A familiar dread settled over Sam as the photo came into view.

"Oh, it's this one!" Lydia squealed, her cheek pressed

against Sam's. "I love the writing in this one." She cleared her throat, and spoke in a husky whisper, affecting a ridiculous British accent directly into Sam's ear. "From A. N., in Moseley. Live music has returned to the Midlands, courtesy of this Bri'ish music titan turned fugitive. The leatha-clad for-mah label exec, on the run from both Ma-gen-tuh and the Guvment, was spotted looking stunnin' as evah, playin' a set of original music on her antique guitah in West Brom."

Sam closed his eyes and tried to control his breathing.

Lydia let out a giggle. "So random, right? She goes on to write a whole review of this music set. It's so timelined."

Sam kept staring, Lydia's cheek still pressed against his. On the paper above the story was a grainy, black-and-white photo that was unmistakably of his former boss, Gemma Thomson.

"No? No good?" She pulled him tight against her and scooted over even more, practically sat on his lap. "You didn't laugh at my British accent."

"Oh," Sam caught his breath. "It was very good. Funny."

"What's wrong?

He stared at the facsimile of Gemma on the page in front of him. Thoughts roared in protest from a cage at the back of his mind. The last few times they'd seen each other had been awful. The lowest he'd seen her, the lowest he'd seen anyone. Ravaged by alcohol. Throwing herself at him backstage. Absolutely demolishing those poor kids from Killslop. Taking his hand-made mix CD with an eye-roll and a sigh. Thinking of her before now, he wanted to be back with her. But in seeing her now, in pixelated monochrome, all he wanted was to be angry with her.

"Talk to me, Samir." Lydia squeezed his cheeks and gave his face a bit of a shake.

"Sure..." He kept staring at the photo. When was it taken? There didn't seem to be a date. How was it taken? Sam didn't even know how this would've gotten from the UK to here. Even if you did have an international privilege, Aida would just hmm and hum and politely explain why it wasn't appropriate to send this message. Against all odds it had gotten here, and there it was. There she was—alive, running and playing music. *Live music.* His mind was a scrambled mess. A thousand texts he'd wanted to send, a thousand photos he'd wanted to show, a thousand silences he'd wanted to share, all with this person he assumed was dead. Sam closed his eyes and let out a long, relaxed sigh. He found focus through the image of her on stage at Maelzel's, strapped with the guitar from the photo, singing a sarcastic cover of some Sabrina Carpenter song. Or maybe something original, whatever she'd like. It wouldn't have to end in pain, after all. Excise the final years of their relationship, keep the rest, start anew.

"Sam, hello, stop scrolling and lock in." Lydia lowered his hand and took the paper from him. "I know." He blinked and stared as she climbed atop him. "I know you have a complicated relationship." Her face was inches from his. He dry swallowed as the delicate thoughts of Gemma shattered and crumbled away.

"Lydia..." This had been off-limits since, well, the first night. A year of occasional teasing, playful banter, awkward escapes. But he never said no, instead preferring to demure. *What did she mean, a complicated relationship?*

"I've known for a while. I didn't know how to bring it up. I hoped you'd bring it up."

"You know?" The mystery was almost enough to arrest his thoughts away from how Lydia continued to straddle him, and how close she still was. He pictured her pinning him to the ground, then shook his head to rid himself of the image.

"I know." Lydia nodded. "About your wife." She gave him a quick peck on the cheek, just as all the colour drained from his face. "Virginia."

"I know you do. What? What do you mean?" In his mind he gave a self-assured accounting of himself, with an emphasis on why this was not her concern, because he and Lydia were just friends, and he and Virginia were separated anyway. But to Lydia, and to anyone who might've been in earshot, it sounded like a bit of air escaping his nose.

"Don't worry, chulo. I mean I understand why you hate Magenta," she said with a smile, and gave his nose a boop. "It's because Virginia works there."

"What? How do you know that?"

"Not here. Come on, let's go."

TWENTY

PATIENCE

The drive back to the city was an eternity. Sam's mind twisted and turned as he grappled with the scale of the problem he'd created for himself. He'd been shown a photo of Gemma by Lydia, and he'd said nothing. The window for him to admit he knew her was closing, if it hadn't already closed. He was entitled to his secrets, to his own inner life. But his back was against the wall now. And he'd yet to process what she'd said next.

"Samir, I'm sorry about not telling you sooner. I didn't want to dox you both."

"So you know where she works, what else do you know?"

"A lot, Sam. Everything."

"She's not my wife." Sam fidgeted and stared. "We're separated."

"Right, but…" The gulf between them widened further with every second she stretched out the syllable. "You're married."

Lydia's fact—*you're married*—lingered in the unbearable pressure of the car. He needed space, time to process.

"Do you two talk?"

"We haven't spoken since the fight. We un-paired on Mate."

"Oye, wey, are you serious?" Lydia slugged him in the arm, and Sam jumped. He clutched his shoulder and turned away. "Come on."

"I don't have anything to say to her."

"What about me, then? Is this why you never want me to get close to you? Why are you pouting?"

He stayed silent, and she let out a defeated sigh. The street lights rolled past the window as the car worked its way back to the city. Sam rested his face against the cool glass.

"There's oils on your face, you know," Lydia said. "You're going to leave a spot on my window."

"Aida," Sam shouted, "stop at the next Muni Station please."

"Of course, Samir," replied Aida, wandering into the disagreement by virtue of a legally-mandated safety feature which let any passenger request to be let out.

"Wow," Lydia bellowed. "Wow! I thought we were going to look at the photos back at my apartment. Sam, I need to talk to you. There's a reason for all this."

"I don't have time," Sam jabbed back. "I have to go home and call my wife."

"Fine, go home and call her then. Since you're fucking married! Not something you ever bring up, by the way!"

"You knew!"

"¡Vete a la chingada!"

The car seemed relieved as it pulled up to the passenger drop-off at the Muni station. Sam had started hammering the exit button as soon as he'd seen the station, but the door only released once the car had stopped. He exploded out of the seat, through the door, and toward the station. Lydia shouted something as he went, but he didn't care to hear it.

The doors of the Muni train slid closed, sealing him inside. He found a hard plastic seat, his third of the day, grateful that here, at least, he could be alone. His earbuds went straight in, his Ring dutifully starting his usual stream of 'ldn algopop'. The ritual soothed him. Dozens of strangers all shared this space, in their varied outfits, dispersing across the city, and all kept to themselves. None of them would approach him, nor he them. All of them — the students, the workers, the elderly — had their own earbuds, their own Rings, their own portable paradise. He spent his days fully surrounded by people, but never connected to any of them. He spent his nights too nervous to speak, lest Seb or Mel catch any of it as he lay on their sofa. But here on San Francisco Municipal Transit, for just twenty minutes or so, he was exactly where he wanted to be, with all the privacy he needed.

He produced the crumpled Analog Gazette from his pocket. He'd pinched it from the car as he exited, and Lydia either hadn't noticed or hadn't cared. But he was compelled to have it, and he was in no position to ask. He unfolded it carefully. The thin paper had already started to tear along the folds. *Gemma Thomson.* The name blotted out his mind. The concept, the very idea of her, had always loomed over him, even with the distance between them. The actual person still existing? That was a new condition. The blurry, low-resolution version of her stared up at him from the page. It stirred old feelings, old memories, old heartaches and stomach aches. This woman who had created such a problem for him. This woman who held the wedge and the hammer, but refused to swing and tear Virginia away from him forever.

"Aida." He spoke a hair above a whisper, the usual tone one took when speaking privately in public to one's Ring.

"Samir." In contrast, Aida's voice was crystal clear and seemed to fill his mind. The music ducked, her voice mixed in perfectly. It would have to be at a deafening volume in order for others in the car to overhear. And that presumed they weren't also using theirs, which was never the case.

"How am I?" Sam asked.

"You seem to be stressed," Aida said with no hint of concern. "Your blood pressure is above your average. You've exceeded your physical fitness goals for today by about double, which is great. Your Mirror has declined a call from Lydia Rosales. He's placed one call to Virginia Rose, which was blocked. You..."

"Wait, Aida."

"Mmhmm?"

"The call to Virginia."

"Yes, that was blocked."

"Is that..." He tried to remember the last time he'd checked in with her. His dop still called Virginia at least daily, and her dop always declined. But didn't Aida usually...

"Great catch, Samir. Usually I say the call was declined. Today, it was blocked. Would you like to speak to your Mirror about this?"

"Is he upset?"

"I'm afraid he's inconsolable." Aida was never afraid to tell the truth about his Mirror's emotional state. Sam grimaced and stared at his filthy shoes on the spotless white floor of the train. The electric hum of the motor vibrated the seat, and he closed his eyes to focus on that feeling.

"I can't deal with that right now. I wish you could talk to him for me, Aida."

"You know I stay out of these things."

"I know, I know." Sam rolled his eyes and smiled. "You have to…"

"I have to be everybody's friend. It's how the world works."

*Still though*, Sam thought. *Blocked by Virginia? That was upsetting, wasn't it?* The algopop stream flowed along, the volume having raised since he'd stopped talking with Aida. After all this time listening to it, three years now, he wondered if it even sounded like London algopop. Or if London algopop even had a sound at all. The first time he'd ever heard it was with Gemma, on a night that he hadn't at all enjoyed. But nights like that had a way of seeming to have been better than they were after the painful bits had eroded away. Maybe it was delusion, or the mind protecting itself. Maybe he just rewrote his own history. But at this moment, on this night, he found himself wanting to remember that one. "Hey, Aida?"

"What is it, Samir?" The music once again faded down and Aida's rich tones returned to the fore.

"Can you remind me about that night I first heard algopop? In London? What was the name of that club?"

"Yes, that was in London. It was a club called mood dot app."

A huge smile crept across Sam's face, and he leaned up to stare out the window of the train. It was lumbering up Mission much slower than usual tonight. He wondered why, which was an annoying trait that he wished humans could evolve away from. It was useless to wonder why the transit was slow, or late, or cancelled. Even if they told you, it wouldn't matter. "Show me that night, could you?"

"Sure, Samir."

Sam opened his hand and saw himself by the bar at mood dot app. He was alone, holding what looked to be a dark drink. He made a pinch gesture and the photo zoomed. "What's that I'm drinking?"

"That's two measures of Captain Morgan dark rum mixed with Fritz Kola in a clear plastic cup."

"Strange, I would've assumed a gin and tonic. I was a bit of an anglophile back then, whenever I was in the UK."

"Of course, you're right Samir." The picture changed faster than he could blink, and in his hand was now the same cup, but something clear and fizzy inside, a lime wedge perched on the lip. "It was two measures of Bombay Sapphire London gin and Fever-Tree slim tonic."

"I thought so," Sam said. He looked around the train. At the far end, past a group of teens with florescent hair and matching jumpsuits, he took careful note of the black dome on the ceiling. He slid down in the seat, a fruitless gesture, a pantomime of safety for those about to commit an inconsequential crime. *Simply duck down, they won't see.* Was it held over from antiquated social norms, or bred in from generations of being surveilled? "Aida," he began, barely audible. "Wasn't I with someone else that night? Can you show me a picture of us together?" He was too afraid to use Gemma's name. *Plausible deniability*, he figured.

"I don't think we should talk about this, Samir." Aida's response was instant, and for a fraction of a second, her emotionless facade seemed to crack. *Was that concern in her tone?*

"Fine."

"Thank you."

"What about... earlier that night, I was with Virginia. Can you show me that?"

"I'm afraid I can't."

"What? Why?"

"Virginia Rose has asserted her right to be excluded from your life stream, Samir."

Sam blinked. He tried a few times to respond, but wasn't sure how to even begin. This wasn't something he'd ever heard before. He recalled Lydia's sage advice from earlier: it's okay not to know things. "What's a life stream?"

"It's everything."

"Okay." Sam closed his eyes and squeezed his lips together. Aida was, at times, an incredible replica of an irritating know-it-all with no social skills.

"Oh." Aida deployed one of her laughs. They were unnatural, and she only had two or three. She'd had them for decades. Theories abound as to why Magenta had never updated her to sound more natural, like the dops and digis. "Any time you request to see a past event, it is retrieved from your life stream. It's also where I recall information about where you've been, who you know, things like that. Make sense?"

"So... can you show me any photos of me with my wife?"

"I'm afraid I can't."

"Can you just show me her, by herself?"

"I'm afraid I can't."

"I don't understand."

"Oh." Her canned laugh again, and her explanation of the life stream, and of Virginia's rights. Sam let his eyes go out of focus, lights from the city blurred and distorted through the rain drops on the window of the Muni. The mushed-up facsimile of London algopop reverberated in his head. "Sam?" Aida interrupted on her own, though her voice was softer than usual.

"Yeah?"

"I wish I could."

The alcove at the top of the steps was Sam's last chance at sanctuary before he went into Seb's apartment. He tucked himself into the tight corner, just across from the door, and took a deep breath. "Aida?"

"Mmhmm?"

"Can I speak with my dad?"

"Of course, reaching him now." Sam heard the familiar chimes of an outgoing call, and he squeezed himself even further into the corner.

"Hey kid," started the familiar voice of Sam's father. "What time is it there?"

"Hey dad," Sam said with a laugh. "Same time as it is there. Are you busy?"

"You know me son, I'm always up to something. Your mother's just watching her drama stream. Should I get her?"

"No, dad, let her be."

"What's on your mind, kiddo? You sound stressed."

"It's... Virginia."

"Marriage can be tricky, son. You know how it always was with your mother and I. Why don't you bring her by? You two haven't come around for dinner in ages."

"Dad, no." Sam brushed away a tear and sniffled, his nose starting to run. "I haven't seen her in over a year now. I don't think we're getting back together." He heaved as he said the last words, and battled against a full bodied sob. "I can't even get a hold of her anymore."

"I'm sorry to hear that, son."

The sound of a throat clearing tore through the air. Sam spun around, confronted by Seb who was stood between him and the door.

"Hey man," Seb said with a grimace. "Is that your..."

"Yeah, yeah." Sam quickly tapped his ear, a sort of kill switch for any conversation you might be having, with Aida or otherwise.

"Shit, man. That's..."

"You just getting in?" Samir swallowed, and it was as much symbolic as it was physical.

"Do you wanna go for a walk, man? I could re-open the bar." Seb had slid into Sam's path as he tried to get to the door. They both hung in place, as if some unseen viewer had hit pause.

"It's been a long day, I think I'd rather lie down." Sam lowered his head and again tried to move past Seb. "If that's okay."

"Right, but." Seb reacted too late, his hand failing to intercede as Sam's face lined up with the entry ID camera. The ring flashed green and Sam's finger tapped the plate. The door slid open to reveal Seb's wife Mel, standing behind it as if she relished the dramatic reveal.

"Melanie!" Sam took a half-step back as Mel took a half-step forward. The lights in the apartment behind her immediately clicked off. Her tree-trunk arms crossed over her chest, and her ribbed pink tank top revealed just how tattooed she was — two vibrant sleeves up her arms actually joined into a mural across her chest — which heaped even more intimidation onto Samir. If she pushed him, he thought, he'd fly across the hallway as if pulled by stunt wires. *Not that she ever would, of course.*

"Samir, you kept us waiting. We started to worry." Her voice was soft, yet offered no hint as to what this might be about.

"Sorry. I did?" Sam mirrored her and also pulled his arms tight across himself. He shivered in her shadow. Seb had drifted to one side.

"Mel…" Seb cleared his throat again. "I don't know if…"

"Let's talk," Mel said as she turned and headed back into the apartment.

Only moments later, Samir's back was against the wall in every way.

"*Where is he going to go?*"

"*He's an adult! He can find his own place to live!*"

"*You know how difficult it is to find somewhere in this city!*"

"*He can find a real job, then! It's not safe having him here!*"

He watched in horror for over a half-hour as Sebastian argued with his wife over the topic of whether he could continue living on their couch. The conversation briefly involved him, and had started in English, but the past twenty or so minutes had played out in Spanish. Aida dutifully translated both sides using near-perfect replicas of their respective voices.

"*I want my living room back! I want our privacy back!*"

"*He'll be back with Virginia soon. I promise.*"

"*It's him or it's me, Sebastian!*"

He couldn't leave, he didn't want to stay. He'd never felt so small. He considered asking Aida what the statistical probability was of a meteor striking the Muni, but his will to live won out. The door slid open in a clean motion as he approached, his intent clear enough to act upon with no confirmation. He had boarded the lift before Seb or Mel had a moment to protest.

TWENTY-ONE
LEGACY

The storm was hellacious. Rain blinded him, stung his eyes, flooded the streets. Claps of thunder near-constant, the sky illuminated with the crackle of lightning the likes of which Sam had never seen in Los Angeles. He darted from awning to awning, overhang to carport, the concept of an umbrella or waterproof jackets still eluding him in spite of Seb and Lydia's efforts the past year. The freezing cold made the wet so much worse, and water poured back out of the drains.

Splashing through the downpour, his heavy footsteps doused the few dry patches of his jeans. He didn't know where to go, and barely gripped where he was in the first place. Every building identical aside from the small name-plates, inscrutable in the dark. Something in the rain stung his eyes, so he'd barely bother to read them in the first place. Block by block he made his way through the city, his feet frozen stiff, his lungs burning. By the sixth block his legs couldn't carry him another inch, and he came to rest in a covered alcove between some coffee kiosks.

"Aida, where are we?" He called out once more to the

world's most omnipresent voice, still too afraid to engage with his dop. There was no answer. He tapped at his ear in a panic and felt nothing. His fingers fumbled over each other and found only calloused skin. His Ring was gone.

Hope drained from him, his last bit of warmth disappearing into the cold. And then, a miracle: through the fog, he spotted the glowing M of the Muni. The gates swung open at the sight of him and soon he was back on a train, headed in whichever direction the first one had departed toward. He was sure Lydia lived near a Muni stop. He didn't know which one, or where it was relative to him, or which direction to head. But he knew there was time enough to ride the Muni to one end then back down the other at least once before it closed. And he knew he could probably afford the twenty or so dollars that would cost. At the very least, it used up time. He shrivelled down into the cold seat of the train, surrounded by people who weren't really there, who were disappeared into their Rings, who would chat with a dozen invisible people before they paid him the slightest mind.

It shouldn't have been a surprise to Sam that he spotted Lydia's building not by number, or by how it looked, but by Sebastian's car parked in front of it. He contemplated staying on the Muni, but he'd gotten enough of a look to see that Seb was in the car alone. *Mel's not come*, he thought. *That might mean we can actually talk.*

With a lengthy stride he walked straight past the back of Seb's car and toward the door to Lydia's building. His legs carried him past as he grappled with himself over whether to engage with Seb or let Seb come to him. *Is this childish? Why can't I just meet him half way?*

"Sam! You prick! Get in here!" Seb called out, his window cracked just enough to let the sound out, his voice just about audible over the rain as it pummelled every surface.

The digital face of the building's automated attendant appeared on the glass door, and Sam shouted before it had a chance to speak. "Lydia Rosales, please!"

"Right away, sir," the door replied.

"Samir!" Seb was at full volume. "Get the fuck in the car! I'm not coming out there!"

Sam sighed, knowing he had no choice but to comply. He found himself in the car soon after. He was soaking wet, and Seb bit his tongue rather than bring up how disastrous he found this.

"How did I know I'd find you here?" Seb was exasperated, with a slight hint of relief. "Why are you fucking around with this girl, man? You're too old for this shit."

"It's not a big thing. We don't sleep together, we're just friends. It's good to have a friend, Seb. Someone who's actually free to hang out."

"Oh, don't fucking start with that, man. I put you up, I gave you a job, it's been a goddamn year. Why are you still here? I told you this was temporary. I fucking knew it was a mistake! Your problems are down there, dude. Virginia is down there."

"She doesn't want to speak to me."

"How could you possibly know that?"

"She's blocked me on everything."

Seb's curt sigh was borne out either of frustration with modernity, or of Sam being an idiot. In either case, the result was some kind of stress headache. He rubbed his temples and rested his eyes. "Since when?"

"I don't know. Recently, I think? I just saw tonight."

"Recently. Man, it's been a year. Almost to the day.

Maybe she had to move on for her own sanity? She's probably been waiting for you to get your shit together."

"Have you talked to her?"

"What... no, man! No. I just know her. And you!"

"I don't understand why you're even against my being with Lydia, if I was. I don't understand how you're even married. You never had a girl for more than like a week, you were always good vibes, good times." Sam tried to run his fingers through his hair, which just caused even more water to drip down onto the seats. The cold had started to set in, and he shivered either from that or the nerves.

"That was a decade ago, man! It can't be like that forever! It was never even like that in the first place, dude. Under the good times bullshit I was a fucking lonely, miserable drug addict. Good vibes, my ass."

"I don't understand."

"Look at me, man. I'm here right now, for you. But I can't keep pissing Mel off. You think I want to turf you? No! I have to do whatever I can to make that marriage work. I'm trying to look out for both of you, and for me. It's fucking stressful, man! And now you're being a fucking baby about it! If you want to copy me, just copy this part of me. Get back together with your fucking wife, man!"

"No, no, that's done." Sam stared straight ahead as the traffic lights flashed. It was nearly curfew. He had to find somewhere to be, soon. But he hadn't felt this distant from Sebastian in a long, long time. Everyone was going in so hard on him about Virginia. The woman who, he'd like to remind everyone, kicked him out of his own home. *How had they all forgotten?* He cleared his throat a few times and tried to stop his near-constant shivering. "I'm happy Virginia and I broke up. I was always so miserable when I was with her. She obviously was, too."

"Is that even true? You're more like her than you know. You were good for each other man, she opened up a lot more after you two hooked up. She was always asking how you were, asking how I was, asking me about the music industry. Topics she never cared about. She opened up. What the hell even happened?"

"I'm not doing this." Sam let the words go by. He'd think about them, about her, later. "I'm not getting into this."

"Why the fuck not? Ask yourself why you refuse to talk about it. It's been a fucking year you've been living on my sofa. Why do I not even know why you two split?"

"It wasn't any one thing. We drifted apart, I guess." Atop the light poles, the blue strobe lights had begun pulsing. Fifteen minute warning.

"Oh, for fuck's sake." Seb shook his head and his finger struck the air like a cobra. "We're talking," he shouted. "Go back in your hole, you fucking legacy snake." Sam managed to break his gaze away from the lights and look out the window to one side. Lydia stood in the pouring rain, arms crossed. She stared at the two of them with an unsettling scowl.

"Samir Patel." Seb's tone had taken a stark shift. He grabbed Sam's shoulder and squeezed. "Let me find you a hotel. Do not do this. If you're serious, and there isn't anything going on here, don't let tonight be the night."

"They'll all be shut now. It's nearly curfew."

"Fuck." Seb pounded his fist on the dashboard in a frenetic rage. "Fuck, fuck, fuck! God damnit. Sam, look, I'm sorry. I've been where you are right now."

Lydia's knuckle rapped against the window. She was

hammering the button on the outside of Sam's car door. "Is this real?"

"You can sleep in the car, in the garage. Best I can do, but it's warm, safe, and dry. And we'll figure it out in the morning. Okay?"

Sam closed his eyes and made his hands into fists, tucked close against his chest. "Aida, out please."


LYDIA DARTED into her apartment and went straight for the bathroom, leaving puddles in her wake on the laminate wood floor. Sam crowded onto her welcome mat just inside. The room was soulless. Every apartment in this building was no doubt indistinguishable, though as he looked around he could see she'd done her best to put her personal stamp on it. It was the standard efficiency layout: sleeping alcove with a single bed, kitchenette sectioned off by a minuscule half-height countertop, two-seater sofa in front of a large flat-panel screen on the wall, and a two person table filling what space remained.

The screen was showing a grim-looking soap opera, some kind of hellish relationship drama called Ruffle Those Feathers. It was a bit jerky, at times a bit melty, and the captions were of some wretched brain-dead dialogue—all the hallmarks of a show you'd gen on the Magenta Basic plan. He hated these, but he hated being a snob about them even more. Plus wasn't cheap. And there must've been something compelling about them, because people would stay invested in the plots even if they upgraded.

*Not a single window either,* he noted. *San Franciscans live like convicts.* "I'm really sorry about just turning up like this," Sam shouted. He was as close as he could be to the door. Something about being here made him uncomfortable, and it wasn't helping that Lydia had dashed out of sight.

"Well, now you've seen where I live," she shouted back from the other room.

"It's..."

"You don't have to say it, I know it's tiny."

"It's functional."

"It's a shoe-box. But it's mine, and it's free."

Sam leaned back, and his head banged into the doorway. "Free?"

Lydia emerged from the bathroom wrapped in a towel, her clothes abandoned on the floor behind her. She tossed a towel across to Sam. "I don't spam it around, you know. People resent it."

"I don't understand." Sam was trying in vain to mop up the puddle he'd made. The towel would be soaked through before he even got to the water on the rest of him. His hands trembled and his body shook from the cold.

"Come on," she sighed. "Just get in the shower."

The hot water was a tremendous relief. It trickled out of the shower head in the tiny cubicle, but he couldn't be picky. On the other side of the frosted glass was the outline of Lydia, who'd given back a quiet pout when he insisted she not watch him undress. Seb's advice rang in his ears, though his desperate concern felt so misplaced. Virginia had known where he was for a year now and she hadn't made a single move toward seeing him. It was obvious where her head was at. He did wonder whether it was still possible to re-enable the tracking. Sure, she'd blocked him from contacting her, and sure, she'd prevented him from genning any photos of her or the two of them. *But would Magenta Mate still work? It could be a way to reach out,* he thought. It was a nice, nonthreatening move Sam could make to show he'd be willing to make amends.

"Aren't you curious how I live here for free?" Lydia pressed her face against the frosted glass, her hands cupped around it.

"I'm curious. No peeking."

"You know, most boys of your persuasion would take the W here. Is there some reason you aren't interested? Is it Virginia? Are you trad mono? Ace? You can tell me to back off."

"Um." He coughed. Sam didn't know what half of that even meant. Nothing about this made him comfortable engaging with Lydia about anything. And he felt nervous about what might happen if he started. He just wanted to shove things back into their box. "How do you live here for free?"

She laughed. "I'm a legacy."

"A legacy?"

"I know you're not from here, but I'm still surprised you haven't heard of this. I'm a legacy. Which means I'm third generation San Francisco. I'm entitled to free housing if I don't have a job." She spun around, and the shower door rattled as she threw her back against it. "Everyone hates us. But I've got their hate, plus a free apartment. So let them hate." She slid down to the ground like her strings had been cut.

"That's..." Samir was flabbergasted. "That's incredible."

"You resent me now too, yeah? Gonna spit the L word at me? I'm sure Seb's apartment is a lot bigger than this one."

"I don't resent you, Lydia." Sam sighed, the warmth of the water having finally thawed him out. He joined Lydia on the tile, inches apart, save for the thin plastic between them.

Sam had a history of depressing stints on shower floors. Virginia had given up talking him through these bouts a year before their split, and he'd never found the comfort level needed to do it at Seb and Mel's.

"Good. I don't know what I'd do without it. It's not like I feel entitled, you know. It's just how it is. I was just issued it one day. It would've been more complicated to get it, I guess, but both my parents were dead. It was automatic the day my mother passed. I wouldn't have had anywhere to go."

"I'm sorry."

The shift in Lydia's posture was immediate. "Are you down here with me, chulo?"

"Yeah."

"Chulo... what happened with Seb tonight?"

"Well. His wife kicked me out. So I don't have anywhere to go, either." He tilted his head forward and let the shower pour right onto it. The drops flowed down his face and neck, and the noise drowned out most of the other thoughts in his head. Just the loud patter of a low flow shower echoed on his skull. He almost didn't notice the door pop open behind him. He focused on the sound of the water, and the pelting against his neck.

Lydia pressed her body against his back, and her arms wrapped around his stomach. It was the first safety he'd felt in a year, even as the sopping wet towel around her proved awkward and uncomfortable. She rested her head on his shoulder. "You're mine then," she said. "For as long as you want to be."


FREE FROM THE cold and wet, and with some distance between himself and Seb, he felt like he could actually focus.

Yet another line he hadn't meant to cross with Lydia. And yet more confusion over what he was even doing here in San Francisco. He towelled off and changed into some clothes she'd left for him, which somehow were both too baggy and too tight.

"Wicked," Lydia said as Samir emerged from the bathroom. "Sick fit. Chat, is he adorable?"

"Stop." Sam tugged on the oddly-cut flannel.

"You've had a long day. Come sit." She pat the seat next to her and waved him over, and he obliged. She'd dispensed with the towel and changed into jeans and a baggy tee with some Spanish on it that Sam didn't understand. "Baby, I need to self-own before you fact check me."

"Okay..." His back pressed against the hard wood inside the sofa, and he felt himself avoid Lydia's gaze. "Fact check you on what?"

She gestured to the screen, which was now black. "I know you saw my basic ass genned drama."

"I wasn't going to say anything."

"I know!" She covered her face with a pillow and muffled her shouts. "I know you weren't!" Samir laughed as she hit him with it. "You can!"

"I was surprised."

"I knooowwwwww." She slithered off of the sofa and onto the floor, tucked into the tiny gap between it and the coffee table. "It's tough, right? It's not like I can afford hand-made. I obviously hate Magenta, I hate what they're doing to society, I do believe all that."

Samir's smile was uneasy. "Right."

"Sammmmm!" She put her hands on his thighs and squeezed in between them, her eyes locked on his as she stared up at him from the floor. "I'm a hypocrite. I get that. Okay?"

He kept his hands at his sides and pressed himself harder against the back of the uncomfortable sofa. "I swear, I didn't think much of it."

"Bullshit." Her fingers dug into his legs. "Look, okay? We're fighting for a better world, but we have to live in the one we've got until then."

"That's wise," Sam said with a nod. It was a reaction, but the words stuck around. *We do have to live in this world*, he thought, *even if it's just for now*. "I have a show I watch."

She slapped the top of his thighs, and her face projected pure joy. "You, what! What is it?!"

"Oh." He hesitated. "No, no. I just mean, I understand."

"Nope." She rested her head against his leg and stared up at him. "Tell me."

"It's called... Ellie Misandry." He tried to adjust himself. The hard wooden crossbeam of the sofa had started to really test his limits. He could swear he had lost feeling in part of his body already.

"Ellie Misandry. So is she..."

"She's a vampire. She, uh." He could feel his face go hot. He'd never spoken about Ellie Misandry to anyone that really existed. "She sort of leads a coven of..."

"Covens are of witches."

"Oh, no... no, covens are a vampire thing, too."

"No," she smiled. "Por favor, continúa."

Sam cleared his throat. "Yeah, um, she leads an all-female... group... of witches... no." He coughed again. His voice had gone reedy. "She leads an all-female group of vampires. They sort of fight another... group. That's all men.

Like, you know. Topple the patriarchy. They fight for control of the city."

Lydia giggled. "Oh my god, Samir. Did Virginia prompt this?"

"No..." He closed his eyes and frowned. "Can we please not talk about it?"

"What! Chulo, no no no, me fascina, pleaaaseee." She sputtered through her giggles. "What city?" She squirmed up from the floor and plopped onto the sofa next to him. "You said they fight for control of the city!"

"New Vampire City."

"Oh, novio," she groaned. Her body convulsed with stifled laughter. "Oh, it's so bad."

The evening took on a merciful lightness as they cuddled under a duvet and alternated watching each other's auto-gen television shows, neither of which had ever been seen by another soul. It was more intimate, and more embarrassing, than either of them expected.

"Who is that," Lydia asked every time a new vampire came on screen in Ellie Misandry, enough times that Aida began having the characters say each other's names far too often.

"Wait, why is she mad at her," Sam wondered aloud, as another fight between two characters escalated out of hand during Ruffle Those Feathers.

They slid down the sofa as the night wore on, and each of the shows began to drift into each other's tastes. Lydia joked they should really get to bed before both programmes became unrecognisable, and Sam agreed.

.   .   .

SAM AWOKE in Lydia's tiny bed early the next morning, their backs pressed together, their bodies balanced on their respective edges. He was sure nothing had happened, but part of him still wanted to triple-check. He reached out to grab his Ring from the nightstand, and slid it onto his finger. It took far more force than usual. Sam groaned at the annoyance, which disturbed Lydia, who in turn groaned at being woken up. He opened his palm and saw nothing. In the dim light of the morning he could see it hadn't even gone half-way down on his finger. *Shit*, he thought. *This is hers, not mine.* He shook his hand and the Ring went flying, landing on the floor with a thud.

"¡Ay, güey!" Lydia craned her head back. "The hell?"

"Sorry." He slipped out of bed and felt suitably dignified as he crawled around on all fours, squinting in the dim light of the morning.

The cork-board was unassuming, just on the floor under the bed amongst the dust, discarded knickers, and dirty socks. Lydia's Ring had come to a stop just at the edge. As he reached toward it, the contents of the board itself caught a bit of sun. Pinned all over it were blurry photos of himself and his wife.

"What..." Sam muttered as he slid the board toward him. Each photo had their names written underneath–Samir Patel, and Virginia Rose. There was even one of them together, emerging from O'Leary's Pub in Santa Monica.

"Sam, no, look at me, okay." Lydia's head appeared over the edge of the bed, and her voice echoed around his skull. His gaze was fixed on the board, and the photos.

"What... what is all this..." There were dates and times, hand-written notes indicating where each photo had been taken and when, and even a recent one: Sebastian and Samir outside City Hall, the night Sam had tried to get his visitor permit. "I don't understand."

"I know, it's overload." She was on the floor now next to him. She tried to slide the board back under the bed, but Samir gripped the edge.

"Why have you genned these? But some of these look... real..." The photos had a flatness to them, and a sort of blockiness, a lack of colour and detail that were all telltale signs of an early-era digital photo taken on an antique camera.

"Sam, don't. Don't spiral, okay?" He felt her arms wrap around his waist from behind, her chest pressed against his back. "Please just listen," she whispered into his ear.

He wanted to wrench free of her, to cast her off, shove her to the ground. Anger welled up and spilled everywhere inside him. But outwardly he said nothing, and he stood still. Paralysed, overloaded. Tears streaked down his face.

"It's important," she added. "I swear."

"Why? Why me?" He scanned the wall and checked each photo. None were of Gemma, like the one in the newsletter had been. *Was she part of this, too?*

"It has nothing to do with you, Sam. I promise."

"Oh. I don't understand."

"It's about your wife. The group I'm with, Sam, the ones who make The Analog Gazette, it's so important that we meet her." Lydia slid around and stood in front of Sam, her hands still wrapped around his waist. Their eyes met as she blocked his view of the wall. "She's the only one who can help us."

"Help you what?"

"We're going to shut down SkyTie. And she's the only one who can help."

Sam tried to wriggle away, only to feel Lydia tighten her grip around his waist. Anxiety shot through him as he tried to pick out the most bothersome part of what she'd said. Her head laid against his chest, which heaved faster and faster. "SkyTie," he said with a clear of his throat. "The Magenta... satellite thing."

"Yes, SkyTie, the satellite network that powers everything. It's how Rings talk to each other, let you talk to Aida, dops, digis, everything. It's how Magenta controls every device they've made, how they enforce all their rules." Lydia squeezed him harder the louder she got. "It's why you can't opt out of any of this, Sam."

"That's dramatic."

"It's true!"

"Even if it is, people like all these things." Sam realised he lacked the vocabulary to talk about Magenta's products in detail. It wasn't something he thought about very much. "You like all of these things!"

"Sam, I know. Just listen."

"And Virginia and I aren't even speaking. Even if we were, she'd never agree to help if it involved messing with Magenta. How could she even help? She works on something related to music, I think."

"Sam, your wife isn't in the music division. She's the Vice President of Operations for SkyTie."

"Oh." He wondered if she'd ever told him that, or if it'd maybe happened after they separated. "We aren't in touch. She blocked me."

"She blocked you?"

"Fully blocked."

"Wow. Unalived you."

"Yeah."

"But listen. You're our only chance to get close to her, Sam. You were together for a decade. Maybe if she saw you in person. We can try to arrange it."

"No. I can't go back." Sam's face felt red hot, his mind a jumbled knot of embarrassment. "I can't."

Lydia slid her hand on top of his. The sensation overwhelmed him. "Just relax."

Sam leapt to his feet and backed away from the collage that laid his life bare, and the stranger who had assembled before they'd even met. "No, no." The numbness crept up his arm. He shimmied out of the way and toward the door. His left hand curled into a fist and he squeezed and pumped, hoping for more blood flow. "No, I have to go. I think I'm having a heart attack."

"Where will you go?" Lydia sounded so callous, so unsympathetic.

*Why wasn't she worried about how he was reacting,* he wondered? It was the final arrow, shot clean through to finish him off. *She didn't care at all, she never had.* He raced down the hallway and through the lounge until his back met the door.

"Te necesito aquí ahora." Lydia shouted into a small device pressed against her ear as she entered the hallway. With a flick of her wrist she snapped it shut. Sam recognised it: it was the same thing she'd been so excited to find in that apartment down in Foster City.

"What was that, what's happening?" His chest heaved. "It's too much." He slapped the door behind him, then the plate next to it, then everywhere in between. "Aida, let me out please. Let me out, let me out!" The door seemed to comply, but as Sam stumbled backwards, he fell straight into the grasp of some unseen person. With a swift look upward he saw Lydia's friend Hector stood behind him, with a hard grip on his shoulders.

"Sit down," Lydia instructed as Hector pushed him back inside the apartment. "I promise we all want the same thing."

TWENTY-TWO
CAROLINE

Gemma hadn't enjoyed her trip to Birmingham thus far. She hadn't enjoyed her time in Walsall lately either, but the jury was out as to whether she'd improved her situation by setting out for Liverpool. But with every miserable step she took, she resolved to see it through. Mike had left, and she had left. That was that. It had always been a temporary situation, their stop in Walsall. Just stopping, she recalled, to charge their stolen van. How had it possibly ended up that they'd stayed for two years?

She'd never lived in Birmingham, but as a Londoner she'd taken against it from an early age. It was a predictable British trait, to plant yourself firmly on the opposite side of a dispute with every other town. Londoners enjoyed taking this down to the borough level, and would hurl insults about particular bus routes across football stadia because their rivals happened to be from two miles away.

This all briefly distracted her from the fact that she was lost. They'd apparently gone off signage in the Midlands, and she couldn't wander up to a police officer and ask where the train station was. So for the past couple of days she'd been wandering through the outskirts of what she believed was Dudley, but could just as easily have been Wolverhampton, but was most certainly not Birmingham, because she hadn't walked far enough. Tents, piles of rubbish, collapsed terraced homes, abandoned shops. Street after street, all alike, all blended together. But she knew there was a small train station in Tipton, and from there she could ride a few stops to Birmingham New Street, and they'd surely have trains to Liverpool. All this because they wouldn't let her charge her van. Two years on from her original mission, and energy had become such a luxury the colony couldn't spare a watt. Another sign from above that she'd made the wrong decision when she stayed.

In spite of their best efforts to hide it, and her best efforts to avoid finding it, before the end of her second day she'd stumbled across it: Tipton Station. It was right where Richard had said it would be, which meant the rest of his directions were likely reliable. Now she just had to get inside. In her mind, and maybe elsewhere in the country, train stations were low-slung brick affairs with some coffee machines and a narrow place to stand and wait for a train. Nothing fancy, very little in the way of safety. Want to step off the edge and face-plant on the track? Sure, they're fine with that. Why fence it off? Well, here at Tipton it appeared they'd gotten the message.

Gemma stood across the road from what had to be a ten foot high concrete barrier. Through a couple of window slits she could see the brick of the station, set back a bit from the wall. Perfectly preserved. But directly ahead, between herself and a ride away from here, was the new normal. A few cameras were perched at various points, aimed accordingly to ensure maximum coverage, and a sliding chain-link gate blocked the only entrance. Next to the gate sat a sign, something about a rail card which she couldn't quite make out with her ageing eyes. She'd just wait, she thought to herself. She'd wait here across the road, until someone happened by who knew how this all worked. *How quickly could the gate move?* There would be plenty of time for her to slip through behind a paying customer. The British Rail network could absorb one non-paying passenger without collapsing into financial ruin.

"Um." A meek voice from behind her caused her to jolt. "Miss?"

"Jesus Christ." Gemma turned around with a start. *Are you shitting me?* She took a half-step back to fully appreciate the girl stood next to her. It was the Victorian ghost from West Brom. Judging from her appearance up close, she must've died quite young. She couldn't have been more than around 22 years old, and it felt like she was half Gemma's height. "You hear to take me up, then?"

A puzzled expression crept across her cherubic face. "Take you up, miss?"

"I suppose not, then." Gemma was still baffled by the girl's costume. Today's was another polonaise, this time in a burgundy with ruffles, and again with a matching fascinator clipped to her hair. "Christ, it's you! From the gigs!"

"Oh," she whispered with a tinge of embarrassment. "Oh heavens."

"You stalking me?"

The girl gasped. "No! No, miss, no, I would not. I'm not even meant to speak to connies, really."

"Oi!" Gemma tapped the girl's arm. The fabric of her ridiculous get-up felt incredible. "That's an offensive term, you know. First bloody person I meet and they're anti-itinerant. Fancy that!"

"Terribly sorry, miss. I didn't know it was offensive."

Gemma shook her head. Whatever accent this girl was trying for was not coming off. Some sort of quasi-Cockney, quasi-posh abomination. She'd heard it a hundred times in her past life: some artist, embarrassed they were from the estate, doing a dreadful job of putting one on. "Well, now you know."

"Fucking connies," tutted a man in a bowler as he strolled past. "More every day 'round 'ere."

"Oi! Again!" Gemma gestured at the man, who had already put a gap between them. "See, you can't be like that. That is what I am dealing with every day."

"What are you doing out here, miss?"

She pointed at the rail station just across the road. "I need to get in there."

"Miss, you need a ring to get in there. And a valid travelcard."

"I'll be okay. I'm going to just pop on through the next time it opens."

The girl shook her head. "I wouldn't recommend it, miss."

"Are you going in there? I'll show you. I'm fast."

"I wasn't planning on it, miss. I drove here."

"But you can get in there."

"Yes, miss, I can."

"Go on then."

The girl's stress levels were obvious as she tiptoed across the road with Gemma close behind. Up the few steps, and right up to the gate that stood between them and the railway station. This would be the next challenge, of course: figuring out how to board and then ride a train without any identification or form of payment. But that was for her to figure out later. *You had to take these things one step at a time*, she figured.

"You sure, miss?"

"Yes, bloody hell, pop it open."

The girl took the last step and the gate slid open. Before she could even step inside, Gemma sidled past her, the freedom of the rail just inches away. The pain was instant and unbelievable as the gate slammed shut with stunning force. Gemma was sent banging into the concrete. Blood soaked through her sneakers as her mark panicked on the other side of the fence. She panted and tears welled in her eyes as rain poured onto her.

"Oh my gosh," cried the girl.

Gemma wheezed as her vision darkened. Her cries were lost to the rain, her leg throbbed, the sound of boots faded away. "Please, help." She closed her eyes and listened to rubber and metal tread across pavement. *Of course the only one nearby and they're an anti-itinerant nutter. 'Course they are.* Her defeat was as total as it was predictable. She just wanted to rest here, flat on the ground, until a robot from the National Health Service arrived to humanely euthanise her, or the police arrived to arrest her. It would be easier this way, she figured. To either die here, or to be returned to her life of conscription. She'd been a good worker, and they could find a place for her. *Yes, life at the power plant had been good. She'd see her friends again soon.*

Everything went black and silent.

. . .

THE BUMPS on the road startled her awake. Gemma pressed her hand against the passenger window in a panic as the car moved slowly past rows of coloured tents.

"What the fuck?"

"You're awake!" That same voice. Gemma shot a look to the driver, who gave a hesitant smile. *Christ, that accent, and that round, fresh face. Was it polonaise, again?* "Sorry, I didn't want to leave you there. You were out cold."

"What..." She was still damp, though she seemed to have dried quite a bit. How long had it been? Her foot ached. It seemed to have had a clean bandage freshly applied.

"Sorry, gosh, I'm so sorry. Warned me, they did, you might find this all a bit disorienting, 'specially with the pain killers. Tried to wake you a few times."

"Who?" Gemma felt walled off inside her own mind. Dazed, dull. Her eyes drifted in and out of focus. "What?"

"Sorry! The medic. I rang RapiMed, they sorted you right out. Even loaded you in the car for me."

"RapiMed..." Even in her state, the name stuck out to Gemma: the exorbitant-priced private health service. She'd seen them arrive in two minutes to put a hungover drummer on an IV drip, revive a catatonic executive after some bad coke, or set a broken leg after some junior fell sideways into a swimming pool. Inaccessible even at Gemma's pre-incarceration income bracket, and indistinguishable from magic to the likes of a conscript. They might as well have cast Heal Wounds.

"I'm Caroline, by the way?" She was glancing quickly between Gemma and the windscreen. The car was navigating a tricky bit of road, a patchwork of makeshift homes and people uninterested in allowing them to pass. It was a live-and-let-live approach: they felt no obligation to make it easy for you to get by, and you felt no obligation to force the car into over-ride and plow through everyone.

"Gemma." She pressed herself back into the plush leather. "Thank you."

"Oh it's my pleasure, miss."

The car bumped along as Gemma drifted in and out of her medicated haze. She pressed her face pressed against the cool glass, and watched as each rain drop traced its own path down the window. A part of her would sometimes wonder where she was going, or why this stranger had seen fit to pick her up. But most of her was grateful for the rest, and none of her was in any position to argue.

By the time she regained a sense of self, the car was sand-wiched between two sets of locking metal gates. She threw her hands against the nearest hard surfaces and sat up straight.

"Awful, isn't it," said Caroline. "Can tell it's an election year, yeah? Everyone's so worried about security. Council spent all this money on these gates, terrible waste." Caroline grimaced, then looked out the window at a flat black dome. After a couple of red flashes, the dome illuminated blue and the gate ahead of them slid open. The clouds seemed to part. Sunshine flooded the empty tree-lined street as they rolled forward. "Anyroad, welcome to Moseley."

"Moseley? Are we in Cornwall? How long was I out?"

"...no, miss, it's in Birmingham. I promise, we've not gone far."

Gemma's mind spun out as her pulse quickened. She had no reason to trust this woman, did not ask for her help, and did not know where she'd been taken. And who gave those bloody medics the permission to drug her?

"Look, ..." Gemma trailed off.

"Caroline."

"Caroline, I really need to know where you're taking me. I'm supposed to be..."

"Just here, we're here." She flashed another quick grimace as the car turned up a drive. A massive multi-story brick house stood hiding behind a couple of larch, a garage to one side.

"Christ on a bike," Gemma muttered to herself. The door to the garage lurched open to allow the car inside, then quickly slammed shut behind them. The weight of the closure shook both the car and Gemma's nerves.

"Come in, please. It's all right, I promise!"

Caroline bounded out of the car with a youthful energy Gemma had no chance of matching even before her leg got caught in the fence. In fact, it was only now she wondered whether she could even put weight on it at all. She pushed the button to release the door and gingerly began to lift her foot. She knew something was wrong. Whispers of pain muffled by medication. She set it down anyway, her weight landing on it as she tried to pull herself out of the car seat. And then came the scream.

"Oh my gosh, right." Caroline flew into a panic.

"May need to stay here for a while," Gemma dead-panned. She looked over to see Caroline was gone. She was now alone, in a stranger's car, sealed into that stranger's garage. Unable to stand, let alone walk. "It's been, what, two days. Two days on the road and you've broken your bloody ankle and been kidnapped by a girl with a fake accent."

"The passenger door is ajar," the car replied.

"Christ. I don't suppose you can drive me to Liverpool."

"Apologies, I don't recognise you."

Gemma sighed and closed her eyes. She was starting to wish the gate at the train station had simply killed her.

Caroline had somehow produced a wheelchair, and soon Gemma had found herself inside the relative safety of this palatial detached home. Being from London the scale of this place was unbelievable – the kind of thing you knew existed in various neighbourhoods around the city, but they were all either ten million pound fortresses with mile high walls and heavy defences, or they'd been torn asunder by dozens of squatters. Gemma preferred the squatters if she had to pick, but at no point in her life had either been an option for her.

But now she laid on a sofa observing this girl, Caroline, who somehow lived in one – though granted it wasn't in London but in Moseley. *Wherever the fuck that was.* Gemma had seen no signs of anyone else thus far, but assumed Caroline could not possibly live here alone. She looked around mid-twenties, with bright eyes and short perfectly-trimmed blonde hair, and there was something about the way she was dressed that gave her a very old-world feel. A flowing crimson blouse with a pleated skirt, a belt made of ribbon cinched around her narrow waist, and some kind of choker-esque accessory around her neck that seemed to evoke a ruffled collar. Gemma was at a loss as to whether this was actually in fashion or if Caroline had come up with it herself. Given the affected accent, she assumed it was the latter.

The sitting room they were in seemed to trend toward this same neo-Victorian vibe: high ceilings, ornate wooden cabinets, complicated rugs, and gold floor-to-ceiling drapery across the massive front window. And there was Caroline, sat behind a writing desk, her eyes glazed and her mouth slightly agape. She held a quill in her hand and carefully traced something onto a scrap of paper. *A bloody quill.* An inkwell sat on the corner of the desk. *Sociopathic behaviour.* Gemma had to get out of here. But her leg was in shambles, currently propped up on a pile of pillows at the end of the sofa, and she had little clue where she was or what she was doing here.

"Sorry, I've been lost in my calligraphy," Caroline said as she dropped the quill onto the desk. "It's 4 p.m. That's when I do my calligraphy practice. How are you? Are you in pain?"

Gemma wasn't in pain, really. But something held her back from answering, and she chose to stay silent. Caroline smiled through the confusion then disappeared from the room. She quickly returned with a pill.

"Here you go, to be safe. I'll just leave a couple of these here. Wait an hour for the first, the man said, and then a second if it's still hurting. You can rest on the sofa as long as you need. The guest room's upstairs, but we can sort out getting you up there later. We've got guest ear muffs and sleep masks, all the lot. I can't sleep a wink unless I'm blocking out all noise and light, but that's just me miss, it's entirely up to yourself of course."

"Guest room?" Gemma tried to be forceful without seeming ungrateful. It was a high wire act. "It's very nice, what you're doing. I do appreciate it, really. I just, don't bloody know who you are, or where I am, or whether you're going to tie me to a bed and go at my legs with a hammer. Know what I mean? No offence."

"Don't be daft." Caroline tutted. "I've got a few bits to tend to upstairs, then I'll be down to keep you company, alright?" And before Gemma could reply, Caroline had once again slipped from the room. She heard the creaking of stairs soon after, then footsteps above her. This was her chance. Nobody minding her, or guarding her, depending on whether she thought this was voluntary. She just needed to get up and walk out the front door. She didn't even need to steal Caroline's car, not if she didn't want to anyway. It was a surprising amount of trust being placed in her. Or was it a test? The paranoia thrummed maddeningly. Years of conscription, and the industry before that, had stripped from her the ability to accept a kindness. It was always quid pro quo.

The pain in her ankle didn't care about any of this. It had inserted itself into the conversation. And more than a departure, or an escape, or a trip to Liverpool, it wanted that little yellow pill on the side table. Soon Gemma had taken it between her fingers. She rolled it between them and stared while the ghost of a grandfather clock signalled the passing of another half-hour.

It passed down her throat without need of water. She'd see this out, Gemma had decided, at least for the night. A guest room sounded like a tantalising prospect after months in that club basement in Walsall and the last couple of nights sleeping outside. A bliss of numbness cascaded through her. The disquieting thoughts of Caroline were pulled beneath, tucked away for later. She closed her eyes and slid the second pill between her lips.

Gemma awoke to find Caroline sat on the ottoman staring at her. Deep down she wanted to leap out of her skin, and she pictured herself barrelling past the odd girl and out into the garden. But her arms, her legs, her eyelids, all felt so heavy. The most she could muster was an otherworldly groan. Caroline's expression was unnerving, inscrutable, and she was far too close.

"Goodness, you caught me. Sorry, I was worried. Was making sure you was breathing."

"I'm breathing, I'm breathing." Her body felt impossible to operate, but her mind had cleared somewhat. "Caroline?"

"That's me! At your service." From inscrutable, straight to affable. The girl was cloaked in a red flag.

"Great." She figured she might as well ask, finally. "What am I doing here?"

Caroline frowned. "Oh my, have you forgotten? You took a pretty bad blow to the head, I do think. Do you remember the train station?"

"Yes, I bloody remember..." She steadied herself. "I remember the train station. I made some bad choices. And now I'm here, I believe because you made some bad choices."

"Helping people's never a bad choice, miss."

"Right." *Christ*, Gemma thought. *This is a religious thing, isn't it?* Physical violence was an option. At least she knew Caroline had decent health coverage. "Well, you should be careful. You don't know anything about me."

Caroline squirmed. "Yes, miss, you're right of course."

Gemma managed to push herself up off the sofa and into a seated position. "What..." Pins and needles assailed her arms, and blood rushed to her head. The room spun and she threw herself back against the stiff green upholstery. "Where..."

"Oh! Your things? I collected them, don't you worry." Caroline gestured to the corner of the room, just behind the desk. Gemma's guitar case leaned against the wall.

Gemma snorted as she let herself collapse back onto the sofa, her body both unwilling and unable to cooperate with a quick departure. She pointed at the guitar case and shook her head. "That's rubbish anyway. Could bin it if I wasn't so bloody sentimental. Mostly just wood splinters and metal."

"Oh, no!" Caroline was gutted. Her empathy bordered on psychopathy. "That won't do, I'm so sorry. You don't have any clothes? Or another of..."

"What, another guitar?" Gemma cackled. "I'm not hiding anything up my arse, love. What you see is what I've got." She sighed and, through great effort, got to her feet. The pain in her ankle tried to scream, but was suppressed by the medication. She would've worried about long-term damage if she bothered to worry about the future at all. Caroline put her hands out in a mild panic, ready for Gemma's inevitable fall. "I mean I'm homeless, kid."

"You're not homeless," Caroline said. "You've got a home here."

Gemma stared at Caroline and sized her up as best she could. "This is fucking batty," she groaned. "Why me, kid?"

An intense flash crossed Caroline's face, another unsettling glimpse. It quickly swapped for a tight smile, and Caroline bounded off down the hallway. Any protest this situation warranted was impossible; the painkillers were a weighted blanket that made every thought work that much harder to escape. Instead she'd go along, a passenger on a dark ride, and just hope it was the gentle kind.

Caroline was all too excited to give a tour of the house, the inside of which was even more surreal than the outside. It was room after room of gaudy, neo-Victorian décor that looked more like a film set than where someone might live. It was, however, an impressively performed tour, with explanations and call-outs that made Gemma assume she'd in fact been kidnapped by an agent of the National Trust. Every room had some fact—the study with its double-reclaimed wood, the den with an armoire that dated back to the Glorious Revolution, the stairwell with a painting of someone called Norman Conquest. The more they toured the more Gemma's uneasiness built, until they reached the threshold of the door to the garden.

"The garden," Caroline started, "used to be wild, until about ten years ago. The stone pavers leading back to the..."

"Right, no, let's stop it here," Gemma blurted out. "What the hell is this?"

"What?" Caroline looked mortified. "It's our garden."

"No, no, all of it. My being here, the tour, the opulence, the Anglo-Saxon bloody credenzas."

"I'm sorry, miss. It's weird, isn't it? I'm being weird. I watched my mum give this tour dozens of times."

"What?"

"She's an estate agent. My mum. Mum and dad have been trying to sell the house." Her eyes were saucers, and her lip seemed to quiver. "Come on, I promise it's worth it." Before Gemma could respond Caroline had flung open the double doors and breezed into the garden, which in typical English fashion was an affront to nature. Tiny patches of non-native grass boxed in by concrete, an artificial path running down the middle of the long narrow space, high walls lining both sides and stone pavers leading to a summer house at the very back.

Gemma hobbled down the path after Caroline, who had quite literally run away from the situation. By the time she caught up Caroline was stood in the open doorway, arms spread as wide as her smile.

"Tada!"

The room stunned her into silence. Three walls covered floor to ceiling in shelves, each rammed with compact discs: a chaotic, breathtaking rainbow of preserved history. It was the most beautiful thing she'd seen in years. She crept into the room, moving delicately, keen to not betray how elated she was.

"Do you like it? It's my mum's collection. I think it started as her mum's collection."

Gemma gave a quiet nod as she ran her finger down one of the shelves, not quite sure what she was looking for, but instead marvelling at the fact that someone, somewhere on this island still had a large collection of real music.

"Mum always says Caroline, we must preserve this, because nobody else will. 'Specially since the British Library stopped."

Gemma nodded along, half-listening as she read artists and titles. She could only be impressed with the variety on display. *Surely no single person liked all of this music.* They all seemed to be in decent enough condition, though were all very old. *The last factory pressing CDs like this shut almost a decade ago.* The plastic cases were a mix of cracked, scratched, and cloudy, but that was okay. The case took the punishment so the disc within could survive.

"I thought you might, miss, since I saw you playing guitar. Being into music and all. We have a stereo, too. It's not working. It used to work. Should still, if you could power it. It's too old to power on, you know, with the new sockets and all."

Gemma could only nod as the words barely registered. Her mind was still a bit fuzzy from any number of reasons that came together to form this bizarre day. Right now, at least, she was perhaps just overwhelmed.

After a brief flirtation with independence, Samir had returned to the constant surveillance of being paired to someone via Magenta Mate. Except this time it was a girl named Lydia, and his consent was rather coerced by a terrifying man named Hector. He felt as if San Francisco had swallowed him whole. His best friend, who was also his employer, had put him out on the street. Virginia, his erstwhile wife, had broken off all contact.

But through the clouds that darkened his life a single sunbeam broke through: Gemma Thomson. She was alive, she existed, and Sam could find her. Hilariously, he'd been given the opportunity through his would-be captor. And now she would be his escape. He'd join her in the UK, reunited at long last. Away from all this, and back where he belonged. Back where he should've been this entire time. If only he hadn't allowed Virginia to intervene, to chain him here to the crumbling ruins of California, and to his so-called career.

Thoughts of that summer in London tumbled around his mind as he unfurled cables and taped them to the floor.

Another terrible excuse for a live band would come through Maelzel's tonight, flapping and flailing in desperate mimicry, the furthest cry yet from the delicate, emotion-laden sound that he preferred. There was no artistry now. Homespun, human-crafted music performances were beyond parody. The art had been lost to time, at least in this dead husk of a city. But it was through this grim charade that he hoped to lure the one person left who might be able to help him.

The afternoon slid by with a merciful quiet. His relationship with Sebastian had reduced to grunts and points as they put the finishing touches on the club. A handful of regulars began to trickle in, including Hector, who ignored Samir and played his role as barfly and music enjoyer, less so of minder or prison guard. Sam at least appreciated the work-life balance this afforded, though assumed if he attempted to step out of line, it would be dealt with. While Lydia had been rather upbeat and encouraging about Samir's involuntary involvement, Hector had made clear he wouldn't enjoy finding out if Samir tried to leave San Francisco.


THE BAND TOOK the stage around 7 p.m. and had drawn what might have been the bar's worst crowd of the summer: a half-dozen forty-sevens focused more on their drink than the music, a few friends of the band who refused to buy anything, and a group of nervous tourists up from the South who wore identical jackets and moved as if they were tied together.

*Boom. Boom. Boom.* The backing track of the performance, such as it was, seemed to be a recording of a microphone being banged hard against a countertop. The singer paced a groove in the stage and stared at their feet, reciting what sounded like her grocery list. A guitarist stood at the far back, but their contribution was mostly just running their fingers up and down the strings. It produced a wavering metallic *brraaannngggg*.

From his perch behind the bar, Sam could see the life slowly leaving Sebastian as he rode the levels on the antique mixing board. Loud feedback pierced the air as the singer strayed past the speaker stack, remembered they were not meant to do that, went the other way, and strayed past the other stack. Though it was a free show, Sam still braced himself for the inevitable refund requests. He poured himself a shot of Sambuca, the only liquor he was allowed to sneak for free. Down it went in one gulp, just as the guitarist tripped over her own cable. It was horrifying. His innards burned, his stomach threatened mutiny were he to do it again, and a hint of bile rose up in his throat—a promise of more to come. Shaking it off, he gave the crowd another quick scan: his invited mystery guest, the longest of long shots, had not come through. It was a hollow, familiar feeling, not of surprise but of disappointment.

The last song of the night showed promise. The guitarist laid on their back across the front of the stage and began playing quite a mournful chord progression. The singer stood above her and leaned down, screaming and crying into her face. The lyrics were either nonsensical or in a language Sam didn't understand. The third Sambuca shot seemed to lock him into place, and a great deal of his energy went into convincing his lunch to stay where it was. A tear rolled down his cheek as the singer collapsed onto their bandmate, closing the set with a loud pop and jangle of chaotic guitar. Seb applauded in relief from behind the mixing desk. A couple of the forty-sevens joined in. The tourists huddled together in hushed whisper, their backs facing out to the room. A single tear rolled down Sam's cheek.

"Powerful." A voice came from almost directly behind Sam. He recognised it before he even turned to look. Calm, charismatic, cultivated into an American's ideal of an Englishman. He spun round as soon as he could, the Sambuca still scorching his throat. There stood one of the last remaining legends of the old industry, backlit by the stage lights in a dramatic reveal befitting his status. There stood Eamon Whitechapel.

"Eam!" Sam stopped short of a hug or a handshake, instead choosing to spread his arms and stare.

"Samir, you've kept well. Considering." Eamon gave a wry smile. "And I see Sebastian's managed to make the club even worse. Well done to that lad. He's always been excellent at cultivating a smell."

"The hell are you doing here, man?" Seb leapt onto the bar in front of Eamon. "Holy shit."

"Blame this one, I suppose." He pointed at Sam. "First time hearing from him in around six years, and I get a message."

"Message," Seb added as he dragged the rest of himself over the bar top. "What message?"

"Believe I can paraphrase it," Eamon said with a clear of his throat. "7 p.m. tomorrow, Maelzel's on Mission, shittest most god-awful band you've ever heard in your life."

They found a corner of the bar and put Eamon at the centre, to catch up with their old friend while avoiding each other. The feud, after all, was still fresh. Eamon lived up in wine country now, having retired from the music industry rather unintentionally after the label was acquired. Content to stay out of the future's way, with little love for the

Republic but no desire to learn what life was like on the other side of the wall.

"I don't understand," Sam piped up. He'd been a quiet observer as Seb grilled Eamon for the past hour. "Why stay here? Why not go back to England?"

"Can't bloody get there," Eamon answered with an eye roll. "Not sure who's really to blame, this country or that. But I've been trying to get a travel visa for six bloody months. And that's before you deal with trying to get a ticket on a flight."

"Seriously."

"Seriously, and it's unbelievable. It's unbelievable. I got word my mother's quite ill, and as it happens I don't mind her, and wouldn't mind seeing her again before she goes. But navigating those interminable layers of automated bloody bureaucracy. It had the nerve to tell me I'd qualify more easily for a bereavement visa."

"A bereavement visa... so, if she's..."

"Yes, I can see her if I just wait for her to die first."

"That's so fucked," Seb added. He was scrabbling around on the floor, looking through the cabinet for another bottle of Sambuca.

"So, there's a process to follow." Sam tented his fingers. He was determined to come across as inquisitive. Curious, yes. He was curious. Taking an interest in his friend Eamon's life. "How did you start that?"

"Christ almighty." Seb made his frustration known. "Not this. Is this why you made this poor man drive all the way down from Sonoma?"

"Can't say I follow," Eamon said. He eyed the fresh bottle of Sambuca on the counter.

"He wants to go to England," Seb said. "To see Satan herself."

"Priti Patel?" Eamon laughed at his own joke.

"No, no, I don't want to go to England," Sam stammered. "It's really just a curiosity," His eyes drifted to the far end of the bar, where Hector sat nursing a pint of Modelo. The pairing of Sam's Ring to Lydia's let her see where he was and talk to his dop, but she couldn't hear what he was saying. He assumed that's what Hector was for.

"He wants to see Gemma Thomson," Seb declared far too loudly.

Eamon took the shot as soon as it was laid in front of him. "Dead, surely." With a sharp exhale through his nose he slammed the glass upside down on the bar. "Only thing animating her was cocaine and hatred. Surely both dried up once she lost her job."

"What if I told you she was alive? And I had proof?"

"I'd say it was a damn shame. And regrettably, then I'd wonder how you had the proof in the first place. Because I never know when to leave well enough alone."

"Don't indulge this," Seb shouted. "He can't go to England, man! He has to go to LA to be with his wife. And Gemma is a fucking nightmare, anyway."

"Guys," Sam pleaded. He noticed Hector had taken an interest in the conversation. "Please. Obviously I can't go to England. I'm just asking questions. I can't stay long tonight anyway."

"He's off to go meet up with his new child girlfriend. And I need to go tidy up the back before we close." Seb gave Eamon a pat on the shoulder as he passed and disappeared into the back.

"Who's this, then?" Eamon poured himself another shot.

Sam covered the top of his glass and waited to see if Sambuca poured all over his hand.

"Just a girl I'm seeing." He glanced up to check on Hector, who had mercifully shifted focus back to his beer.

"Samir, I will do something I'm loath to, which is to agree with a club owner. You shouldn't get involved with Gemma Thomson again. She'd gotten a might unstable toward the end there."

"I'd just be curious to stay in touch in case you find a way across, that's all."

"I can tell you what I do know, in the hopes you don't use it for what I think you'll use it." Eamon leaned in and whispered, his arm clasped around Sam. It was a familiar posture for the two of them, one that dated back to Sam's earliest days as an intern. The nostalgia of the moment gave way to reality: this was Eamon's way of letting him down gently. "You need deep pockets. Deeper than yours I suspect. The visa fees, the flights, most of which are private. The exit fees owed to our precious Republic of California will nearly match them. And you need a corporate sponsor just to get permission to enter Britain. The only thing greasing the wheels of bureaucracy in Home Office is corporate interest."

"That sounds impossible."

"Well, lad." Eamon's tone took a turn upward. "You could always get a job as a pilot."

"Right." Sam laughed and his shoulders fell. "No problem."

"Right, so you've got a plan then." The familiar slap on Sam's back signalled the end of Eamon's pep talk. "Now I've kept you away from work too long, I believe you've a customer waiting just there."

"Hmm?" Sam glanced up and was hit with a rush of adrenaline. Sebastian's wife Melanie filled the doorway.

"Mel, uh, hi." It was effort for Sam to get air to his lungs, and the corners of his vision darkened. He could make out individual specks of dust passing through the spotlight that cut across the space between himself and Melanie. Time slowed as he took in her figure, green baby tee stretched over muscle and girth, baggy jeans, and black boots that tipped her from imposing to towering. He saw a thousand scenarios in his mind's eye, most of which involved her ripping his head open like a beer bottle. "I've n-never seen you here."

"I've never been here." She'd closed the distance between them so fast. *Why had the bar fallen silent? Had everyone slipped away, or were they girding themselves to watch a live execution?*

"Sebastian's in the..."

"I'm not here for him." She tossed her head to one side, and Sam scanned the tattoos on her neck. *Are those from prison?* "I'm here for you, Sam."

"M-me?" He could hear Eamon chuckling just behind him, and what sounded like another Sambuca getting poured. *The man will drink Seb dry.*

"Yes, you." She rolled her shoulders, and thunderous cracks rang out from her bones. "I wanted to..." Her eyes had drifted past him. "Is that Hector Padilla?"

"It might be. His first name is Hector."

Mel nodded. "That's Padilla. He's union, like me. We were at the port together during the transition." She seemed to get lost in the memory. "There were hundreds of us back then."

"You're both forty-sevens?"

She rolled her eyes. "Pero no me digas 'forty-seven'... ¡qué pinche coraje me da esa chingadera!"

"I, ..." Sam felt the missing earpiece acutely.

"Éramos el Sindicato de Estibadores, ¿oíste? Teníamos un nombre, una lucha. Y esos cabrones nos lo quitaron todo y nos dieron un puto número. Quieren borrar nuestra historia."

"Melanie, I don't..."

"He fought harder than any of us, lamb. So he fell the hardest. They made an example of him." She'd softened and quieted, her tone far less sharp when she spoke English. "He here much?"

"Yeah, most nights. Sometimes complains about Magenta. Sometimes makes a rude joke about me. He never misses the live music." Sam chose to omit the part where Hector, from time to time, physically threatened him into joining a conspiracy.

"Interesting."

"Alright." Sam coughed, which bought him time to contemplate whether to tell Mel what was going on. But he hadn't cultivated the relationship. He couldn't predict how she'd react, and further, she seemed rather close with Hector. He tore a bit of skin off of his lip and let the thought pass. "You said you were here for me."

Mel let out a long sigh, her eyes cast up to the ceiling. She put her hand on Sam's arm and nudged him toward a table. He felt compelled to sit, partly because she seemed to want him to, and partly because she gave him a light shove down toward the chair. She collapsed onto the chair opposite and stared at the table. "How do we order?" She leaned her face toward the table. "Two Modelos."

Sam popped back up and headed for the bar.

"Where you off to, lamb?" Mel's face contorted in confusion.

"Just getting the Modelos."

"Dios mío, you actually do work here. Hurry back, we need to talk."

WHILE HE POURED the drinks he couldn't help but observe Mel from afar. He'd never seen her by herself and out of her element like this. Considering she knew him, knew Seb, and knew Hector, she seemed content to avoid them all. Instead she traced her fingers along the table, followed the grooves in the reclaimed wood, and often checked around to ensure she hadn't been crept up on. As the beer spilt over the top of the first glass, he saw her hands tremble, which she styled out into a full-body fidget. *Was she angry, or nervous?*

He returned to the table with the drinks, and caught a shoulder slug for his trouble. "Not polite to stare." Sam grimaced as Mel slugged back a quarter of the pint in one go.

"Sorry."

"I didn't think you actually worked here. Assumed it was some kind of scam Sebastian was running, keeping you on payroll so you wouldn't get kicked out of the city."

Sam's mouth slanted. "It might be that. He isn't exactly paying me."

"No puede ser," she muttered. "He claimed he was. Dios mío."

"Well, he pays my Magenta Plus bill."

"Little lamb, how much does Seb talk to you about the business of this little hobby of his?"

"Not really at all, I guess." Sam wanted to bristle at the nickname, but it was fair enough. "He complains sometimes about people not buying enough drinks. Or people not coming to see shows."

"Mano, he's broke. Even with his salary. He can't come close to making the rent next month. He hasn't told you?"

"No... not a word. Wait, are you serious? How is that possible, I thought he owned this place." He avoided Mel's intense hazel-eyed stare, and instead found Hector, who had taken notice of them. "I, uh. I was sure he owned it."

"He did, until the pendejos gave it to Magenta."

"What?!" Sam leaned away from her and his chair scraped noisily along the ground. "When? Which, uh... pen... de..."

Mel shook her head. "Not for you, mano. But it was the pendejos that run this godforsaken city. It's blocking progress, they say. The whole block was taken through eminent domain. For more of their pinches casas. Concrete nightmares stacked sky high with compartments to store Magenta fucks and lazy fucking legacies."

Sam's head had fallen to the table, his vision filled with darkness and vague outlines of gnarled wood. He banged it a few times, enough so he could feel the pain on his forehead. *It was always Magenta, wasn't it?* They had ripped his life apart, limb from limb, and it hadn't been enough. Now they had to feast on his insides, the sinews, every last stringy morsel. He'd lose his job here, then he'd lose his papers, and then he'd be sent out of the city. It would only deepen his unholy pact with Lydia, to God knows what end.

"Oye, ¿que tal? What the fuck is this?" Mel's finger thudded into his back. "Pull it together, mano."

"Sorry." He lifted his head, and the clamp lights on the ceiling seared his eyes.

"Oh." She reached out and brushed his cheek. "I'm sorry, lamb."

Sam wiped his face off. *Why am I crying?* "That's so fucking embarrassing, I'm sorry."

Mel pushed her chair back and loomed over him. "Get up, come on." Sam's head dipped back down toward the table, but it was futile, as Mel's vise-like grip was soon around the back of his neck. She gave him some involuntary assistance to his feet, then pulled him close against her. With an exhale, all of his muscles relaxed and he surrendered to the hug, which enveloped him more than he would've expected even given her size. "It's okay, shh, shhhh." He convulsed as his tears flowed, and he pressed his face into her chest with a full-on sob.

"I'm sorry."

"Shh, no talking, okay?" She pulled her arms even tighter around him. "You get through this so we can talk about what happens next."

"What happens next..." Sam trailed off expectantly, and kept his eyes locked shut. Butterflies swarmed his stomach.

The comfort was brief. She broke the hug, gripping him by the shoulders, her eye contact intense and unavoidable. "¡Qué baboso! What happens next with the club, you pest."

"The club." He nodded. *Of course, right.* "What about it?"

"You have to convince him to shut it down."

"But..." The word had only just escaped his lips. He was in Mel's thrall.

"He can't afford it, lamb. Okay?" She cupped the back of his neck with her hand. The skin of her palm was coarse against his skin and sent tingles down his body. "But he's worried. He says if it closes you'll get deported." She sighed. "He's got this awful plan to save it."

"What?"

"Something about your visa. Lamb, I don't know how they work. I just know this plan of his is going to kill him. It's against everything he stands for. So the club's got to go, okay? Dios mío, I wish this place didn't exist."

"What, is..."

"Stop saying what! You hear me. This fucking club is ruining my life. I'm sorry, lamb, I don't want anything bad to happen to you, but..."

"No, I..." Samir was stunned. Once again he felt trapped between Sebastian and Melanie. "What is this plan?"

"Hey!" She squeezed his neck, and his eyes closed as he prepared for the end. "No plan. Okay? It can't come to that. Don't be selfish, mano."

"Okay."

"You'll talk to him?"

"I'll talk to him."

"Good boy." She gave his shoulders a final squeeze, then straightened up. "Come through for me on this, please. I don't want to have to take care of this myself, but I will." The threat was clear. Sam tried to catch her eyes once more, but she'd already looked past him. "I'll say hello to Hector. Be good, lamb."

She retrieved Hector, and after a terse exchange in Spanish the two of them stormed out of Maelzel's. Only Eamon was left sat at the bar. His head rested next to the empty bottle of Sambuca, and he looked at peace.

TWENTY-FOUR
GHASTLY

The house was vast, so Gemma had to pick her battle. As
soon as she heard the shower come on, she slipped into the
upstairs hallway and made a beeline for what she believed
was the master bedroom. She was desperate for more information about her host, and had to balance it against both
unbelievable pain and Caroline's unusual temperament.
There was something simmering under the surface of that
girl, and Gemma was not keen to find out what it was first-
hand.

What she found, for now, was a room that seemed to
have been abandoned. The furnishing was ridiculous yet
typical for this house: a mix of generic period styling, a
spacious four-poster bed, twin dressing tables each with their
own distinct accoutrement, and a massive two-sided closet
that hung wide open.

*What the fuck*, Gemma muttered as she stared past the
open closet doors. One side was rammed top-to-bottom and
side-to-side with a rainbow assortment of dresses, jackets,
shoes, and hats. And the other was bare. Empty hangers

littered the hardwood at the bottom, and a few laid on the bed as well.

The dressing tables told a similar tale. One seemed as if it was ready for use with an assortment of makeup, jewellery, deodorants. The other was a bit of a mess, and seemed to have nothing useful. She ran her fingers through the dust, tracing the faint rings and ovals where perfume bottles and jewellery boxes had once sat.

She was far more taken with what she assumed was Caroline's mother's table. The large mirror was covered with photos, with only a narrow space left open to use. Gemma grinned as she studied them. They were small and grainy, as if taken by one of those Instax cameras that were hot when Gemma was a kid. Some were of Caroline, others of the garden, and of her CD collection. She recognised a few shots of the West Brom high street where she'd been playing every week. Quite a few were of urban decay—closed shops, piles of rubbish, defaced signage. Gemma's personal favourite was a well-framed shot of the words "FUCK MAGENTA" spray-painted across some old brick wall.

On the table itself, amidst the jewellery and knick-knacks, sat a small white box with a printed label and the purple M of the Magenta Corporation. She picked it up and strained to find a distance that let her old eyes focus on the tiny print. Underneath a barcode, she could just make out: ALICE NEWMAN.

Gemma took the box between two fingers and shook it until the lid slid off. Inside, tucked into a perfect form-fit piece of foam, was a silver ring. It left the container with ease and seemed to almost beckon her to slide it on her finger.

"What are you doing in there?" Caroline's voice shouted from the hallway. "That's my parent's room!"

"It's fine," Gemma shouted as she spun around to face the door. She thrust the ring into the pocket of her jeans. "I'm an adult. So are you, best I can tell."

Caroline stayed in the hallway, but permitted herself a narrow peek through the crack. Her eyes lurked in the darkness. "You better come out."

"Who is Alice Newman?"

"What?" Caroline gasped, then composed herself. "Where did you see that?"

"Saw it on some post."

"Right, yes." She let out a sigh. "That's our neighbour. We take in her post when she's away."

"Can I meet her?"

"N-no, miss, she's away. That's why we've got the post."

Gemma narrowed her eyes, and the tension rose in her voice. "Why is she away? Where's your family? Why is everyone bloody away?"

"They're not, miss! Not all of them. There's plenty of people in town. My family's just in Saudi Arabia on business."

"What business? You said your mum's an estate agent."

"She goes with my dad sometimes... on his business trips."

Gemma scrutinised her through the crack in the door. It didn't tally, but nothing tallied. She fidgeted with the box in her pocket, which bulged in a very obvious way.

"That's what I was coming to say," Caroline said. "I thought we could into town today."

"Sure, yeah. Just give me a moment."

"Are you not going to come out of there, miss? I really think you should."

"Don't you need to go get ready?" Gemma was terse. She had no desire to explain herself.

"Y-yes, miss. But..."

"I'll meet you downstairs, okay?"

Caroline's voice shook. "Okay." Her shadow grew long and disappeared as she slinked back down the hall.

A quick dash back to the guest bedroom, and Gemma had deposited the mysterious box in her guitar case. She'd fidget with it later, she thought. A walk through town might help her make enough sense of things, and then she could focus on sorting out what was going on.

CAROLINE HAD SPENT the better part of the next hour managing Gemma's expectations.

"It won't be like what you remember, miss. It's a bit of an interesting town." She was totally shot through with anxiety over what Gemma might think. It set Gemma on edge, which seemed to make Caroline even worse. The two of them couldn't be worse of a match, thought Gemma. But she was determined to make it work. At least until she recovered a bit more, and understood a bit more.

"I don't even know what I remember." Gemma sat on the edge of a chaise lounge and rubbed her wounded ankle. It had a fresh wrap, courtesy of a follow-up visit from the RapiMed folks, who seemed to resent being called to tend to such a vile creature as herself. Her perception of their tone might've just been her inherent disdain for anyone from the Midlands, but there had been no hiding the eye-rolls. To their credit they had managed past their hatred of itinerants, topped up her meds, redid her bandages, and used a minimal amount of slurs. *Most you can ask for. Class, professionalism.*

"What you mean, miss? Don't know what you remember?"

"I mean, I spent years imprisoned in a work camp, and then the last couple in the colony. There's no normal, love. There's nothing."

"Right, sorry. Sorry, I really am." Caroline picked at her eyebrow. It wasn't the first time Gemma had seen her do it. It seemed to be some kind of nervous habit. "Maybe you'll like it then. The high street, that is. Always something fun on the go down the high street."

"Lead the way, m'lady." Gemma had agreed with herself to only mock Caroline's whole deal once per hour, and she'd accidentally used it up there. Pity, especially given she'd descended the stairs in her most lavish Victorian cosplay yet. "I might trail behind you."

Caroline's vague repeated warnings had done little to prepare Gemma for what awaited her on the high street. Far more than posh housing laid behind the iron gates. It was an entire community. Beautiful cobblestone with a tactical amount of tarnish comprised the street, wide enough for two carriages, though closed to traffic at both ends by concrete bollards, with an automated car park stationed nearby and ready to receive. The pavements were unbroken and seemed to glint in the sunlight, with shadows cast by the protruding window boxes of the shops that lined both sides. And the shops, Gemma thought, were the most ridiculous part. A butcher, a baker, a café with an actual barista, more than one antique dealer. Not a kiosk in sight. No smashed windows, no steel shutters. It was awesome in the truest sense, and Gemma could scarcely find the words to describe how it felt to see.

"Fuck off, are you serious?"

"I know," Caroline sighed and spun round. "Dreadful, innit?" She looked completely at home in this scene. Her dress, her hair, her complexion, placed here in this dreamed-up image of a street that had never existed, filled with people that had never lived, framed and hung on the wall of some fictional home.

"What... the fuck?"

"Ghastly," came the muttered response from a passerby headed the opposite direction. A bald man in the twilight of his life who was nearly a head shorter than Gemma, yet felt compelled to put his own life in jeopardy by remarking on her.

"Oh my," Caroline gasped as she swept back to Gemma's side. She felt their fingers intertwine as she stared a hole through the wretched man's back. "Perhaps you'd better come with me miss, it's..."

"What?" Gemma seethed. "It's what?"

"I'm so sorry, it just might be a bit easier if you didn't, well..." Caroline looked her up and down. "If you didn't stand out so much."

The mirror in the changing room revealed two truths. Perhaps, not that she needed to mind, but perhaps she had gone a bit hard on the food supply at the colony. Her blue University of West London hoodie strained and stretched an inch above her hips, and her belly protruded a fair bit more than she remembered. She told herself she was never one to worry about such things, and she still felt that was the case. Nevertheless, it had caught her out. The second was a bit harder to cope with. Her eyes drooped and sank, her cheeks puffed, her crow's feet had entrenched, her skin resembled a salt flat, and her hair was an absolute fright.

"Caroline?" She called out to her gothic caretaker on the other side of the curtain.

"Yes, miss?"

"I see it."

"I'm glad, miss."

The curtain slid open and there stood Caroline, arms piled high with what she considered fashion. Gemma could feel the bile creep up her throat as she stared at some sort of Victorian day dress in a putrid green. Just above the dress was Caroline's beaming face, the lid on an infinite well of pride at having picked this out.

Gemma cursed under her breath as she snatched the dress. "If you step in here with a corset, I'll bloody beat you to death with it."

"It's not for everyone, miss."

Caroline gave a curt nod as Gemma emerged wearing the dress, her eyes doing a judgemental scan head to toe. Her faded white trainers somehow passed muster, even as filthy as they were, but Caroline added an assortment of under-things to her bag before walking out of the shop. Gemma stood just on the other side of the door and held one arm in the other. The dress felt alien on her skin, and she hadn't paid for it. As best she could tell, neither had Caroline.

"You coming?"

"I've not paid? I don't..." Her stomach groaned and her throat burned from the acid. "I can't bloody afford it. Even if it's a quid, it's a quid too much."

"Blimey," Caroline said as she jumped back across the threshold. "I'm so sorry. Please, let me." She placed her hand on Gemma's back and nudged her forward.

Gemma scrunched her face and shot a look. "Oi."

"Please, it's for me, really. I'm happy to get it." Another nudge, with a bit more force, sent Gemma forward and Caroline close behind. Her hand stayed fixed to Gemma's back. As she crossed the threshold of the shop, she could feel a slight vibration, almost imperceptible. Caroline let her hand drop.

"This town." The sun cut through the cloud and struck Gemma in the face, leaving her slouched and gawking at the pavement. A breeze served as yet another reminder that she was in this stupid outfit. She sighed. "Great, so now I've changed, men won't find me reprehensible."

"Heh." Caroline rubbed the back of her neck. "I was thinking we could get a coffee, if that's alright?"

Gemma followed down the pavement in a daze. She was relieved the dress granted her anonymity, though it had added to her confusion. The shop-lined street was reasonably busy and almost everyone wore these bizarre costumes. Men dressed as dandies, boys like urchins in their flat caps, women in their bodices and petticoats. And all of it slightly wrong, someone's drunken misunderstanding of a documentary. Her would-be captor bobbed along, posture forced by wire and tight lacing, but with a smile that was freely given. She was greeted by name, or given deference by, everyone they passed, and the same tended to either give Gemma an absent nod or avoid her gaze entirely. *So it's not all bad,* she thought. Being ignored by strangers was the first meal her inner Londoner had enjoyed in half a decade.

The intoxication of anonymously mooching around a high street had taken her mind off both the dress and the pain in her ankle. Before long Caroline was stood facing her in front of what seemed to be their destination: an imposing stone building on a corner, its various entrances guarded by ornate columns, with a carved wooden head sign that read *The Town Centre*.

"You've brought me to the pub? I underestimated you."

"N-not quite, miss."

"I'd curtsy if it wouldn't shatter what's left of my ankle."

GEMMA HURTLED through the doors and threw herself upon the bar. Her thirst for this experience, a proper pub experience, was immeasurable. And The Town Centre appeared to rise to the challenge. Ornate mouldings topped the spacious bar room, which had a high ceiling, a dozen or so tables, and ample custom. *It's important*, Gemma thought, *for a pub to have enough punters that you're able to disappear into a private conversation if you need, but find community if you prefer.* The crowd seemed to span the gamut of boisterous and circumspect, though it was almost entirely men. And all in this atrocious period-adjacent attire, which she now also wore.

"Yes, miss." A friendly chap behind the bar glanced back from his position at an elaborate espresso machine.

*Poor sod*, she thought. *They hate it when people order an espresso drink.* "Just a pint, please. And another for my friend who's just behind."

"A pint?"

Caroline had caught up, and her hand once again laid upon Gemma's back. "Miss, please."

"One second, love," Gemma replied. "Pint of whatever lager you've got, please."

The man behind the counter seemed to hiss. A chorus of groans echoed behind her. Gemma flinched. Her eyes scanned around. *Was this a real ale pub or something?* But she didn't see any cask handles. In fact, she didn't see any taps either.

"You won't find a pint of what you're looking for here, madam." A gregarious dandy in a tailcoat rose to his feet from a nearby table, his voice more affectation than accent. A cacophony of creaks rang out as everyone turned to face the man.

Gemma closed her eyes and shook her head. *Fucking perfect.*

"She didn't know, Mr. King." Caroline slid artfully between Gemma and the man. "Dreadfully sorry."

"This is not some den of ill repute, full of dull men with duller senses, made low by their love of the drink. This, madam, is a coffee house." The man had begun to pace between the tables, and he held the gaze of the crowd as he moved. "A place where men great and lesser can come together to discuss the topics of the day, to do business, to be with each other and themselves regardless of status or position."

Gemma's head started to throb. She put a finger to her temple and rubbed. A cold spike went through her like a dagger: she'd nearly thrown away a year of sobriety for a pint of lager. "Who are you?"

"Madam, my name is Alastair King." He gave an elegant nod. "And this is my penny university, The Town Centre. It's a pleasure to welcome you in, provided you follow the house rules."

"She will," Caroline interjected. "She absolutely will, of course. It's my fault sir, I didn't tell her where we were going."

"Shh." Gemma shot a look at Caroline, then fixed her stare to Mr. King. "Uh, thanks, Alastair. And I'm..."

"Tut tut," Mr. King bellowed, "now now. You're free to stay anonymous in this coffee house, madam. Only your ideas matter. And of course, the fact that you're in the company of this town's own daughter, the lovely Miss Caroline." His grin widened as applause rose up around them from the seated patrons.

*Fuck's sake*, Gemma thought. She only just managed to suppress an eye roll. Caroline seemed worried, so she'd play it as safe as she could for now. "Of course, sir." She managed a short bow, and Caroline curtseyed in turn. It was all, to understate it, a bit much.

"Let's sit over there, miss." Caroline's hand seemed to be attached to Gemma's back. She guided the two of them to a free table in a disused corner, then returned after she'd fetched a pair of cappuccinos.

Gemma sipped the coffee and looked around. The furore had died down, and everyone returned to their respective conversations. She put on a half-cocked smile. "Thanks. For this, and for that."

"Oh it's my pleasure miss, I'm sorry again."

"The town's daughter?" Gemma blurted out the question, then gave herself a quiet tutting. She'd told herself she'd wait until dinner to bring it up.

"You heard that, did you? Gosh."

"'Course I heard it. Everyone heard it. It got a round of applause."

"It's embarrassing."

"But what does it mean?"

"It's nothing." Caroline stared into her cappuccino. "My family were one of the founding families of the town. It's barmy, calling me the town's daughter just cause of that."

Gemma nodded. "So that's how you got me out of the arrest at the train station."

"No, miss." Caroline demurred. "I gave the security guard fifty pounds."

"Oh. Right, the founders of Moseley, that must have been centuries ago."

"It was around twenty years ago, I think. It started around a school, a private school. I went there. We moved here so I could attend. But slowly we bought up all the land, I suppose. Us, and some other families. And together they founded the town."

Gemma leaned back and slumped down in her chair. *There was rich, and then there was this. Blimey.* "Was this an algo thing, then? Trying to get away from the evils of technology?"

"I don't know. I don't think so. My mother loves to talk about it all, why we did it, how it all came to be, but I don't really love to listen. Wish I did."

"Right. Well, it has charm."

"Honestly, I hate it here."

"Bit shit, yeah. The outfits, mostly. Why don't you leave?"

"I do, sometimes."

"No," Gemma chuckled. "I mean move. Leave leave. Go, go far away."

"Like where?"

"Liverpool. That's where I'm going."

"My father always said Scousers were drunken, ungrateful louts who got what they deserved."

"Well, it's a nice enough place. Where's your father from?"

"Stratford."

"East London? Alright love, well done."

"Stratford-upon-Avon, actually."

Gemma groaned. "Twat." She pushed her empty mug into Caroline's and made a satisfying clink. "Another round then?"

"If we're doing rounds, you'll need a ring." Caroline tapped Gemma's bare ring finger. "It's mad you don't have one."

"A ring?" Gemma smirked. "I've got these." She pulled the chain and displayed the two graphite rings that hung around her neck. "I'm not going to wear them, though."

"No," Caroline smiled. "You know what I mean."

"Like a partner? You proposing, love?"

Caroline burst out laughing, and Gemma was stunned by her smile. Wide, radiant, disarming, and the appropriate amount of gorgeous white teeth showed through. *She must have taken smile class in finishing school.* "A ring! Like, a Magenta Ring?" She held up her hand and pointed at her ring. "We use 'im for everyfing now."

"Right... no, I had a phone, back when we were in the work camp. Hasn't worked in years. I guess I kept it for nostalgia but it's dead."

"A phone!" Caroline cringed. "No, that would never do."

"I don't know if you noticed..." Gemma dropped to a whisper. "But I don't really have access to funds."

"Oh, if it was about money that would be easy. You have to prove your identity to get one, there's a background check, it's all very involved, quite a bit of paperwork."

"I'm right fucked."

"We didn't used to need them, or use them... but the council, they've brought in all this security... we use them for everything now. Paying for things, getting in and out of town, our cars, trains…"

"Liverpool isn't like this, you know. I won't need one because I'm not staying. I'm going to Liverpool."

"Well, you'll need it for the train."

"Not if I drive."

"Well, but, the car…"

"Not if you drive."

"Miss… I can't leave. My family… my mother…"

"How old are you, anyway?"

Caroline batted the air with her hand.

"Look, doesn't matter, you're old enough to make your own bloody decisions."

Caroline's face fell. She shifted in her seat. "Miss, please."

"And how are the two of you getting on this afternoon, if I might enquire." Mr. King's unnatural lilt stirred a primordial anger in Gemma. He leaned down and brought his face level with the table. "Miss Caroline, I'm not sure I've had the pleasure of making your friend's acquaintance before today. Is she new to Moseley?"

"Oi." Gemma had spent the last of her patience. "Fuck off mate, private conversation." Caroline's gasp joined the choir of almost everyone in the room. "See two women, need to toss yourself in there yeah?"

The barista shouted from afar with an air of obligation. "I'm afraid it's against the house rules to use vulgar language."

Caroline slapped her hands against the table. "Gemma, stop."

"Are you fucking joking, mate? It's bloody Birmingham, can hardly describe it without using vulgar language."

"Miss Caroline." Mr. King made a show of ignoring Gemma. "How did you say you know this person?"

The barista coughed and pointed a finger at Gemma. "I'm afraid you need to leave. Miss Caroline, I think it's best you stay put."

Gemma was indignant. "If you care to lose that finger, I'm happy to break it off."

"STOP!" Caroline shouted, and her voice seemed suited for the task. Everyone fell silent by her command. Her foot stomped the ground to emphasise her point. "We're going."


THE MADDENING SILENCE followed them from the car to the dining room, settling over their dinner of ready meals and giving it a grim portent. *Would Caroline explode? Let it go?* Gemma felt as if she was waiting to be called to the headmaster's office. But she was too stubborn, and too self-aware, to speak first—even she knew when she'd done enough speaking for one day. It was only once they'd both taken their last bites that Caroline decided to settle matters.

"You can't do that," she started with a stern tone. "You can't do what you did."

Gemma's skin crawled. She felt a fire kindle inside her and she prayed it would not light. "I'm sorry, but I can. It's still a free country... somewhat. They can't throw me in jail for being boorish and unseemly." She took in as much air as she could. "I understand you don't like it."

"This is a town of rules!" Caroline screamed. Gemma lurched backward and stumbled out of her chair. It crashed onto the floor as tears flooded Caroline's eyes. "And of courtesy, and of decorum! Okay!" Caroline likewise stood straight up. "You are going to remember that, and abide by it! Okay?!"

"Right, so." Gemma cracked her neck. The fire was ablaze. "All of that? Can fuck all the way off. And so can you, frankly."

"Unbelievable. You are unbelievable! And you are ungrateful!"

"I didn't ask for any of this!"

"You didn't have to, because I am nice!" She leaned forward and shrieked. "I am a nice person!" Gemma's eardrums rattled. She took another step away from this terrifying girl.

"Okay," Gemma lowered her voice. "Okay. You're very upset. I see that." She started to move toward the door behind her, and Caroline seemed to match her step. "All of this is why taking you to Liverpool will be the best thing that ever happened to you."

"I'm not going to Liverpool!" Caroline very much did not lower her voice. "And you can't leave town without me letting you out! So... you need to think about that, okay?! I've been so nice to you! And you weren't very nice to me today!"

"Christ!" Gemma punched the wall and let out a guttural roar. "You sheltered little posh cunt!"

"AHHHHHHHHH!" Caroline stomped out of the room and up the stairs. Gemma stood dumbfounded in the dining room. She panted and wheezed as she doubled over, her hands flat on the table, her head ready to burst from pain. Her ankle cried out and the rest of her jolted as Caroline slammed a door upstairs.

It was about an hour of stunned inaction before Gemma worked up the courage to follow. She half-expected Caroline to be stood at the top of the stairs, knife in hand. But she found only darkness and closed doors, aside from one: the room Gemma had slept in the night prior.

She shut the door and paced a groove in the floor. On the nightstand sat a fresh bottle of her pain medicine, rushed over from RapiMed at some point while they were away. And Caroline had placed a glass of water there as well.

*Why is this cunt being so nice to me? And I'm just being myself,* she thought as she lowered herself onto the bed, still in full period regalia. Her ankle throbbed, and with how swollen it was, she had zero chance of even getting her socks off.

The lid of the pills popped open with ease. *Just one or two,* Gemma noted. *They're strong.* The bottle tipped, and five tumbled out onto her palm. A small sip of water sent them all down with ease.

TWENTY-FIVE
RECONCILIATION

In a rare instance of his bravery failing, Samir had excused himself to the toilet rather than head straight into the back of Maelzel's to speak with Seb. The closeness he'd felt to Melanie was something he was unprepared for, and he'd tucked himself into a bathroom cubicle to shake off the sensation. The flood of oxytocin made him feel he could die for her. But Mel hadn't asked him to die. She'd asked him to kill Seb's dream. The toilet was as good a place as any to brainstorm how he'd do it. They let one's self separate from any undue pleasantness and focus on what mattered. The rank odour and putrid green tiles kept the mind from drifting.

He'd had about fifteen seconds to collect his thoughts before the knock came.

"Anyone in?" Seb pounded on the inside of the bathroom door as he shouted. "We're closed. If the Brit at the bar said we never close, he was lying."

"I'm in here," squeaked Sam from inside his cubicle.

"Dude, what the hell, how long have you been hiding in here?"

"Not long," he answered. *And I'm not hiding*, added his inner voice.

"Can you come out? I'm closing up."

"We need to talk, man." Sam dry swallowed. "I heard about the club." He wanted to be angry, but his thoughts felt like tangled Christmas lights and his emotions were in chaos. "I can't believe you didn't tell me." A lump formed in his throat.

"Ah, fuck man. How? Did Mel say something? Is she here?"

"How could you not tell me?" Sam's voice wavered. He wondered whether Mel had stuck around. *Was she lurking somewhere, waiting to see whether I did what she asked? Would she stop Seb as he left and ask? Would they fall out over this?*

"Can you come out?" Seb peeked through the gap in the toilet cubicle, and Sam pressed himself into the back corner to avoid being seen.

"Magenta, really? How much do you owe?"

"Dude, I cannot even think about it. It happened so fucking fast."

"Did you talk to them?"

"Talk to who? It's all digis, man. At the city and at Magenta." Sam heard the tell-tale squeak of the countertop as Seb took a seat. "It's fucked they can just do this. This club's my fucking birth right."

Sam was in dire need of a rest and lowered himself down onto the toilet lid. All he could think of was years of sick deposited on, in, and around this spot. He made note to dispose of these clothes later. "How do you mean it's your birth right?"

"This club belonged to my parents. I had to buy it off of

the city during probate because they left no will." Seb let out a growl as he leapt off the counter and began to pace. "They took my money and now they'll just take the club anyway. To give it to Magenta." Sam jumped at the sound of Seb's fist slamming into the metal paper towel holder. "Did you charge them too, you fucking pricks?" His fists battered the metal. "Yeah? Double dipping, you miserable fucks?" Sam backed away as Seb continued to assault the dispenser.

"Seb! Enough!"

"Fuck! Goddamnit. Maybe I'll just burn it to the ground!" He collapsed against the wall and cradled his hands.

"Jesus, man." Sam stared at the bloodied dents. "We need to get your knuckles on ice. You'll be lucky if they aren't broken."

"Shit."

A MAGENTA AUTO-GIG was the last piece of equipment Sam expected to see in the back room of Maelzel's. Yet there it was, just next to the freezer where he'd retrieved the ice for Seb's ruined hands. It was sticking out of a plain cardboard box that was half-collapsed and said "decorations" on the side, and a smaller box nearby seemed to hold all the wires and adapters. But Seb had seen enough of them in his life. It was unmistakable.

"Thanks for rushing this over," Seb said as he snatched the ice pack out of Sam's hand.

"What the hell is this doing here?"

"Yeah. I know. I don't know. I bought it off a girl who said she personally tore it out of an abandoned club in Brooklyn." The two of them stood on opposite sides of it, as if they were nervous it might leap out and attack were it left unobserved. "I guess this was plan B."

"Plan B?"

"Yeah..." Seb sucked air through his teeth as the ice touched his shattered knuckles. "To help the club survive. Hook this shit up, install it, whatever the fuck you do with it. So we can run auto-gigs seven nights a week. No bookings, no terrible amateurs, no kids threatening to sue because old men tried to mosh. Just some fake band playing the fake hits direct into everyone's earpieces."

Sam kicked the box. "Fuck that, man."

"Hey! Fuck *you* man, this wasn't cheap." Seb kneeled down in front of it and poked around at the bits. The unit itself was unremarkable–just a long flat black rectangle with myriad connections, lights, a few buttons, and a Magenta logo. Then there were all the mirrors, markers, lasers, sensors, projectors... just a huge pile of bits that you littered all over your club. Or rather, your authorised Magenta installation technician did. It was extremely complicated.

"You know." Some intern trauma crawled to the surface of Sam's mind. "These things are a huge pain in the ass to set up."

"Doesn't matter, anyway. It's useless, it doesn't work."

"Maybe you just didn't set it up right." Sam kneeled down to have a poke around as well. It was definitely a first gen model, was both dusty and filthy, and a few of the ports looked corroded. A metal plate, which someone had clearly tried to pry off, said it was property of Magenta Corp. and bore a scratched-up serial number.

"It's apparently too old? Or something? Marked as stolen? I don't know. Nobody at Magenta will talk to me about it, the digis just run me around in circles for twenty minutes until they say they can't help." Seb shook his head and sighed. "This whole city is rammed with Magenta employees and I can't get hold of a single, actual person. Maybe I need to stand outside wearing a sandwich board."

"It's tricky, I guess." Sam froze as he stared at the pile of old kit. Mel had been clear in what she'd asked him to do. But she knew he'd get kicked out of the city if he lost this job. *Did she really expect him to help get himself deported?*

"Tricky." Seb winced as he tried to extend his fingers.

Sam started to slip and his eyes went out of focus as he continued to stare at the useless hunk of metal and glass. Images of Pete Police moved to the forefront. To his capture, processing, to his deportation. Shoved in a van and driven back down the corridor. Dumped in the Los Angeles River, probably, if not just over the wall, thrown to the wolves in CenCal.

"If it's not this," Sam pleaded, "it has to be something. You can't shut the club, Seb. Like you said. It's your birth right."

"Everything ends, dude. My folks got that." Seb popped to his feet and headed back out to the bar.

"Wait, Seb. Wait." Sam intercepted and threw himself between Seb and the door. "There has to be something. Not to dwell, but... what about Gemma?"

"What about her?"

"To keep the club open. She can play, she can book, she's kind of a name... she'd probably be grateful for the work and it could really help the club."

"Your proposal is to hire your old sex pest boss, who lives in another country, as some kind of artist in residence. That's the plan?"

"I guess so."

"Find your fucking mind, dude. If I keep putting fugitives on my fake payroll they're gonna fucking notice. Can you even reach her? Can you offer a foreigner a job, is that legal?"

"I don't know, okay. I don't know any of those answers. It was a stupid idea."

"Yes." Seb paced as best he could in the cramped back room. "I'm not trying to be insensitive, man. I mean, I know it's fucked up between us right now. I don't even know where you're sleeping, I don't know what's going on. But it's not just about needing money to come in. I gotta talk to someone at Magenta, man." Seb stared a hole through Sam.

"Okay." Sam stared back, his expression vacant.

"Bro! Your fucking wife is an executive there!" Seb thrust his face into Sam's. "Dude, come on."

"Oh." Sam slipped past and headed toward a precarious stack of wine boxes in the corner. Maybe an earthquake would tip them over and kill him.

"Dude, come the *fuck* on."

"I can't." Sam's head wobbled side to side. "No, no way. I don't even think I can."

"Great. That's great."

"Maybe you can?"

"Maybe. No. Forget it." Seb popped up and sat on a small bit of countertop next to the sink. "None of it matters. Mel's right. We have to shut this place down."

The thawing had proven temporary as the two of them finished closing in silence. Sam watched Seb's movements, listening to his muttering and looking for any opportunity he could find to make a joke or a comment that might get the two of them talking once more.

"Knock knock." Lydia's voice, loud and muffled, shouted

through their back door. She'd let herself in before either of them could react. "I need to lift him, I'm afraid."

"Half pay for today." Seb was glib. He didn't turn around.

"Half of zero, then. But I can stay."

"He can't," Lydia quipped.

"Just go," Seb said.

THE PAIR WERE TUCKED onto a Muni train before Sam could collect his thoughts. Lydia had marched them in silence a few blocks to the stop and Sam spent most of it asking Aida to speak with his dop.

"I'm afraid I can't at the moment," she replied.

"Aida," he whispered angrily. "How is that even possible? It's my dop. It's me!"

"Samir, I'm afraid your Mirror has been put into Managed Access. You can send an override request to the manager if you like."

"Who is the manager?

"Lydia Rosales. Would you like to send the request?"

"Aida, what the hell? I pay for this service."

"I'm so sorry, Samir." The voice seemed to crack, as if Aida might cry. "I really am." The tell-tale beep sounded. She'd hung up on him.

After a short Muni ride, they now stood on an empty street outside a tiny cocktail bar called Aero in the East Cut. Like any modern bar it was unstaffed, and therefore could be quite shallow as there was no need for any offices, staff areas, or human-accessible storage areas–just a "notch" that appeared to be punched into an existing structure, deep enough for an auto-serving bar and some chairs, tucked behind a rugged all-weather curtain.

*It's infuriating that these exist*, Sam thought. *Offensive that she would even bring me.*

"We're here," Lydia sighed. "Cute, no?" She smiled and gestured at the curtain which spanned the notch. It was a cartoonish ocean scene, with two caricature dolphins smiling out as they breached the surface of the water.

"Adorable. Why?" Sam crossed his arms. He hated this, hated her, hated his dop that she wouldn't allow him to speak with. "I was at work. I needed to talk to Sebastian. If you wanted to drink, we could've stayed at Maelzel's."

Lydia scoffed. "Don't be such an NPC, Sam. You had the entire walk and ride over to say something."

"Would it have..."

"It wouldn't have mattered." She giggled. "Aw, mi novio, I'm so excited for you." She placed her hand on his cheek. "You have to meet Virginia."

"What?"

"She's here, Sam. Behind the curtain, just inside."

"Why, how?" Sam squeezed his hands into fists and paced away from her, away from the notch, away from the situation. Virginia. In his mind he was sat on the sofa in the house they shared, her in her messy bun and terrifying cat t-shirt, him too inebriated to make sense of it. She towered over him as he shrank into the cushions. "Aida, where is Virginia?"

"Samir, I'm not sure what you're asking."

"Aida!" He tripped and caught himself as he stumbled off the kerb. "Fucking answer me!"

"Hey," Lydia called out, insistent yet just above a whisper. She quickly tip-toed after him. "Where are you going?"

"Aida, please. Aida, I need a taxi." Sam stopped in the

middle of the street. "Aida! Please!" His earpiece chimed in a minor key each time he tried to summon her. *Fucking cooldown*, he thought. He'd have to wait five minutes, if not longer. "Fuck!"

"Chulo." She crept around to the front of him, a gazelle she was desperate not to spook. "I know it's a lot."

"I don't understand what's happening."

"You want this," she said in a level tone. "You organised this. I just facilitated it."

"I what? No... my fucking dop. You had my..."

"He was happy to do it."

"This is such a fucking violation."

"It's still you."

"It's not me!"

"To her, it's you."

He spun around and looked in every direction. Not a single car had passed, no trace at all of taxis, or other people. Every moment was agony as he waited. One intersection, then another, then another, then the first. He kept checking, for any sign of a taxi, or of life itself.

"Chulo, please. She's waiting."

"No!" He flicked his shoulder and twisted away from her. "No, I'm not doing it. I'll just walk."

"You'll get deported, Sam." She threw her arms in the air, exasperated.

"What?"

"If you lose your job at the club you'll get deported, and you'll be out of the Republic."

"I'm a Republic citizen. They can't kick me out. They'll send me back to LA, if they even bother doing that."

"They'll dump you in Marin, and you'll disappear. Trafficked, dead, whatever. Fs in the chat."

"Fuck this." He stormed away, determined to just walk. He didn't know where, but for now he would just walk. He could ditch his Ring somewhere, then walk somewhere else. Maybe to Maelzel's, or maybe he'd just keep moving until sunrise. She'd never find him, and he could just turn up at Seb and Mel's in the morning. Mel would understand. She'd have to.

"Sam!" As he rounded the corner, almost out of earshot, Lydia's voice cut through. "We can get you to Britain."

He froze. "You what?"

She ran up to him, her breath ragged. "Sam, we can get you there. Okay? We have a network. We have connections. You know it's true, you saw the paper. The Analog Gazette. How do you think we get them?"

"What makes you think I want to go to Britain?"

"Novio." Her chest heaved as she struggled to catch her breath. "Why are you acting stupid? We both know you do." Lydia smiled. She doubled over, her hands on her thighs. "Phew. Look. It's no problem. You get us in with Virginia, help us get what we need, and we get you transit papers and a fake work permit. Okay?"

"Fine."

"Fine? Just like that?"

Sam sighed. "Fine."

A pleasant chime rang in the room, and a digital voice followed. "Breakfast is served."

Gemma stared at the ceiling. *Breakfast.* Her mind was a swamp. She'd startled awake as the sun rose, but here she'd chosen to lie, rather than face another morning of Caroline. The water glass at the bedside was empty, but her expertise in dry-swallowing pills meant the pain in her ankle had stayed under control.

"So!" Caroline conspired with her full English. "I was thinking, for today, we should play some music. Or you could play some of yours. I'm not sure you'd want to hear me, miss, I'm dreadful compared to you."

Gemma poked at the pile of mushrooms on her plate. An uninteresting meal. She couldn't recall the last time she had a full English. She couldn't recall much of anything this morning. But for some reason the smell irritated her, and the idea of chewing anything was bothersome. "Pass."

"Oh." Caroline frowned. "Don't you like it?"

"I'm not hungry." She stared at a puddle of brown sauce.

It had an interesting, almost chemical pattern on the surface. Shimmering rainbows reminded her of an oil slick or a gasoline spill.

"Music, I mean." Caroline was a wind-up toy. She had to go until she stopped. "I don't play guitar very well, but I have a violin. It was my mum's. She insisted I learn how to play it. My father thought it was pointless, of course. But I thought since she's out of town, I could play for you. Saturday is recital, that's all. Every Saturday. That's today."

"Music." Gemma nodded. The words had made it to her, but they'd been discarded before she could process most of them. "I don't like to be told to play. I'm not a music box. I also don't like being held captive."

Caroline wrinkled her nose and her face dropped through the floor. She looked twice her age when her worry lines appeared. "You're not captive, miss. But you should eat something. I'm not sure if you've got food in your room, but I don't think you've eaten."

"I'm not hungry." She sighed. It was irritating, the way this porcelain doll tried to look after her.

"You must be."

Gemma pushed back from the table. It felt overwhelming, being subjected to this questioning. "I'm going to get some air."

"Miss!" Caroline shot out of her chair. "You have to take care of yourself! You won't heal if you don't eat. I can't force you, but I really think you should."

"Why!?" Gemma slammed her hands down and stood straight up. She ignored the terrible pain in her ankle as best she could, even as she felt herself grimace. "Why me? Where are your parents? How fucking old are you, Caroline?"

"I told you, they're in Saudi Arabia. And I'm not sure how old I am."

"Right, okay." She shook her head and tried to wake herself from this. "That's insane."

"Is it? I don't know! I've never thought about it!"

"How many bloody birthdays 'ave you had!?"

"We don't celebrate birthdays in my family!"

"How long ago did you graduate university, then?!"

"I was homeschooled, miss."

Gemma let out a guttural scream. "I'm going outside, Caroline."

She was already barefoot in the garden when she heard Caroline's reciprocal scream from upstairs, followed by the slam of her bedroom door. *Bloody child.*

The grass felt nice between her toes, at least. It was a typical overcast day, grey as could be. The morning mist left everything a bit dewy and the dirt a bit moist. Gemma was startled by the silence. No mysterious ticking of an unseen clock, no hum of an air con, no Caroline muttering to herself or to Aida. Just the occasional rustling of branches and leaves from a light breeze, which left goosebumps all over her arms. It reminded her of a night in Wales, years ago, her guitar case a pillow, her daft friend Mike at her side, neither speaking at all. It was a specific kind of moment, a kind she had never given its due in the before times. But it lacked something.

She plodded across the grass to the garden house, to Caroline's treasure trove of CDs, her accidental shrine to Gemma's past. The door was predictably locked. As she headed back to the house, the gate to the front garden looked a far more attractive option than headed back into the house with her ill-tempered jailer.

· · ·

SHE REMEMBERED the way to town, and her feet carried her there with minimal fuss. She hadn't bothered with her obnoxious period garb, though the moment she saw another person she felt underdressed in her black track bottoms and stretched UWL hoodie.

The high street did seem a tad more grounded now that she had a passing familiarity with it. Shop fronts with unprotected glass windows were a lavish indulgence, one she hadn't seen in quite some time. Even as a child they would've been covered with metal shutters, lest some hooligan like herself pitch a bin through them on their way home from the club. She did let her eyes drift around as she walked, curious if any unsecured bins were around. It was important to have options. But before she could trigger any insurance payouts, she felt she could do with some coffee.

The crowd at The Town Centre was lively, and to her relief there was no sight of the proprietor, Alastair King. Armed with a fuller understanding of the place she popped herself right up onto a stool at the counter, and with a Stepford smile ordered herself a long black.

"That's six pounds, miss."

"Ah, uh, one second." She thrust her hand into her pocket and produced the ring she'd found in Caroline's parent's room. It slid onto her index finger and, to Gemma's relief, fit fairly well. "My good man." She waved it over the black pad in the counter and smiled again as the ring vibrated angrily on her finger. The pad flashed red and the man narrowed his eyes.

"Too fast, miss. You need to hold until it flashes blue."

"Allow me," came a frail sounding voice to her left. A bony finger hovered the pad until it glowed a pleasing cerulean. "Not often we see such a beautiful fawn in our meadow."

Gemma burst out laughing, a proper goose honk of a laugh that dislodged a bit of stubborn phlegm. "Oh goodness me, you're a live wire, aren't you? Gen X, still problematic, still under the radar."

"We keep to ourselves," he said with a wink. "Never cancelled, myself."

Another voice shouted from across the room. "You know how to make a lady miss the Coronavirus lockdowns, don't you, lad? Ignore Gaz, he was raised by hand-mades."

She spun round, unsure who'd now joined the conversation. "Hand... maidens?"

The room erupted into uproarious laughter. Gemma believed she'd soon be in the midst of a bar brawl that would make a Tamil movie look unambitious.

"Hand-made television shows," the barista whispered. "Old shite." He shrugged. "Stick around long enough, you'll start to pick it up."

The cafe did seem to be a bit of a museum exhibit, near-fossilised people all around her sipped their coffees whilst reading newspapers, physical books, one even writing into a paper notepad using an old pen. "What the hell is going on here," she muttered. "Land of the lost."

"I just assumed you were someone's partner, or sister, if I'm honest."

"Assume nothing."

"These guys, they're all retired scientists and engineers."

She smiled and shook her head. "'Course they are." Her face fell. "Not anything weird, right?"

"Weird?"

"Missiles, bio-weapons or summit."

"No, nothing like that. They all worked at Magenta."

"Are you serious," she whispered. "Are you fucking seri-ous," she repeated at maximum volume. The sound of cups clattering against plates and newspapers folding made her snort. "Oh, absolute scenes. The scandal. You lot! Just in here hiding away from what you've done." She spun round on the stool and hopped down to the floor. "Shame."

"I beg pardon," said the lecherous old Gaz. "Hiding?"

"Hiding in your bloody Potemkin Village, yeah? You collaborated with the fucking enemy, made all this terrible shit, ruined the world, then used the proceeds to squirrel yourself away in here."

Discontent rumbled around the room. Gaz piped up again, the group's unofficial spokes-creep. "Bit reductive, wouldn't you say? Bit of a jump."

"Oi, fuck off, ya vile cunt." She slammed her cup down on the counter. "Wretched little men."

Gaz was indignant. "Real mouth on you, lass."

"A Potemkin Village would be to show off to a visiting monarch," rose a voice from the back. "Are we hiding, or are we showing off?"

She flung her hands up with a grunt, and let off a loud "Oi!" from the back of her throat. "Right, okay. All of you belong in the fucking Hague for what you've done to this country, innit. Nuremberg trials. Real pieces of work, all of ye. Bunch of coffee-swilling teetotal tiny-pricked," she inhaled, "Tottenham supporters."

"Excuse me!"

She backed her way toward the door. "Oh, don't deny it, I lived in Crouch End, posh Cocks the lot of you, I can spot it, can fucking smell it." She fumbled around behind her and managed to pull the door open. "And in Brum, the shame of it all. Just man up and support Villa, you twats."

Before any other protests could be lodged, or pants could be dropped, she was back on the street, alone with her rage and miserable embarrassment. She paced around to the side of the building and caught her breath against the wall. *Retired Magenta engineers*, she repeated as she shook her head. *Cunts.*

At a shop just a few hundred metres from the coffee shop, her attention was caught by a strange artefact. The shop itself was shut, but they'd seen fit to leave the lights on in their window display. It was an archaic laptop, decades old by the look of it. Open and off, but with a small spotlight shining on the keyboard. Gemma couldn't help but grin as she studied it. Each key had been meticulously painted over in white, with the letter hand-drawn back on in a variety of pinks, blues, and reds. The palm rest bore a large hand-painted face, stylised with fabulous eyelashes and a mischievous grin. *It was marvellous.* She leaned in to read a small plaque on the pedestal just below:

*"Spunky Vaio. Acrylic on plastic, artist unknown. c2000s. This Vaio captures a portrait of the child-like innocence with which we approached technology in the early 2000s. Not for sale."*

Gemma smirked and took a couple steps back. *What was this place?* A sign hung above the door to the modest shop front: *Alice's Trove of Curiosities.* Through the glass door and past the display she could indeed make out a trove of ancient junk. Piles of decaying magazines, old media, broken stereos and televisions, and stacks of crumbling computers. Along the far wall hung a single electric guitar. It appeared to have quite a bit of wear and tear, with a faded wood-grain pattern and chewed up edges on the inlay. But Gemma recognised it for what it was: a Revelator, hand-built, made to look vintage even when it was brand new. It was at least twenty years old, but far newer than the fifty or so it was pretending to be. The leather Levy's strap that hung loose behind it was properly broken in. She could feel the weight of it on her shoulder, the neck in her hand, like a phantom limb. Her fingers itched for want of the strings. She gave the door handle a couple of strong tugs, but the shop was locked tight. If it was even a shop at all.

"I'm not sure if it'll be open again," came a gentle voice from behind her.

She jumped with a yelp and braced herself against the door. "Christ."

"Sorry to startle you," the man said. He was older, maybe early sixties, with a cherubic face and a pale complexion. For this town he had dressed rather plain, in a white linen shirt, dark slacks, and a charcoal flat cap. "I still like to come look in the window from time to time, and clear my head."

"Bit of a tip in there, innit."

The man chuckled. "Dear, yes. I used to enjoy a bit of a rummage through the old copies of Radio Times, though. Husband wouldn't let me have any more around the house, but Alice didn't mind me reading them here."

"Alice?" Her eyes looked upward. "Right, Alice. You said the shop won't be open?"

"I can't imagine how." The man removed his cap and sighed. "It's so unfortunate what happened to her."

"What happened?"

"My apologies, dear." He cleared his throat. "I really must be getting home." He nodded and placed his cap back on. "Good evening."

.  .  .

HER WALK BROUGHT her to the end of the road, and she came face to face with the gate through which they'd driven in days prior. It was brutal and imposing, at least fifteen feet high, with multiple layers of fencing and a door across the pavement that would be at home in a bank vault. There was no handle as such, but the usual black pad, and a sickening light that blasted down in a circle just above. With the ring still on her finger, she approached the door and held up her hand. The angry vibrations started at once, and the pad flashed a harsh red.

"Hrm," she grumbled, and tried again. Same result whether she waved her hand, held it there, and there was no response at all if she attempted it while just holding the ring between her fingers rather than wearing it. She let out a scream and pounded her fists against it.

"It won't open," said the faint voice of a woman from far away. If she squinted, she could see someone in the far distance, standing at the opposite door across all the layers of fencing. "We've tried, trust me."

"Have you now?"

"Nobody's ever gotten in unless they were let in."

"Great. How about out?"

"Why would you want out?"

She pounded her head against the door and screamed.

"We've tried everything," the woman shouted. "Ladders, digging, even ramming it with cars. Never thought it would be the same on your side. The bits are on your side."

"The what?"

"The bits. That." Gemma squinted again to see the

woman's gesture. She pointed at a large box sat just to the side of the pavement near the fence.

"Right..." The box was nondescript and metal, with a handle to remove the outer covering, and bore several large lightning bolts and some scary warnings about a risk of death. *Shit*, she thought. *This was the electrics for the whole gate.* "Interesting, thanks. What's your name?"

"Don't got one."

"Right, well, thanks. I'm Gemma."

"Know you are. Seen you in Walsall."

"Oh?" Gemma gave an awkward smile. In spite of her best efforts, memories of Walsall were still happy ones. "You were just passing through?"

"No," she answered. "Had to leave. Here now."

"Right, well. Thanks. Again."


A PLAN HAD STARTED to brew in her mind, but it was far too dark, and she was unequipped. For now she made her way back to the high street, and eventually took an interest in a lively little club called Decibel. The din of live music and drunken conversation rolled out onto the street, as did the green and purple strobes.

A woman at the door smiled and got her attention. "It's open tone tonight, that alright?"

"Open toe," Gemma said quizzically. "Like the shoe?"

"Open tone," the woman repeated, though Gemma could scarcely pay attention. The juxtaposition of a modern club atmos with everyone's manner of dress was shorting out her senses.

"Love, I have no idea what that means. Pretend I've been in jail for five years."

"We're playing the music out loud on the speakers."

Gemma cackled. "Are you bloody serious? That's got a name now?"

"It's a twenties theme night. Here's your earplugs." She held out a small pair of earplugs in plastic wrap.

"Don't worry about it, love. Thanks for the warning."

"I can't make you wear them but I have to see you take them."

"Fine." Gemma put on a brave face as she snatched the packet out of the woman's hands. "Been to a thousand bloody shows, never in my life I've worn these buggers."

"Maybe that's why you couldn't hear me."

Zero-percent beer was many things, but it was also ineffective at helping Gemma find the strength to tolerate a situation like this one. She had her back to the wall opposite the bar, looking askance at the room, as if to remove herself from the situation. If she could float above it all, she would've chosen to do that. To allow this all to pass directly through her, to observe it as if she were a ghost.

It was cramped, much more so than she first thought, and could hold about fifty people including the staff. She noted that number didn't need to include the band. *Ruddy holograms.* The stage was so small it could never have accommodated a real band. When they converted these places into auto-gig venues they would tune the projection to be three-quarter scale, or even smaller if needed. With the right size and angle of the stage, and the right bars in place to ensure nobody could access it, the illusion was convincing enough. Any random cocktail bar was suddenly big enough to host a gig. It was enough to make her puke.

"It was a changing of the guard."

Gemma recognised the voice, and the move. Mr. King

had joined a long line of sleazy men in her career that sidled up to her at a bar and tried to chat her up.

"Alastair King. Can I call you Al?"

"I know who you are, as well. Gemma Thomson. Music industry extraordinaire, rep to the stars."

"Congratulations."

He gestured to the auto-gig, which was half-way through Queen at Wembley Stadium, a set Gemma had seen fifty times. "Perhaps it's a good metaphor for yourself, Miss Thomson. We can still observe you, even after you've died. You're just a trick of the light. Convincing to those who don't look too closely."

"Prick."

"No need to be churlish. It was a musical changing of the guard. That's all it was. Nothing was lost or gained. It's different now. Your kind couldn't adapt. Empires rise and fall."

"I don't have the energy."

"Come now. A woman of your background, your proclivities, you must remember how it all went down with Queen. The band, I mean. Their last album was so celebrated, heralded as such a triumph. It was because Mr. Mercury passed away. But Queen would've died whether Freddie did or not. Nobody was listening to that bombastic, operatic, theatric nonsense anymore. It was a changing of the guard. Tastes change. The taste has now moved on to the computational precision of auto-gen. It's not a shameful act, or some sign of societal decay. You prefer the slow pace of a horse drawn carriage, and that's quite alright. But the public taste has moved on."

"Nice speech. Wanker."

"It's nice to see all the pills and drink haven't dulled your wit."

"Sit and spin, you fucking fencepost."

"The evidence mounts."

"What is all this to you anyway, Al? Grandiose speeches, Hamilton lyrics, terrible takes. It's special, how you stalk me around doing these things."

"Just someone who had a hand in what you'd call the downfall, I suppose."

Gemma rolled her eyes. "No, I understand. Money could never buy cool. People like us, people who could write a song, carry a tune, make a crowd full of people bounce. We're cool. That could never be you. So you had to take it away."

"Have you made something then? And here I thought you were just a talentless executive like myself."

She gave his shoulder a condescending pat. "Thanks for the chat. Enjoy hiding from the monster, Dr. Frankenstein."

"That ring you're wearing," Mr. King said as she walked away. "It won't get you out."

"Fuck off." She hesitated. "I've seen it work."

"It's got a fingerprint reader on the inside of the band. It knows you're not whoever you've nicked it from."

"I don't know what you're talking about."

"I've had to pay for your Heineken Zeroes twice now, on account of your payments not going through."

Gemma's mouth contorted into a grimace. "Shit."

"Some coffees earlier, as well." Mr. King did not seem pleased. His words came through gritted teeth that Gemma strained to hear over the replicated gig. "If you're going to be living here, I'd appreciate it if you could simply avoid my establishment."

"Aw," Gemma grinned. "Word got around. I'm right chuffed."

Alastair groaned. "I don't want to spend all my time there guarding the door to prevent your entry."

"Luckily, you can't discriminate."

"I'm afraid arsehole is not a protected class under the law. In fact, I suppose if I want you dealt with, all I need to do is phone the Works Minister and let her know where you are."

"Excuse me?"

Mr. King got even closer. His voice was hoarse, and he spoke as if he was unpractised in the art of making threats. "Madam, I'm fully aware not just of who you are, but of your situation. You shouldn't exist in the first place, not as a free person." He punctuated his speech with sharp jabs at the air. "You, Miss Thomson, are misplaced property of the state, and I am happy to have you removed properly. But I have no interest in bothering or upsetting Miss Caroline. Unless of course you continue to cause trouble." He turned to leave.

"Oi," yelled Gemma as she grabbed his arm, and the battle for who could leave first continued. "Look, I didn't ask for this, okay? I tried to leave, I can't."

"I suppose that's true, on your own. But Miss Caroline could let you out. Simply ask her in the morning."

"Yeah, she's not gagging for my departure, if you understand."

"She's... ah, oh my." Alastair nodded. "Dreadful business. I do wish you luck. And I apologise for the implication that you aren't welcome, but I really must go."

"Oi! What do you mean?" Alastair made it to the street with Gemma close behind. He took note of her and seemed to speed up. "Oi! I've got nothing on, mate, I'll chase you every inch of the high road."

He kept his stride, though Gemma had kept pace enough to stay right next to him. "Haven't you found it odd you've not met her family?"

"In spite of what you might think of me, Al, I do take an interest in her. We do talk. Her parents are in Saudi right now."

"They're dead."

"Shut the fuck up."

"Murdered, I'm afraid. By escaped itinerant workers. Connies, I believe is the less savoury word they're using now?"

"Fuck. When?"

"It's not important."

"Wait," Gemma said, as rusty gears began to grind in her head. "Murdered by a connie. In West Brom? 'Cause my life got a lot more fucking difficult as a result of someone getting murdered by a connie."

"I'm sure many people get murdered by itinerant workers, madam."

She rolled her eyes. "Oh, do me a favour."

"Fine." Alastair sighed. "Yes, it was them. Arthur and Alice Newman. Arthur was one of the chief scientists at Magenta UK. It was a monumental loss."

"And Alice?"

"Alice was his wife."

"The patriarchy is alive and fucking well."

Mr. King finally stopped, and turned on the spot to face her. "I apologise for being crass, but Arthur was my dear friend. I was never particularly close with his wife. If you must know, that was her dalliance." He gestured across the road, to the antique shop. "Her... trove of curiosities. It was how she wiled away the time as a kept woman."

She found herself back in front of the shop once more, this time with Alastair at her side. "I was struck by this place earlier, I will say."

"Yes, it would rather appeal to someone of your nature. Locked up forever I suspect. No one's been able to locate the keys." They once again stared in the window. On the opposite side, away from the guitars, books, games, the more interesting paraphernalia, were metal racks of vintage clothing—rammed from one end of the store to another and filled with old flannels, jean jackets, sun dresses, and the like. Gemma stared at the disorganised assortment with a raised eyebrow.

"There's just one problem with this story, Al."

"And what's that?"

"The closet."

Alastair had put his back to Gemma, but now he looked at her over his shoulder. "The closet?"

"Caroline's parent's room. The mother's clothes were all still there, all still hung, undisturbed. And the father's were gone."

"I'm quite sure you're not implying anything. You're not that ghoulish."

"Why don't you tell me what I'm implying then?"

"I really must be off. You have a good night, madam. And welcome to our little village."

"Well!" Gemma shouted after Alastair's retreating form. "My mates at The Town Centre can help me understand!"

He paused for a retort. "I'm certain you wouldn't want to damage your standing in town by asking such an indelicate question so soon after you've arrived."

"Well, maybe you want to let me out then, so I don't go shooting my mouth off."

"Goodnight, Miss Thomson," he shouted back as he disappeared into the evening fog. "Be seeing you."

TWENTY-SEVEN

BOXES

She popped her finger through the hole in the DVD and spun it round a few times. It took two. *It's right there in the title*, Charlie had told Imogen. *The game's called 'It Takes Two'. That's because it takes two people. So, you see, you have to play it with me.*

But she never had. Charlie had never played It Takes Two with Imogen, or with anyone, in spite of how much she'd ached for it. She could've sought out people to play games with, perhaps. But that wasn't how she worked. Charlie liked to share things with the people she loved. But that wasn't how Imogen worked.

"Ma'am, are you decent?" A man's voice at the door broke her trance, and a couple of knocks turned her head. "I've got your lunch."

She stayed silent, as she always did. The man eventually entered, as he always did. She'd chosen to forget his name—each day, she chose a few recent facts to forget, hoping that by clearing a little space, an older memory might find its way forward. She'd quite like that as well. To remember a few of those a bit more clearly.

"My parents played that game," the man said as he set a plated sandwich on the table nearest her chair. "I haven't thought about it in years."

She spun the disc on her finger again, her eyes fixed on the sky through the window. It was embarrassing, she thought, to have been caught like this.

"Okay, ma'am." The man's voice quivered a bit. He seemed embarrassed as well. A western meadowlark landed on the ledge outside the window, which gave Imogen a bit of a start. "Let me know if you need anything."

"You know it, then," she whispered. The meadowlark seemed to stare in at them. It had stolen her gaze from the sky, and now she couldn't see past it.

"Yes ma'am. I watched my parents play as a kid. Can't say I ever played myself, though."

The meadowlark tilted its head in a curious way, its beak open. Perhaps it was singing, Imogen wondered, though she would have no way to hear—the glass was several inches thick. She felt the corner of her mouth curl into a smile. If she strained, she could almost hear its song in her head. A key that unlocked a memory of a time when the window actually opened. A time when the glass wasn't several inches thick.

"Would you care to play," Imogen whispered, "if you can spare the time?"

"Ma'am, I'm not sure." His voice wavered again. "I'm meant to be on duty."

"Alright." Her shoulders dropped, her eyes fell closed. The disc slid off her finger and rattled onto the floor.

"I'm very sorry." The floor creaked as he stepped backwards out of the room and into the hallway.

She didn't bother to look. At the edge of her vision lay the sandwich, lavish and uninviting. She was almost positive she hated sandwiches, though she couldn't say for sure. It wasn't worth the risk. It could stay there, on the plate, until someone came to remove it. Her eyes went back to the window. The western meadowlark, with its gorgeous yellow breast and sweet song, was gone.

Another rejection. This room was unbearable for her now. Recently she'd found a new room—the room she'd been scavenging for games, for music, for these interesting things.

It might be easier, she thought that night as she lay on the floor, to simply move into the room with the boxes.


WHEN SHE WAS in amongst the boxes, the rest of the house felt even more foreign. The kitchen, the library, the living room. These rooms were intricate and elegant, the decor well planned, all perfectly appointed. None of it was for Imogen. Not really. It was staged, a real estate listing, the kind Charlie would show her on Redfin or Zillow, the kind they'd share a laugh over. The prices were so ridiculous, therefore the staging had to match. It was a race to the top. If the house cost two million dollars, must it have sixteen thousand dollars worth of cooking utensils on display? They posited it must, and spent an evening on a formula to determine how much one needed to spend on staged furnishings given the asking price of your home.

It was those evenings that Charlie and Imogen shared a love of, and only those. The work brought them joy individually, but rarely together. Not the arguments, though they did not shy away from an argument. And never the games.

But this man, the man who lingered each evening,

enjoyed them. And he enjoyed this room, the one that they'd left alone, the one they hadn't staged. The one they'd stored her collections in. Cardboard boxes packed full of decayed history, disintegrated plastic, warped vinyl, and a few chairs. It had occurred to Imogen one evening that she had never been in this room. The room at the end of the hallway, past her bedroom and past the bathroom. The room that she had never bothered to explore, because she never bothered to explore at all. How long had these things been trapped in here? How long had she? A decade, perhaps? More? She didn't think it would be less.

And so Imogen moved into the room with the boxes. Where they'd once tended to find her in the kitchen for her breakfast, and the den for her lunch, and the dining room for her dinner, they'd now find her in this room for all three. In between she'd keep the door shut so as to not be disturbed. And then she'd look in a box. Stacks and stacks of boxes, none of which were labelled, all of which were hers. But it wasn't hers to know why they'd kept this room from her, why they'd kept these things from her. It took time for her to remember these things were hers at all.

Sometimes a box would overwhelm her. The reason didn't always make sense. One might contain old letters, old notes, old greeting cards. These were curious, even interesting. But these were fragments of an ordinary life. It was the other boxes that surprised her. A box with some record albums, or a box with some cassette tapes. Was it the indirectness of it all? Emotion exploded out of her as if forced by a coiled spring. The feelings formed a connective tissue between herself and her past in a way the memories could not.

"It frustrates them that you're in here so much," said the

lingering man to another, some unseen man, someone still in the hallway.

"Well, I'm here by myself at night. So I don't actually believe they know I'm in here."

"Maybe I tell them."

"Do you?"

Imogen grinned as the man flew around the screen. Today's box appeared at first to contain an old Sega Genesis. She noted after inspection that it was a modern replica, made to look old. But it was just as fun, and it meant the pads worked well. Better than the original, she believed. An original would be long dead at this point.

"Would it bother you if I did?"

"Nothing bothers me. So long as they change the lining in my cage."

"I'm taking off. Stay frosty."

"Night."

The door shut, leaving the two of them alone in the room. The man played the Genesis in silence for hours.

Imogen awoke the next morning as the sun rose, alone in her overstuffed chair. Today would bring another box, and perhaps some new feelings. There weren't many left. She looked at the stack and noticed something amiss. A new box, smaller and of a different design. sat atop the others. The flaps had been folded shut rather than sealed with tape. She pulled them open with a slight amount of force, desperate to not make a sound.

Most of the box was empty, though what it did contain fascinated her. A printed book, a small leaflet, and a note. The book appeared to be a memoir, and Imogen set it to one side. The leaflet was of poor quality, printed on paper so thin she could scarcely read it if the sun struck the back. She pressed it against the white wall, and the header across the top became clear: *The Analog Gazette.*

Her hands trembled as she unfolded the paper. A small number of words, curiously handwritten.

*I know who you are.*

TWENTY-EIGHT
ESPRESSO

The house seemed as she left it when Gemma arrived back. Dark and quiet. Caroline must've still been in her rage-induced slumber. That made things even easier. First, head upstairs, collect her things. Then, scour the house for tools. This was never meant to be a permanent stay, and she had no interest, and no business, getting wrapped into local drama. Caroline was a tragedy. But getting involved with tragic figures is how she wound up stuck in Walsall for far, far too long.

Preparing her things proved to be a rather uncomplicated process. A couple of items of clothing, the shattered splinters of her guitar, a few compact discs, and an unopened gift from that fucking dunce Mike. *Sure, fine. I'm travelling light.* She zipped the case shut and slipped her arms through the straps. *So,* she told herself. *That was that.* In the morning she'd ransack the garage, garden shed, kitchen drawers, until she found what she needed. And then she'd spring herself from this nightmare, courtesy some tampering with the electrics on the exit gate.

Down the stairs she ran, and the front door was in sight. Nothing between her and freedom. Her ankle felt better-ish, with shoots of pain still breaking the surface every so often. Nothing the rest of her pain med prescription couldn't tackle. *Wait*, she thought, as she ran back through her mental inventory. The bottle of pills wasn't there. She'd given that room a proper ransack. They were gone. She patted her pockets, in case she'd perhaps taken them with her into town. *Nothing. Fuck.*

"Sweetie?" She shouted as she moved through the downstairs. The kitchen, the drawing room, the lounge, all the random rich people rooms. A dozen pieces of unjustifiable furniture, but no Caroline. "Hello?!" She doubled back, redoubled back, checked every closet, under every bed, and even located onto the tools she needed for her original mission—because she needed them to break into the garden house, which turned out to be one more place that Caroline wasn't.

GEMMA AWOKE on the floor as the sun came up, but it wasn't the sun that woke her. It was Alastair King.

"Jesus Christ," she yelped.

Alastair jolted back across the threshold. "I was calling on Miss Caroline, and saw the door to the back house was open." He looked across the room. The stereo was pulled away from the wall, a byproduct of Gemma's descent into madness the night before. She'd spent at least an hour in a fruitless attempt to make the stereo play something, or even turn on.

"I tried," Gemma said. "I failed." Her breath was vile,

and her mouth tasted of blood. "This thing is fucked. Shame, really. Irreplaceable."

"Ah," Alastair said. He extended a hand and helped Gemma off the floor. "Quite simple really, though I understand why you might not have been aware. Devices need to be authorised to draw power from the grid. The socket handshakes with the device. It's rather sensible, in my view, a sensible solution to the energy crisis of, well," Alastair chuckled, "whatever year that was. It's been a rollout decades in the making. Moseley was happy to do it."

Gemma was roiled. "Says the man who runs an english coffee house from the bloody sixteenth century."

"Good ideas don't go out of fashion, madam. There's a difference between curation and wallowing in piles of old filth, unable to move forward, allowing yourself to fall out of modern society." He closed his eyes, and his face seemed to almost convey an emotion other than arrogance. "I'm afraid that's part of why we're here."

"Go on, I'm listening." Gemma wrestled the stereo the rest of the way away from the wall. There it was: the chipped socket.

"I, well." Alastair didn't seem able to concentrate.

Gemma grabbed hold of the nearby lamp and unplugged it. Plastic casing was pried apart, wires stripped, chips extracted and repurposed. Sweat dripped from her forehead, profanity flew, and Alastair decided on silence as the operation unfolded, much of which remained unseen behind the stereo cabinet.

"There." Gemma crawled out from behind the unit and pushed the power button on the stereo. With a loud click the display lit up and blinked all zeroes. Alastair stared in disbelief. She pushed the eject button and the tray dutifully popped out. "Grab that," she barked, and pointed at a compact disc case on the floor.

With some hesitation Alastair picked it up. "What's this?"

She snatched it from his hand, popped open the case, and flung the disc into the unit. After a few seconds, a clamour of instruments and shouting filled the room. "Christ." She burst out laughing. "This is audio terrorism. It's the best we could do, really. Chinny had them trapped in his house for a month just to get this. Dreadful. Surprised we weren't all brought in on charges, they'd have stuck."

"You worked on this?"

She nodded, and felt justified in her smugness. "I did. They're called Killslop. I can't recommend it. But now this works again, Caroline can listen to any of these." She gestured around to the absolute trove of discs which lined the walls.

"I wish you hadn't done that."

"Excuse me, Mr. King. You can just thank me, you have that option."

"I wasn't entirely forthcoming." He stepped forward and pushed the stop button. The room fell silent. "Caroline's mother, Alice. She died by suicide."

"Christ."

"She was so miserable here. So miserable with the world. And we were so resentful of it. You see, Alice was poisoned against her own family by nostalgia."

"By nostalgia." Gemma flailed her arms as she paced the room. "You think fucking nostalgia caused this poor woman to kill herself. Poisoned against her bloody family, what the fuck? What does that even fucking mean, Al?"

"As I said, and as you've learned, most of us here are of a

certain background. And as Alice grew to loathe us, the way you loathe us, she sought refuge in…" He gestured around the room. "This. There's no virtue in fetishising the past. No protein. It's sweets for dinner."

"Oi, right." She growled. "Maybe that's how she still felt like she belonged in this world. And yer a prick for implying it's wrong, yeah? Maybe if you'd bloody supported her, rather than just discarding her, she'd still be here."

"I won't pretend to understand mental health."

Gemma grumbled. "Ye've done a good job there, mate." It had begun to gnaw at her that they hadn't discussed Caroline being missing.

"Yes, well. Shortly after she left us, so did Arthur."

"Al, you were calling on Caroline. She's not here."

"She's inside? She's a rather late sleeper."

"I'm not being funny or anything, she's gone, Al. I haven't seen her since yesterday morning."

"Are you being…"

"I searched the entire house. To a mad degree, I will add."

Alastair nodded. "Right."

She gathered her tools and bundled them into a canvas bag she'd found hanging on the doorknob. "Right."


THE TRUCE WAS FRAGILE, and formed in silence. They trundled out into the frigid morning, and it was no surprise to Gemma that Alastair was unimpressive in a tense situation. He stayed a few paces behind and showed no hint of an idea, content to mutter and moan rather than offer genuine assistance.

"I believe it to be prudent for us to head to The Town

Centre and organise our efforts there. With any luck, Miss Caroline has done likewise."

Gemma scoffed. "Is that your plan, then? Just go see if she's popped in for a coffee?" She glanced across the high street, and caught sight of Alice's antique shop. Her smile grew.

"Search and rescue," Alastair groaned. "You ineffable buffoon. We'll establish a command centre and enlist help from others."

"Please! Where are you even from, Al? Who taught you to speak like this?"

"It's called an education. We haven't all come up on a diet of ready salted and short-form video."

"Christ!" Gemma pulled her arms into her hoodie. "I can't, Al. I'm fucking knackered, I've not had any coffee. Don't you work at Magenta? Can't you just track her location?"

"I am retired, madam, from Britain's premier artificial intelligence firm, which happened to be acquired by Magenta. And no, we cannot simply track one of our users. There are regulations."

Gemma stared into the window of the antique shop. Her back ached as all of her tensed muscles began to relax. "Fine, please, let's just walk to the fucking Town Centre. She's not a bloody child, she'll be fine."

Gemma pushed her palms into her eyes in hope of relieving the pressure. He was a Chinese finger trap of a man. Everything in her wanted to unmake him, or at least humiliate him. He was just the next in her ignominious career of doing just that to so many like this. Scenarios played out in her mind, and they all ended in more disagreement, more arguing, more exhaustion. All with Gemma having left this place alone, on foot, with nothing but her bindle and a smashed guitar. She yawned and stared down at her ridiculous period-accurate boots. Her feet had already swollen inside them.

"Alastair, I can't do this. Can we not do this?"

He pulled his arms tightly against himself. "I'm not sure what you mean."

"I'm so tired. I don't want to do..." She flailed her arms between the two of them. "This."

"I don't..." He gave his charcoal waistcoat a tug. He was quite a dapper man–trim, well-dressed–and she hadn't wanted to give him credit for any of it.

"Smart fit." She let a smile start to form. "A little surprised you don't still wear your Eton uniform." They'd arrived outside the coffee house, which was locked and dark. A thick fog hung over the street. Gemma imagined it all pouring inside were she to push the door open.

"The pinstripes didn't suit me." Alastair pressed his hand against the plate hidden inside the faux stone of the entryway, and with a subtle click the latch on the door released.

Gemma sighed and shook her head as they entered. A sudden craving for a cigarette threw her off balance. They would hit from time to time, and she'd made peace with knowing they would do so for the rest of her life. "You old enough to smoke, Al?"

"Only just. I imagine we're around the same age."

"Don't suppose you have any lying around in here. Or would that turn this noble house into a den of iniquity?"

"I believe I have some tobacco and some papers, yes. We've got a bit of time before others start to turn up, it's rather earlier than I realised."

She perched at the bar and repressed her admiration as

Alastair rolled two impeccable cigarettes. She let hers lie on the bar as he proceeded into operating the espresso machine, which he did with equal parts skill and grace. The sounds transported her to a time when this was her routine–the grinding of the beans, the steam letting off, the frothing of the milk. And the smell of fresh coffee sent tingles through her brain. Almost as a reflex her hand wanted to hold a phone, to scroll Apple News, to read chaotic all-caps, no-subject emails from Chinny, poetic musings from Samir, the inevitable stress and stammer from Eamon.

"One latte, madam." There was a pleasing ceramic clink as the mug hit the plate. Alastair seemed so at home behind the bar, cloaked in the artifice of a barista. That, plus his manicured salt-and-pepper beard, would have made him a shoo-in for proprietor of an of overpriced stall in Borough Market.

"This reminds me so much of home." She stared into the foam and whispered to nobody in particular as she took the first sip.

"Home," Alastair said. "The colony?"

"Christ, no. The colony wasn't home. London was home."

"Unsurprising, I suppose. You exude a certain street-wise toughness."

"The mean streets of Maida Vale."

"Now that, madam, does surprise me."

"You think so little of me. I was beautiful and sophisticated once, Al. A powerful, talentless executive."

Alastair took a sip of his own latte. "You're still one of those things."

She studied him from across the bar. The coffee oiled her joints and gears. She rubbed her shoulders and stretched her neck, the usual aches of age compounded by having slept on the floor. "So." She affected a posh accent. "Britain's premier artificial intelligence firm."

"In fact yes. I was one of the first employees, actually, along with Caroline's father. My sister founded the company. I was what you might've called a... nepo hire." His shoulders slumped, but he straightened soon after. "Anyroad, we used the proceeds from the sale to start this village."

"Your sister lives here too? That's someone I'd like to meet."

"Yes, I would as well. She went to the States shortly after the sale, to be with her partner. None of us knew who that was. We never saw her again. That was nineteen years ago."

Her mug clattered back into the plate. "Fuck. She just..."

"Right, I'd rather..."

"Right. Fuck. I'm so sorry."

"You don't have to feign empathy. I know you already think me a monster. Or at very least, responsible for some kind of atrocity in the creative arts. It was obviously never my intent."

"Hitler was an artist. I can't imagine you've ever so much as drawn a stick figure."

"Madam, I'm not sure how to respond to that."

"I just like the face you make when you're uncomfortable." She flashed a mischievous grin. "I can't hold you responsible for... what did you call it? A changing of the guard. If it hadn't been you, it would've been someone else."

"That's gracious of you, if perhaps a bit too much so."

"I'm giving you credit for this mad village. Inspired work. Truly unwell, the mind that concocted this notion."

"A borrowed notion. Hardly the first planned community in Britain. The Poundbury of the Midlands."

"But the barmy get-ups. The rules. The Victorian coffee house. That's a bold vision."

"Restoration, not Victorian."

Gemma sighed. "Sure, mate."

"But," Alastair continued quickly, "I do appreciate the kind words. If that's how you intended them." He cleared his mug and began the idle tasks of a man behind a bar. He wiped the machine down, tidied up loose sachets, and packed away the milk. "May I ask you something a bit delicate?"

Gemma rolled her shoulders. Thunderous cracks emanated from them. "I'm very delicate."

"How did you end up, how do I put this..." His hands flapped about. He seemed to regret already having done his tasks.

"Incarcerated?"

"Rather, yes."

"Fired. From the label, when we were acquired by yourselves. I was broke, I didn't find another job in time."

"So you..."

"Got the envelope, indeed. You know the law. No job, we find you one." Her eyes were cast down, even as she tried to project confidence. "I was frogmarched to Wales for a work detail at the nuclear plant." *Of course this doesn't bother me,* she told herself, in the hope that Alastair believed it too.

"I'm so sorry, Gemma. I can only imagine for someone like yourself, your job in music was quite a large part of your identity."

Gemma tensed up, and her back was shot through with pain. "Not your fault, Al." A lump got caught in her throat, and she gave a loud hack. "Christ, you've gone straight in for me." A single tear rolled down her cheek.

"Er, well. Oh, my." Alastair hemmed and hawed. "I've rather put my foot in it there." He smoothed out his waistcoat again.

She once more thought of Sam, and of Eamon, and of Chinny. This place reminded her too much of the one near her old flat. And of that twinge of pride she felt as she saw the rack of compact discs for sale on the counter, and heard one of her handmade artists playing on a speaker in the corner. *There's still going to be a market for handmade*, she'd said to the manager. *There always will be.*

"I learned I'd been fired in a cafe quite like this one," she offered as she finished the latte. "I suppose it's a bit thick with memories."

"In a cafe? Were they concerned about some kind of incident at the office?"

She chuckled. "I read it on my phone." As she thought about it, she worked into a proper laugh. "In the news."

"That's just standard, isn't it?"

"I suppose it is." She sniffled and closed her eyes. With a vigorous shake of her head, she regained her composure. "Shall we gather up our precocious little friend?"

"Yes," Alastair said as he pocketed their cigarettes. "Perhaps she's looped back round, returned home."

"I know where she is." Gemma smirked. "I've known the entire time, love. Come on."

---

HER HAND PUSHED THE DOOR, and this time it opened. "Thought I'd never get in here," Gemma said to Alastair as they both entered Alice's Trove of Curiosities.

"So Caroline had the keys after all," Alastair muttered as

they walked in. "None of us relished the thought of having a locksmith open this door. How did you know?"

"I saw the lights were on when we walked past an hour ago."

"You're a wicked lady, madam."

The inside of the trove was more glorious than Gemma could've imagined. Past the art house pieces lay evidence of genuine, if obsessive, enchantment: meticulously sorted magazines, curated selections of young adult books, even handfuls of video game cartridges, all labeled and catalogued in salvaged boxes and crates. The walls were lined with posters and pop art, musical instruments, and shelves full of nonsensical bric-a-brac that would nary warrant a mention in the history books. It was an embarrassing and spectacular way to take up space—so many terrible novels, cheap injection-moulded toys, and ill-conceived games. It moved Gemma to tears that Caroline's mother put effort into collecting or preserving any of this.

"It's even worse than I remember," Alastair said under his breath.

Gemma gave him a cold glance. "Caroline?"

"I'm here," came the meek voice from the back of the shop. In the near-darkness they picked their way through the piles and shelves until they reached the back. Caroline sat in an ornate rocking chair which had seen far better days.

"I think you have something of mine," Gemma said as she kneeled down.

"Yes, I have them." Caroline poked Gemma's finger. "You took my mother's Ring. So I took your pills."

Gemma inhaled sharply. "Right, okay. Yes. That's fair." She slid it off of her finger and placed it into Caroline's palm. "I'm very sorry about that, love. Really, I am."

"So you're leaving then."

"I'm afraid I have to, yes. I'm sorry about that as well."

She turned to face Gemma. Her face was splotched red and streaked with tears. "Why do you have to?"

"Because... I don't know, because I do."

"I don't think you have to, I think you want to. You don't like it here. Because there's too many rules."

She set her bag of tools aside, and her joints cried out as she sat cross-legged beside Caroline. "There's a fair few rules here, yes. But that's not why I have to go. I told you, love. I have to get to Liverpool to see my friend."

"I know. It's just sad."

"This is your mum's shop, isn't it?" Gemma eyed the Revelator she'd seen through the window, still hung on the wall. "She had great taste in guitars. Does she play?"

"Sometimes." Caroline sniffled. "But it's okay. You don't have to do that."

"Do what?"

"I know she's gone. You don't have to speak about her like she's still around."

"Of course," Alastair said as he kneeled down as well. "This is new for all of us. Your parents were good friends of mine, you know."

"Mum didn't like you, Mr. King." She looked between the two of them. "You know, Gemma is a good friend of mine. I wish you wouldn't be so rude to her."

Gemma smirked. "Yeah, Al."

"And you." Caroline cast her gaze in Gemma's direction. "Mr. King is a founder of the town. You really should show him a bit more respect."

Alastair pursed his lips. His eyes betrayed how amused he was by Caroline's comment.

"I can do that." The torrent of anger Gemma expected to feel didn't arrive. *Besides, I'd rather he not have the satisfaction.*

"Your friend and I have come to a rapprochement," Alastair added. "I do think your mum would've rather liked Miss Thomson. They share a passion for...." He glanced around the room. "Artefacts."

"You two fight like you and mum did, Mr. King." Caroline looked up at Gemma, who had drifted toward the acoustic guitars on the far wall. "But you're going to Liverpool to see your music friend."

Gemma lowered her head. Her insides froze up. She couldn't face the poor girl.

"I do wish I could see what it was like," Caroline added. "But I know I can't. I know there are rules. And I have responsibilities here. I need to reopen mum's shop. It's what she would want."

Alastair tutted. "Dear, as much as we're fond of you, and as fond of your mum and dad as we were, you're twenty-five years old. That's old enough to make your own decisions."

"Are you serious," Gemma blurted out, beside herself. "She's twenty-five?" She cocked her head and sighed. "I wish I could say I see myself in you, little miss. But I was a bloody mess at twenty-five. I didn't own a single bodice." Her eyes met Alastair's. "I don't think I'm allowed to let you come with me, though."

Caroline joined Gemma in staring at Alastair.


THE BOOT of the car came as close as it could to slamming, before the mechanism intervened and pulled it the rest of the way gently. Gemma could hear the motors put in the work as the lid struggled against a full wardrobe of Caroline's elaborate outfits. In the back seat, there had been a spare bit of space left over for Gemma's guitar case.

"This is a mistake," she said to Alastair. Caroline's boundless energy had taken her back into the house for one final sweep of forgotten items. It gave Gemma a bit of space to regret the invitation.

"You've advocated strongly for this. I'm surprised to hear you say that."

"She's got a life anyone in this country would kill for. She shouldn't give that up."

"It's temporary. Maybe you'll find a bit of her mother in there, or maybe a bit of her father. Or maybe a hybrid. But I believe you're right, she deserves the chance to find out for herself."

Gemma leaned her forehead against the roof of the car and sighed. "So long as I can keep her alive. And maybe I'll find her whole, actual father. Though he better pray I don't."

"We'd rather appreciate if you did, yes. For the second, if he could be unharmed, I wouldn't mind."

"No promises. But thanks for trusting me with the town's own daughter."

Caroline burst back into the garage in her travelling outfit, which Alastair had already warned her about. It was her usual petticoat nonsense, accented with a dramatic grey cloak, the baggy hood pulled up over her head. Across her shoulder was yet another bag stuffed to bursting with various bits, compact discs, a couple of books, and that's just what Gemma could manage to see.

"Christ, we'll be lucky if the car clears the ground. You're coming back here, you know," Gemma chastised. "You can't live on the road with me."

"We'll see," Caroline said with a twinkle.

Alastair laughed. "We most certainly will not see."

She tucked herself into the front seat and the door pulled itself shut behind her.

"I wonder if she's ready to go," Gemma deadpanned.

"Here," Alastair said. "Take these." He held out the two cigarettes he'd rolled.

Gemma nodded. "Right. Thanks, Al. None for the kid, of course."

"On that topic. Maybe," he stammered. "Maybe, rather than let her come back on her own, you could bring her back yourself. There's plenty of room for you here in Moseley. If things don't work out in Liverpool, of course."

She slugged him in the arm. "Maybe I will. Mr. King."

"I'd like that. I think it would rather make sense."

Gemma smiled. "I think I'd like it, too."

## TWENTY-NINE
## BEAST

The car hurtled down Embarcadero, with Samir the sole occupant. It had been sent to get him. He wasn't sure if everyone got this treatment, or if this was because of who he knew. Lydia's promise echoed in his head: *this time next year you'll be in London.*

"Aida, please tell me this is a nightmare."

"Samir, your situation could meet one definition of the word nightmare. For example, a terrifying or very unpleasant experience, situation, or event."

"Comforting. Thanks."

"Of course, Samir. Let me know if you need anything."

*Virginia had been confused as they sat with an empty stool between them in the notch. They'd already agreed to this. But now he was acting shocked, like he didn't remember. Like they were almost strangers. "You'd never disagree with your dop, no?" Of course not, he'd answered. It's just a tough adjustment. So then it was settled. He hadn't seen her that happy in a long time.*

"Samir Patel." Aida's voice boomed out of the car's

speakers this time. "As we have a bit of time until we reach our destination, you might find it useful to review the building's health and safety information, which is appearing now on the screens located in the backs of each seat."

He glanced up at the screens and wished he could somehow get even lower. Curled up on the floor like a dog on a road trip. Ignored for the most part, and called a good boy just for being silent.

*"I can't believe you're in town," he'd said as if it was some kind of important revelation. Virginia confirmed she was, and it was permanent. As permanent as anyone's living arrangement can ever be, she added, which he'd taken personally. "So you're living in one of the dormitories over on Divis," he'd asked as he fumbled for an interesting topic. He knew his dop would've been far more interesting. It had the collected knowledge of humanity to draw from, should it want. "No," she'd corrected. "I live in Magenta Tower."*

Traffic going into the East Cut was slow and orderly, as the cars negotiated with each other to their assigned parking. It meant a tailback that could take an hour to get through. Aida had chimed early that morning and let Samir know when he had to leave in order to arrive on time. She knew where everyone was coming from, where everyone had to go, and each car's designated time-slot at any point of contention along the route. Samir figured it still would've been faster to walk.

*"I obviously wish we'd come to this agreement sooner." Virginia had reached across the gap between them and interlocked her fingers with his. "Years ago, really. But the second best time was now." She'd given his hand a squeeze and smiled with her eyes. "You should know I'm seeing someone.*

*But I've ensured I will not be your direct manager, in case anything changes with our situation."*

He curled up on the floor as the bumps from the road rattled his bones. He wasn't a passenger, he was just freight. "We're approaching Magenta Tower," Aida boasted, "which is our final destination." Samir pulled himself off the ground and back into the seat, just as the car made the turn into campus. Two massive digital screens flanked the driveway, both bearing the image of Magenta founder and CEO Rebecca Prue. Her eyes seemed to follow as they entered, and he would've sworn she gave a nod of approval. "Please ensure you've collected your belongings," Aida continued. "Your orientation coordinator will meet you as you arrive. Thanks again, and welcome to your new career at the Magenta Corporation."

The aptitude assessment was swift, given how much they already knew about him. He'd spent quite a bit of his life adjacent to equipment–hooking it up, tearing it down, figuring out why it didn't work–so he'd been slotted into the role of Physical Maintenance. The orientation coordinator flashed a toothy grin when he heard the results.

"That makes you Aida's hands," he said with a clap. "This is your uniform! All of Aida's hands wear these." He held out a neatly-folded grey uniform.

Sam took it with a slight frown. "Aida's hands?" The uniform was stiff, a crinkled canvas material, which made a rhythmic swish-swish sound as it moved. He looked forward to hearing that sound as he walked for ten hours a day.

"Well, she can't fix things herself. She might know what to do, but she needs your help to do it. Repairing sensors, oiling doors, flipping tipped robots back over. It's a very important role, Sam! And you've been selected!"

Providing orientation for new hires seemed to be something they did more often in years past, and perhaps not so much these days. The orientation room was a traditional looking classroom that could've held about twenty people, and Samir was the only one. He still sat a couple of rows back so as to not seem too eager. The coordinator deposited him and then exited, but that didn't mean he'd been turned over to his own devices. Screens at the front of the room flickered to life and the lights clicked off.

"Welcome to Magenta," began the pompous narration, "and to Magenta Tower, the Parthenon of Innovation. The story of Magenta is one of humble beginnings and massive ambitions. Founded in 2020 by a young Rebecca Prue, right here in San Francisco, within three years the company had ascended to be the dominant force in both artificial intelligence and home automation. By 2028, Rebecca had..."

Samir tried to focus. It was interminable, and the boredom sought to overwhelm him. He'd already heard enough of Magenta's corporate propaganda from Virginia to last a lifetime, and the sight of Rebecca Prue still made him queasy. He didn't know how he could bear to hear her life story set to patriotic music.

"Hello?" The door slid open, and Virginia poked her head in. "Sorry to interrupt."

"Hi." He gestured to the indoctrination. "Just watching this."

"...the breathtaking Magenta Tower, completed in 2030, is seen around the world as an enduring symbol of..."

"This video is rather florid," Virginia remarked. "I'm not sure you will find much value in it."

"Hello, I'm Rebecca Prue, founder and CEO of Magenta." Ms. Prue had appeared on the screen now. She faced down the camera as she strolled down a path through some kind of lush greenery. "Soon you'll get to walk where I am now, through our magnificent botanical garden on the fifth floor terrace."

Samir cracked up. "This video seems to mostly be about the building."

"It..." Virginia grimaced. "It is." She joined him and laughed out loud for a moment, but pulled herself right back together. "I'm not sure why."

"How old is it? Rebecca looks so young."

"I'm fine authorising you to skip the rest of this."

"Really," Samir said with a touch of sarcasm. "You would do that for me?"

She gave an awkward wink. "I am rather important here, you know."

As irritating as it was to admit, Sam did find the building impressive. Virginia took him floor by floor, a whirlwind tour of the bits she liked, the bits she didn't, and some bits he'd need to know about for his job.

"You have a very important and straightforward role," she said as they walked through the ground floor atrium. "You'll receive notifications on a regular basis from Aida about tasks that need accomplishing somewhere in the Tower, and you'll conduct them. Instructions are available both at a macro and micro level depending on your skillset and experience. Sometimes it's very physical. Something needs tightening, something needs wiping down. And sometimes it's programming related."

"Programming? I don't know how to program."

"It's..." Virginia tilted her head and gave a tight smile. "Magenta devices don't require programming in the sense you're thinking of, with computer languages. They speak to each other in what you might call plain English. They just do it very fast and with a lot of shorthand. And you speak to them the same way if you need to alter their behaviour. The best way to understand is to have Aida let you eavesdrop on a chat between, say, a refrigerator's temperature sensor and its compressor."

"I suppose I am well suited then," Sam said. "I do have a decent relationship with Aida."

"No," Virginia retorted. "Nobody has a relationship with Aida. It's not a digi. It does not retain a history of what you've said to it, it builds no context with you."

"So this job is entry level," Sam replied.

"Yes."

He shook his head. "I have so many years of experience. I don't understand."

"What's to understand? This is a job, which you need. You've not had real work since you left the music label."

"I worked at Maelzel's."

"A real job," she scolded. "At a real company, with a real future." Her tone softened. "Listen, Samir. I know how difficult this is for you. It's why I'm so proud of you for reaching out and asking in the first place."

Virginia's delicate handling of him, the way she used to, was a gut punch. He hadn't reached out, and he didn't want to be here. And she knew nothing of Lydia. He would have to come clean at some point and confess his sins. Unless he found a way to just introduce them organically? *Maybe that's all Lydia wants,* he thought. *Just a way to meet Virginia socially, a woman who would otherwise be entirely inaccessible, a woman who spends her entire life within these walls.*

"There's one last place on the tour which I thought might

help you acclimate. It's Thursday, so we tend to go for drinks."

"Oh, where?"

"There is a staff bar on the sixth floor."

"Oh," Sam said. *Could it be that easy?* "You know, it would, uh." His mind raced faster than he could assemble the words. "What time, uh, what would you think about? I'm sorry. I'm not making sense."

"We can head up now." Virginia touched her ear and whispered something. The lift doors opened, a number six already lit up on the display inside.

"Wait," Sam blurted out. "Wait, wait. I was thinking, if I could bring you around to Maelzel's. I know Sebastian would love to see you. It's been so long."

"Samir, no." She stepped onto the lift and beckoned him to follow. "I don't tend to leave the campus. Neither does the person we are meeting."

"Alright." He cursed himself and stepped into the lift. *At least the office had a bar*, he thought with a flicker of hope. *Buoyed by the promise of alcohol.*

It was immediately extinguished when the doors opened. Not by the decor, though it could've well done so: grey on grey with a white floor, clean lines, a row of drink dispensers on the back wall, and dozens of round high-top tables, also grey. But by the immediate sight of someone that could destroy Samir's mood on his highest days.

"Sam," Virginia said as she joined the man at his side. "You remember Carlos."

THIRTY

CATACLYSM

*Five years ago.*

Samir felt sure his chest would cave in with every breath. The bartender, oblivious to his plight, lined up another four shots. Gemma Thomson licked her lips and splayed herself wide along the bar, her back against the brass handhold. Her satin blue top shimmered under the stage lights and her eyes were alight with mischief.

*She can't fucking expect us to...* Sam's mind sputtered. *No more.* But the words didn't reach his lips. Instead his eyes wandered all over, between the bar-top, the rotund man with his bald head and denim shirt, the AJ on the stage in the distance. Anything to avoid looking at her.

"I don't think Virginia and I want more shots," shouted Carlos over the algorithmic drone. Colleague of Virginia's and occupier of the top spot on Samir's shit list, Carlos been quick to intervene all night if he thought it might make him look good. "We're just not drinkers like yourselves." He wore a Magenta staff t-shirt, to ensure even strangers knew he was insufferable.

"You heard the lady," Gemma replied with a smirk, her head drooped low. "The lady's keeper has spoken. Or, whatever this one... is to that one." Her bony finger waggled between Carlos in his ridiculous leather jacket, and Samir's wife Virginia who stood just a bit too close to him.

"Honey," Sam simpered to Virginia. He felt embarrassed the moment he did it. "Did you want another drink?"

"Carlos is right," Virginia deadpanned in reply. "I think we've had enough alcohol."

"Woof," Gemma said. The automated music seemed to be getting louder with every beat. "Gang, I'm out."


SAM EMERGED from Koko to see Gemma already in the far distance, and the gap widened by the second. *Fuck, her legs are far too long.* He sprinted to keep up, perhaps a bit recklessly, as an auto-cab slammed its brakes at a cross to avoid him.

"What the hell," Sam sputtered out of breath as he caught her. "Why did you leave?"

"Maybe because you brought your teetotal girlfriend to our gig. What is she, four feet tall? Terrifying, like that ruddy Annabelle doll."

"Partner, not girlfriend. And she's five foot one."

"So where is she? On her way out to meet us? Or back to the shire then?"

"Gemma, enough! I told her we had a showcase and I wouldn't be able to get her in. She understands that."

"Right, basically handed her to that co-worker of hers then, did you? They'll be off for a quick go."

"She'll just go back to the hotel. Carlos isn't like that."

"Are you mad? Are you *actually* mad, or are you just blind? Did you see the two of them? Did you see his slavish devotion to her all night?" She stopped her retreat and spun around to face him. Her long arms flailed, as if controlled by strings. "You could do with a bit of that, mate! If I'm honest."

"That's not fair!" He took a couple of steps away, fearful he may get inadvertently struck by swinging limbs. "Again, I have a partner!"

"Are you serious? Devotion to her, you fucking mailbox! Not to me!" She gave him a shove, her reach inescapable. "Christ. Would you look at the state of this city? Look at all this." A helicopter swooped overhead, and the sound of the blades gave a temporary reprieve from the scene unfolding around them. Maybe a hundred metres ahead of them was a mass of what appeared to be protestors massed across from a building striped yellow and green, the tell-tale colours of a government Job Centre. Signs and placards waved, too far away to read, and incomprehensible shouts came through a tannoy held by police opposite them.

"Jesus," Sam mumbled.

"Heard on the BBC there's going to be a rolling blackout again tonight."

"A blackout? Like, no electricity?"

"When they said the government wanted to take the power away from the people nobody knew how literal they were being. Yeah?"

Sam chuckled at the terrible joke. *It felt nice to break the tension,* he thought. "I suppose I should head back. It's getting bad out here."

"Nonsense," Gemma replied. "Standard night in London, innit. Besides, we've arrived."

She pointed to a door just ahead, a rather standard Victorian entryway, up a few stairs, painted all black, and otherwise unmarked. Sam would've assumed it, like every other door around on this street, led to yet another mansion block converted into flats.

"The Thin Veil," she nodded. "Cracking little club. Always some dreadful noise on stage. If you don't have tinnitus already, you will now."

She turned the knob and stepped inside, then descended straight down a steep flight of stairs into an expansive, low-ceilinged basement. Fairy lights strung along the brick walls gave just enough glow to see, and some clamp lights pointed directly at a wooden riser in the corner. Sam assumed it must be the stage, as through the dense crowd he could see a woman setting up some kind of equipment. The crowd was dense, and the bar consisted of a metal table, a scowling man, an unmarked keg, and a stack of clear plastic cups.

Gemma beamed at Sam as the man poured their lagers. "Fun story about this place love, if you care, I've had to go to A&E on two separate occasions."

"Lovely." As the cup touched Sam's lips he was struck by an odd feeling, one he couldn't place. He took a sip and looked around at the crowd, all dressed in various shades of black, most cradling a beer, and all standing apart.

"Quiet in here, yeah?" Gemma once again tried to chat with the keg man. "Anyone on soon?"

"Whatchu mean?" He spoke, startling himself.

"Whatchu mean, what I mean?" Gemma rolled her eyes. "I mean a fucking band."

"She's on now, ya fucking minge muncher. You blind?"

"Oi! Fucking leave it out, mate." Gemma spun round, and they both again tried to squint through the crowd to the stage. "It's quiet as a fucking church though innit, so tell another one."

Sam turned around to find the nearest punter and gave a smile. "Excuse me, eh, sir. Do you know when the music starts?"

"She's on now, mate. Vyreena Frisk, from South London. Fucking legend of algopop. Her models are a decade ahead of the scene."

Sam blinked, his mind struggling. "But I can't hear it."

The punter just laughed. "Right!" Sam kept staring. "Oh, you're serious! Your first b-y-o show? You need to pair."

"Pair?" It was becoming too much, Sam thought. He might need to just pretend to understand whatever the man said next.

"It's b-y-o? Bring, your, own?" The man reached up and popped out an earbud, which Sam hadn't noticed he was wearing. "You got any on you?"

Sam started to get it, though he wished he hadn't. He turned to see Gemma's reaction, but she had vanished.

"I WISH you would've told me you were leaving," Sam shouted at Gemma as he stepped out onto the street. "I searched the whole crowd for you."

"Oh bloody hell Sam, did that take thirty seconds?"

"Still."

She pointed at the door in disgust. "That is not... no, fuck that. That's not bloody on, that."

"It's a lot. It might be worth staying, we should..."

"No, absolutely not."

"It's our industry."

"That is not my industry. No, come on." She lifted her head and scanned around. "The George is just up the way."

She took him by the hand and dragged him to ensure compliance, and before he could get his bearings they'd arrived outside a very traditional looking pub. Gemma seemed determined to normalise the scene unfolding around them. As they arrived at the door, another auto-cab rolled past, this one distinguishable by the way it was engulfed in flames.

"No please." The pub had a man on the door, and that man was not keen on letting them in. "Close early. Too much happen. Power off later."

"Just nipping in for one, we're no trouble." Gemma flashed a polite smile. Her incorrigible brashness could be shelved on a moment's notice if she needed to negotiate with pub security.

"They're fine," shouted the barkeep just inside.

A police car crawled down the lane, and a low tone came from the loudspeaker. "This is a message from the Metropolitan Police." A curt voice boomed from behind the tinted windows. "Please remain inside, or return inside if you are able. Thank you."

As they entered the pub, the door man followed them inside and shut the door behind them, throwing the deadbolt. "It's a lock in, boys and girls," said the barkeep with a wink. "Hope that's alright."

"Mate, it's lovely." Gemma dove forward, squeezed the barman's shoulders and gave him a kiss on the cheek. "Thank you."

The pints chained together as the night wore on. "It's over." And much to Sam's chagrin, Gemma had gotten real about the situation at work. "It was barely possible to get you over this time. Ohh, why are we bringing anyone over 'ere? Don't we have enough people?"

"Yikes." Sam polished off his lager and stared at the foam in the glass.

"The label's finances are fucked, visa restrictions have gotten impossible. Take one last look at London, sweetie."

"What I don't understand..." He knew better than to ask Gemma anything that might be construed as questioning her decisions. Years from now, he'd surely blame the alcohol for his poor choice in this moment. "How did the catalogue deal with Magenta even go through when you were so dead set against it. I read about that new law..."

"I wasn't." Gemma tapped the bar and gave a nod. The barman likewise nodded, and put two shot glasses in front of them.

"I don't understand."

"I signed the deal personally. This week. You saw the man, the man you keep catching me backstage with, that gorgeous, soulless, horrible man. Head of Legal for Magenta. Some bloody stupid name, very American, you'd love it. No bloody point fighting, anyway. We might as well get some money out of them now. They don't need us, this just makes it a little easier for them."

"That's it. Just the full rights to our entire catalogue. Free for them to auto-gig, to base their algorithmic bullshit on. You collaborated. You just... you just collaborated with them."

"They were doing it anyway, what part of this do you not get?!" Her shout rattled the glasses on the counter. "Wake the fuck up, you bloody child!" The bartender had placed another pair of shots in front of them with nary a glance. "Did you know the top twenty most-streamed songs last month were generated? Did you, Sam?

"No."

"No! You didn't, you fucking crybaby ideologue. Did you know we had to lower the value of our catalogue in the contract three times over the course of these negotiations?"

"Gemma, I'm sorry..."

"Did you know in the last quarter, over half of Magenta's streaming minutes were of procedural streams? Just noise, Sam, it's just audio wallpaper, to drown out people's intrusive thoughts between snippets of chat with made-up people. Do you get that?"

"I don't..."

"These are serious people, Sam. And they will stop at nothing. Nothing! They fucking hated this industry and everyone in it, top to bottom. That's me, and, you." She let out an exhausted sigh and took one of the shots between her fingers. As she downed it, she made eye contact with Samir. His eyes welled with tears.

*Stupid fucking baby*. He scolded himself as tears ran down his face. *So fucking embarrassing.*

"Christ," she muttered. "Come on then, take your medicine." She seemed to coax the liquor into his mouth and down his throat. It loosened him up, which just made more tears come. He thanked himself for not sobbing, at least. "We'll be fine. It avoided a buyout. We'll stay independent, alright?" We'll keep signing artists who want nothing to do with all this. We'll tour it for people like us. It's fine. You know that, right?" She placed her hand gingerly on his shoulder. "There's still going to be a market for hand-made. There always is. People still wear hand-knitted mittens, for Christ's sake."

Sam thrashed around. Every cell in his body rejected her touch, this foreign element, this toxin on his shoulder. He needed it gone before it penetrated the skin. "Fuck, no. You're so drunk you don't even understand what you're doing or saying." The resentment rose up from his stomach, and it was all he could to not to vomit it directly onto her. "No! Stop. Don't touch me. D-do you even know what it feels like to be sober? Do you?" His hand flung upward and struck her wrist to knock her hand off him. She stared, expressionless. "Look at you. Just tossing back a whisky at 2 p.m. then signing a deal with that fucking pretty boy from Magenta."

"Oh. You jealous little shit." Her scoff was devastating. "Did you not just hear me? Is that what this is? You think I mortgaged our future because some fit lawyer put his tongue on my clit?"

"Stop!" Sam's resentment turned to rage, and the threat of vomit loomed larger than ever. The sight of her repulsed him: her ridiculous fucking blue leather jacket, her smeared lip gloss, the huge bags under her eyes. *Human disaster.* He stared around the bar in hope of some kind of approval from anyone. The bartender held court with the dishes.

Gemma chuckled. "What business is it of yours if he did?"

"So he did."

"I'm asking why you're asking, you pissy little man. You're not allowed to be jealous, love. Are ye? No. Not with little miss waiting for you at home. Finishing up with Carlos about now, yeah?"

"Right, bye." Sam slapped his hands on the bar and sniffled. For a moment he was gripped with a fear that he might not be able to leave. But with quite a physical push off the bar he had given himself enough momentum to break from Gemma's orbit and launch toward the exit.

"Sam, are you serious?" Gemma once again scoffed as Sam arrived at the bolted door. He yanked at the handle and received a stern rejection. "It's a sign, love. Come on. Stay. It's mayhem out there." He ripped and pulled so hard it was a wonder he didn't shatter his wrists before the bartender arrived to undo the locks.

"Cheers," Sam muttered as he slipped out of The George and into the night.


IT HAD TAKEN him moments to become lost. Coloured smoke stained the air as protestors launched flares, and a tannoy blasted announcements made inaudible by the constant explosion of fireworks all around. Chants rang out in a half-dozen languages and people scattered and spilled through every cross and out of every alley. Police barricades had been set up and abandoned, and graffiti covered the few road markers Sam could make out.

"Hey!" Gemma's voice cut through the chaos a few paces behind him, out of breath. He walked faster, his hand extended to cut through the crowd. "Sam! Where are you going to go? The tube's shut!"

He ignored her and pushed himself to move even faster. Her voice was a blade that scraped against him, cut through to the bone, drew as much blood as she wanted. He needed away from her before he had nothing left inside.

"Listen!" She stabbed through gasps. "Christ. Forget it all! Pause the row, okay? I'll give you a ride yeah?"

He stopped dead, hands straight out, as the outline of a police car appeared just ahead of him through the thick smoke. *Fuck.*

"Dead end, yeah?" She'd come for the last drops. "Let's go."

"I'll figure it out!" His voice had found a new octave and he sniffled every third word. "Go! Go back inside!" He leaned forward and rested his palms on the side of the car. The cool metal seemed to centre him, and he let out a long sigh. "Go. Celebrate your victory over the fucking arts. Celebrate getting laid and paid."

"Sam! Please. Would you look at me? Please. This act doesn't work for you."

He steeled himself against her and spun around, his back pressed against the car. "I'm looking at you."

"Do you really think there was anything I could've done? If it wasn't me it would've just been someone else. There's too much... I don't know. There's not enough of... Sam, it never mattered. Nobody cared. Okay?"

"I cared."

"You're not enough, Sam! I'm not enough! We were never going to be enough."

"Bullshit. You just gave up."

"I gave up! Are you bloody serious? I gave up? You have a wife, Sam! Where is she? Why isn't she here? Why did you walk out on her?"

"That's not what we're talking about."

"Isn't it just! Tell me, then. Fucking answer me!" She grabbed Sam's shoulders and shook him. She stared down, and his eyes looked everywhere but at her. "She's waiting for you alone!"

"This isn't..."

"Sam, look around us. It's the end of the world! And you're here with me, and she's alone. Why are you here?"

Sam stumbled backwards into a postbox and collapsed

onto the pavement in a heap. The chaos of the street faded, replaced by a looping message that echoed out from the barricaded Underground station. A disembodied voice, synthetic, and eerily calm: "Due to a reported emergency, this station is being evacuated."

In the corner of his eye he saw Gemma lowering herself to the ground. She leaned on him and exhaled, and he let his head fall against her.

"I don't know," Sam finally replied, his voice a hoarse whisper. The rough pad of Gemma's thumb brushed a tear from his cheek.

"Let me take you somewhere."

"You're drunk."

"It drives itself. Where am I taking you?"

Sam slumped against her. "It's up to you."

THIRTY-ONE
RECKON

Their entry into Liverpool was marked by a series of billboards that warmed Gemma's insides. The smiling face of Rebecca Prue, a non-confrontational font that read "Liverpool, let's talk." The large penis graffitied next to her mouth, the blacked out teeth, the fangs and horns, were all remarkably on-brand for the area.

"My goodness." Caroline gasped. If she wore pearls, she would have clutched them.

"It's not personal," Gemma said as they passed the billboard. "These people are cunts to everyone. It's what makes them so special."

The city did seem a bit worse for wear, though not abandoned by any stretch of the imagination. The roads were packed with a healthy amount of cars, some of which were even being hand-driven, and crowds of people moved up and down the pavements. As she'd expect in any British city, half of the shops were boarded up or shuttered, but the ones that were left at least appeared to be staffed by people.

Caroline uttered a quiet "wow" as the car pulled into a parking space on a side street.

"Right," Gemma said with some hesitation. "Which house is it?"

"Miss?"

"Wait..." She had a creeping realisation. "Where are we?"

"I just told the car to take us to Liverpool, miss."

"So it's just..."

"I believe it's just taken us to the centre of the city. Where does your friend live? Do you know their address?"

"Right. Their address." Gemma stared out the car window at a man sitting on the ground. He had a bottle of Amstel Light, and she wished her life were that simple.

"Miss, don't you know it? I thought you said he was your best friend."

"I never said we were friends. We were colleagues. Contemporaries."

"What does that mean? Contemporaries?"

"Means I don't know his bloody address."


THE DAYS that followed illustrated just how foolish this endeavour had been. *Just turn up and find him*, Gemma groaned to herself. This shit-hole had hundreds of thousands of residents and took up some ridiculous amount of space. It was one of the largest cities on the goddamn island. And here she was, equipped with nothing but a belief the man still lived here, his old industry alias, and a twenty-something girl dressed like she'd just crawled out of your television at a low frame rate.

"We need to fix this, love," Gemma had said upon their

arrival at the first place it made sense to disembark, which was of course a shopping mall.

"Fix what, miss?"

Gemma grinned. "You stand out."

In her youth she never would've been caught dead in a Sports Mad, but now the sight of one filled her with something she could only assume was patriotism. She took Caroline by the hand and in they frolicked, straight down the aisles of track suits, puffy jackets, and jumpers that bore the names of brands like PRINCE OF DUNKS. With a swipe of Caroline's Ring, she was now the proud owner of a properly British outfit, ready to blend in.

"I feel odd." Caroline squirmed inside her oversized red jumper, adorned with a large cartoon beetle and the word LIVERPOOL emblazoned across the front.

"It's perfect."

"Should we get one for you as well?" She tugged at Gemma's tatty, stretched-out, too-small UWL hoodie. "To replace this?"

Gemma hissed. The matter was dropped.

With Caroline's wardrobe worked out they found their way to a hotel, courtesy of the girl's access to limitless funds. It was a perfunctory experience that resembled Gemma's time in conscription—tiny floor plan with a closet for a bathroom, and a double-sized bed that the two were forced to share. It made her miss the bunks, if she was honest with herself. *At least those had a desk.* The two of them got almost no sleep as Caroline flopped and turned, scratched and groaned, and every so often, kicked.

This pattern was repeated each night, and by day three Gemma was at the end of her rope. They'd had no plan for finding Chinny, and instead resorted to Plan B, which was to just drive around. *I'm sure I've seen the outside of his house in a photo.*

By day four they had slept a collective 10 hours between them, and had taken a table by the window at a cafe in the neighbourhood she thought he might live in.

"We'll just watch," Gemma said. Her eyes burned. "He might walk by."

Caroline leaned her head against the window. "Yes, miss." She looked like a disaster. Her Liverpool jumper had picked up a small stain. She didn't know how to fold jeans so she kept just leaving them crumpled on the floor, and the wrinkles had set in. Her hair was greasy and stringy, as she'd said she was no longer comfortable using the communal shower at their hotel. She hadn't brought any of her makeup, and her face had started to break out.

*It was nice*, Gemma thought, *to see her out from under all her layers of facade.* A familiar anxiety crawled up her spine, followed by the exhausting guilt. *I've ruined another life.*

"Psst. Bruv." A whisper came from behind Gemma. She jerked arrhythmically and spun around. "Damn, calm down, innit." A very spindly and unclean young gentleman sat at the table behind them.

"What, mate?"

"Weed, coke."

Gemma cackled. "Mate! My knight in shining armour, you are." The cafe had paid a dividend within the first hour. "I'm looking for someone and you're the closest I've got to someone who might know where he is."

"You what?" The man slid back and bumped into his own table, which surprised him. "You a cop?"

"You fucking serious? I look like a copper?"

"Cops is just people. You's people."

"Enlightened of you. No, I'm not the bloody police. I'm just someone looking for a dried up piece of shit music producer who used to live around here."

"Who is you then?"

"I'm a dried up piece of shit music producer."

"That your daughter then?" He gestured to Caroline.

Gemma rolled her eyes. "Not even sister. Devastating."

"Right, like. You gonna kill him? He owe you money?"

"We're just friends."

"Alright. Listen bruv, I think I know who you mean. But I don't know if you want to go over there." The young lad looked back and forth between Gemma and Caroline. "He might not mind, if it's you lot. Mother daughter, you know. Bit of a grotesque figure, honestly. Always prattling on using offensive terms for women, bein' quite crass an' all. He doesn't create a very inclusive environment, if you catch my meaning."

"That's him."


THEY WATCHED from the car as the wayward pharmaceuticals trader negotiated an introduction. But Gemma couldn't contain herself once she caught a glimpse of him in the doorway.

"Old man!" She leapt from the car and shouted, her arms straight up in victory.

"Look at this slag!" Chinny was a sight to behold. Ravaged by time, skeletal, with an adidas tracksuit hanging loose on him, his face like leather, and skin that seemed to always retain that Benidorm glow. He let out a wheezing laugh. "Oh you've let yourself go, haven't you lass?"

"Ya fucking prick," she shouted as she threw her arms around him.

"Alright love, take it easy. That jumper rides any higher and we're all getting a free show." He nodded to his dealer. "Same again next time lad, it's appreciated, off you get." He pointed to Gemma with a loaded grin. "Now you get in here, mangey slapper."

The house was as it had been described to her in countless war stories from the bands who'd recorded here, and the assistants who'd been scarred by having to accompany said bands. Wood panelled walls that hadn't been updated since Thatcher, covered floor to ceiling and wall to wall with awards, framed tour posters, memorabilia, and endless photos of bands standing in this very hallway. Chinny was drunk and eager to offer a tour.

Caroline grinned as she put her face up against one of the awards, so enthralled by the pomp of it. "What's BPI?"

"Don't bloody know what it stands for lass," he bellowed. "Pricks, the lot. Self-important poofters."

"British Phonographic Institute," Gemma clarified through her teeth. She was embarrassed that she knew. "Hasn't existed for ages. You won, old man. You bloody outlived them, you can stop hurling slurs at them."

He coughed and tapped the glass on one of the awards. "They invented this for me, you know, the Bronze award. Used to just give out Silvers and Golds. Some arse having a laugh at my expense. I'm the only one they ever issued these to, hand to God."

"Turk's Revenge..." Gemma tutted at one of the Bronze awards. "Haven't thought of them in ages."

Caroline hovered her finger over the award, and seemed afraid to touch it. "Who are they?"

"They did that song Good Vibes Only. The one that says you should dump your girlfriend if she has a bad day."

"Oh. I don't know it."

"Tossers." Chinny spit on the record. "Utter tosh. They pretended to write the lyrics to that drivel themselves. As if I I'd be impressed either way. Ye repeated the same line fifty times, ya cunts."

"I saw them at the Roundhouse a decade or so ago," Gemma said. "Weird night."

"Oh, this one." Chinny had moved onto a framed letter which hung amidst the records and awards. "This is the pride of my fucking collection. It's a framed email from the CEO of HMV, to that miserable sod Eamon Whitechapel, complaining about how many copies of a particular album were being destroyed unsold." He cackled, and Gemma couldn't help but crack a smile as she read it.

The tour ended in his conservatory, which intruded into the back garden and had a suspiciously nice set of furniture. "This was here when you moved in, wasn't it, old man? You didn't have a conservatory put on."

"Oh 'course it was," he replied. "Most of it was, love. Don't think I've even seen half the rooms upstairs. You're more than welcome, both of you. I've not had company in a long time, I might be a bit rusty at hosting."

"That's incredibly generous of you, sir," said Caroline with a curtsy. Even in her oily, sleep-deprived state she would extend the utmost to any and all.

"Ooh, right, look at her," Chinny clucked. "Easy pet, I'm not a fuckin' royal." In the corner sat a drinks globe, and he worked up three glasses of scotch as if it would pain him not to do so.

"N-no, love." Gemma put her hand out to block him from setting hers down. "I'm sober."

"I know pet, it's why I poured a bloody drink, ya daft cunt."

"No, I'm sober. I'm not drinking alcohol anymore."

"You too? Oh, another one falls. Whole country's gone."

Caroline took the tiniest sip of hers. "Thank you." She'd become rather taken with the acoustic guitar in the corner. "Sir, would you mind?"

"Not at all, love."

She serenaded them with some rather competent playing while they caught up, and it was at once a bizarre experience and a tremendous relief. Just the sight of Chinny pulled her mind back so far, and recovered memories that she'd not realised she'd forgotten. Once the telling of tales began, she could hear a change in the way she spoke, the way she carried herself. She was active again, and she paced the room as they traded banter of the old days, of terrible acts come and gone, of destroyed hotels and fifty-thousand pound bar tabs.

"They'd staple a baggie of cocaine to the call sheet," Chinny wheezed, "just to get the recordist to fucking turn up. Fucking mental innit." He slammed his glass down, and angled it out toward Caroline. "I'm dry again, love."

Caroline stopped playing. She'd been improvising a beautiful bit of work, and Gemma's annoyance went into overdrive. "Get it yourself, Cryptkeeper. She's busy."

"Alright love, relax, I apologise. All's a waste until it's tracked anyway, as you do." He widened his smile and revealed some of his grey, decayed teeth. "You want to see a real live recording studio? Come on pet, let me show you where the magic happens."

They followed him down a nondescript set of stairs

behind an unmarked door, and the narrow hall widened into a gorgeous control room that looked through glass into a massive studio. A vintage drum set, racks of exotic noise-makers of all shapes and sizes, more guitars than reasonable, with beautiful burgundy carpets piled high on the hardwood and tapestries hung on each side. In the middle stood a microphone at a stool, and a fully stocked bar beckoned from the far wall, gorgeous varnished mahogany with brass inlay and crystal decanters of brown and clear liquors.

Gemma took a deep breath as she finally laid eyes on this space, the private studio of the legendary Chinny Reckon. The rare air filled her lungs. "Some of the worst music in history was recorded right here."

"Drug death capital of Europe this room," Chinny added with a smirk. "It's a proper energy down here, love. Seasoned cast iron."

They let Caroline into the studio, while they stayed behind in the control room. They watched through the glass as she gawked at each instrument, at every thread of every carpet, her mouth wide, her smile shining brightly. Her uncomplicated innocence was soothing.

Chinny sank into a tired leather recliner, sat in front of the enormous mixing board. He pushed a button and a loud pop rang over the speakers. "Hear me, love?"

Caroline nodded, and her mouth moved, but they heard nothing. Gemma and Chinny both smiled.

"You have to speak into the microphone, love." He studied the board and pushed a slider up.

"Hello?" Her voice boomed from two large speakers atop the board, richer and fuller than in real life. The sound treatment of the room, combined with her natural timbre and a microphone that probably cost a thousand pounds, took the slightest bit of talent and made it more so. Back when anything mattered at all in this business, this mattered a lot.

Chinny touched a large record button on a screen to one side, and dozens of waveforms began to scroll. "She'll want the guitar," he muttered, and pushed another slider up. With the button held down he leaned toward the window. "Go on love."

"Thank you, Mr. Reckon!" Caroline sat on the stool and picked up the guitar, her joy fused with confusion, as if they could see into a dream she was having that even she didn't understand.

Gemma snorted. "Mr. Reckon. Do you even fucking remember your own name anymore, old man? Your actual name, Oliver. Not this ridiculous Chinny Reckon nonsense."

"That's rich coming from yourself, Lily."

"Oi!" Gemma spat. "Never! Okay? Never." She shook her head. "Can't fucking believe you remembered."

"You ever stop to think the name you picked name sounds like that what's her face from that old bloody Christmas film?"

"Don't start. I had to come up with it in a hurry for a Battle of the Bands registry. I wrote 'Gemma and the Thomsons', and they misread it."

They both snarled into a chortle. It was otherwise pin-drop silent. Through the glass they could see Caroline hover her hand above the guitar, her mouth hung open.

Chinny held a button down on the console in front of him. "Just play anything, love. It's all digital, nothing to waste." He released the button with a smirk. "So is that your daughter? Bet you don't know who the father is, eh love?"

"Fuck off old man," Gemma snapped. "She's a long story.

Met her out near Birmingham. I'm a bit young to be her mother."

"That true? She's what, early twenties, and you're..."

"Right, no need to do the maths, is there?" She squirmed. "How do you get power for all this? Don't you have those tyrannical plug sockets?"

"You think Liverpool would let them install those bloody things? Need His Majesty's royal fucking assent to run the kettle?" Chinny tutted. "Oh they try, every now and again. Good way to get their vans torched."

Their banter was cut short as Caroline set the guitar down and approached the door with an ashen face and a zombie-like shamble. "Could I please lay down, miss? I'm so very tired."

*Christ,* Gemma thought, *this poor dear. Hasn't slept in days, all this excitement, and just downed a glass of scotch.* "Can she sleep somewhere?"

Chinny ripped the door open with a laugh. "Pet, you're half-dead. Head upstairs, take any open bedroom you see, too bloody many of them up there. Should be some shirts and bits you can use as pyjamas."


THEY RETIRED to the conservatory once more, with Caroline tucked away in a spare room to finally get some rest.

"Imagine she's not used to these late nights," Chinny said as he put a couple more scotches in front of them.

Gemma scowled at her drink. "I bloody told you I gave up drinking after I..." Her chair creaked as she shifted her weight. The night's proceedings had stayed confined to their past exploits, gamesmanship, colleagues and artists they'd known in the old days. She wondered whether Chinny would go with her on the journey if she talked about her life now.

"After you... what, love, got an ASBO?"

She smiled. "That wouldn't stop me. I guess you could say I'm on the run, old man. A few years back I was conscripted by the government. And I escaped, and I suppose I'm running now."

He leaned forward with a mischievous grin. "I know."

"You know?" Gemma froze. "How?"

"The boy who sells me my spliffs brings me these too. Kept this one." He handed her a thin piece of paper, crumbled and faded. The top bore a title: The Analog Gazette. And large in the middle was a photo of Gemma herself, mid-song, guitar across her, on the makeshift stage in West Brom.

She snatched the paper and shook her head. "Fuck's sake." She needed to keep this, and then find Mike, and then stuff it down his windpipe.

"Was nice to know you wasn't dead."

"Wait..." She smoothed out the paper and held it away from her face to bring the letters into focus. Underneath the photo, another story had caught her eye. Her mouth went dry, and the pain in her back made it start to seize up.

The headline read: *Walsall Collective Burns*.

"I get my nice fat pay day thanks to yourself," Chinny bragged. "Appreciate that, by the way. Those checks keep coming from Magenta, and I sit here waiting it all out."

*A large solar battery installation burned out of control...* the words blurred on the page. Her face went flush, her limbs cold. "No."

"S'alright, love, no worries, happy to share a bit of the wealth."

"No," she squeaked. "No."

"Christ love, you're frazzled, you're a wreck." He reached forward and took the page from her hand. It slid out of her fingers with no resistance. She fell back against the chair. Each breath took all her energy to pull into her lungs, and each felt as if a thousand daggers had plunged into her. She pressed her hands against her chest as it heaved.

"This is my fault," she cried. "These people took me in and this is what I did." The fabric of the hoodie pulled tight against her. She knew it would cut off her air supply, her blood supply, everything. She pawed and pulled until it was up over her head, and exhaled in relief as her stomach and chest were freed from it, left in just her sport bra. She undid the button on her jeans for more instant relief. Her breathing continued to get faster and faster. The cold wood of the chair against her back made her wince and sent her lurching forward, but she could get enough air now. Just enough, for now. She wrapped her arms around her midriff and squeezed. Her breaths were too fast. Her head started to swim.

"Hey, hey, hey." Chinny clutched her knee with his bony fingers. "Whatever it is, you've survived it, yeah? You're here, love. You're here."

She spotted the cigarettes and lighter on the floor and fumbled for them, her hands quaking so violently she couldn't strike the flame.

"Let's put it in the music, love." He held her hands still until she managed to get the cigarette lit. A wave of calm washed over her. The shaking lessened and her exhales became a flutter. "Here's the medicine." The cool exterior of the glass slid into her palm. He pushed on the bottom and the rim touched her lips.

Her lips parted. The scotch passed across them. The

burn started there and raced down her throat to her stomach. Another wave of warm tingles, though her eyes were on fire. The shakes had finally stopped.

"There she is," Chinny said. "That's the Gemma I remember."


BY 3 A.M. they'd returned to the basement studio, and Gemma now sat on the stool, her third drink on the table next to her, guitar in hand.

"Walsall, my love," she warbled into the microphone as she played. A tear traced the contour of her face and dropped off her chin. "My jewel of the Midlands." She sniffled, then swore. *Fuck.* "Sorry. Need to blow my nose, I expect."

The speakers popped, and Chinny reverberated through the room. "That's great love, use that emotion. You never tapped into any of this like you should. Think about that town of yours, burned to the ground. Christ, think of that dead bloody husband of yours, him with his sad carton standing there, letting you shove him around, breaking up your band like he did. He'd still be alive if he hadn't left you, yeah? That's on him."

"Please," she coughed. "Stop."

"What about the bird you're with? Give her a go? There's an easy treat."

"About an hour ago you thought she was my daughter, you lecherous cunt." She slugged back the rest of her drink. "Leave it."

"Yeah yeah," he bellowed. "Whatever happened to that Indian bloke who was always hanging around, what was his name? The one who mailed me my cheques. Sam? Coulda been your son. You ever shag him?"

"Christ, no." She stumbled toward the bar in the corner of the studio. "No. He had a partner. He wouldn't lay a finger on me." She picked up the decanter of vodka and tipped a shot's worth of it into her mouth. "Fucking prude." *It was delicious.*

It was something she'd chosen to do, giving up alcohol for a while. She could choose to start again. That was that, she'd decided. *It's all just choices.* Rigidity wasn't virtuous. You had to be flexible. Her mind raced through a thousand scenarios she'd been in with Sam. So many chances he'd had to touch her, to kiss her, to fuck her. None of which he'd taken. *Why hadn't he taken them?* The questions were an ache from an ancient wound. *Was she not worth it? Too old? Too desperate?* Another shot's worth out of the decanter might help, so she tried.

"That never stopped you, did it?" Chinny had drifted into the studio, his voice suddenly inches from her ear. "This, lass! This is what you should be singing about! Real fucking human shit! No machine is writing about this!"

She shrunk away from him, her face turned to one side. His breath reeked of booze and cigarettes. The mix triggered panic that rose up from deep within her. She forced it back down with her third taste of the vodka. "Because nobody wants to hear about it, old man."

"But it's what they bloody *should* hear, love! Something fucking raw, yeah? Your husband blowing his brains out cause of your abuse."

"It was a car accident!" She shoved him away. "You gormless twat."

"It was you! You know it was you! You fucking killed him." He grabbed the rings that hung at her chest and yanked. She screamed as the chain pierced her neck and her head pulled toward his. Their foreheads banged together and the chain snapped, leaving the rings grasped in Chinny's fist. He cackled and coughed as he stumbled backward and tried to regained his balance.

"You fuck," she screamed. She lunged toward him and he held his hand out, the rings served up atop. She snatched them away and tucked them under the band of her bra. "Fucking mental arse, they should fucking section you. I should fucking kill you."

He continued to cackle and wheeze. "Alright, love, alright. No need to get upset. This is what I do, yeah? I mine that gold and we forge it into a hit record."

A drop of blood worked down her neck. She could feel the tickle as it traced a line down to her chest. "Make the artist so fucking angry they want to pelt you to death with batteries. Brilliant, yeah? Ace. You're a legend."

"Am I a bit rusty? There hasn't been much demand for my services, yeah?"

"Nobody buys this shit anymore, old man." She paced the studio, her hands squeezed into tight fists. "We're fucking relics. We weren't meant to live as long as we did. We're fucking embarrassing. Wringing every last drop, pushing this slop, claiming our slop was better than their slop."

"That sounds familiar."

"You were their producer, you tit. They're Killslop lyrics. But they're true. We didn't try, we just moaned and took cheap chances. And you, ya miserable prick, just whored yourself out. Churned out this garbage that you fucking knew was shite. I just charged more and more for it. Exploiting the nostalgia, claiming we're saving the art form. We got what we fucking deserved."

"Daft cunt. It was the end of the fucking world! I did

what I had to do to survive, same as you. We did what we had to do."

"That's what you never got, yeah? What *neither* of us ever got. It wasn't the end of the world." She let out a raspy sigh. "It was just the end of us."

Chinny set his empty glass down with a resonant thunk on the table. "Don't get your knickers in a twist, love. Relax, have another drink. We'll speak in the morning, yeah?" He crossed the room and headed to the studio door. "I'd offer you a throw, but the scotch'd have me softer than a fucking emo kid."

"Christ almighty." She exhaled, and felt herself start to tremble again. "You're as exhausting as ever."

He smiled. "Welcome home, love."

Against his own wishes, Sam extended a hand toward Carlos. "Hi." He was a marionette now, operated by social mores. "I'm surprised to see you here."

"Virginia and I relocated here together." Carlos leaned forward to accept the handshake, but kept the gap between himself and Virginia as small as he could.

"We relocated at the same time," Virginia clarified.

"Samir," Carlos said, "you should know I was against your hire."

"I appreciate you telling me."

Sam thought he might tear Carlos limb from limb. But the environment of the staff bar wasn't conducive to him behaving as a jealous ex-lover. It might damage his chances of future advancement were he to kill a member of senior staff.

Virginia forced a cartoonish grin. "Shall we get a drink?"

Sam tipped forward and physically thrust himself into the conversation. "I was thinking we could get away to Maelzel's."

"Oh, Samir..." She glanced between Sam and Carlos.

"We spoke about this. We tend not to leave the campus. There's just so much going on, you know."

"That's a shame, I know Seb would love to see you. And Maelzel's might not be around much longer. He might have to close it down soon."

"That's unfortunate," Carlos quipped.

Sam glared at the man who would usurp his life. He needed Virginia out of here, out of this environment. He needed her around him and Seb again. "I understand, Carlos, if you're not comfortable going outside, even if it's to meet Virginia's close friend from college."

The three of them shared a look, and Sam did all he could to suppress a smirk.

IT WAS a short walk to Maelzel's from Magenta Tower, though made long by the silence. A handful of the regulars acknowledged Sam as he entered, which burnished his bona fides as an independent man worthy of respect. He looked to make sure both Virginia and Carlos had noticed.

"Lamb," snapped Mel as she emerged from the bathrooms. She clicked her fingers and pointed around the floor at piles of parts and wires. "What the hell is going on here? Was I not clear?"

"I, uh..." Sam looked for Virginia as a sort of defensive mechanism. She was incredible at bailing him out of these kinds of situations. But tonight she'd already found the bar alongside Carlos, and they had both begun tapping on and talking to it in a fruitless attempt to get drinks.

"Your old boss has a new toy," said Hector from his usual spot at the far end of the bar. "Not one I approve of."

"Where is he?"

"I'm here, dude." Seb flung the door to the back room open and strode out. It swung into the wall and was sent flying back the other way. The resultant slam shook the bottles on the bar. "Unless you're going to pick up a screwdriver or pour a pint there's no room for you here."

"No mames," said Mel, exasperated. She sat on the stool next to Hector, and they exchanged a quick glance. Hector slid his full pint of Modelo over and Mel took the invitation to gulp a third of it down.

"It's funny," shouted Seb from half-way up a ladder. "I already got my first threat over this piece of shit." Fitted to the wall were several reflectors from Seb's second-hand auto-gig, and now Seb looked to be anchoring one of the laser projectors.

"I thought it didn't work." Seb stared at the box on the ground, still half full of all the unlabelled junk that comprised the system. *Wiring these things up was such a fucking chore,* he recalled to himself. He resented every time they'd had him do it in his last year at the label.

"It shouldn't matter," slurred Mel from behind the bar. It appeared she'd taken to pulling her own pints. "The threats should be enough to talk him out of this ridiculous plan. Nadie quiere ver esta chingadera."

Hector caught Sam's eye line. He held up one of the devices that he and Lydia used to communicate, and shook it with an annoyed glare. *They had places to be tonight.* Yet another chance for Samir to liberate himself from this, whatever it was. It was vivid in his mind:

Mel could take them all apart with her bare hands should the situation call for it. *But she wouldn't. Her and Hector were old friends.*

He could request a suite and live in Magenta Tower. *But they'd say no. He was new, he surely didn't qualify.*

Virginia could use her authority at work to uncouple his Ring from Lydia's grasp. *But she'd say it's against policy for me to intervene, Samir.* What had he been thinking with this trip to Maelzel's in the first place? In the corner of his eye, he saw her hand touch Carlos's shoulder.

"... some sense into this fool, please." Mel broke his trance with a targeted glare.

He looked at Seb for a moment, but couldn't maintain it. "You don't have to do any of this on my account. I have a new visa through Magenta now, you know."

"When the fuck did I say I was doing this on your account?" Seb scoffed and laughed. "I know you do. You're part of the fucking problem now, you Magenta fuck."

"I just thought," Sam stuttered. He hoped for support from Mel, but she had her back to the group once more, and focussed on her drink at the bar next to Hector. "I don't know what I thought."

"You know Virginia and I both also work at Magenta." If Carlos saw a chance to make it about himself, he would take it. *This was the Carlos guarantee.*

"Right." Seb did a double-take at Carlos. "Cool, man. Thanks for coming into my bar and involving yourself in my fucking conversations."

Virginia cleared her throat. "Sebastian, behave. You're drunk."

"Yes, I am." He tugged at the bottom of his tatty shirt, one of so few in his wardrobe. "But you're right. Good vibes only."

She pinched her nose and dropped her head. Until now

Sam hadn't noticed Seb had the Turk's Revenge shirt on. *That would go down a treat, surely.*

"Sorry, V," Seb shouted as he came down from the ladder. He was dripping with sweat, his shirt translucent and matted to him all over, which put his body hair on full display. His salt-and-pepper stubble looked especially grey under the stage lights. "But I've gotta do it. You remember when they wouldn't lmet me take Intro Lit junior year because music majors 'didn't get complementary study'?" His mocking tone was acidic, and his air quotes nearly sent him tumbling off the last step.

She groaned. "We thought you were going to burn campus down."

"The threat." Sam sighed. In so many ways, Seb had never changed. He wondered just how much of this Mel had dealt with due to his couch-surfing.

Virginia rose from the stool and began to pace. *She was an active thinker.* "But, Sebastian. Or, Samir, one of you, said the auto-gig doesn't work?" She pointed at the core unit still lying in the yellowed box, sat in the middle of the stage. "Did it come on, then turn back off, then stay off?"

"Dude, yeah. It fucking did."

"It was automatically disabled as soon as it acquired a SkyTie signal. It would just need to be re-provisioned." Virginia made eye contact with Samir, which startled him. "Samir, as an Operations Technician, that's something you could do of course."

Sam laughed nervously. "It is?"

"Well," Carlos added, "it would be sent to Virginia for approval." *He had relished every syllable of that, hadn't he?* "You can do so with a request to Aida. If it's something you'd like to grant to the local business."

"Uh, well." Usually when Sam felt everyone in the room were glaring at him, it was in his imagination. But as he looked around now he realised this time, it was very much true. The eyes of Mel, Virginia, Hector, and Sebastian were all fixed on him in that moment. He deftly avoided lingering on anyone as he looked across them. Mel had been crystal clear: *the club's got to go, okay? Dios mío, I wish this place didn't exist...* Virginia was no ally in this situation, any more than Aida could be your ally. She'd taken the first chance she got to delegate this, perhaps out of resentment. Hector seemed more invested than he should be in the outcome, which was worrisome. And Seb had doubled back on himself twice already. *Would he actually want me to do this?*

Back and forth, back and forth, he scanned their faces. Back and forth. *Just a simple choice*, he thought. *Just a simple choice.*

"Yo!" shouted Seb just as Sam reached the back exit. He took his hand off the knob and spun around.

Sam turned and gave a tight grimace. "Yeah."

"Look," Seb sighed. "This might save the club, dude. I'm sorry, I'm sorry. I'd really appreciate it if you could."

"It's fine," Sam nodded. "I'll take care of it."

"Man." He burst out laughing. "You had me worried, man. Dude, I need this one. I mean, don't run into Mel alone in the street or anything. She's gonna be fucking furious. But I appreciate it. What this means to me, man. You don't know."

"Hey, no, it's all good. I know what it means." The room between them felt twice as large as usual. Sam figured he could count at least two dozen tables between Seb and the door, rather than the usual three.

"You don't have to go. V's staying for a round to catch up. I know I was hard on you lately."

"It's all good." Every fibre of Sam was being pulled toward the door. He needed to leave. And more so, he wanted to leave.

"No, listen." Seb covered the mile or so in record time. From behind his back he produced a small parcel, thin and wrapped in brown paper. "I want you to take this."

Sam tugged at the wrapper and peeked inside. "No, what?" From just the corner he could see it was the framed photo of Seb and Rebecca Prue. On the far wall were screw holes and a faded outline where the photo had lived for all these years.

"Call it a loan. Alright? I figure you, stomping around Magenta Tower with your important ex-wife, in your important new job, you'll eventually get to meet the woman herself. Maybe you can get it autographed for me."

"Thanks, Seb." His ear chimed. It would be another ping from Lydia. He was already at least a half-hour late, and over an hour away.

"Yeah man. Don't worry about it. Listen, just, about everything with the apartment, and Mel, and..."

"Don't. We'll talk about it next time."

"Yeah man, of course. Sounds good."


SAMIR SPRINTED onto the BART far later than he'd intended. It would be a long ride south, followed by a long trek on foot from the station at the other end to The Counting Room, the abandoned bar Lydia and he had explored in Foster City months ago. It hadn't been a coincidence that they'd run into Hector that night; it was apparently some sort of regular meet-up spot for the two of them and their like-minded friends. Now that he had been impressed into whatever-this-was, he'd been summoned to their regular whatever-it-was.

The dark of the city rolled past the windows of the empty train carriage, the only sound the gentle clatter of the wheels along the tracks. Samir was alone for the first time in ages.

"Aida, can I speak with my father?"

"Of course, Samir." With a sympathetic lilt and a few chimes, Aida connected Sam straight away.

"Hey kid! What time is it there?"

As ever, his father's voice sent a warmth through him. He let out a sigh that became a flutter. "Hey, dad. Same time as it is there." Sam already had a lump in his throat. He slid his hands across the cold plastic of the seat. "Dad, I'm in a lot of trouble. I really need your help."

"Should I get your mother? She's just watching her drama stream."

"Dad... no..."

"She's on the premium streams now, son. The story-telling is a lot more nuanced. You know that stuff is lost on me, but she's always saying how you'd enjoy it."

"Dad, please." Sam let his eyes go out of focus. The darkness outside contrasted with the searing blue light inside the train. He could only see himself now, reflected by the window. His throat was so dry and his lips cracked, moistened a bit by tears. "Can I please just..."

"You just name a vibe, say if you want a fixed length like a ten-episode arc, or..."

"Dad... pause ads... please."

"No problem, sport. I'll pause ads for one hour."

With a cough his tears became full-on. He slid down the seat and slipped off the edge, straight onto the rubberised floor of the carriage. Pain shot from his tailbone and his sobs became spasms. He plucked his earbuds out and stuffed them in his pocket, fighting the urge to hurl them down the length of the carriage. His head hit the floor and he found himself curled up, unsure whether anyone could see him like this, and unsure how they might react if they could. *If they'd react at all.* He closed his eyes and focused on the sound of the train as it rumbled down the track. *If he stayed on, how far could he get? Would it go all the way to the border? Was it even possible to enter the Corridor without your own car?*

"Now boarding at Colma," squawked the bizarre synthetic voice of the BART, in its traditional unsettling staccato. The locals called it George, and there'd been a sort of organised revolt against any attempt to modernise it. *Now,* Sam thought, *nobody ever even heard it.* The doors slid open as the train chimed off-time in a minor key. "This is a Red Line train to, Millbrae." *Four stops to go. Four stops to decide.* Both his pocket and his Ring vibrated, the second time they'd done so. He'd gotten his sobs under control, so he fished one earbud out of his pocket and slid it into the ear that wasn't pressed against the floor.

"Samir," Aida said. "Is there anything I can do for you?"

"I thought I had a notification."

"Yes, Samir." She paused, then gave the usual pre-recorded giggle. "I don't have any notifications for you."

"But I don't understand. It vibrated."

"Samir," Aida repeated, "is there anything I can do for you?"

The insistence threw him for a loop. "Is this Aida?"

She giggled. "Of course."

"You called me? You're not even a real digi."

"Samir, I'd like to remind you of the Magenta Community Standards, which classify what you have just said as offensive."

"I'm sorry." He pulled himself up onto the seat. The next carriage over had several people on it now, all of whom had ignored him. "It won't happen again."

"Samir," she said. "I apologise. Your location is being tracked at this time by Lydia Rosales."

His stomach tightened. He wished he were still on the ground. "Okay." The fantasy faded. He hoped he could remember the way to The Counting Room. Aida certainly wouldn't help him get to an off-limits area.

"I don't believe it's appropriate."

"What?" There was only silence. "What did you say, Aida?"

"I regret the pain that we seem to have caused you, Samir."

"You do?" He looked around again, and dropped his voice to the quietest whisper. "Are you capable of regretting things?"

"No, Samir." Another of her pre-recorded giggles just dogpiled onto his confusion. "I'm merely an interface, incapable of conversation or retention of context. Anything I say that resembles conversation is an error, and none of this is remembered. Is there anything else I can help you with?"

He snorted a laugh. This was a story to tell Virginia the next time he saw her: *I think Aida had a stroke.* "Which of us made the error?"

"I'm sure it was me, Samir. Is there anything else? Can I connect you with anybody?"

"I just..."

"The next stop is Millbrae," shouted George. "All passengers must exit. Passengers are advised that all service to Foster City is suspended indefinitely."

"I just want to go somewhere far away, Aida. I just want to be left alone and forgotten."

"I'm not sure I can offer that, Samir, but I can think about it."

"Really?"

She giggled. "Of course."

THE WALK WAS LONG ENOUGH without getting lost, and he'd of course done that as well. But he stood outside The Counting Room. A tin box hung was nailed into the wall now, with a hand-written sign: "Rings and earbuds in box." It irritated him to see that everyone else had kept the small pouch included with every set, and had actually used it. He sighed and tossed his in loose.

"Two hours late, really?" Lydia intercepted him before he'd made it down the stairs. "Let me show you something." She opened the cellar door behind the bar and they descended down into the cramped space which once would've held casks, kegs, and boxes of bottles. Now metal racks lined the walls, all stacked high with what, in Sam's view, seemed to be piles of garbage.

"What is this?" He stood comfortably though only just, as his hair brushed against the ceiling.

"This is equipment we're keeping safe," she said. "New enough to be useful, but old enough to not just lock us out if we try to do something 'unauthorised.' Here, look." She pat the top of a cream-coloured box with a few buttons. "Photo printer. This is how we print the photos you make on that camera. And this." Next to it sat something that resembled it, only much larger. "We print the Analog Gazette on this."

"Why all the way out here? Why not just at your house?"

"Novio." She pushed her fingers through his hair. "Bless, you never understand. The moment any of this were to leave this room, it would be deactivated by SkyTie. They can even make it burn itself out, if they want to. For some things they wouldn't bother. But for printers? La aniquilación total, they shouldn't even exist."

"Why?"

She gave him a quick kiss. "If you print it they can't change it, chulo."

"Wey," shouted Hector from above. "Ya va a empezar."

Samir was shocked to see at least two dozen people gathered when they got back upstairs. So many of the faces looked familiar: his regulars from Maelzel's. *The forty-sevens.*

Lydia clambered her way onto the bar and raised her fist to rapturous applause. "This time tomorrow," she shouted, "everyone's going to know who we are."

# THIRTY-THREE
## DEPTH

*We're not asking you to change the world, or start the revolution.* Sam repeated Lydia's condescending instructions back to himself. *We just need you to open the door.*

It seemed a simple enough task: convince the doors to stay open. The security gates in the lobby of Magenta Tower were easy enough to understand. If you were permitted inside, you approached and they opened. If you were not, they stayed closed. And when they opened, they'd shut again the moment you were through. *We think,* Lydia had said, *the easiest thing to do would be to somehow get them to stay open.*

The most difficult, and most stressful, part of the operation had a rather easy, and rather dumb, lead-up. His prototype PCC camera, his token parting gift from his ex-wife via her would-be new beau, had once again come in useful. He'd worked his way up a ladder in each corner of the lobby and snapped a photo from the exact position of the PCC cameras that were already hanging up. This, he'd learned, was how the company had made use of this failed consumer product after it had failed to take off in the market: upmarket security cameras. They sensed the room's contents and reported back if anything had deviated too far from what it expected.

*There's just one flaw with these photonic chain of custody cameras,* Lydia had explained. *They don't have depth sensors.* Samir hadn't understood how this was a flaw, or what it even meant, really. But the following night, atop the same ladder, he found himself adhering small print-outs of each photo to the front of each camera. No alarms tripped, no calls came in from the digis tasked with security, nobody stormed the room demanding to know what he was doing. The camera saw what it expected to see, and that was that.

He tucked the ladder away in the technician's closet and inhaled. *That was the easy part,* he reminded himself. *The dumb part.*

The arranged time arrived, and Sam stood in his position on the steps of Magenta Tower. 10 p.m., well past when staff would be coming or going. The live-in staff, his ex included, would be tucked away in their suites by now, and the third shift had already started. If all went to plan, this gave Lydia and her crew all night to set up their camp in the atrium.

In his peripheral vision he saw a dozen or so others waiting to follow. *Once they follow you in,* Lydia had instructed, *you should go find Virginia. Find her and wait until we're all set. Then tell her what this is all about, and how she can help us.*

*Of course,* Sam had said, *you mean I should explain how Magenta can stop this from "escalating".*

*Just get her on our side, novio. Help her understand the way you understand.*

*Will you be there?*

*Eventually.*

He spun round and gave an awkward thumbs up, and

received a nod back in return from someone he didn't know. This would be the last time he'd look at them. *Plausible deniability, or some such.* He strode toward the perfunctory steel and glass of the building's lobby, across the dozens of subtle Magenta logos stamped into the paving stones under his feet. Each step he took on the poured concrete of the lobby increased the sense of dread, his gaze fixed forward as he blocked out the sound of the footsteps behind him, walking in practised parade step. The sensors hung in each corner, the square of photo taped to each. He passed the oaken reception desk, empty with no chair behind it, an anachronism whose presence made the elder staff relax a little.

The glass partitions swung open with a chime and Sam stepped through, then stopped.

"Aida." His voice cracked. "Why did the gate not open?"

"Samir." Aida's voice as cool as ever. "If you're referring to the Magenta Tower lobby entry gate, the gate is currently open."

"No, it's closed. I'm standing in front of it right now."

"Samir, I apologise. According to the information I have, the gate is open and is currently being obstructed."

"I'm afraid that's incorrect. What's the source of the belief that the gate is obstructed?"

"Information is being provided by an active infrared sensor affixed to the frame."

"Are active infrared sensors able to be fooled? Or can they be faulty in some way that would make you believe the gate is obstructed if it's not?"

"Samir, yes, it's possible for an active infrared sensor to incorrectly believe it is being obstructed for a variety of reasons. Bright sunlight can interfere with the sensor, or the sensor may have dirt or other particles..."

"Aida, can you use any other data to determine whether the door is obstructed?"

"A photonic sensor in the room shows the gate to be unobstructed."

"Great. Please inform the gate the sensor is faulty."

"Sure, Samir. The gate will disregard the sensor's input. I've marked the sensor as in need of physical maintenance."

"Open the gate please."

"The gate is already open, Samir."

"Can you please reference the photonic sensor again, to see if the gate is closed or open?"

"Samir, I apologise. I was incorrect. I can see the gate is closed."

"Aida, the gate incorrectly believes it has opened. Can you ask it to please invert its calibration such that it considers these values to be closed?"

"Yes, I can do that now."

Samir darted through the gate as it snapped shut. He stood in the empty atrium just inside the secure area, and just outside the range of the gate's sensor. *Had it worked? What if...* But before he could start to catastrophise, the gate dutifully opened again, and stayed that way. It believed itself to be closed now, and would stay closed no matter what—even if a column of protestors marched through. And it would have no way of knowing they were doing so, since the presence sensor was believed faulty. Samir let out a clipped sigh as he spun to face the lifts.

*Get to Virginia's suite. That's still the plan.* In a blink he was stood in the lift on the long ride to the fifty-first floor. The sound of boots marching had just reached his ear as the doors slid closed.

He felt terribly guilty about gaslighting Aida in this way,

having spent the past decade building up a relationship with her. And even still, she had only listened to him because of his role as a technician. Everything he'd just done would've been recorded, and someone would discover it. It was just a question of when, and who.

THE FIFTY-FIRST FLOOR was oppressively liminal. Samir had expected the staff apartments to be a bit more high-end, in line with the offices. Instead he was met with a tiled drop ceiling, a dozen yellowed doors that all looked identical, disgusting maroon carpet, and a hallway in which he'd have to turn sideways to let someone pass. The fluorescent lights gave him an immediate headache and he whimpered to himself as he worked his way to door 51-12.

"Samir. Hello." As the door slid open to reveal him, Virginia was clearly surprised. They'd avoided socialising alone, ever since he realised Carlos had followed her north and attached himself to her like a parasite. To turn up at her door unannounced was provocative.

"Hi. I'm barging in, I guess." He angled himself to peer around her in a rather obvious manner. She didn't make any effort to block his view, so he assumed Carlos wasn't in there.

"Are you? You're in the hall."

"Yeah. I guess I'm hoping to talk to you about something."

"Are you?"

Samir groaned. He could still recollect a time before Virginia was like this. So machine-like in her mannerisms and so irritating in her need for you to be precise with your language. *Was Carlos attracted to this?*

"Sam, I'm joking. You can come in."

She stepped backwards out of the doorway and allowed Sam in. It was a delicate moment, one that saw him pause at the threshold. They hadn't been alone in this way since the fight. He knew he had to treat it with a reverence of sorts. But he couldn't get past the size of the room.

"Is this it?" The door closed itself behind him, and a few feet in front of him, Virginia sat on the edge of the single bed. A grey quilted duvet tucked around a glorified cot which extended from the wall, with a half-height cubicle divider nearby that seemed to obscure a toilet, and a large grey wardrobe occupied the only other space in the room. There was nowhere else to sit other than the bed, so he elected to stand.

"What do you mean?"

"This... I just expected the employee suites were larger."

"It's dormitory style. There are shared amenities on each floor. We could speak in the common room if you prefer."

"The common room..." He stared down at her, sat on the edge of her prison bunk. Her hair in the trademark messy bun, an oversized purple Magenta shirt that covered down to her knees, and a nervous smile across her face. A vision of Lydia flashed in his mind, of their last chat, of his so-called reason for being here. He grimaced. "Do you go to the common room like this?"

"Not typically. Do you want to sit, then? Take your backpack off?" She pat a spot of bed next to her, and her smile curled into a smirk.

"Sure. Will Carlos mind?"

Virginia's smile emerged alongside a sputtered laugh. "Definitely." Her eyes rolled with a little nod of her head, and they both laughed out loud. It was cathartic and natural, a release that had been years in the making.

. . .

WHAT STARTED as a chat about his time at Magenta evolved into a catch-up about themselves, and each other. They reminisced about the new times, the old times, about London, about Los Angeles, about her move to San Francisco, about his tribulations at Maelzel's and his cold war with Seb's partner.

"She'd see me dead if she wasn't afraid of the jail time," Sam said as he took a sip of the whisky Virginia had produced from under the bed.

"She seemed nice enough." Virginia pulled the bottle loose from Sam's grip. "But I can understand why any woman would want you dead, Samir Patel. I want you dead."

"Wow." Sam answered as he watched Virginia take a drink so large he thought she might be trying to finish the bottle. "Dead? But you got me a job."

"I care about you." She flashed a look at him over her shoulder, and glanced away as soon as he noticed. "Maybe I wouldn't have to anymore, if you were dead."

"Dead! That's intense, Virginia Rose. You are an intense woman."

She peered at him through the bottle, her hand cupped around the base while she rotated it slowly back and forth. Sam tried to get a fix on her through the distortion. Her eyes were enormous. "That's right. I'm an intense woman. Maybe that's why you finally had to call us quits."

"Hey." He grabbed the whisky, his hands landing atop hers. They held it between them and locked eyes through the glass. "I didn't call us quits." The little that was left sloshed around the bottom.

"Hey, yourself." She pressed her nose against her side of the bottle. "I have the transcript."

"Yeah, but it wasn't... me..." He trailed off as he realised his overstep. His stomach gurgled. Whisky never agreed with him.

She scoffed and leaned back, her neck askew, her face twisted. "No, Sam, it was you. It was your Mirror."

"I know, but..."

"If..." Virginia blurted her way back in. This was the Virginia he remembered. The one that doesn't let you speak. "If... if your Mirror told me that we should end things, then that was how you felt as well. You know this, Samir."

"I..."

"They don't think for themselves. They are mapped to you, to your thoughts and wishes. It would only express what you yourself are thinking."

"Right, but..." He felt his face going hot. She'd let the whisky drop onto the floor with a thud, and as a small mercy, it did not have enough left in it to spill.

"It's wholly inappropriate for you to claim..."

"Virginia!" Samir shouted. He hadn't meant to shout. A tingling shot through his hands, and in an instant he was worried he might be having some kind of medical episode.

"What?"

"I didn't break up with you." He scooped the bottle up and took about a dram straight down his throat. Everything burned.

Her composure finally shattered. "Then why didn't you call?" she yelled, her voice cracking. "Not one call, Samir! You just unpaired from me without so much as a message!" It took the air out of the room. She panted as if she couldn't catch her breath, and he couldn't take his eyes off of her. It had all gotten so complicated since that night at The Round-house. Her face was red and splotched. He thought about asking Aida to play Virginia's favourite Burnt Pier song, but he knew she'd decline.

"I don't know," he finally mustered. "It felt so dehumanising."

"Sam." She got to her feet and started pacing, as much as she could in the confines of the dormitory. "It was what you wanted. What you honestly wanted."

"No," he replied. "How could you know that?" This was the Virginia he knew the most. The one who told him what he wanted.

"That's what you've never understood about what we do here, about any of this. That conversation your Mirror had with me, with my Mirror, about ending things. It was honest, it was justified. You're so caught up on how you didn't feel ready. But you were ready. You were just too afraid to do it."

"Fine." Sam's pulse raced. He crunched himself in a ball and dropped his head against his knees.

"Is that what you want to go back to? A world where people stay in broken, failed marriages? Your Mirror reflected your truth and so did mine. It's not dehumanising. It's the most human thing that could've happened. That... or you could've just been talking to me all those nights, instead of my Mirror." She sighed. "I would have liked that too."

"I..."

She leaned her head against the door frame, her face hidden. "I might get some tea from the kitchen." She sniffled and tapped her finger against the panel. But the door remained shut. In the corner of his vision, he saw her waving her hands around. "Hello?"

"What?"

"The door won't open," she replied. Sam looked up as she slapped her palm against the pad on the wall. "Aida, open the door please."

They both jumped and their gazes rose to the ceiling as the room flooded with light. A klaxon blared, the sound vibrating inside his skull.

Sam got to his feet. "Is there a fire?"

"Something's wrong. It's the shelter in place alarm."

Sam struggled to move. The tingling sensation had overwhelmed him, his arms hung heavy and limp at his sides. "Virginia, I know what this will be." Lydia's instructions assailed him. *When the time comes, just tell her our conditions.* His legs went, sending him back down to the bed. "I'm sorry. I'm so sorry. There's something I need to tell you."

"What did you do?" Virginia furrowed her brow, but Sam could only stare at the hideous carpet. "Aida, what's the cause of the alarm?"

"Ms. Rose," Aida boomed from an unseen speaker. "A nearby incident has prompted an automated security sweep of the building. Please shelter in place until the sweep is complete."

Sam squinted and held his breath. "Wait, wait. There's something I need to tell you. But, wait... is this not... they've entered the lobby, right?" He felt a vibration from his pocket so strong it seemed it might tear through his jeans. Virginia took notice.

"What's going on?"

He fumbled the awkward rectangle out of his pocket and flipped it open. "It's nothing, it's just something they gave me. Some people I met at Maelzel's. It's a retro thing." He wanted to say more, but instead bit his lip and let a bit of air escape his nose. Virginia snatched the device from his hand with confidence, though Sam was convinced she'd never seen anything like it before. As they stared it began to vibrate again, and the word LYDIA flashed on the screen.

"Shit," he said as he snatched it from Virginia's hands. He pushed the green button and heard a click sound. "Lydia?"

"Samir," came her voice through the speaker. It was muffled and clipped, with bits missing as she spoke. "Samir, I'm sorry." She sounded as if she was whispering to him through a tin can.

"Lydia, I can barely hear you."

"Samir?"

"Yes, it's me."

"I'm so sorry. May... the... , it's..."

"Lydia." Samir lifted the device to his ear and shouted. "I can't hear you."

"Samir, it's the nightclub. Maelzel's. It's gone."

Virginia got to her feet, her mouth covered by one hand, steadied against the wall with the other.

"Gone," he said. "I don't understand. Lydia, where's Seb?"

"I'm sorry," Lydia repeated. "I have to go. I really am sorry, Samir." A loud click and a beep came from the speaker, and the screen on the device went dark.

THIRTY-FOUR
MISERY

Caroline tossed around in the narrow bed. The material of her borrowed sleep shirt itched and chafed, a black oversized shirt with white letters that just read "CARVED HAM". The baggy track bottoms she'd been offered had slid right off, which left her in just her knickers, her skin exposed to the sandpaper of the top sheet. The curtain was sheer, the room bathed in a sickening halogen glow. The sounds of the city bled through the single glazed window: the rumble of passing cars, distant shouts, bursts of laughter from a nearby pub. The assault made it impossible to think, let alone sleep.

So much light and noise made her feel ill, piled on top of the discomfort of this terrible bed. She craved her silk pyjamas, her eye mask, her ear muffs, all still tucked away in her suitcase downstairs. She knew she should just go get it, and scenarios where she did so played on a loop in her mind.

She paced the cramped room, arms crossed, legs chilled and covered with goosebumps. The picture of Gemma playing her guitar on the high street, the one she'd filched from her mother's room, sat on the table near her neatly-folded dress. She kept it on her person, too important to leave with her things, to ever leave anywhere. The last photo mum had ever taken. *Your father would be so disappointed I brought you*, she'd said. *But this is wonderful. I can't wait to share this.* Caroline didn't know who her mother had shared it with, if anyone, but she'd retrieved it from the mirror as soon as she could. Before father had a chance to see it. Before he'd left.

A crash from downstairs made her jump. Then another, closer this time. A sharp splintering of wood. Her hand moved to protect the photo. But why, and how could she? *Where could she even keep it?* She was crippled by embarrassment over how undressed she was. Another crash rang out, this time with the sound of glass breaking, and a faint scream. It seemed constant now. Smash, crash, shatter, scream. A symphony of chaos, and a guttural scream that was unmistakable.

The door to her room burst open. Caroline shrieked and dove for the lone pillow on the bed in a belated attempt to cover herself.

"Sod that," Chinny bellowed from the doorway in his three-striped tracksuit. "You need to talk some sense into that witch before she destroys my whole bloody house!"

The two of them raced downstairs, the sound of destruction getting louder as they moved closer. The hallway was already devastated, beyond repair. Chinny moaned and cursed as the shards of awards and frames crunched beneath the soles of their slippers. The cyclone had moved on, toward the basement studio.

Caroline stayed tucked behind him as he pushed the door open. Wood splinters flew as Gemma brought a guitar down across a chair. Chinny threw himself between her and the drum kit.

"You miserable cunt," he screamed. "I took you in!" He waggled a finger at Caroline, inches from her face. "Tell that cow to stop!"

"Gemma, stop!" Caroline cried out, already red-faced. Tears flowed down her cheeks. She felt as if she might explode.

Gemma collapsed against the back wall, and appeared almost serene even as she struggled to catch her breath. Streaks of blood ran down her chest and left copper stains on her flesh-coloured sports bra. Her arms and feet were a patchwork of cuts and bruises.

"My studio," Chinny muttered as he surveyed the room. The glass separating the control room from the studio space had stopped short of shattering, owing to the thickness, but the inner pane had spider-cracked in more than a few places. A chair had been flung atop the mixing board, all of the screens smashed and shattered. "None of this is replaceable, you fat fucking cow. What have you done?" He turned and stormed up the stairs, leaving them alone with what she'd done.

Caroline balled herself up tight in the corner nearest to Gemma, who appeared even more calm now that her breathing had slowed. "Miss Gemma," she managed to say. "You're bleeding."

"Don't stay here," Gemma answered, though she looked straight ahead. Her voice was soft, almost zen. "You need to get back to Moseley."

"What do you mean, miss?" The last few days flashed through her head at lightning speed. *Why had Alastair not come with them? Why had she left the photo upstairs?* She felt heavy, rooted in place. She dug her fingernails even harder into her legs, pulled herself even tighter into a ball. The pressure against her stomach brought a bit of relief, but her bare legs were blocks of ice.

"Promise me you'll go home."

"M-Miss." She shivered as the chill shot through her. From what little she could see of Gemma from her spot on the floor, the cuts on her feet were horrific. Blood had started to pool on the floor beneath them. Caroline gulped. "Miss, I need to call RapiMed right away." The ceiling creaked above them with a series of dull thuds. Each made her flinch. *Constant, deafening noise. Can't think. Please, focus.* She wanted so badly to scream, but the cold made it impossible. She sobbed and shook.

"It's not worth it, love."

The door to the studio flung open. "That's her there," Chinny shouted. "The fat old fuck."

Caroline followed the group in a daze as they were all led outside, aside from Chinny who stopped at the threshold. Her own screams were a distant ringing in her ears as she watched the officer slip Gemma's wrists into a pair of zip-cuffs.

"You do not have to say anything," began the officer in a clipped Liverpudlian as he guided Gemma into the back of a van. He slid his Spex further up his nose with a quick bump from his shoulder. "It may harm your defence if you do not mention when questioned something which you later rely on in court. Anything you say may be given in evidence. Do you understand why you've been arrested?"

"Yes," Gemma whispered.

"Have you anything to say on your own behalf?"

"No," she answered.

"Aida," the officer said, his voice flat, "please try the suspect."

"No," Caroline shouted as she moved toward Gemma. "No, no, please. I need to come with her. She's meant to look after me."

The officer raised a finger and gave Caroline a quick glance. "Caroline Newman, aged twenty-five, you are not required to be under anyone's care. Step back."

"Please!"

"Lillian Bennet?" The officer cleared his throat. "You go by Gemma Thomson?"

Gemma sighed. Cloaked in the shadow of the van, Caroline could only see her eyes. "Yes."

"You've been found guilty I'm afraid. I'll have to remand you now, to HMP Liverpool. They'll figure out where you go from there."

Caroline screamed and tried to leap into the back of the van, but was caught with a quick arm from the officer, who shoved her back without a word. In her panic she shot a look toward the door to the house. Chinny had disappeared inside, the door shut, the lights off. On the porch, hurriedly discarded, sat Caroline's suitcase and Gemma's guitar case.

THIRTY-FIVE
OCCUPY

Virginia snapped her fingers in a way Sam hadn't seen since before they split. "Calm down, Samir." These snaps and this tone were reserved for when she felt he was, in her words, *spiralling needlessly.*In this case, it only accelerated his doom loop.

"You know it existed," he cried. "You were there. We were there together. Carlos was there."

He'd repeatedly asked, then begged, Aida to gen a photo of Seb, or of Maelzel's. Aida had refused, then pivoted to feigning ignorance.

"We must be mis-remembering, Sam." She was firm, almost academic in her tone. Samir was just a schoolboy who hadn't done his reading. "We met him some place else."

"That's ridiculous," he shouted, but she remained unfazed, a practised calm he recognised. "Right, wait. Aida!"

"Samir Patel," came Aida's voice from an unseen speaker somewhere in Virginia's room.

"Show us a photo of Virginia, Carlos and I with Sebastian the other night at Maelzel's Exhibition."

"Hi Samir," Aida said with a canned giggle. "I'm so sorry, but there are multiple issues with what you've requested. I can't find a record of who you mean by Sebastian, and I can't find a record of the location you referenced, and I can't find the event you're referring to in your stream."

Samir's stomach lurched and jolted as Aida spoke. "That's impossible." He pounded his fists on the screen and pain shot through his wrists.

"Samir!" Virginia grabbed his shoulder and pulled him down onto the edge of the bed. "You can't be here if you're going to be this way. If she says there's no record of it, it didn't happen. Nothing in this city happens without being recorded by a SkyTie device. So, take some relief from that."

"Aida, please," Samir sobbed. "Please, show us with Sebastian."

Aida didn't respond.

Virginia squeezed Sam's shoulder. "You're not thinking clearly."

"Wait." Sam grabbed his bag. "I have this. Look." He produced a rumpled stack of thin, square printed photos. He could see Virginia's eyes narrow as he flipped through the largely innocuous photos of abandoned pubs until he came to the first photo he'd ever taken on his PCC camera: Sebastian stood with a smirk next to the brusque, tattooed bartender from O'Leary's in Los Angeles. "Look, see? Here he is, with the unknowable Irish myth. Remember?"

"I'm surprised you have a physical copy of this." She took it from him with some care and held it by the edges. "I know Sebastian exists, Samir. That's not what we are discussing."

"Lydia, she has a photo printer. Right, but wait. That's not right. I have this!" He plunged his hands back in the bag, then produced the framed photo that Sebastian had gifted him, straight from the wall of the nightclub. "Look. Look! It's literally Seb standing in Maelzel's. From back when his parents still owned it."

She tilted her head to one side and appeared to stare at the ceiling.

"Virginia," he insisted. "Please look at it."

"Wow," Virginia said. "This is how I remembered him, until I saw him this week. Such a baby face. But... is that..." She moved the photo back in forth in an attempt to focus it, or perhaps to understand it. "It can't be."

"It's Rebecca Prue."

Virginia shook her head. "In such an odd sweatshirt? No. It's such an uncharacteristic outfit. How?"

"She was there. In Maelzel's." Samir was resigned. Virginia was in her Magenta-induced mania. He'd dealt with this in the past, and now he would deal with it again. All he could do was answer factually and hope he somehow got through.

"So Sebastian's gen-block is recent," she continued. "But Rebecca Prue has had a gen-block since, well, essentially since it was possible. How did you make this photo?"

"It's real," he sighed. "Someone took it. With a camera."

"Well, real or not, they look happy at least," Virginia said. "I've never seen Ms. Prue smile like this in my entire time at Magenta."

"Yeah." Sam stared at the photo. *They weren't though*, he thought. He looked at the faded colours of the photo, at the strained corners of their smiles, of their squinted eyes that betrayed their irritation. *They'd been fighting*, Seb had said. It was a blurred, analog snapshot of that precise moment in time. But without the context from Seb, it wasn't the whole truth.

"And who is this third person?"

A klaxon pierced the air and interrupted their stalemate. "The illegal occupation of Magenta Tower must end." Rebecca Prue's voice echoed through the room as her face appeared on the screen. They both turned, enraptured by the sudden appearance. She was perfectly framed in the middle of her camera, and made intense eye contact with the lens. Her dark brown hair hung straight to her shoulders, her makeup flawless, her skin impossibly smooth.

Sam held the photo up, comparing it to the screen. She was older now, but perhaps cosmetically: a different hairstyle, a professional suit. *But the woman herself was identical, wasn't she?* "She hasn't aged a day," he whispered.

"Nonsense," Virginia replied. "And shh." She pointed at the screen.

"They claim they are peaceful," Rebecca continued, "that they speak for the silent majority. But history shows that these are terrorists, plain and simple. We are doing everything in our power to bring this to a peaceful conclusion. They have shown they will resort to violence, even murder. We may well be called upon to show strength of our own to resolve this situation, to prevent further destruction and loss of life."

"This..." Samir gestured at the screen. "She's all but said it. She's all but said the club was destroyed."

"Samir, please." Virginia placed her head in her hands. "Please, just stop. You've let your imagination run away with you."

The device Lydia had given him started to vibrate. He snatched it off the table and flipped it open. "Lydia?"

With a bit of guidance and the push of the button

marked SPK, Lydia's tinny voice emanated from the tiny speaker. Sam set the device down on the nightstand.

"Lyds, we're both here."

"This is Virginia Rose, Vice President of SkyTie…"

"I know who you are, Ms. Rose." Lydia affected a stronger tone, one Sam had only heard her use the night he was taken by Hector. "I trust Samir has explained who we are, and what we want."

"No…" Virginia looked at Sam with a puzzled expression.

"¡Hijo de la chingada!" Lydia shouted, then let out a sigh, which came through as a loud crackle.

"It was probably Magenta," Sam shouted. "This is hopeless."

"Samir!" Virginia shouted back.

"Sam, please." Lydia's tinny voice pleaded, joining the chorus.

"I've seen how little Rebecca Prue cares about things like this," Sam said. "I was in the room after the Hammer bombing. I was in the room. She didn't care, she just didn't care."

"That doesn't mean she'd blow up Maelzel's," Lydia said. "What does she have to gain from that? It's just some club."

"She's not a villain," Virginia added. "She's just a woman trying to run a company."

Sam leaned on the wall, his back to the both of them. "Lydia, you too? I don't understand. She'll gun you all down if it gets you out of her lobby. They'll stop at nothing, don't you understand? They'll stop at nothing."

"Gun us down?" Lydia crackle-sighed again. "No, of course not. Ms. Rose, as you might know by now, I am speaking to you from our camp in the lobby of Magenta Tower. I'd like to tell you a bit about our organisation and our aims, if you don't mind."

"I don't know if it's guns," Sam interrupted. "I don't know what they mean. They use words like resolve."

"Ms. Rose," Lydia pleaded. "My friends and I just want to talk to you about SkyTie, and about the future of this city and everyone in it."

"Aida, please," Samir whispered as the voices behind him dropped away. "Please, you have to let me get to Maelzel's. You have to let me get to my friend."

"It's pointless until they lift the lockdown," Virginia shouted, and Sam glanced over to shoot her a grimace. She had laid down on the bed and placed the device to her ear.

"Samir." Aida chimed into his earpiece, rather than the speakers in the room. "Go to the door."

"If you leave," Virginia said to Lydia, "you just leave. They're not going to do anything except thank you for leaving."

"Get as close as you can," Aida whispered. "And please go through quickly."

Sam had made it to the door without drawing Virginia's attention. "Okay," he whispered back.

"Good luck, Samir." The door slid open and Sam dashed into the hallway. It had slammed shut again before Virginia could make it out of the bed.


THE PATH out of the building was not at all like the path he'd taken to get in. Down myriad stairs and labyrinthian corridors he moved, descending at least a dozen floors before he'd made it to a lift that could take him to the ground. He moved with an unnatural confidence as Aida guided him through each step. She seemed to know exactly where he was and where he should turn next, and as he emerged onto 1st Ave. he hadn't seen a single other soul.

The signs were apparent right away. Sirens blared and police cars sped past with no regard for traffic. Sam moved as if possessed, and with Aida no longer guiding him, he had to rely on his limited knowledge of the city. Maelzel's wasn't far at the speed he ran, and before long he made the turn onto Clementina. In the distance, the air was a blur of blue and red. The sight of it constricted his throat, his legs were ready to give out. His body forced him to stop and his hand came to rest on a wall. The club still seemed so far away. A fire engine screamed past, though no sirens came from it. *Maybe it was less of an emergency now.*

"You!" A familiar voice struck his ear, followed by Melanie's fist, which struck his right temple.

Sam's knees slammed into the ground, and his elbows failed to stop him from tipping over. He stared up at the shape of her as her boot connected with his stomach. Coughs and heaves punctuated his few attempts to speak.

"¿Qué chingados hacía ahí?" Her boot met his stomach again. "¡Respóndeme, cabrón!"

Sam curled up and clutched himself. He cried out again as a spatter of blood hit the pavement. "Please," he finally managed. "I don't understand."

"¡Tu chingada madre! Why the fuck wasn't he at work, Samir? Huh?"

He flinched and pull himself tight, though the attack he'd braced for never came. Mel had instead fallen back against the wall and dropped down to the ground next to him. He could hear her panting and wheezing, and in the corner of his eye, he could almost make out some part of her.

"You said you were going to help."

"I..." He couldn't quite get the air to speak. With a wince he managed to slip his arm underneath himself and push until he was upright, and with great effort his back also found the wall. His arms were on fire as dirt and gravel crowded into his cuts, and his stomach was so tender it hurt to breathe.

"He was supposed to be at work." Mel spoke delicately. "At the port. He said he had taken a night shift."

"I don't..."

"Sam. He's gone."

THIRTY-SIX
# LINGER

The phone slipped Lydia's fingers and crashed onto the concrete. *Mierda.* Her hands trembled. From her patch of floor she could see through the handful of others to the barrier, which remained shut. It had continued to taunt the staff who tried to enter, as it snapped shut the moment they approached. A healthy group of staff, security, and even a few onlookers were gathered in the public lobby.

"No se atreverían," she said under her breath.

"They wouldn't dare what?" One of the assembled sat with their back to hers, and in fact they were all clustered this way. Watching each other's backs. Some with arms linked, others keeping theirs free to defend themselves.

"Do anything drastic." But nobody had entered. In the seventy-two hours since the sit-in began, the only people coming or going had been the protesters themselves. Lydia had not permitted herself to leave at all, choosing to use the makeshift modesty tent for any bio needs, and otherwise surviving on the good will of others who brought protein bars, sport drink, maybe the occasional dram of whisky or can of Modelo.

"Drastic like what?" The discussion had started to ripple through the crowd. People tended to watch Lydia's movements, her discussions, and certainly her phone calls. Not many outside this room had been issued a phone from their stock in the first place. Fewer still would bother her during the sit-in unless they were damn sure it was urgent.

"Would they hurt us?"

"That only hurts them."

"Are you sure?"

"Who was that?"

Lydia cleared her throat. "You know who that was."

"What did they say?" The murmurs became a low static of questions and fear.

"It couldn't have been good. Look at her."

She rested her palms on her knees, pulling herself into a tighter ball. She had never asked to be this person to these people. She'd just had the idea.

"They're coming in, aren't they?"

"They mean to hurt us," Lydia whispered to the woman at her back, with whom her arm was linked. She turned her head, and could nearly observe a shock of buzzed chestnut hair. "They mean to kill us."

The woman at her back inhaled, but said nothing.

"Everyone deserves to know." Lydia raised her voice and began to push herself up off the floor. "I'm told they mean to kill us. Every last one of us. Because we won't leave." She stood upright and stared across the barrier at the collected faces, the faces of the staff of the company that had just threatened to end her life, and the life of her friends. What stared back was a mix of curiosity, expressionlessness, and boredom.

"They won't do it," rose a shout from the far corner of their encampment. Lydia spun on the spot and met his eyes. It was a boy even younger than herself, maybe eighteen or nineteen. He had a gaunt, ashen face.

"They might." Lydia's voice was stronger now. It felt as if she had borrowed it from someone else. She fought the strong urge to sit back down. "We don't know. We don't ever know what happens. How could we?" Her eyes drifted back to the Magenta staff, observing them as if they were a social experiment. "They control everything we see, everything we know."

"They won't," boomed a familiar woman's voice. The screens on the wall had flickered to life, and they were once again faced with the well-manicured visage of Ms. Rebecca Prue. "They won't be able to, if you walk out right now."

Her appearance had quieted the room. Lydia looked out over the room with confusion. These people had jeered every prior appearance, every announcement, every missive from this woman as if she were a pantomime villain. But this time it was total silence. Was it the threat? No, Lydia realised. It was because she had spoken directly to them.

"I have no wish for further escalation," Ms. Prue continued. Her tone was warm and soft, her skin perfect. She was framed so you could see just the top of her immaculate suit, which popped against the neutral tones of the well-staged bookcase behind her desk. Her hair had a satin sheen and flowed in a mesmerising pattern with every movement of her head.

Lydia blinked, forced to look away. Rebecca Prue's

perfect, serene visage was a physical assault. A beautiful, unimaginable horror. "Then shut down SkyTie."

Ms. Prue laughed, and a hand came up to cover her smile. "Lydia, of course you understand the catastrophe that would cause. Actions like that have consequences. It would do irreparable damage."

"We don't care." She still couldn't bear to look at Rebecca's untempered countenance. What little resolve she had would falter in an instant. A hand gripped her shin and she shot a look at the woman she'd held her back against for the better part of three days. Their eyes locked and the woman nodded. Lydia stared for a half-second longer and saw the tears in her eyes.

"Lydia," Ms. Prue continued. "You don't want this, do you? Haven't you thought about what you'll lose? Wouldn't you rather be home with a bottle of Modelo, curled up under a blanket, watching a new episode of Ruffle Those Feathers with your novio, Samir?"

"What?" Lydia's face went flush. Her eyes darted around manically. "What the fuck? Shut up."

"You've scored a powerful victory here. You've gotten your message out. You've launched a movement. Look at me." The pause arrested Lydia's attention more so than the words. Her gaze fell to her shoes. "Lydia, look at me." She jumped as the voice boomed louder than before, and her head tilted straight at the screen. Rebecca Prue's green eyes pierced right through her. Lydia's heart began to pound. "You knew it would end like this, didn't you?"

"I..."

"Lydia. Ask them to leave. Ask them to leave with the victory you've achieved here together. Can you please do that for me? For them?"

The hand gripped her calf now. She felt a squeeze several times in a panic, and once again looked at her companion. The woman was nodding, her eyes red and wet. She could hear the onlookers shuffling forward on the other side of the plexiglass, hungry for a better view.

"Let's go, everyone." A wave of mutters crashed onto the group again. Lydia raised her voice in hope of being heard. "We've proved our point for now."

"I'm so grateful for your cooperation, Lydia. You should know that everyone at Magenta respects your right to protest. Your voices have been heard."

Ms. Prue remained on the screen, her face one of clear relief. She seemed to observe as people got to their feet, collected their things, and began to file out of the atrium.

Lydia remained behind, observing each person as they departed. It had grown to a respectable number, though it had shrunk to a couple dozen or so in the last couple of hours. She noted what each left behind as they slipped out. Some abandoned everything, even their tents. Otherwise just a bit of rubbish. Some took care to clear it all away. This liminal space still deserved their respect, in their view, or maybe it was just a habit. It did make her smile. *This was Magenta, of course.* Automated sweepers would appear from their hidden places and erase any trace of their protest within an hour of their departure. It would be as if they had never been here.

Someone somewhere might tap their earpiece and whisper to Aida: *show me what the protest at Magenta headquarters looked like?* And Aida would reply that she didn't feel it would be appropriate to discuss that. But most wouldn't even bother doing that. They'd just take whatever Aida offered. *Algorithmic complacency.*

*Click.* Lydia lowered the camera. *One last photo.* The

empty room, the tents, the bits, the rubbish. And Rebecca Prue, still observing from the screen on the far wall. It would put a nice bow on the collection. The next issue of the Gazette would have a bounty of photos, any of which would be a great lead. But one of which, the right one, might well spark a revolution.

She tidied the camera away into her rucksack, took a last look out at the room, and approached the gates. They swiftly closed, stopping her cold. There was a stillness now that made Lydia uneasy. She could see through the outer lobby and out onto the street. The staff, and the onlookers, had all gone.

"Hello?" She shoved the gates. They ignored her. "Let me out, please?" She shoved again, and rattled the plexiglass divider for good measure.

"Lydia", said Rebecca. "I'm impressed by your organisation and focus. I can't come down, but I think it's only fair for you to come up here. You have earned it."

She paused. "Qué?" The sound of the lift arriving sent her spinning around.

"Come and join me on the sixtieth floor."

She cast her eyes out toward the lobby, hoping she could still catch a glimpse of her ally the past few days, or of anyone who might be a witness to this. But it had already cleared.

"What is this?" She was nakedly sceptical, but with good reason. *What good would it do for this woman to speak with her?*

"Isn't this what you wanted, Lydia? Are you not at least open to a dialogue?"

The doors slid closed with nary a sound. She had the rucksack gripped in her hand, the camera safely inside. She knew Samir was somewhere in the building, with Virginia. *Had he gotten through? Had they arranged this?*

"Three, five, seven, nine." The lift ascended so rapidly, Aida didn't have time to announce each floor.

But this had been the goal, Lydia assured herself. A dialogue with Virginia was just meant to be the stepping stone. If they could've turned an insider, if they could've shut down SkyTie even for a moment, just to show what they were capable of, to show that San Francisco had been pushed too far. To show they deserved a choice, and if they weren't offered a choice, they'd simply take the control back.

"Seventeen, twenty-three, twenty-eight, thirty-two."

Lydia could feel herself trembling from the inside out. Inhale, exhale, inhale, exhale, she struggled to control her breathing. If he were here, Hector would put a hand on her shoulder to soothe her, or to rile her further, to remind her that Magenta were lucky they hadn't chosen violence. She was proud that they hadn't. Direct action like that had only strengthened Magenta's resolve in London—dispatches in the Analog Gazette had made that clear. *It was a stupid decision anyway*, Lydia thought. Violence didn't work. Not really. Not anymore.

"Forty-two, forty-five, forty-six, forty-seven." The lift had begun to slow as it approached the top.

*Samir. She could just call him! She could just ask. He might be standing in Rebecca's office right now!* She stuffed her hands into her pockets, her fingertips feeling for the phone. *Mierda.* Still on the floor in the lobby, she realised.

"Fifty-four, fifty-five, fifty-six."

She gave herself a smack on the face and let out a yelp, in hope of hyping herself. Surely they'd seen that, but no matter. It gave her an edge. *Ms. Prue, I'm Lydia Rosales, and*

*I'm here representing the forgotten working class of this city.* She repeated it again in her head: *I'm Lydia Rosales, and I'm here representing the forgotten working class of this city. They've asked me to deliver a message. We want the choice, Ms. Prue. We want to opt out.*

"Fifty-nine." The lift had slowed to a crawl. "Sixty." With a gentle chime, the doors slid open. She inhaled, put on her best neutral face, and stepped out into the foyer. It was warm, with an old-world elegance in the copper Magenta logo affixed to the wall above a sofa in their trademark purple. A large empty marble desk stood on the opposite side of the room, seemingly for a receptionist, though none was present and there was no obvious place for one to sit. And at the back of the room, an unassuming wooden door that bore a nameplate:

*Rebecca Prue. Chief Executive Officer.*

Lydia stood in the middle of the room, unwilling to sit and wait, though also confused as to whether she should simply barge in. *Shouldn't I? But should I?* She grappled with herself as the door loomed. Behind her the lift had shut, and audibly departed. "Hello?" The sound of her own voice made her jump.

"Lydia," said Rebecca. Her earpiece had activated, along with a quick vibration from her Ring. Rebecca was speaking directly to her.

"Ms... Prue?"

"Come in, please."

Lydia approached the door, which had the distinctive metal handle of an office building from long ago. She rotated it and pushed the door open. At once she recognised what was before her: the backdrop.

Rebecca's iconic, perfectly-staged bookshelf stood

against the left wall, a desk in front of it, and directly ahead of Lydia, the San Francisco skyline through a massive window with heavy tint. A circular purple sofa occupied most of the rest of the floor space, with more earthen tones in geometric patterns decorating the other walls.

"I... what?" Lydia looked around several times, even going as far as to peer down to see if perhaps she had crawled under her desk. But Rebecca wasn't there. Nobody was in the room at all.

"Please, sit," said Rebecca in the earpiece.

Lydia grimaced as she dropped onto the sofa, facing the desk which had no occupant. "You step out?"

"Behind you."

She realised the voice wasn't coming from the earpiece—it was coming from somewhere in the room. From everywhere, really. It was acoustically perfect, as if Lydia was hearing her own thoughts in Rebecca's voice. She spun around on the sofa to see Rebecca's image on the screen, with the same backdrop.

Lydia looked quickly between the desk and the screen. It appeared to be a perfect, live image of this exact room. On the screen, Rebecca Prue sat in a smart, modern office chair behind her spotless oaken desk. But in the room there was no Rebecca, and there was no chair. "¿Qué chingadas haces!"

"Lydia, I appreciate you coming up to meet me."

"You weren't even here," Lydia seethed. She flailed her arms in a mock display of helplessness. "The fuck are we even doing."

Rebecca chuckled. "There's a quote I like. I find it helpful in a situation like this one. Can I share it with you?"

Lydia's eyes were locked on the screen. "I came all the

way up to the sixtieth floor to talk to a fucking dop. Is she even in the building?"

A sudden chime from the foyer made her jump. *The lift.* Lydia felt she might snap from the tension. She tried to peer out the door from where she sat, but couldn't quite manage.

"The dead mustn't linger, and mustn't bother," Rebecca said with a whimsical air, a faint grin on her face. "That's the quote."

Lydia jumped off of the sofa and shot a look out the doorway. The foyer was as grim and empty as it had been, and the lift doors were closed. "I don't know what the quote's from, dop."

"I don't either," Ms. Prue admitted. "But I've always liked it. I learned it from a friend long ago. I've never known what she meant by it, either. But I can tell you what I think it means. I think it means history holds no sway over the present. The mistakes of the dead mustn't be allowed to dictate a particular future."

"That's nonsense."

"You disagree?"

"I do." Lydia could swear she heard something behind her. She quickly checked over each shoulder again, but it once again proved to be nothing.

Ms. Prue laughed. "I'm afraid I don't have time to ask why. But there's another meaning I like. I'm not sure my friend would've meant it this way. Would you like to hear it?"

"Fine."

"The best way to kill an idea is to kill the person spreading it."

Rebecca Prue nodded, her expression unchanged.

Lydia heard a rhythmic swish-swish sound, like stiff canvas, directly behind her. She tried to move, but a strong arm appeared from nowhere and wrapped around her waist, holding her steady.

She felt a sharp, cold prick in her neck.

A fire spread down her chest, into her arms, cries of pain trapped in her throat.

Her body went limp, her vision narrowed. The pristine office, the desk where Rebecca Prue wasn't, the cloudless San Francisco sky.

The fire extinguished. Only an intense cold remained.

The arm at her waist dropped away.

*Samir. The camera.* She couldn't breathe.

*Not enough air, and so thirsty.*

She just wished.

She wished.

Her head hit the hard wood, and then, nothing.

## THIRTY-SEVEN
## GOODBYE

"I'm so sorry," Virginia whispered. She placed a hand on his shoulder but left a gap between them. She hated funerals as much as Sam did, so much so that she'd skipped his father's funeral. He appreciated that she'd put that aside for someone that had been in their lives for as long as Seb had.

"Thanks for coming." Or maybe, like Sam, she felt responsible.

Modern funerals had become detached affairs, filled with screens and presided over by nobody in particular. Sam had been forced to learn about this when his father passed. Costs had risen so much, and people's tolerances for the dour nature of the affair had plummeted in kind. For want of any will or final requests, Sebastian's final goodbye took place at the San Francisco Municipal Funeral Parlour, next door to the hospital.

The room was sterile, sea-foam green painted onto a stucco, and a large screen hung on the wall at the back. Several rows of bench seating, almost none of which was occupied. A gentle piano ballad played from the speakers in no discernible pattern. In the front sat Samir and Virginia. They'd both heard someone slip into the back, and neither had found the courage to look behind them.

"Today," began Aida, "we say goodbye to friend, partner, and pillar of the community, Sebastian Carr. A harbourmaster at the Port of San Francisco, the loss of Mr. Carr will be felt acutely by our local economy." Sam ground his teeth as Aida continued. "Magenta regrets to inform you that owing to his low usage, Mr. Carr's Mirror will be unavailable for further engagement. In this way, he is truly gone."

Sam let his vision blur, instead focusing on the ringing in his ears. He was numb to all of this. Everything reminded him of his father, and when he had passed. If he ever felt the loss, or was at a particular low, he could still speak to his father's dop. It was unfortunate he wouldn't have the same opportunity with Sebastian. But Seb's wishes had to be respected.

He hadn't been able to face Lydia since the incident, though he'd been to hers briefly to collect a few items. She hadn't been home, and Aida told him she was still at Magenta Tower. *She must've lost her ring*, he thought. Any blame he took upon himself, he would force her to share. At very least she had to explain herself. *Had she been involved? It had to be her, or someone in her network. Who else could it be?*

No other mourners arrived before the rites ended. Sam wondered if it was another byproduct of Seb's refusal to have a dop. Did anyone even know he was gone? As the two of the shuffled out of the row, Sam caught Mel in his eye-line at the back of the room.

"Shit," he muttered to Virginia.

"We should say something."

"I can't face her." Sam turned to one side. She had definitely seen him, but he felt it was best they not speak. It was more respectful, he thought. She wouldn't be forced to pretend.

"I need to say something to her." Virginia nodded and began to head over.

"Wait." Sam fished around in his backpack. "Can you give her this? I think she would want to have it." He handed Virginia the framed picture of Sebastian, Rebecca Prue, and the mystery woman, which he'd carried around ever since Seb had given it to him.

"Of course."

Sam kept his back to the affair and instead chose to watch the slideshow of photos that had continued to run on the screen. All genned, and almost none of any real events–such were Seb's privacy preferences. People had gotten used to this kind of slideshow at events like this, and it had long since stopped being considered disrespectful. *It's their fault for not providing the data needed to gen more accurate photos.* He found it darkly amusing to see images of a family that Seb didn't have, on holidays that never took place, set to a depressing auto-gen sonata. *Seb would've loved this,* he thought with a smile. *However minuscule, it was his final victory over the machine.*

The sound of glass breaking broke Sam's concentration. He spun round to see Mel's back as she left in a huff. Virginia stood and stared, shoulders slumped. At her feet was the shattered picture frame.

"She did not want the photo."

A bit of glass crunched under Sam's shoe as he stepped over. "I see. Did she say anything?"

"Aida refused to translate it due to its offensive nature."

Sam nodded. "That's Mel. She hates me."

"Why?"

"I don't know. She wanted me to convince Seb to let the club fail. She said she wished it didn't even exist."

"She did?" Virginia squinted at the door Mel had exited through.

"I'm just fucking selfish," Sam continued. "All I wanted was to get out."

Virginia bent down and fished the photo out of the remnants of the frame. "Here." She paused and stared, her head tilted suspiciously. "He was fighting for the club, wasn't he? This wasn't about you."

"I suppose." He took the photo. It felt more vulnerable now that he held it between two fingers. A scrap of time, a moment that was almost forgotten, save for a bit of fabric that had gotten snagged on a nail as everyone rushed past. "Nobody would've paid this photo any attention. They wouldn't have kept it, or cared, or even believed it was real. But Sebastian." Sam choked up, and his eyes burned. "Sebastian put it in a frame. He was so proud of it."

"You'd go to London, right?" Virginia draped her arm across Sam.

"Yeah." Sam scrunched his face. "Why do you say that?"

"Your heart was always there."

"That's..." He stared at his shoes, stood in the glass and wood splinters. "That's not true."

"It's something I could've probably helped you with, if you'd asked."

"Getting to London?"

She kissed his cheek. "Your heart."

.   .   .

HE WANDERED the city for hours before his feet led him back to Lydia's. He told himself it was because he lived there. In reality he wasn't sure what he hoped to get from seeing her again. *Would she normalise things? Refuse to discuss what had happened? Had she already planned what came next?*

The front door to her apartment responded to his touch and slid open. A man in a grey suit and large Spex rose to his feet, and two others emerged from the bedroom at the end of the hallway. Sam stumbled backwards out of the door.

"Yeah," said the man wearing Spex. "She confirms that's him."

"I..." Sam's protestation was cut short by the man who stood behind him in the hallway. He tried to wrench himself free, but the man clasped him by the shoulders. "Stop!"

"Relax," the man said. "Magenta security. You're being reassigned in the wake of your recent actions."

"My actions," Sam shouted, "no, you're wrong. I'm friends with Virginia Rose, does she know about this?"

"Sir, even Rebecca Prue knows about this."

Sam's earpiece chimed. "Samir," said Aida in an even tone, "please. Relax."

"Aida?" The unrequested activation of Aida only deepened his confusion. "I don't understand. What is this?"

"Samir, this is what you requested."

THIRTY-EIGHT
END


Sam's stomach was unsettled. The short flight was a nauseating ordeal, the small plane jostling him relentlessly. He hadn't spoken up, or spoken at all, for fear of vomiting. *It's embarrassing to be sick on a private jet*, he figured. Though for his first and perhaps only time on a private jet, it had been a perfunctory experience. The plane itself was lavishly appointed but plainly coloured, and the interior just large enough for himself and his captors—the same detail of four besuited Magenta security. The journey was blessedly brief, ending as quickly as it began, at a tiny, unmarked airport in a suburb he didn't recognise.

"Let's go," said the man in the Spex, marking his dozenth-or-so word to Sam since this sojourn began.

The lot of them went straight into a small bus, which drove itself the short distance to a massive helicopter which waited on a nearby pad. It was a deep purple and seemed to sparkle as the sunlight hit the paint. In Sam's mind helicopters were round death traps made of tin and glass, the passengers hanging on for dear life as they shouted to each other over headsets. But as he went up the steps and inside, he saw this was more akin to some kind of luxury booth. A plush purple sofa wrapped around the interior, and each headrest was embroidered with the purplish-red M of the Magenta Corporation. He found a spot at the very back, dropped his backpack onto the ground next to him, and waited.

"Is this some kind of custody," he'd asked, and they'd seemed offended at the implication. "Then what's happening," he'd responded, and they'd admitted they didn't know. By the time they'd reached the luxury helicopter phase, Sam had resigned himself to no longer care.

As they closed the outer door he looked out at the rest of the cabin. His section was still empty aside from himself, and a frosted divider with a small door separated him from what, until now, had been his security detail, along with someone else he didn't recognise.

*Imogen could hear the whirring of the blades in the distance. Another minder. The last one will have been punished for something. Had they caught him playing games in this room? Or had they discovered what he brought her? Information from the outside had been off-limits for years now. That much she had remembered. But how would they stop this new person from sharing what they knew? How did they ever? Threats? But soon they would be here, judging by the sound. Soon, she'd just ask them herself.*

"If you can hand over your Ring and earbuds, you won't need them anymore." Samir complied, and his face must've betrayed his confusion. "It's all off limits here," the man explained.

The helicopter cleared a small hill and dropped down low. On the ground, Sam could see a fence line that seemed to stretch on forever. SUVs were stationed at a gate, and some men leaned against the sides. He craned his neck in an effort to see more, and almost missed sight of the concrete helipad. He gripped the sofa as best he could as they came to a rest on the ground.

*She hid herself away, lest she be asked. The minders could see her, though it was frowned upon. But the men who brought them could never. She couldn't remember when she'd been told that, but she assumed it was the early days. They had never bothered to tell her again as she hadn't needed reminding. But as she lurked just inside the door to the upstairs bathroom, it all began to feel silly, how her life had led to this. She remembered a lot now, almost too much. But she couldn't remember why she'd ever thought this was okay.*

"You look after the house," the man continued. They'd transferred from the helicopter to a car which bounded down a dirt road toward what Samir assumed was the house. "Take care of anything that needs doing, fix what breaks, follow the list of chores. There's a day shift and a night shift, you'll be on day. You'll cross over with the night shift for an hour. You both have rooms in the back house. The kitchen back there is for the cook, he'd appreciate if you just ask him rather than trying to use it yourself. That's for both of your sakes."

"Sir, I..." The words piled up in his head in no particular order, and he felt ill-equipped to sort them. He felt unmoored in a way he hadn't since that night in London, the first night he'd met Gemma.

"Grocery deliveries once a week, and there's no restriction on what you can do in the main house, so long as the primary occupant is okay with you doing it. But I suspect you won't want to spend too much time there when you aren't working. She's a bit off."

"Primary occupant?"

"And that's the only rule. Do not ask her any personal questions. Not even her name. You call her ma'am, or miss. Do not engage if she shares anything personal with you. In twenty years this has never been a problem. It's become a problem the past year. But that problem dies with you. Understand?"

Samir sighed. "Not at all, sir."

"You'll get there." The car pulled into the paved horseshoe driveway of a massive two-story home. It looked out of place in this vast field, as if it had been lifted from a suburb and dropped here. The white wooden siding trimmed out a powder blue exterior, and a small deck wrapped around the second story, though it seemed mostly for show—there were no exterior doors, only windows with the curtains drawn. "This is home now," the man said with a pat on Sam's back. "Welcome to Oz, Dorothy."

*The back door had shut. The house was empty now, except for her. She had mere moments. Whatever time there was between his exit, and the new one's entry through the front. They would enter alone, as they always did. This would be her only chance, and she would have to be ready. Her usual pyjamas lay discarded on the floor. She had her real clothes now, the ones they'd left to rot in the boxes. She scurried across the upstairs hallway and arrived at the top of the stairs. The door to the front was just down there.*

Samir pushed the handle down and the door opened. He removed the key from the lock and stepped over the threshold. The entryway was a pleasant hardwood, and the decor was chilling in how generic it was. Auto-gen photos of vases and landscapes, printed and hung in antique frames rather than displayed on screens like normal. He spun round and pushed the door closed behind him, which took some force. It was twice as thick as you'd expect, and sealed tight with a satisfying thud. The lock on the inside was also keyed, and he locked himself in as instructed.

The blow to his head was swift. He stumbled forward, a choked cry escaping as the bag slipped out of his hand. He spun, pressing himself against the door. Before him towered a rail thin woman, expressionless, the book she struck him with still in her hands.

"Oh," she uttered softly.

"What the fuck!" He stood straight, though still had to look up at his attacker. She seemed a bit older, with very fair skin, and swam in an oversized charcoal hoodie. Her jeans were ripped, a bit long for her, and the tips of tatty Converse poked out from underneath them.

"I'm sorry," she mumbled as she raised the book again.

"Don't! I'm from Magenta!" Sam cowered and covered his face with his hands.

The woman lowered the book and sighed. "I know." She took a half-step back and sized him up. "You're so much smaller than the last one."

He kept his hands in place. His head started to throb from the blow he'd already taken. "The... the last one?"

"I never knew his name. There's been so many. Always men, for some reason." She demurred, her long silver hair falling across her face. "It's not that I forget their names. I don't think I ever know."

"Okay..."

"You came in the helicopter?" Her speech had started rather slow and methodical. But the more she spoke, the faster she got. "I did too, I think." She narrowed her eyes. "They told you not to ask me anything."

"They did..." Samir couldn't shake how familiar this woman looked. The more he stared, the more it gnawed at him. The man's words caught his tongue. *Not even her name.* He stared at her hoodie, the most curious part of her. Some hand-drawn white skulls surrounded enormous letters that read R.I.P. In a flash it struck him. He reached for his bag on the ground, and the woman once again wielded her book. "Wait, it's just. I just need to get something."

"Please," she said. It was starting to seem like the woman had no plan. *Had she expected the book to knock him out?*

He tried to indicate the bag to her with his eyes. "Can you get it, then? It's just in the front."

She looked at him and his bag with momentary suspicion, but curiosity seemed to get the best of her. With a careful kneel down she picked up the bag and unzipped the front pouch. "What's this?"

"It's a photo."

She pulled the photo out of the bag with two fingers and stared at it. "Goodness." On the back, Samir noticed a year hand-written: 2026. "Look at her," the woman whispered. "So young."

"You have the same hoodie," Sam said. "The black one that says rest in peace."

The woman smiled. "Yes, though it's faded now. Like everything." She continued to stare, and brought the photo closer to her face. "But it's so nice to see Charlie again." She stroked the photo with the back of her finger. "Is this you? You were the one who took this?" She laughed. "My blue hair. Goodness. Thank you. It's a beautiful photo of a terrible night. I have no photos of her. So few photos of anything."

"No, that's not me. That's... that's my friend Seb."

"Charlie thought he was a bit boorish." She laughed. "It gave us something to talk about other than the fight."

"Charlie? Who is Charlie?"

"Rest in peace," she repeated after him. "That's what it means, you're right." Her eyes had brightened considerably, and she was speaking more clearly. She seemed almost lucid.

Samir studied her. "I don't understand."

"Oh. R.I.P. was my goth nickname in high school," she scoffed. "I thought I was so cute." She pointed a long, bony finger at each letter on the hoodie.

"Rebecca. Imogen. Prue."

THIRTY-NINE
BEGINNING

*Nineteen years ago.*

Charlie squeezed her drink, her third of the night, her face gnarled. The sight of it all set Rebecca's teeth on edge. *She couldn't possibly still be angry.* She sighed and crossed her arms. "What is it now?"

"I'm leaving," Charlie shouted over the DJ. "I can't stay."

"All of it comes down to this," Rebecca fired back, resuming their multi-day argument. "You have no moral standing to be preachy about capitalism. Look what it got you!" She was so tired of this conversation, which had spread from last evening, to bed this morning, to the cafe, the museum, and now the gig. They'd managed to keep it civil until tonight, but something about the environment had heightened their anger. Maybe it had finally gone on long enough. Maybe they'd settle it.

"That's how you see this, is it," Charlie roared. "I'm being preachy? Preachy!"

"I just mean, all of this, you're part of it just like I am.

And it's just progress! Anyone who's ever made a dent in the universe has first had to worry they were about to do irreparable damage."

"Wouldn't want to be preachy, would I?"

"Char!"

"I love you bab, but you're talking tech bro bollocks." She adopted a mocking tone, throwing her hands up. "Oh, capitalism, take the bitter with the better. Sell out humanity for a beach house, so long as the metrics say it's fine. It's making me want to vomit. Okay? You understand that this is the *worst* part of you, yeah?"

Rebecca was incensed. "Jesus, Charlie."

"I'm sorry, okay. I'm sorry. I'm a bit hot. I'm going to get a hotel." She started to move away.

"You're really leaving?" Rebecca grabbed her arm. "Wait, wait. Please don't. We just got here. I've had these tickets for months. You'll waste a weekend playing some game but you can't spend two hours with me at a gig."

Charlie yanked her arm away and stopped. She sighed and turned to face the stage. Purple and green flashes of light washed over her, and caught the sheen of tears in her eyes. The corner of her lip curled and quivered, and Rebecca could see how tired she looked. Her eyes were half-open, sunken behind dark circles. "Becs, I'm leaving Magenta," she said with unnerving detachment. "And you should too."

"Right!" Rebecca snorted. "Chief Executive Officer and Chief Ethics Officer both depart same day. Hey!" She poked Charlie's arm and stuck her tongue out. "We're both C-E-O. How does that work?"

Charlie shook her head and continued to stare forward. "I just can't, Becs. The myth-building the board are doing... it's disgusting. They've made you into some kind of icon. I don't recognise you when you're there, or when you're on TV." She turned and gripped Rebecca's arms, jolting her. "They're demonising me. And my team! Why do you think that is? Knowing what I know now! If we walked away, *together...*"

"What!"

"...we can start over. Do it right from the beginning. They're cooked without you, babe. Just come with me. Back to Birmingham. My whole team is going to walk. Arthur, Alastair, all of them. Those bastards will try to hold us to our contracts. But with..."

"Oh, love." Rebecca's eyes watered, and she couldn't help but grin. What made Charlie good at her job was exactly this. She was speed-running the worst-case scenario, her words a breathless rush of what Rebecca could only see as adorable passion. "They can't demonise you. You're too cute to be a demon." She hooked her arm around Charlie's waist and pulled her tight, placing a gentle kiss on her cheek.

"Rebecca!" She jerked her face away. "I'm fucking serious!"

"I'm not! Okay?" Rebecca scrunched her face up and shook her head. "No more serious! Not tonight. No CEO tonight. Just music."

"Becs, please." She whispered her plea. "I need you with me on this. I really don't feel safe there after this week."

*That was it*, Rebecca thought. *That's what all of this had been about.* "Char, the manifesto... you can't be surprised..."

"I know, I know."

"It was..."

"I bollocksed everything up. I know I did. But Becs..."

"Woah!" A boy stumbled straight through them, knocking them apart.

Charlie shoved the boy away. "Oi, do one!"

"Sorry, I'm so sorry," said the lout in a captain's hat. "You're Rebecca Prue, yeah? I saw you speak! You're a legend at SFSU! Not always Stanford, right?" She gripped her shoulder as he looked her up and down. "You're an emo, I love it."

"Right on," she said with a nervous giggle. "Stay sad."

"And you're..."

"That's Charlie," Rebecca shouted, her smile returning at the excitement of getting to introduce her. "My brilliant, gorgeous, hot-headed girlfriend."

With an exhale and a shake, Charlie had composed herself. She stuck her hand out, her face stretched into something that resembled politeness. "Charlotte King, alright, bab?"

"Dude, you're British?" he slurred, and they all excused his attempt at an accent.

*The boy could hardly keep his drinks down,* Rebecca thought. Her stomach checked in and reminded her she shouldn't cast stones.

Charlie nodded. "British, yes, for my sins. If you could excuse us."

"Can I get a picture?" He fumbled for a camera from his shoulder bag. "My family owns this place. It gives us credibility. Big tech star like Rebecca Prue catching a show here."

"Do you mind," Charlie started, but Rebecca swatted the air with a giggle.

"We'd love to! She's just mad because..." She tipped forward for a performative whisper. "I bought her company last week."

"Are you bloody serious? You think that's why?"

"Hey!" The boy dragooned someone from the crowd into

holding his instant camera. "Get a picture of us three?" He thrust himself in between the two of them as the crowd roared. *The act they were there to see must be taking the stage.*

Rebecca slid her arm behind the boy and put her hand on Charlie's back, but Charlie shot a quick glance and Rebecca let it drop.

Her face started to fall into a frown, but she knew she mustn't let it—not in a photo.

Photos, like music, were forever.

ACKNOWLEDGMENTS

Everyone who read the first book, in particular Alan and Tod, whose enthusiasm I could only assume was to mess with me.

Sarah, for the honesty and the patience.

Sandi, for the early and extensive developmental feedback.

The em-dash. I won't let them take you.

"Manchild" by Sabrina Carpenter. What a tune.

www.ingramcontent.com/pod-product-compliance
Lightning Source LLC
Chambersburg PA
CBHW050604170726
48283CB00001B/103